OVERWHELMING ACCLAIM FOR CHARLES WILSON'S CUTTING-EDGE THRILLERS

GAME PLAN

"Mr. Wilson plays with scenes like a master director, pulling in his audience subtly and surely, until, in a Hitchcockian move, he twists the story into an unexpected direction . . . Do not miss GAME PLAN." —*Bookbrowser*

"Wilson weaves a complex plot, made all the more interesting by the science behind it . . . This is my first encounter with Wilson's work, but I guarantee it won't be the last."
—*Colorado Springs Gazette*

"As fresh as today's headlines and as scary as tomorrow's news." —"Daybreak Today," USA Radio Network

"A tautly interwoven story line that seems to go at an SST pace . . . a game-winner." —*Midwest Book Review*

DONOR

"DONOR reads at the speed of light . . . Wilson has hit a home run again." —*The Clarion-Ledger* (Jackson, MS)

"If you haven't already picked up Charles Wilson's latest book, you're missing one of the best I've read in a long time."
—*Brazosport* (TX) *Facts*

"Symptoms: quick pulse, shallow breathing. Diagnosis: DONOR, the new thriller from Charles Wilson."
—"Tuesday Talk with Brad Link," KDTA Radio, Denver CO

EMBRYO

"A highly entertaining, chilling story about an experiment that will no doubt soon become fact rather than fiction—and we can only wonder about the consequences."
—William T. Branch, MD, University of South Florida College of Medicine (listed in *Who's Who in the World of Educators*)

"With EMBRYO, Charles Wilson jumps into the ranks of the best storytellers on the market today. His extensive knowledge of the medical field brings a believability to his novel's cutting-edge technology and futuristic expectations that no other writer can deliver. Back that up with fast-paced plot and taut dialogue and you have a book that's worth staying up at night to read."   —*Bookpage*

"With the release of EMBRYO, Charles Wilson joins Stephen King, Robin Cook, and Michael Crichton as the Fourth Horseman of the Apocalypse."
                    —*Under the Covers Book Reviews*

"EMBRYO remains the only book, out of our weekly book-review series, that both the host and the producer went out, bought and read. It is simply that good."
—"Daybreak with Larry George," KUIK Radio, Portland, OR

EXTINCT

"A nail-biter that those planning a seaside vacation might want to save for beach-house reading." —*Publishers Weekly*

"The best work of fiction I've ever read about a sea predator."
—Dean A. Dunn, PhDs in Oceanography and Paleontology, and former shipboard scientist for *Glomar Challenger* expeditions in the Pacific and Western North Atlantic

"Meticulously researched."   —*Entertainment Weekly*

St. Martin's Paperbacks Titles
by Charles Wilson

Direct Descendant
Fertile Ground
Extinct
Embryo
Donor
Game Plan

GAME
PLAN

CHARLES
WILSON

St. Martin's Paperbacks

GAME PLAN

Copyright © 2000 by Charles Wilson.
Excerpt from *Deep Sleep* copyright © 2000 by Charles Wilson.

Library of Congress Catalog Card Number: 99-055724

ISBN: 0-312-97443-4

Printed in the United States of America

St. Martin's Paperbacks edition/ December 2000

St. Martin's Paperbacks are published by St. Martin's Press, 175 Fifth Avenue, New York, N.Y. 10010.

10 9 8 7 6 5 4 3 2 1

acknowledgments

A SPECIAL THANKS to my youngest son, Destin, who came up with the idea for this novel and has always helped me with ideas for my other books. And to those whose expertise I then relied upon in developing the story: David Balts, Ridgeland, Mississippi; Colonel Mike Simmons, Vienna, Virginia; William T. Branch, M.D., F.A.C.S., clinical professor, University of South Florida College of Medicine, and listed in *Who's Who in the World Among Educators*; Brian S. Haight, San Francisco, California; E. B. Vandiver, Fairfax, Virginia; Bryan Slade, Pearl, Mississippi; Dr. Craig Lobb, Department of Microbiology, Samuel B. Johnson, M.D., F.A.C.S., professor and chairman of the Department of Ophthalmology, and Bob Galli, M.D., F.A.C.E.P., professor and chairman of the Department of Emergency Medicine, all of the University of Mississippi Medical Center; and Lisa Smith, surgical technician, Plastic Surgery Associates, Jackson.

Finally, my thanks to Jennifer Enderlin, executive editor at St. Martin's; to Matthew Shear, vice president and publisher; and Sally Richardson, president of St. Martin's, without whose faith and backing I would have never reached the point I have. Sometimes I wonder what I do, other than just sit and write. Again, thank you all.

prologue

SHE CAME SILENTLY down the wide corridor, moving swiftly, but not running. The only things that took away from her youthful beauty were two tiny blemishes spaced a few inches apart on her forehead, and the United States Disciplinary Barracks garb she wore—shapeless trousers and shirt in faded blue colors. Six months since she had been brought to this place and they still made her wear the hated garments. Six months and she could still visualize the razor wire of Leavenworth, still smell the concrete walls. She had been sentenced there after killing a sergeant who thought he could use her and then treat her as he wished. And she died a new death every day she was there, trapped in the confining space.

And now, after volunteering for the experiment for which she had been brought here, she was treated no better than she had ever been. The guards still snapped their orders, still stared at her as she walked by—despite how insignificant they were now and all she had become since the surgery. She stepped over the body of the military policeman lying on the floor. His arms were splayed and his features were frozen with the agony he had suffered going to his death. She dropped the gas mask she had been carrying since removing it at the entrance to the corridor, and it landed next to his outstretched hand.

To her sides, steel walls painted a light green reflected the illumination cast by the overhead fluorescent fixtures, spaced thirty feet apart. The military hadn't bothered to veneer the ceiling; it still consisted of the solid rock left when the passageways and rooms had been carved out of the bowels of the wide hill rising above the ground. The door at the end of the corridor was closed, but not locked, and she pushed it open.

Two doctors in surgical scrubs, their plastic face shields still in place, lay sprawled on their backs on the tile floor. A male nurse in similar scrubs lay on his side past the operating table.

On the table, Enriquez, covered to the waist with a sheet, lay bathed in the bright glow of the operating lamps. He was unmoving but not dead. The endotracheal tube protruding from his mouth and funneling oxygen into his air passages had protected him from the gas that had filled the complex moments before. He slowly turned his face in her direction. The two small, round incisions in his forehead had not yet been stitched closed. Blood seeped from the wounds and trickled across the skin. The look in his eyes told her that he was confused by the new thoughts racing through his mind. It was always that way at first, she knew. It had happened with her, and it had happened with the others. He moved his hand slowly out from his side and held it toward her in a pleading motion.

Then his features suddenly contorted into an expression of obvious fear.

He knew. Despite his confusion, the new power surging through his mind was such that he had reached a conclusion without even knowing how he had come by it. This sudden realization wasn't based on any form of psychic ability, but rather a logical conclusion coming from information streaming out of the data banks he now possessed. It was logical that she and the others would have to run when they reached the surface, he had realized. And he knew that even with their enhanced physical strength they could not carry him and run for long.

He didn't make another gesture. But every second now his ability to control his mind would improve. He would soon realize what had to happen after they left. He would try to fight through the lingering effects of the sedation and rise from the table to escape before it was too late. But it was already too late for him. She turned from the room, leaving him staring after her.

Ahead of her now, from beyond the open doorway at the far end of the long corridor, she heard the clanging sound of the grill that had covered the air shaft dropping to the floor. That meant that the others leaving with her had finished piling the folders containing the experiment's research records into the halls and setting them afire. The only thing left was to crawl up the steeply inclined shaft to the freedom above. She kept walking, despite feeling an urge to increase her pace.

She passed one of the old ether barrels, placed against the wall under a wide steel support beam holding up a section of limestone ceiling. Ethers, phosphates, and other chemicals found in the laboratory storerooms had been quickly mixed together, put in similar containers, and placed in strategic locations throughout the complex. The timers were already set. The resulting explosion and fire-storm would put to shame the power of the ordnance being tested on the range above the ground as a cover for the site.

As she reached the end of the corridor and turned into an intersecting passageway, she saw that the other four, dressed in the brown garb reserved for male prisoners, were already starting up the air shaft.

In only moments, the last one's scrambling feet had vanished from view. And the urge to move faster suddenly turned into a growing nervousness.

It was her emotion trying to take over. That she still could feel that kind of sensation didn't surprise her. She still had all the feelings and mental processes she had possessed in the past. The new artificial power she had been given had only combined with the old, superseding it but not erasing it. And now, the old burning desire to be free of confinement had combined with her keen awareness of the explosives to cause the feeling. The timers were ticking,

all set by men she wasn't certain of, set by men who had
sent her to see if Enriquez had recovered enough from the
anesthesia to escape with them—although they had known
that was highly unlikely. And now they had scrambled up
the shaft without waiting for her. If she had brought Enriquez with her, they would have needed to help her get him
up the shaft. They had known that, too.

　　She suddenly broke into a run toward the opening, hat-
ing them for feeling the need to hurry even as she ran faster
and faster.

1

TEN YEARS LATER

THE RAIN CAME down hard, hammering the roof of the Governor's Mansion, splashing against the sides of the buildings along Capitol Street, and forming shallow pools spreading across the pavement. Alfred Wynn drove his Mercedes in what most would consider a reckless manner, weaving around the slower traffic, slashing through the puddles, the sleek vehicle's tires throwing wide sheets of water out to the sides.

But he knew what he was doing. He knew he was absolutely safe under the conditions—the amount of water his tires cut through, the drag that the water caused, the weight of the Mercedes resisting the pull. He knew all these facts without even thinking, and the speed he could drive safely up to the very mile an hour.

A flashy diamond ring on his hand and his large frame encased in an Armani suit, he gave the appearance of someone who knew what he was doing in his business life, too. Obviously rich, the look on his chiseled, square face was one of complete confidence, absolute total confidence; the confidence that came from knowing all there was to know—and being able to instantly assimilate it all into complex thought that served whatever purpose he desired.

He didn't show a sign of panic when out of the corner of his eye he caught the image of a furniture transport truck running the red light at the intersection he should have been safely passing through. All he did was raise his arm against his face for protection, a primitive, instinctive gesture that came from somewhere deep in a part of his mind he had almost forgotten was there.

And then there was the thunderous sound of the truck's front slamming into the steel of the Mercedes' side.

At that moment, on the top floor of the tallest office building in the city, two large men in their mid-forties, dressed in nearly matching tailored suits, sat across from each other near the end of a long conference table. The larger man suddenly flinched. The other man's mouth gaped.

"What . . ." he started, ". . . a truck . . ."

Then their faces swung as one toward the far wall, as if they knew where the collision between the Mercedes and the truck had taken place, many stories below and several blocks away—in the direction they were looking.

Two miles away, Spence Stevens turned his aging Ford Bronco toward the rear of the main teaching hospital located at the center of the sprawling 160-acre University Medical Center complex. He parked out of the rain by stopping under the protection of the second floor of the hospital extending out over the emergency department entrance. But he was already soaked. His white shirt clung to his shoulders like a T-shirt damp with perspiration from a game of hospital league basketball. Even his jeans and sneakers were damp. A droplet of water trickled out from under his hair and moved slowly down his face. He used his knuckle to wipe the drop away, pushed open the driver's door, and stepped outside. Rolling his damp shirt sleeves up his forearms, he came around the front of the Bronco and walked toward the emergency department doors.

As they slid back and he walked inside, an older couple standing in a small waiting room off to the left stared his way. The woman smiled at his appearance. Ahead of him, a tall security guard standing beside the next doorway leading into the heart of the department looked at the wet clothes and smiled, too.

"Left my raincoat at my apartment this morning," Spence explained as he passed the man.

"No kidding," the guard called after him.

As he continued across the floor, doctors and nurses dressed in surgical scrubs went about their business around him. An older cardiologist, wearing a suit and tie and standing at the nurses' station off to the left, looked at him, staring at the wet attire for a moment, and then went back to writing orders in a chart. Dr. David Lambert waited in the corridor past the rear of the department. The aging pathologist wore a white knee-length lab coat over slacks, a dress shirt, and bright red tie: about the only combination of clothing Spence could ever remember seeing him in. Always the red tie. In fact there was almost nothing ever different in the old man's appearance, Spence caught himself noting for at least the fiftieth time in the few years since he had been a medical student and Lambert one of his professors. Lambert's slight build had not seemed to vary a pound over that period of time, his thin neck always making his shirt collars look too big. And, most memorable, he was still possessed of those ever alert, piercing dark eyes that seemed to stare right into you and know all there was to know about you. Not many things could make a beginning student so nervous as meeting Professor Lambert for the first time and being a recipient of that piercing stare. Lambert smiled as Spence walked up to him and stopped.

"You swam?" the old man questioned, looking at the wet clothes.

"Forgot my raincoat," Spence repeated.

"Good thinking, son," Lambert said as they shook hands. Then the old professor looked across his shoulder down the hallway in the direction of the morgue. "Can you believe he carried a donor card?" he asked, remarking on the peculiar fact that the man delivered there earlier that morning, a man guilty of at least two prior murders and a record of abusing others all his life, could otherwise be so caring as for such a bequest to have been found on his body.

Shaking his head in amusement, Lambert turned down the hall, and Spence followed after him.

With the elevator stopping for passengers at nearly every floor, it had taken the two men four frustrating minutes to get from the suite of offices on the top floor of the office building down to the lobby area. When the elevator door opened, they pushed past an old man starting to step outside. He stared after them as they hurried toward the building's entrance, but didn't say anything. They were large, obviously strong men, both of them a good six-feet-two and well over two hundred pounds, and it would be foolish to cause a scene with a pair already proven to rudeness at the least. And their tailored suits and shiny shoes spoke of wealth and power. The shoes especially, the old man knew. He was a shoe salesman. The shoes were Vallys—easily a thousand dollars a pair. He didn't need any problems.

The two disappeared into the heavy rain falling outside the building.

From a few blocks away came the sound of the bells atop St. Peter's Cathedral. It was twelve o'clock in the city of Jackson, Mississippi.

The morgue was fifty feet wide by a little over twenty feet deep, with most of its rear blanked from sight by a tall wall of metal body drawers. A small work area to the right of the drawers contained a white porcelain sink, a washing table, and the stocky body of Tommy Small, lying on his back on a gurney. Shorn of the blood-stained jeans and shirt he had worn when rolled into the morgue, he was naked except for a towel laid across his stomach and tucked up under his wide hips like a loincloth. Dr. Lambert, his thin, straight white hair hanging down across his forehead, stood on one side of the gurney. Spence, now wearing a black disposable full-body apron over his damp jeans and shirt, his hands clad in a double thickness of latex gloves, stood on the other side. In addition to the two jagged holes where police bullets had exited Tommy Small's chest, the left eye, partially protruding from its socket, showed where a round had entered his head from the rear and lodged itself just behind the orbital socket. The force of the shot had caused the cornea to disintegrate, leaving a slight amount of clear-colored pulp at the corner of the eye.

"The right one was usable for a transplant," Dr. Lambert said, sliding a pair of glasses with thick lenses from his lab coat pocket. "You're the only person I know who would be interested in the other one."

Spence hoped the optic nerve wasn't damaged. From the angle the shot entered the head it didn't appear that the trajectory of the bullet itself would have done any damage. But the concussion could have severed or damaged the nerve beyond use even in his experiments. He lifted a scalpel from the stainless steel instrument cart next to the gurney.

His first incision was at the very inside corner of the eye, as close to the bridge of the nose as he could get it.

On Capitol Street, only one car at a time was being let through the eastbound lanes at the scene of the accident. The Mercedes' side was caved in and the furniture truck's cab had ridden up on the sleek car's top. Firemen standing in the driving rain were using hoses to spray the gasoline away. There was no ambulance in sight.

The two large men stared through the windshield of their Mercedes, brought to a crawl in the slowly moving traffic. As the car neared the intersection, the larger man slowed it even more, lowered his window and leaned his head outside toward a young fireman directing a wide spray of water under the truck.

"Where did they take him?"

The fireman glanced across his shoulder but hadn't quite caught the question.

The Mercedes suddenly stopped. The man threw open the door and stepped outside into the rain. "Where did they take him?" he snapped.

A police officer directing traffic through the intersection stared at the man. The fireman hesitated a moment, then said, "The truck driver wasn't hurt. He—"

"The one he hit, you fool!" the man shouted. "Where did they take him?"

The young fireman's lips tightened. He started to come back with an even louder voice. But then realizing he must be facing someone important considering the way the man was acting and the Mercedes he drove, he held his tongue. He had just received his position on the fire department a month before. He certainly didn't need to jeopardize it.

"They took him to University."

As the man slid back inside the Mercedes and it sped past the policeman directing traffic, the fireman stared after the car. As he saw the policeman glance at him, he felt a little embarrassed at having taken the abuse he had. Powerful figure or whatever, he wasn't certain now. But there *was something* he had sensed in the big man's demeanor.

Spence dug the scalpel farther down inside the orbital socket and past it, cutting carefully, ever deeper, around the optic nerve, into the brain.

Dr. Lambert, eyes blurred behind the thick lenses of his glasses, smiled his approval at the dexterous movement of the sharp blade.

"You learned well," he said. "You remind me a lot of myself when I was younger."

Spence glanced at the older man. Lambert wouldn't be a bad model to emulate when it came to working with a scalpel. And not only when he was younger. His skill with operating instruments put him more in the mold of a neurosurgeon than a pathologist. There couldn't be anyone who was more skilled by steadiness and hand-eye coordination— and that intuitive feel that a person who was going to be a skilled surgeon possessed long before he entered medical school.

Of course I'm biased about anything that has to do with Dr. Lambert, Spence thought. He knew that started just after finishing the second year of his neurology residency, when he began to think about making his career one of research rather than joining one of the private practice groups in the city. "You're crazy," everyone had said. "Only two years from beginning a private practice that will set you up for life—and you want to give that up for a researcher's salary and a state pension that will hardly pay off your house before you die." Only Dr. Lambert had said that if research was where he wanted to be, the hell with what anyone else thought. By that time Spence already knew where he was headed, but it was nice for the old doctor to add his encouragement. And he did so repeatedly after that, right up to the day Spence remembered ending his residency and starting work in research the very next day. He smiled a little at his next thought.

"What?" Dr. Lambert questioned, looking across Small's body.

"I was thinking about how you helped talk me into research. I was just wondering what I'm going to be thinking of you about the time I start drawing my pension."

"Hell, son," Lambert said, "the others will have their millions, but you'll have the good feeling." There was the inkling of a smile at the corners of the pathologist's lips. "Of course not much else," he added.

Spence lifted the eyeball, complete with the optic nerve ending in a clump of severed brain tissue, into view.

Siren wailing, the ambulance swerved off North State Street through the rain into the University Medical Center complex. The driver followed the narrow pavement circling around the helicopter pad toward the emergency department at the rear of the main hospital. The paramedic in the back of the ambulance, a slim female in her late twenties wearing a yellow rain suit, performed her life-saving actions almost by instinct she had done them so many times before— though she knew this time they were of no use. If nothing else, the inch-wide flat piece of steel driven into the Mercedes' driver's forehead just above his left eye told her that.

It had been driven into the skull when the side of the Mercedes, which virtually exploded on impact, was hit by the loaded transport truck. A couple inches of the metal, jagged on one edge and smooth on the other, protruded above the skin. How deep it went she could only guess, but it was obvious it had gone *too* deep. The profuse amount of blood that came from a head wound had quit running out around the metal. There was no movement of the heart to pump the blood. He was in full cardiac arrest. He was asystolic in two ECG leads. She had intubated him, started an IV, and given him a total of five milligrams of epinephrine and three of atropine—all without results. Mr. Alfred Wynn, the forty-two-year-old senior vice president of Computer Resources Incorporated, according to the identification in his wallet, would be DOA at the hospital. He was already dead.

Then, directly below the protruding piece of metal, Alfred Wynn's eye opened.

The paramedic's eyes widened.

The blood began pumping out around the metal.

The paramedic jerked her head toward the readout on the electrocardiogram monitor.

The man driving the Mercedes suddenly tightened his eyes. He stared over the steering wheel through the top of the car's windshield as if he were looking for something in the heavy dark clouds overhanging the city.

"He was back," he said.

He looked across the seat. "John?" he said, a questioning tone to his voice, a tone that was almost never present in either of their voices.

John had seen the same thing. He looked toward the clouds. But that was only where his idle stare went as he concentrated. What he was seeing was inside his head. The image had come back, for just an instant, and blurred, and then it was gone again.

Now it was back again.

This time a clearer picture—a woman's face, her features twisted into an incredulous expression, looking down at Alfred's face. She had long blond hair tied back in a ponytail. She wore a yellow rain jacket over a light-blue uniform shirt . . . a small hose running from Alfred's face toward a round, steel cylinder . . . the scene bouncing.

An ambulance.

A paramedic.

The flash of the building off to the side.

The emergency room entrance.

The blond paramedic came outside the rear of the ambulance, reached back inside the blocky vehicle and pulled the gurney toward her. Its legs popped down to the concrete and the body of Mr. Alfred Wynn, strapped to a spinal board, came outside. Her partner, a male with his dark hair damp and draping across his forehead, had hurried out of the driver's seat to the rear of the ambulance, and now used the flat of one hand to pump on Alfred's chest while using his other hand to pull the gurney toward the open emergency department doors. The blond rapidly compressed the ambu bag, forcing oxygen down the endotracheal tube into Alfred's lungs. A pair of nurses dressed in blue surgical scrubs met the gurney, grabbing its sides and helping pull it hurriedly inside the department.

"He was gone," the blond paramedic said to one of them. "He opened his eye—he could see, I know he could see. No pulse. No cardiac rhythm, no breathing . . . he could see."

As they passed through the doors into the department, a slim, unusually young resident in green scrubs met the gurney.

The eye popped open again.

The one beneath the section of jagged metal driven into his forehead.

The blond pumped the ambu bag with both hands.

The gurney being turned rapidly into a trauma room caused the body to shift. Alfred's arm began to pull out from underneath the webbing securing him in place. His hand moved toward his head. The resident grabbed Alfred's forearm.

With amazing strength, Alfred's hand continued on toward the piece of protruding metal. His fingers locked around its jagged edge.

The male paramedic caught the man's wrist.

"Stop him," a nurse wailed to the side of the gurney. "Don't let him pull. . . ."

The embedded metal came out of Alfred's forehead with a noticeable squishing sound. His hand, holding the sharp section of steel, trembled. Blood gushed from the wound. Even the resident, stunned momentarily, stared at the blood.

The hand went limp.

The length of steel fell to the floor, clanging against the tile, and lay still.

Alfred's arm fell to the side, his hand hanging limply off the gurney.

A gray-haired black nurse, standing a few feet away, made the sign of the cross across her chest.

2

SPENCE STEPPED OUTSIDE the morgue into the short hall-way leading from the area. He held a plastic bag containing the eyeball and attached optic nerve immersed in a clear saline solution. Dr. Lambert shut and locked the morgue door behind them, and they pushed through the double doors into the connecting hallway.

"How much progress have you made?" Lambert asked.

Spence shook his head. "The first day I started work we could already send electrical impulses into the occipital lobe. It gave a blind person the ability to register fuzzy, distorted bursts of light. We had hoped by this time to have managed some kind of definition that would at least form a general image. About all we've accomplished is to give better focus to the same fuzzy, distorted bursts of light."

An attractive young nurse coming toward them from in the direction of the emergency department glanced at the plastic bag. As she drew closer, she looked at the bag again, and her eyes narrowed.

As she came almost even with them, Spence noticed her look at Dr. Lambert, then narrow her eyes again and then look quickly back down at the bag and the bobbing eyeball. Spence looked at Dr. Lambert. The old pathologist had removed his glasses and had one eye tightly closed. His bony finger pointed toward it and then down at the bag, and he shook his head sadly.

The nurse hurried on past them.

When she glanced back over her shoulder, Lambert had his head turned looking back at her, his eye still clamped tightly shut. "You have an aspirin?" he called after her. "Pain's getting to be something awful." He rubbed his closed eye with his knuckle.

The nurse increased her pace down the hallway. Spence couldn't help but smile a little.

"A new one," Lambert said, glancing back at the nurse once more, this time with both eyes open. "They get younger every day."

He shook his head again. This time in genuine feeling. "Maybe it's just I'm getting too old," he lamented.

"Lazy maybe," Spence said, "but not too old."

"That's a fine way to address your former professor," Lambert came back. Then he added, "Yeah, I am getting old. I've been thinking about retiring lately. About everybody else my age is already gone, though I'm not certain I really want to hang it up quite yet. What do you think about my retiring?"

"Weren't you the one who told me the hell with what anyone else thought—it's your life."

Lambert nodded. "Yeah, I did." A few steps later, he suddenly said, "You'd think a good-looking young guy like you could find a wife." He had a serious expression on his face.

Spence smiled a little. "I have a few years left."

"Spence, the wife and I never had any children. Now with her gone I see the other doctors with their grandchildren coming up to visit them . . ." As Lambert let his words trail off, he turned his gaze back up the hallway. Their steps echoed ahead of them off the tile. "But Carol and I did have each other for a lot of good years," he added in a low voice. "I'll always be thankful for that."

Spence saw the old pathologist's expression was more forlorn than serious now. Even with the death of his wife several years before, he had outwardly seemed to stay his old self, wisecracking in his scolding of residents who didn't perform exactly as he wished, almost funny unless

you were the unlucky resident, but always deeply serious
with his teaching. It was his whole life. Somehow Spence
had never thought about Lambert being absorbed with anything else. Especially being lonely. But it wasn't just the
death of Lambert's wife; there was nobody else, either, no
brothers, no sisters, the old pathologist's parents deceased
long ago.

Now Spence suddenly felt guilty. During his residency
Lambert had invited him over to his house to eat dinner
several times. Spence remembered trying to return the favor
several times by inviting Lambert out to eat. But at the time
it seemed the old man had always been too busy to accept—always something or the other he had to do at the
hospital—and Spence remembered it had been years now
since he had invited his old friend out again.

"What are you doing for dinner tonight?" he now asked.

"Why?" Lambert asked as they stopped in front of the
doors leading into the emergency department.

"Why else, if I'm not asking you out to eat?"

The old man studied him for a moment. "Okay, Spence.
Since you're asking me out rather than trying to subject me
to your cooking." There was already a livelier tone back in
Lambert's voice again.

Spence smiled. "I can't stand my own cooking."

"Good." Lambert nodded. "Good," he said again. Then
he added, "Of course I guess you'll be wanting me to return
the favor to you next week."

"Of course."

Lambert nodded again, and smiled now.

The door to the emergency department opened.

The gray-haired black nurse coming through the door
held it open for them. "You have another one let go of his
soul, Doctor," she said.

"Thank you, Bertha," Lambert said.

They walked inside the department.

The man Bertha had referred to lay on his back on a
gurney in a trauma room only a few feet away. An endotracheal tube was still in place. The young resident working

over him injected an amp of epinephrine into the IV tube running into the man's limp arm. When the doctor stepped back, he nodded at a nurse holding a pair of defibrillators in her hands. She slipped one over the man's heart, the other at his side, said "Clear," and pressed the buttons on the paddles. The body convulsed with the surge of electricity activating the muscles. But that wasn't a sign of life. A laboratory frog dead for hours would still convulse when a charge of electricity was passed through its body. And the defibrillators weren't called for anyway; the monitors showed the man wasn't in an arrhythmia but rather in full cardiac arrest. The defibrillators were being used only in a desperate attempt by a young resident not wanting to lose one of the first arrivals he had to face alone. Dr. Lambert, usually quick to point out a mistake, would have normally said something to the resident, even if he wasn't in Lambert's program. But the pained look on the resident's face was enough to keep Lambert silent. The mistake of using the defibrillators wasn't harming anything, only useless.

Spence didn't have to look at the monitors to see that it was time to declare the man dead, if for no other reason than the gaping hole in his forehead, as if a spear had been driven into the brain.

The entrance to the emergency department was down a wide thoroughfare closely surrounded by the rear of the hospital rising to the left and the wings of the newer children's hospital rising to the right and in front of them, causing the pavement to dead-end in a wide strip of blacktop larger than a basketball court. Several empty parking spots, sheltered from the pouring rain by the second floor of the hospital extending out over the emergency department entrance, were spaced a few feet apart. They were reserved for ambulances and for vehicles of relatives and friends of those rushed to the hospital. Currently, only an aging Ford Bronco sat in one of the spots. Parking there would only bring attention to the Mercedes. So the two men parked on the third story of the complex's main parking garage, not much more than a hundred yards away from the department's entrance, and came back to stand at one of the garage doors facing back toward the department. They remained there for several seconds, staring through the rain, thinking. There would be security guards. There would be a need for identification tags. And a need to shed their expensive suits. Then John saw a security guard look their way from across the garage. He carried an umbrella. They didn't need anyone to try and help them through the rain. "Genowski," John said, and nodded in the direction he was looking.

Genowski looked at the guard.

And then with neither Genowski nor John speaking or even looking at each other again, they agreed on what they would do next—and stepped out into the rain.

The young emergency department doctor pulled the sheet up over Alfred's head. A wide circle of blood soaked through the material over the face. An orderly started the gurney toward the morgue.

"Another day, another dollar," Lambert said.

The words weren't spoken in jest. It was the best an old pathologist who had seen too many bodies in his time could do in managing to keep his sanity.

Spence looked at the resident coming across the floor. He was even younger than Spence had first thought, twenty-two or twenty-three at most. One of those whiz-kid types who graduated college in his teens and had already been into his medical school studies while most others his age were still fighting freshman English. But the expression on his face as he stopped in front of them said that for all his high IQ, he was at a loss as to what had just happened.

"The wound to the forehead was enough to kill him instantly," he said in a low voice. "A length of metal penetrated a good eight or nine centimeters into the brain. But he regained consciousness in the ambulance. Then in here again on the gurney. He didn't want to die." The young resident was obviously deeply affected by not being able to help grant the man's wish.

Lambert's statement, spoken in a compassionate tone, showed he knew that, too. "Not everything is in textbooks, Doctor," he said. "There are miracles—and there are some things that start out like they're going to be miracles that don't quite make it all the way. A certain percentage of your cases aren't going to have any basis in medical fact as you've been taught it."

Genowski and John walked into the hospital through a front entrance, just two men among the many men and women patients and visitors of all ages passing in and out of the massive building.

They didn't have to know where the morgue was. They simply asked a cleaning lady mopping the floor.

And they certainly didn't need to go anywhere else but the morgue to find Alfred. They knew that was where he would be taken when he had stopped transmitting the picture.

3

IN THE MORGUE, Dr. Lambert leaned over Alfred Wynn's body, lying before him on a gurney placed close to the washing table. In life the man had been six-foot-three and well built. With the blood now cleansed from his face, his skin was smooth and lightly tanned, marred only slightly during the accident by a few red marks where glass had embedded into his cheeks. With his expensive suit and manicured nails, he had been a distinguished looking man, probably one most women would consider attractive. He still wore his trousers. They appeared untouched, somehow avoiding even getting blood on them from the massive wound in the forehead. Only one shiny shoe remained on his feet. The other must have come off during the collision. His silk shirt had been ripped open by the paramedics. It was blood soaked, as was his bare chest, as had been his face, his neck, and his hands—all from the head wound, for, actually, the man had suffered little other injury during the collision. His chest didn't show any evidence of blunt trauma. With the exception of a laceration on one hand and a wide bruise on his left shoulder, he had come through the accident exceedingly well—except for the flat piece of metal that had penetrated his forehead. Lambert looked at the length of metal now. It had been delivered with the body, and he had set it aside on the instrument cart before beginning his examination. A single piece of metal that, had it missed its mark, could very well have left Alfred

Wynn sitting up in a hospital bed at the moment, sore and bruised, but basically unharmed.

Miracles and almost miracles, Lambert thought. *Good luck and bad luck.* He used tweezers to pick the fragments of glass from the cheeks and deposit them in a small stainless steel bowl sitting on the instrument cart. It took only a few seconds. There weren't many of the tiny pieces present.

Then he ran a probe into the wound where the steel had been, measuring the depth it had penetrated. The young resident had made an accurate guess, more than eight centimeters, better than three inches past the skull into the brain. And a wide penetration. He *should* have died nearly instantaneously, Lambert mused. The resident was correct about that, too. As he withdrew the probe, he felt its tip nudge against something.

Not tissue.

To his sensitive fingers the object felt solid—hard.

Metallic?

Another piece of metal from the mutual disintegration of the Mercedes and the front of the truck? Lambert moved the tip of the probe back down to the area where he had felt the object.

He felt nothing this time.

He slowly brought its tip up the side of the tissue.

He felt it.

Holding the probe carefully at its current depth, he reached to the instrument cart and lifted into his hand a small forceps, which looked little different from a pair of stainless steel tweezers.

He ran the forceps down into the wound, stopped the instrument's tip at the end of the probe, worked a moment by feel only, not seeing the object, felt it, and clamped it with the forceps.

Withdrawing the probe slowly so as to not dislodge the object, he pulled on the forceps—and felt resistance.

He pulled harder.

*Alfred's leg kicked spasmodically. His right arm flipped
up and fell across his chest.*

Lambert jumped back from the gurney.

Alfred's arm slid back to his side.

He lay still.

Genowski had felt the sudden piercing impulse enter his
brain.

"They found it," he said.

A hospital security guard was walking down the hall
toward them. They resumed their pace.

When they passed him, they smiled pleasantly.

He returned their greeting with a nod and continued on
down the hall.

When he turned a corner and disappeared from sight,
Genowski and John turned back in the direction of the
morgue.

They were wearing surgical scrubs now, pilfered from a
storage room's contents, and, except for their damp hair,
looked little different from any of the similarly dressed phy-
sicians constantly moving along the hall.

Their loose scrub suit shirts even sported ID badges at
their chests.

John carried the clothes they had changed out of in a
plastic bag similar to the kind that one would use to carry
items from a supermarket checkout counter.

Dr. Lambert took a deep breath. He stared at Alfred Wynn's
limp body. It was not unusual for a muscle contraction to
cause a recently deceased body to move, even convulse.
Yet he had never seen such a dramatic contraction. *Lingering electrical activity in the brain?* he thought. But he
shook his head no even as he thought that. *Not everything
can be found in a textbook,* he reminded himself.

Nevertheless, he stood where he was for a moment without moving back toward the body.

The forceps, still in the wound, lay tilted against the side
of the deep hole.

He slowly reached for them, clasped them, hesitated for a couple of seconds, then began to feel for the object again.

This time when he found it he waited a long moment, staring down at the corpse's face, then slowly began to tug at the object again.

He tugged harder.

The object popped loose.

Slowly, he lifted it up out of the wound.

It *was* another piece of metal. Tiny. Square. The color of a penny but only a fourth as large.

He studied it in front of his glasses perched on the end of his nose. Its sides were perfectly smooth, with no jagged or twisted edge to show it had been broken off of the larger length of steel that had been driven into the skull.

He deposited it into the bowl on the instrument cart.

Then he lifted a clipboard from one side of the cart and recorded the cause of death and depth of the wound.

As he laid the clipboard back on the instrument cart, his gaze went once again to the piece of metal in the bowl. He stared at it for a moment, then used the tip of his finger to separate it from the glass fragments and slide it up the side of the bowl, clasping it between his thumb and forefinger. He would almost guess it came from something like a radio or maybe some kind of mechanism in the car door. He could visualize a panel from the door being slammed inward and disintegrating, and the flat length of metal driving a tiny fragment of the panel ahead of it into the forehead.

The telephone on the solitary small table against the front wall rang.

He carried the piece of metal with him as he walked to the table and lifted the telephone receiver with his other hand.

"Yes?"

"Dr. Lambert, this is nurse Edith Day on three east. We have an eighty-three-year-old female dead of apparent cardiac failure. She had bruises on her neck and shoulders when her family brought her in, and Dr. Moore thinks an autopsy is called for."

"The more the merrier," Lambert said, lifting the tiny square in front of his glasses again.

"Excuse me?"

"Send her on down. I'll call the coroner." He replaced the receiver. He looked at the wall of drawers in front of him. They were all full, with Tommy Small taking the last available space, and Alfred Wynn needing room. He could store the new body across the hall from the morgue in the area normally used for in-house autopsies, and it could be kept there for a few hours. But more space needed to be made available in the drawers by removing some of the bodies to the human anatomy lab. The professor there was supposed to remove three the day before, but he hadn't. Lambert looked back at the tiny piece of metal, balanced it on the tip of his forefinger for a moment . . . and then, still unable to guess what part of the Mercedes it came from, he dropped it into a stainless steel cup on the table.

It disappeared into the center of a large cigar ash lying at the bottom of the cup.

Lambert frowned. The medical center was a nonsmoking facility throughout, and yet Dr. Chokchai could be tracked through the corridors surrounding the morgue any day by the trail of cigar ashes he left scattered about. "When I arrived from Thailand four decades ago, 'no smoking' was not part of package after medical school," Chokchai would stubbornly say to anyone who dared mention the no-smoking edict to him. "Not part of package then, not change deal now in mid-river. Not around dead patients anyway." Were it not that Chokchai was an old codger who seemed to have been around as long as the complex, the powers that be would not put up with him so easily, whether he smoked only around dead patients or not. Lambert thought again about thinking of Chokchai as an old codger. The "old codger" was actually six years younger than he was—they had starting teaching at the medical school the same year, nearly forty years before. Lambert wondered if anyone thought he was being tolerated, too.

The morgue door opened.

Speak of the devil, Lambert thought.

Dr. Chokchai, all five-feet-six, light-brown, 200 rounded pounds of him, cloaked in a too-tight lab coat, stood in the doorway.

"I'm starving to death," Chokchai said. "You about ready for lunch?"

"If you don't light that thing," Lambert said, staring at the cigar stub clinched at the corner of the man's mouth.

"No smoking allowed around live patients," Chokchai said.

Lambert frowned again, walked back to the gurney, lifted the instruments he had used and washed them hurriedly in the porcelain sink set back in the corner of the room past the edge of the metal drawers.

After dumping the glass fragments from the bowl into the sink, rinsing the small container, then carefully drying the instruments on a paper towel and placing them and the bowl back in their proper positions, he pulled off his surgical gloves and dropped them and the towel into the small, box-shaped, biohazard disposal container sitting on the floor next to the table with the telephone. Then he stepped to the door to walk with Chokchai to the cafeteria.

He paused a moment and looked back at Alfred Wynn's perfectly still body. "Not everything can be found in a textbook," he murmured.

"What did you say?" Chokchai asked.

"It's over your head, Chok," Lambert said as he stepped from the room and pulled the door closed behind him.

It locked automatically.

Even though the rain had finally ceased, Spence had remained in the Bronco after he stopped it in the parking lot fronting the building where his team conducted their research. The blocky, concrete structure, one of the oldest buildings at the medical center, was actually home to a half dozen different research groups; his group's laboratory and offices took up the right half of the first floor. The vehicles parked in front of the building were mostly midsized and similar in age to his Bronco, a far cry from some of the late-model BMWs and Mercedes in other doctors' parking lots at the center. He lifted the plastic bag and stared at the eyeball and optic nerve floating in the saline solution. He certainly *hadn't* gone into research for the money in it. He didn't regret that. Yet at times it was frustrating to think about the number of hours he and his assistants had put in trying to work around the limited research dollars they were allocated—and how little they had accomplished. At least as a private, practicing neurologist he could have sealed off a brain aneurysm, felt immediate gratification at what he had done.

Also frustrating was that many researchers kept whatever progress they might have made a closely guarded secret. There were the patents that could be applied for if the work was kept secret until a breakthrough was made. Patents meant money. Untold riches when you considered what the blind would pay to see again, the paralyzed would pay to walk again. But the secrecy could be the very thing preventing the sought-after breakthroughs. If everyone was sharing their research, there would be a chance that what one group was doing would combine with the progress another group had already made. As much as he hated government regulation, he still almost wished there was some law that medical research *had* to be shared. Then, irritated with his thoughts, he opened the Bronco's door and stepped outside.

He entered his lab through a rear door.

As he did, Flo looked his way from where she stood next to the long counter at the far side of the laboratory. She wore a knee-length white lab coat, stained at her hip where she had spilled some chemical or brushed against something. More likely, the coat was somebody else's, he thought, one she had hastily lifted from among the others hanging on the rack in the open closet a few feet away from her—for she never spilled anything, never made the slightest wrong move when she was engaged in work. Joining his team the year before, she was one of the most meticulous research assistants he had ever known—and the only person who had ever worked in the laboratory whom he was certain was smarter than he was.

She didn't care about little things though, whether it was her lab coat or someone else's she wore, whether her hair was in place—a dark curl now hung twisted over one eye and she wasn't wearing any makeup, though she was definitely feminine, with a slim, tight figure and big eyes highlighting a perfectly molded face. He thought she could easily pass for someone younger than he, though she was older. Her personnel file said she was thirty-six. She saw the bag.

"Is it a good one?"

He nodded as he stopped in front of her.

"I'll test the conductivity," she said.

When he didn't immediately hand the bag to her, her hand reached for it impatiently. "It's been nearly four hours since he was shot, Spence—it's already deteriorating." She was always very professional, calling him Doctor or Dr. Stevens when they were in the midst of their work. Calling him Spence was reserved for when she was irritated with him. He handed her the bag.

She walked toward the far side of the lab and the equipment she would use to quickly test the tissue, then preserve it. She looked back across her shoulder.

"Dr. Brimston is in your office, Doctor."

That announcement alone was enough to take away any enthusiasm that Spence might have felt for the day.

4

DR. RICHARD BRIMSTON, chairman of the committee in charge of research funding allocation at the center, was a notably overweight man in his sixties with an equally noticeable pink glow to his face brought about by chronic high blood pressure. The staffs of the various research units at the hospital had placed bets among themselves for years about when he would keel over—and few would have been overly depressed if someone betting on an earlier demise of Brimston than they had won out. But he had gone on year after year, actually outliving a couple of those who had bet against him, his skin assuming a slightly pinker glow all the time. He was standing at the window in Spence's office staring out across the parking area. His hands were crossed behind his back at his waist. He didn't bother to turn around as he heard the office door open and close.

"Where are we, Doctor?" he asked in his typically nasal tone. "I have people who will be asking questions at the board meeting at the end of the month—hard questions."

He still didn't turn from the window.

Spence walked around behind his desk and settled into the leather chair there. His answering machine light was blinking with the tape jammed full of calls. "Would you like a cup of coffee?" he asked.

Dr. Brimston turned around. His hands were still crossed behind his back. He rose a little on his toes and then settled back to his heels. The hands remained where they were.

"No, Dr. Stevens. Thank you. I need a progress report on your work. Detailed enough that I can explain it fully. Funds are getting tighter every year."

Spence held his hand out in a gesture across his desk to the straight chair at the front of the desk. Dr. Brimston stared at it a moment as if studying it, then walked to it and slowly settled onto its flat seat.

"A report on your progress," he repeated, adjusting his weight to where he was most comfortable and crossing his legs. "There's actually not much new to report, is there?" he said. "I hope there's *something*."

Discovery didn't always come in a neat progression. Often it wasn't one-two-three-four, but rather one-two then back to one again and starting all over after a dead end was reached. But even a dead end wasn't all bad, Spence knew.

"Nothing is wasted even when we learn what *won't* work," he said. "It tells us that much, where no one will waste research hours in going in that direction again. And even some of the dead ends might not be true dead ends in a literal sense. It's simply that at this point they didn't take us where we wanted to go. They're all cataloged—every last thing we have tried. We can never tell when one thing we've learned, even in a failed effort, might connect with something else we try later and result in a breakthrough. It's going to happen."

"Do you often plan strategy with the heads of the other research units?" Brimston asked, folding his arms across his chest.

"Excuse me?"

"I've just come from Dr. Ambrose and he basically says the same thing you do—no progress in his field either, but there are all kinds of reasons why his program should continue, he says. In fact, he claims his funding should increase. I imagine that's what I'll hear from you next. And all of this based on what *hasn't* worked?"

Before Spence could respond, Dr. Brimston added, "Have you given any more thought to Mr. Quinlan's suggestion?"

"Dr. Brimston, I—" The telephone on his desk ringing interrupted him. "Excuse me," he said, and lifted the receiver. "Yes?"

"Dr. Ambrose wanted to know if he might speak to Dr. Brimston," Flo said over the line.

Spence held the receiver across the desk. "Dr. Ambrose," he said.

Brimston frowned but leaned forward and took the receiver into his hand. "Yes, Dr. Ambrose," he said in a dry tone.

Spence leaned back in his chair. Mr. Walter L. Quinlan, he thought. A name that always drew immediate attention when it was mentioned at the center. Based on his longtime interest in medical issues and the several million dollars he had donated to research at the center over the past several years, the man was a very prominent member of the medical center board. Maybe the *most prominent* in some members' minds considering the rumor that since he had no close relatives, his entire billion-dollar-plus fortune—made in timber and building chicken houses as a young man, then processing chickens for fast-food restaurants nationwide over the last couple of decades—was to go into a permanently funded trust for research at the center at his death.

He was a good man, a great man considering what he had already done for research at the center. But he was not a scientist. There were two different methods in which scientists were working to create artificial vision. Both ways started with the same basic ingredients they all had to work with: light enters the eye through the cornea, hits the retina, and is converted into electrical energy. Then that energy runs through pathways back to the occipital lobe of the brain. An individual actually *sees* when those electrical impulses get back to the lobe. The difference between the different scientific groups' methodology was that one had settled on working to replicate only an artificial retina for those patients who had damage there. An artificial retina, actually a small computer chip as it was envisioned now, would be implanted behind the cornea, where focus would occur on the chip, and the chip would send electrical energy back into the optic nerve. That was the method Mr. Quinlan had suggested might make better use of the funds he donated. But Spence wanted to keep going in the direction of the groups working on total eye replacement, where an individual had suffered complete destruction of the eye, as happens in many injuries. This was where his research on the miniaturized camera occurred, a camera so small that it could take the place of the cornea, capture light, and, through a converter placed in the back of the eye as a retina, change the light to computer language, which is exactly what a digital camera does, and then run the wires directly into the occipital lobe and re-create vision even when the optic nerve itself was damaged beyond use. It was his dream.

And something else. Somewhere in his work, in the transmission of electrical energy through the brain, was the key to how we learn and retain. Though he hadn't voiced his hope to anyone other than Flo, it was his *real dream.* To understand and be able to duplicate the process whereby the brain learns and retains, and then be able to use that process to implant knowledge directly into a person's mind, would jump humankind thousands of years ahead of its normal evolution. He thought of the oft-quoted wish of college students who said, "Wouldn't it be great if you could just record a professor's lecture and play it back into earphones at night while you slept, waking up with all the knowledge freshly implanted in your mind?" All knowledge could be implanted rather than simply learned. Man could become a walking encyclopedia; doctors could become specialists in all fields at the same time. Mankind could learn anything, everything, become anything they desired. And not with any more effort than flicking a switch on whatever machine that would be developed to implant the knowledge. Tens of thousands of school hours could be done away with; mankind could turn that saved time to accomplishments. What couldn't the world become with everyone able to be enlightened to the fullest extent they desired? "No," Dr. Brimston said now in a tone so sharp it pulled Spence back from his thoughts.

Brimston had finished his conversation with the abrupt rejoinder and was holding the receiver back across the desk.

Spence took it and replaced it in its cradle. "I would think about Mr. Quinlan's suggestion," Brimston said, and stood.

Spence shook his head a little. "To change our focus now would be throwing away tens of thousands of dollars we have already spent."

"It's Mr. Quinlan's money," Brimston said, "and his wish."

Before he turned toward the door leading from the office he added pointedly, "And I think he's about reached the end of his patience."

At the door Brimston paused and looked back toward the desk. "I don't mean that to threaten you," he said. "Mr. Quinlan hasn't specifically voiced any impatience to me. But while he's a great humanitarian, he's also a human being. And though he's been totally unselfish in all he's done for the medical center to date, you and I both know he has a vested interest in retina replacement. I would think about that."

Just before he closed the door, Brimston added, "Maybe a compromise of some sort. Part of what Mr. Quinlan wants, part of what you want."

Mr. Walter L. Quinlan, in his late fifties, tall and thin, but with ropy strong muscles running along his arms and legs, wore only a brief bathing suit girding his hips, exposing the majority of his deeply tanned body. He stood at the edge of a rain-dampened balcony outside his sprawling home in Rose's Bluff, a luxury subdivision perched on a rise along the northwest shore of the Ross Barnett Reservoir. With the heavy line of thunderstorms mostly gone north now, and the sun once again beginning to peek through the remaining clouds, his view was a magnificent one, sweeping out over the thirty-three-thousand-acre body of water and across it toward the buildings and trees along its far shore. But he viewed it with only one eye.

The other was covered with a black patch held in place by a thin string looping around the back of his thick shoulder-length dark hair. Not that there was any noticeable marring of the eye in question—its only damage was a retina that didn't work any longer. But if he couldn't see out of it, he preferred it be covered. That was what he wanted, and he always got what he wanted.

To anyone who might be looking at him, he appeared totally relaxed, slumped lazily against the balcony rail, a paperback novel held loosely down in his hand, propped against the edge of the rail. But he wasn't relaxed. In his mind, he watched the morgue door swing open in front of him. The view swung to the right of the morgue, and he saw Alfred's body stretched out on the gurney, his silk shirt ripped open and still wearing his pants and a shoe. The body seemed to move closer and grow larger in the same way it would if the picture he was viewing was from a television camera being rolled forward toward the gurney. Genowski's forearm came forward into the picture. Behind his hand, his arm was covered with the blue sleeve of a set of surgical scrubs. The blood had not been cleansed from Alfred's body. Dried and turning dark, it coated the side of his neck and his chest in a solid sheet running down from the deep wound in his forehead.

Genowski's hand moved to the wound, and his forefinger was suddenly digging down into the jagged hole, feeling in the spot where the microchip was implanted.

Genowski dug his forefinger deeper, twisting it, probing for an area in the brain matter where the piece of steel driven into the skull during the collision might have driven the chip deeper.

But even as Genowski dug deeper, Quinlan knew it hadn't happened. The last quick signals that had come from Alfred had come when someone purposely tore the chip from its attachment. Genowski jerked his finger back out of the wound and moved his gaze to the instrument cart.

Quinlan had the same view. There was nothing there but the stainless steel instruments.

"He took it with him," Genowski said.

Who was "he"? The emergency room doctor? No. The doctor who would have been using the instruments on Alfred's body.

The pathologist.

5

THE CONTROL PANEL in the cafeteria cash register was malfunctioning, and the manager, a short, bald-headed man with an irritated expression across his face, worked hard to fix it. An older, heavyset woman in a cafeteria uniform looked at the items Dr. Lambert held in front of him.

He said, "Coffee seventy-five cents, ham and cheese sandwich a dollar fifty, apple pie a dollar fifteen—three dollars and forty cents."

The woman stared at him. "I can add," she said. She held out her hand.

He handed her a five-dollar bill. "That's a dollar sixty back," he said.

The woman frowned, then reached past the man still working over the open cash register drawer, lifted a dollar bill from one of the trays, counted out two quarters and a dime, and handed them to Lambert.

He dropped the coins inside a quart jar labeled JIMMY DAWSON BONE MARROW TRANSPLANT FUND and turned toward a table.

Dr. Chokchai carrying a salad and tea as he walked beside him, said, "Why do you irritate her like that?"

"We're old friends to start with. She's been here almost as long as I have. Secondly, looking at them working so desperately trying to fix that cash register irritated me. I'm surprised with it not working that they didn't have to shut the cafeteria down. I mean who can add and subtract any more, let alone multiply or divide?" He set his items on a table and pulled the chair back. "It's calculators, computers . . . ," he said, "they're taking the place of brains."

He lowered himself onto the chair. "In my classes—and we're talking about supposedly bright medical school students—if there is math mixed in with anything I say, I look out and see a half dozen of them grabbing for their calculators. One of their batteries go dead, they might as well be brain-dead as well."

Chokchai looked across the table at the piece of apple pie. He smiled. "Smells good from even here, Dave."

"You know where you can go back and get one, Chok."

"No. I'm sticking to diet this time," Chokchai said. He speared a tomato slice with his fork and lifted it toward his mouth. "You don't like modern? Had you rather go back to a pit latrine behind your house like your fathers' had?"

"That's my *great-grandfather*, Chok."

"Only a matter of expression."

"Chok, the kids need to understand what they're doing before they get into artificial intelligence."

"Learn something new? School is already too long. There's not time to learn all the old and all the new."

"Maybe we should take the time—understanding what we're doing before we really screw up."

"Sounds like different subject, now."

"Same subject, Chok, scientific advance without an underlying knowledge. We jump into things without really knowing—what about the polio vaccine that was being administered before the fifties?"

"Not certain it causes cancer, Dave—only preliminary study indicates a possibility. Even if does, in meantime many will be saved from crippling disease for fifty years."

"What about your field? Grain yields are greater with crop plants' resistance to herbicides, no doubt. But now weeds are showing up resistant to weed kills—genetic propensity is jumping from the crops to the weeds."

"Still more food."

"Did you know there was a possibility of resistance jumping?"

"Human genetics, not crops, is my project, Dave. But, again, the intended good outweighs the unforeseen bad. That is the usual case in science. We cannot know everything before we start experimenting. If we did there wouldn't be any breakthroughs to seek. So when overall good outweighs bad, that's science. That's progress. To not go on with science is no problem certainly, but no advance. Leave worse in problem place—people starve."

"What did you say?"

"What part didn't you hear?"

"You said, 'Leave worse in problem place'?"

"You make fun of my English? Would you like to speak Thailandese to me?"

"Thailandese?"

"English slang word, Dave. That's not my fault."

"Dr. Lambert . . . "

The voice came over the hospital speaker system.

"You are needed back in your lower office."

It was hospital code telling him that a physician who had just pronounced a patient dead was requesting an autopsy of the body. To actually spell out the message in language understandable to everyone would be traumatic to many of the more seriously ill patients and their relatives waiting anxiously by their beds or in the family waiting rooms.

Lambert looked at his sandwich.

"You can take it with you," Chokchai said, "or I'll eat it for you. Diet is one thing, but letting food go to waste is another."

Lambert wrapped a napkin around the sandwich and lifted it and his coffee with him as he came to his feet.

"You can have the pie," he said.

"Thank you, Dave."

"You owe me a dollar fifteen."

"I figured that, Dave."

*   *   *

Several minutes later, after a long walk down empty, winding corridors, Lambert stopped outside the double doors leading into the short hallway to the morgue. He looked at his sandwich. He thought about the odors in the morgue, the bacteria and viruses often left behind in blood splatters on the floor. Just the day before a group of medical students had worked on the corpse of a patient who been infected with spinal meningitis. *Even my touching the doorknob,* he thought. *Every medical student and professor working on corpses always had to touch the doorknob to leave.* He knew it didn't matter if he was a pathologist for a hundred years, he'd never be able to stomach the idea of eating inside the room. Cradling his cup of coffee in the crook of his elbow, he awkwardly unwrapped the ham and cheese.

He ate the entire sandwich in four big bites, took a couple of quick sips of the coffee, and set the paper cup on the floor next to the wall.

Then he turned to the doors, stared at them for a moment, and finally used his elbows to push them open rather than touching them with his hands.

At the morgue door he fumbled inside his pocket for his key.

The latch clicked when he unlocked it, and he stepped into the room.

The first thing he noticed was that Alfred's body was the only one lying out in the open. That meant that the body of the person who had just expired hadn't been delivered yet. He wouldn't have had to be there when it was—the routine receiving of bodies wasn't in his job description. But whenever he could, he came to the morgue when a body was on its way. He would place it on the washing table if it needed it, cleaning it with the jets of water that came out of each side of the table. He remembered this propensity of his coming about long ago. Usually a corpse didn't need any cleaning. What had been needed was done by the nurses on the floor in preparation for anyone coming to the hospital to view the body before it was moved. But on rare occasions, there was still some cleaning to be done. That had happened to him with a sixty-year-old daughter who had just arrived in town and gotten to the hospital after her father had vomited his life blood away when an aneurysm had ruptured, and a fresh drainage of blood had soaked the man's chest as he was being moved to the morgue. He had to use a damp paper towel to clean the blood away as the woman had been restrained from entering for the time it took. Besides, there was Alfred's body to be moved into a drawer out of sight if a relative of the latest deceased was to arrive. He moved to the gurney and caught it by its end.

It was at that moment that he must have sensed rather than heard something, for Genowski and John made no sound, and he looked back across his shoulder at the two large men stepping out from behind the end of the metal drawers.

Though still slumped against his balcony rail at his home overlooking the reservoir, Quinlan could see what was happening in the morgue as clearly as if he were there:

Genowski slammed the old pathologist into the wall and grabbed his skinny neck in his big hand, squeezing the throat cruelly.

The words were clear, too.

"The chip."

Lambert could only make a gurgling response.

"The chip!" Genowski shouted into the old man's face.

Quinlan concentrated on the view of Lambert's terror-stricken features. But he wasn't witnessing the fear through any ability of his eyes. The view was inside his mind alone, electronically transmitted there, box-shaped and smaller than the larger view his eyes still held of the water of the reservoir spreading out before him. Together, the views were juxtaposed in a position similar to two separate scenes showing at the same moment on a TV equipped with a picture-within-a-picture feature.

The morgue door opened.

The view inside the small box swung to a red-haired

orderly standing in the doorway. His mouth gaped in shock. He flung the gurney he had been pulling behind him back out of his way and sprinted toward the double doors leading back into the hallway.

Quinlan's view now changed from Genowski's perspective to what John's eyes saw, with John rushing through the open double doors and racing after the orderly.

The orderly sprinted down the hallway.

He screamed in terror.

A security guard hurried around a corner at the very end of the corridor and stared toward the running orderly. The guard reached for the gun in his holster.

John's view abruptly swung back toward the double doors. Genowski, carrying the large plastic bag stuffed with their clothes, came through them and dashed past John down a corridor leading toward the far side of the hospital.

Now John's view was bouncing as he ran, going past lines of metal lockers against the corridor's walls; Genowski fleeing ahead of him, and then turning back to disappear into another narrow intersecting hallway.

John swung around the corner into the hallway, a much narrower one. Genowski raced ahead of him up a steep set of stairs leading toward a closed steel door.

He threw the door open and rushed out into the bright sunlight.

Quinlan clenched his fists in anger.

He concentrated a moment, vanishing the scene from his mind, the box-shaped cubicle disappearing and his view once more only that of the reservoir spreading out before him.

At the hospital, the security guard threw open the steel door, rushed out into the sunlight, and looked to his left and his right. Nursing students on their way to class along the sidewalk stared at the gun the guard held in front of him.

The two large men had disappeared.

*   *   *

Spence leaned back in his chair as the last message on his answering machine began to play. The voice was that of a female, speaking softly.

"Spence, your secretary said to leave you a message here. She said you were real busy today. I hope I'm not bothering you. I'm in town for the next three days—at our drug reps conference. I'll be at the Holiday Inn on fifty-five north if you get time to talk. Maybe we could catch lunch."

There was a pause of a few seconds, then the sound of the receiver being replaced. The machine gave the time of the call and ended with, "No more messages."

Flo stood in the doorway. She looked at the answering machine, frowned, and then at him. "If you're ready to go to work," she said.

He pushed his chair back and stood. "You don't like Jennifer?" he asked. He knew she didn't.

"I'm not your secretary, Spence—and she knows that. You ready to work?" She turned and disappeared back into the laboratory. As he came around the desk he heard her mutter, "But she's no *dumber* than any of the others who call."

He smiled a little and followed her out the doorway.

Freddie Crawford, a twenty-six-year-old lab assistant and the third and final member of their research team, stood in front of a double-barrel microscope sitting on a stainless steel counter off to the side. Freddie's thin frame was clad in a white knee-length lab coat over jeans and a sweatshirt. His brown hair draped casually across a lightly tanned forehead. "Jennifer," he said, looking back across his shoulder. "She's the tall blond, isn't she?"

"She would eat you alive," Flo said. "Spence doesn't attract any who wouldn't," she added. "Now, Spence . . ." She nodded toward the eyeball and optic nerve now strung weightless between fiber optic conductive wires immersed in a clear liquid inside a rectangular glass tank that looked much like a fish aquarium. "Do we go to work or continue to discuss bimbos?"

Spence heard the sirens as he walked toward the counter. At first he didn't pay any attention, as there was always the sound of sirens at the center. But then he realized he was hearing several sirens at once.

He looked toward the raised window Freddie had opened to take advantage of the pleasant scent of the storm-washed, spring air. The noise of the sirens continued to grow louder.

So many he couldn't really tell how many there were.

Coming from different directions.

Flo walked to the window and stared out across the complex. In a pen just outside the window, Tank, the small, potbellied pig used in their experiments, had come out of his home, a wooden structure resembling a doghouse, and stared in the general direction of the sirens.

The telephone next to Freddie rang.

When he answered it he said, "Lab." Then his eyes suddenly tightened at what he heard.

Spence watched Freddie's face, a look of shock twisting his features, turn toward his.

"Dr. Lambert's been . . . been murdered," he said.

6

A CROWD OF doctors, nurses, and orderlies filled the hall-way. A pair of hospital security guards stood at the doors fronting the hall leading to the morgue. Spence pushed his way through the throng, speaking among themselves in low voices.

Through the glass panels in the double doors, he could see the gurney that had been flung to the side by the orderly, Benjamin, when he had opened the morgue door to see the two men attacking Dr. Lambert. The body of the old woman on the gurney had nearly been jolted from it when it had slammed into the wall. One of her bare legs hung down from its side. Her far arm hung limply off the other side. The sheet had been pulled back up across her face.

A second gurney stuck halfway out of the morgue into the short hall, exposing the lower half of Dr. Lambert's body. The old professor's feet were angled out to the sides. He had lost a shoe in the struggle with the man who had killed him, and the worn black sock that showed had a hole in its heel; Lambert's skin looked almost chalky white.

The bright burst from a police photographer's camera reflected out into the hall.

Dr. Chokchai squeezed past Dr. Lambert's body on his way out the morgue door. He never looked down at his old friend. A moment later he was coming out through the double doors. He didn't look at anybody. A tear seeped silently down the man's rounded cheek, leaving a glistening trail along the light brown skin. In a few seconds he had disappeared into the crowd lining the corridor.

Spence felt a hand placed softly on his shoulder.

He looked around at Flo. She had a sad look of her own on her face. She stared directly into his eyes. And, somehow, her expression suddenly caused his eyes to moisten, and he turned his face away.

She patted his shoulder. "He was a good man," she said in a soft voice.

Spence nodded rather than trust his voice.

Then he saw Benjamin looking at him from the morgue doorway. A stocky police detective in his early fifties and wearing a sport coat and slacks stood next to the orderly. Benjamin said something, and Spence saw the detective's gaze come toward his, and the man walked toward the double doors and called to him.

Spence stepped forward past the security guards and swallowed to clear his throat. "Yes."

"The orderly says you were one of Dr. Lambert's closest friends."

"I was."

"How long have you known him?"

"He was a professor of mine in medical school."

"Did he have any enemies you might know of?"

"None."

The detective nodded, turned his gaze back toward the morgue, and scratched a side of his broad chin with his forefinger before speaking again.

"It wasn't an enemy, anyway," he said. "There's a lot better places to deal with something like that than in the middle of a hospital in the middle of the day. Somebody came for something—something that wouldn't wait. Something they wanted badly enough and quickly enough to dress up in scrubs and break into the morgue knowing that they could be discovered at any moment." He shook his head as he paused. "But what in the hell could somebody want from a morgue?"

Spence watched the stocky man's questioning eyes come back around to his. "You have any idea, Doc?"

Spence shook his head no.

"Come on in here with me for a minute," the detective said, walking back toward the morgue. At the door, he turned sideways to squeeze past the gurney containing Lambert's body.

As Spence followed along, turning sideways himself, he looked down at the awkward angle Lambert's head set on the shoulders. "They broke his neck," the detective said. Spence lifted his eyes from the sight. "Somebody strong or somebody who knew what he was doing, or both," the detective added.

Inside the morgue, the camera was still being wielded by the police photographer. He was taking shot after shot of the shallow, wide area in front of the metal drawers, slowly moving in a circle, only slightly changing the angle of the shot after each flash.

Spence knew the important photographs would have been the ones taken before Lambert's body had been moved from the floor. Before anything had been touched. The shots now were meant only to lock the surroundings on film in an attempt to preserve everything in sight—and hope something out of the ordinary might be noticed later.

But there was nothing out of the ordinary noticeable now, the body drawers tightly closed, the table and telephone undisturbed against the wall. Alfred Wynn's body still lay on its back on the gurney. Benjamin stood in front of the drawers.

"You can go," the detective said to the orderly.

Benjamin nodded and slipped past the gurney toward the small outer hall.

"Look around, Doc," the detective said. "See if anything pops out at you."

Pops out at you? The stocky officer was fishing for information. The same as with the photographs. The police had nothing. But they had . . . "Didn't Benjamin get a description of the men?"

The detective shook his head. "Not much. Only that they were big and he was scared. They stole some scrubs and lifted IDs off a pair of lab coats lying at a nursing station. They ditched them in the parking garage. By the way, my name is Dunlap. Go ahead, look around."

Spence stepped closer to Alfred Wynn's body, to see into the small work area at the end of the metal drawers.

There was nothing but the solitary porcelain sink and the washing table.

Behind him, Dunlap opened a body drawer and stuck his head inside, looking to the left and right.

"You know I can't get over this," he said, still staring inside the drawer. "Before I looked the first time, I thought they were each in separate drawers. They're just . . . sliding racks. You can see 'em all. Like a beehive, sorta." He shut the door. "Well, anything catch your eye?"

Spence shook his head no.

"That's what Dr. Choka . . . what that other doctor said. Not much in here to see, is there? You think of anything that the victim might have had on him that somebody could have been interested in?"

"To murder . . . No."

"His pockets were turned inside out."

Spence looked toward Lambert's body. They still were, both of the lab coat's side pockets.

"The man that stayed inside while the other one chased the orderly, killed him," Dunlap said, "and then went through his pockets. Or had already gone through his pockets. Looking for something. Whatever it was, it was important enough that they didn't want to leave any witnesses behind."

Dunlap paused a moment, then said, "My guess is they got it."

"Got it?"

"They had something in a bag—when they were running. I figured at first it was their clothes—carrying them with them after stealing the scrub suits. Maybe it was that— along with something else."

Along with something else, Spence thought.

As Dunlap paused again, he shook his head in irritation. "Not a damn thing makes any sense. If Lambert had something they wanted, why not wait until he left the hospital? No sense at all. But that doesn't mean I'm going to quit trying."

Dunlap's words were only a meaningless drone in the background as Spence now stared at Alfred Wynn's body. *Along with something else,* he thought again.

"It was nothing that one had on him, Doctor," Dunlap said, noticing where Spence's gaze was fixed. "After he was declared dead, emergency department people say they kept all his personal items: billfold with a few hundred bucks and credit cards, a watch, a big diamond ring. Nothing came down here with him but his clothes and the skin he was born in. Big man in town. Real big. But no matter what you got or haven't got, that's all it really amounts to in the end, isn't it—skin."

Dunlap looked at the back of his hand, then turned it over and looked at his palm. "Skin," he repeated, nodding to himself. "Skin—and then eventually dust. Just like the Bible says."

Spence continued to stare at Alfred Wynn's body. Joey had told him about that *something else* before. In bodies shipped home from Vietnam, it had been bags of heroin and cocaine. A group in South Africa had taken its cue from that tactic and used bodies from a terrorist explosion at the American embassy there to smuggle stolen diamonds into the United States. Nobody filled Alfred Wynn's body cavities with anything. He had been brought straight from the scene of the accident that took his life. Yet his body *was* the only new thing in the morgue. The only thing that hadn't been lying there overnight when it would have been no problem to break into the morgue without the chance of being discovered. His body—and Tommy Small's body.

Spence's gaze moved to the body drawers.

7

WHEN SPENCE CAME back inside the laboratory and walked toward his office, Freddie looked at him for a moment, then lowered his eyes back to the microscope on the counter before him. Spence noticed that Flo, a concerned expression across her face, continued to watch him until he stepped into his office.

He came slowly around his desk and eased into the large chair. He sat there for several seconds, then reached for the telephone.

Flo appeared in the open doorway. "You alright?" she asked.

"Fine," he said.

He lifted the telephone receiver. He had the number memorized and quickly punched it in.

"Joey McDonald Investigations," a female voice answered on the other end of the line.

"Patricia, this is Spence Stevens. Is Joey in?"

"Hey, Dr. Stevens. Let me tell him it's you calling."

"You sure?" Flo asked from the doorway.

"Sure," he said, and she nodded and turned back into the laboratory, closing the door behind her.

Now Joey's deep voice came across the line. "Spence. What's it been—three months? Thought I was going to have to find me another father confessor."

His voice sounded good, lively, no depression apparent, nothing out of the normal.

"You don't need a confessor."

"Rather have a confessor than a shrink. They cost too much. I'm still paying Dr. Bower off."

"He told me he wasn't going to charge anything."

"When I started back to work, I started paying. My idea, not his."

"How *has* it been going?"

"Never been better."

"We went through that the first time we met, Joey."

"It's okay, really, man." Joey's voice was lower now. "There's times, but nothing I can't handle."

"Good, I knew it would work out." He paused for a moment. "Joey, I need a favor."

"You've called the right man, Hoss."

"Dr. Lambert is dead."

"Oh, sorry, Spence, I hadn't heard."

"He was murdered."

Joey didn't say anything now, and Spence spoke into the silence. "It happened just over an hour ago. Two men were waiting inside the morgue, killed him and got away. The only description the police have is that they were large. It sounds like a nut case, I know—in the middle of the day, right inside the hospital. The detective on the case says they had to be after something and didn't feel they had the time to wait."

"Or repaying a debt," Joey said.

"With Dr. Lambert—what kind? He didn't do anything. He didn't have any enemies. He hardly ever left the hospital except to go home and sleep. He was eating lunch with another doctor and got called back to the morgue. He came in on whoever they were."

"What do you want me to do?"

"There's nothing in the morgue anybody would want. The only new thing there was a couple of bodies. I started thinking about what you told me about the bodies from Vietnam and the embassy. How they were used. I know it's not going to be like that. But it made me think. I know that's crazy but I don't know what else would have attracted anybody."

"You want me to run a background on them?"

"Sounds nuts, I know. That's why I didn't mention it to the police. I can't even imagine anything that would connect them to what happened. But somebody came for some reason."

"Dr. Stevens, a Miss Christen Dantonio from the *Clarion Ledger* here to see you."

The voice was Freddie's, coming from the intercom on the desk.

Spence continued to speak into the telephone. "Their names are Tommy Small—he was a thug the police killed early this morning—and Alfred Wynn, an executive with Computer Resources Incorporated, who was killed in a car accident. This won't bother you, will it?"

"It's what I do for a living," Joey said.

"I know. But you have to tell me for me to know what bothers you."

"I haven't been to see Dr. Bower in six months."

"I know."

"No, Spence, it won't bother me."

"I know it's crazy."

"Crazy is my specialty, Spence. I'll check around and get back to you."

"Thanks, I appreciate it." As Spence replaced the receiver, Freddie's voice came over the intercom again.

"Dr. Stevens, there's a Miss Dantonio from the *Clarion Ledger* here to speak with you."

He leaned back in his chair and stared at the ceiling for a moment. What he had asked Joey to do *was* crazy, much farther out than the fishing expedition the detective had been on with the extra camera shots and the rambling questions. But Lambert had no one else. To not try to do something, no matter how crazy it was on the surface, seemed like nobody . . .

"Dr. Stevens," Freddie's voice came again.

Spence frowned. The last thing he wanted to do was to

answer questions from a newspaper reporter about Dr. Lambert's death. He leaned forward and depressed the speaker button on the intercom.

"If you will, explain to her that I'm way behind schedule on a—"

He turned his eyes toward the unusually attractive young woman who had opened his door and stood in the doorway. "They said you were off the telephone," she said.

In her mid-twenties, with her slim figure clad fashionably in a silk blouse and linen skirt and her lightly tanned, oval-shaped face framed by perfectly coiffured shoulder-length dark hair, she looked as if she had just stepped from the cover of a fashion magazine. In addition to her striking physical appearance, she wore a noticeably expensive bracelet studded with small diamonds and a matching set of earrings.

Daddy's money, he thought. Certainly it wouldn't be easy to buy such jewelry on a young reporter's salary. He summed her up as probably not long out of college, finally graduating after too many years of sorority partying, and now wanting to quickly move up the ladder in her chosen field of journalism. Pushy, as in coming into his office without waiting to be invited, and more often than not used to getting her way all her life with her good looks and her daddy's connections. She walked to the chair in front of his desk.

"May I?" she asked, nodding down at the chair.

"I'm behind on some work, Miss Dantonio."

"Christen," she said, and moved around in front of the chair. She looked back over her shoulder at it now, and then smiled politely at him.

He nodded, and she settled into the seat.

"Thank you," she said. "I would like to ask you a few questions for a story I'm doing."

When he didn't immediately respond, she added, "It has nothing to do with Dr. Lambert's murder."

It was as if she knew what he had been thinking.

"It's a feature story about the different types of research

being conducted here," she explained. "I would think that a story on the promising research you're doing could help your funding in the long run—for the kind of research *you* want to continue doing."

It was as if she also knew about Mr. Quinlan wanting him to change the direction of his research.

But, of course, she probably would know if she had spoken with any of the other research groups in the building. It wasn't a secret that Quinlan was anxious to turn the eye research toward concentrating exclusively on overcoming retina damage.

And she might be correct in how a feature story in the state's largest newspaper could help, too—if he could hype the story along the line of how his avenue of research was the most promising route to take. There *were* other board members besides Quinlan and other research monies besides Quinlan's that could be moved in his direction, too.

He nodded. "Alright."

Instead of pulling a pen and notepad or tape recorder from her purse, Christen simply smiled at him again.

"I've been on the run all morning with nothing to eat," she said, "I wonder if you would mind too awfully much if we did this over a late lunch in the cafeteria. Have you eaten yet?"

He shook his head no.

"Good," she said, standing up, "it's settled then. It'll be on me—the paper."

She smiled politely again and waited.

He stood and walked around his desk. She walked beside him to the door.

As they stepped through it into the laboratory, she lifted a tape recorder from her purse. A red glowing light at the top of the recorder told him that it had been on since she had entered the office.

Joey McDonald, in his mid-fifties, barrel-chested, with his brown hair cut short in military style, had remained in his chair after ending the conversation with Spence. His thick forearms resting on his desk, his broad, chiseled face not moving, he stared at the wall, thinking.

"What did Spence want?" Pat asked as she came through the doorway into the office. Slightly younger than Joey, her hair was similar in color to his and also cut short. A loose yellow print dress covered a rounded figure that was slightly overweight, and she had a smile on her face.

Then her eyes tightened slightly.

"You have that look," she said.

Joey forced his features to relax and leaned back in his chair. "No," he said, lifting his hand and cupping it, signaling her toward him. "Nothing raging in your husband's brain," he added. "At least not at the moment. I was just thinking how down Spence must be. You remember that old doctor who was like a father to him?"

As Pat came around behind him, she nodded. "Uh-huh."

"He was just murdered."

"No," Pat said, "that's terr . . . where did it happen?"

"At UMC. In the morgue. Two men who got away."

She placed her hands on his thick shoulders and began massaging them. "Your muscles are tight," she said.

"Maybe that means I haven't gone all the way to pot yet." He looked up over his shoulder at her. The deep scar running from the bridge of his nose up across his forehead to disappear into his hairline was plainly visible. "Spence asked if I would check on a couple of bodies that had just arrived there."

"Why?"

"He doesn't know. He's just trying to do something. If you will, call UMC and see if a Tommy Small and an Alfred Wynn have been delivered to funeral homes yet."

Pat didn't immediately move toward the doorway or reach for the telephone on the desk. Instead, she continued to slowly massage Joey's shoulders.

"You certain that look didn't mean anything?" she asked.

He smiled and looked up at her. "Nothing," he said.

"I'm serious," she came back.

"Nothing," he repeated. "Really, nothing, honey."

Spence had used a pen and napkin to sketch a cross section of the eyeball complete with the optic nerve running toward the occipital lobe. "Conceptually, if we're able to carry this to the point we would like to, by using an implanted miniature camera we'll do away with the cornea, the retina, even the optic nerve, and wire the electrical impulses directly into the occipital lobe. The principal problem has been to get enough separate impulses to enough separate areas of the lobe to recreate a recognizable pattern. And, of course, getting the camera and electrodes implanted in a manner in which they can stay in place over a period of time without infection or rejection."

"You're convinced your way is the only way?" Christen asked.

"No, not the only way. But nobody knows which way might reach a breakthrough first. So why not take the path that will provide the most benefit if it works? Total eye replacement rather than just an artificial retina. If we can make that come to pass, then all the components will be in place to use whatever part of the total package a doctor might need with a particular patient: total replacement, or only the retina, or only the optic nerve, or a combination of components. It will all be there in the package to be used as needed."

They were in the cafeteria. He still hadn't felt like eating and had settled on a cup of coffee. Christen had chosen little more, only a salad and a glass of tea. She obviously hadn't been as hungry as she let on. He had decided that the reason she had asked him to the cafeteria was to get him out of the confines of his office into more relaxed surroundings, where she might get him to talk more freely.

She *was* smart. No doubt about that. Every time he explained something she seemed to immediately grasp it and then come back with an even more detailed question. And now she had a questioning look on her face again. "Doctor, there must be . . ." She searched for how she wanted to phrase her question. "The visual image has to be broken down into innumerable separate dots of light, or whatever you call them—electrical impulses."

He nodded.

"So, Doctor, if I'm understanding you correctly, hundreds of thousands of impulses being directed into the brain, each trying to find a specific connection between an equally large number of possible receptor points in the occipital lobe . . . That sounds almost impossible to sort out."

He nodded. "It would be if each impulse had to go to an exact specific receptor point predetermined at birth. But that's not the case. Just getting the impulses into the occipital lobe in general appears to be all we'll need. We feel it will be able to sort them out itself. In a more understandable example, scientists for years have been able to bypass certain damaged brain passageways, but remain close to the passages with artificially directed impulses, and have the brain rewire itself, so to speak, with a part of the brain close to the old pathways taking over the original function. You see this occurring naturally in some stroke victims, where a certain amount of locomotion is lost, then regained over time, though the original pathways that carried the impulses directing the function remain dead. The brain has rewired itself. Maybe not to the degree of complexity that the stroke victim once enjoyed in using his limbs. But, nevertheless, the function is taken over and a great deal of locomotion regained. We've already gotten the occipital lobe to register flashes of light from impulses beamed into the lobe's mass in general. And we're rapidly becoming more specific with our targeting. There has been a great deal of study of the lobe when a war injury carries part of it away. For years scientists have known that with certain parts of the lobe missing, the patient sees only the top half of what he's looking at, or the lower half, or one side or the other. The rest of the image is simply not there. So we basically know what part of the lobe in which to beam each part of the overall image."

"And what else can you put in the brain, Doctor—thoughts, ideas, schemes, intelligence itself?"

The question caught him off guard. It was something he had never discussed with anyone but Flo.

"I know schemes can be put into the brain," Christen continued. "Brainwashing, for example. But that would be prehistoric compared to running commands down wires into the brain, using computer language to set in concrete what someone thinks or does. What about that, Doctor?"

He looked at the glowing red light on top of her tape recorder lying on the table between them. "If I get into that type of speculation I would sound like some kind of wild visionary," he said.

"And that wouldn't go over well at all with the people who control the funding, would it?" she said, and lifted the tape recorder into her hand and switched it off.

She held it up for him to see. "Not on the record, but because I'm curious," she said.

When he hesitated she said, "I give you my word there won't be a sentence from you about it in the story. In fact I'll let you read it before it goes to press."

He nodded. "It's possible. No . . ." He looked at the recorder. "Not just possible. It'll happen. Maybe quickly—from some breakthrough that comes out of the type of research I'm doing or others are doing. Or maybe a hundred years from now. But it will happen."

"Humans meshed with technology," she said.

"It's already happened physically—everything from pacemakers to artificial joints and limbs. It'll happen mentally, too."

"A computer meshed with the mind."

"Or computer chips implanted in the brain."

"Humans could do anything then, couldn't they?"

He nodded again. "Become anything they dreamed."

"That's what you would really like to be a part of in the end, isn't it?"

He nodded again, maybe too enthusiastically, he decided, when she said, "That's your real dream, isn't it?"

She was one of the most perceptive people he had ever met, or one of the smartest. He looked at the tape recorder, still switched off in her hand.

"It will happen," he said.

"I CALLED AND spoke to your embalmer a few minutes ago," Joey said.

"Oh, that's Byram," the receptionist said, looking up at the barrel-chested investigator standing in front of her desk. "Last doorway on your right."

Byram was in the embalming room, leaning over a corpse. He appeared to be in his mid-twenties, had long red hair tied in a ponytail hanging down his back nearly to his waist, was so thin he looked anorexic, and wore jeans and a muscle shirt hanging slack from his thin shoulders and cut off at his midriff. Steel-rimmed glasses perched near the end of his long nose. He took them off as he looked toward Joey's big figure stepping into the room and shutting the door behind him.

"Sir?" Byram questioned.

"I'm Jack Boyd," Joey said.

"Oh, yes," Byram said, nodding. "Your prices did sound very low."

"I'm not really here about the embalming chemicals," Joey said. "I collect autographs."

"Autographs?" Byram said, his eyes narrowing. "Sir, what do you mean autographs?"

Joey looked at Alfred Wynn's naked corpse, lying on its back on a long, porcelain table just behind Byram. Byram glanced back at the body.

Joey pulled a scrap of paper from his pocket and held it

up. "Whose autograph is this?" he asked, walking toward
the redhead and stopping at arm's length, where he held
the scrap of paper out for him to see.

The scribbled words were easy to read.

Byram's eyes narrowed in a questioning expression.
"Pope John Paul?"

"No, it isn't," Joey said, suddenly raising his voice to
take command of the exchange between them. "I just wrote
his name down on this before I came in here." He wadded
the paper into a tiny ball in his big hand and held it up in
front of Byram.

Byram looked at the clenched fist, at the scar running
up from the bridge of the big man's nose into his hairline,
and then glanced toward the door.

"A fake, boy," Joey exclaimed, still speaking louder than
normal. "How do you know when any autograph's real?
Even if you compare it to known signatures of somebody
it could have been done by a duplicating machine. With
the high-tech writing stuff they got nowadays anything can
be pulled off. You don't know when a celebrity sends you
a signed picture if he even touched it or not."

Joey waited for that to sink in. "Do you, boy?"

Byram said, "Mister, I think maybe you better—"

"What I better do," Joey said, "is get Alfred Wynn
here's autograph certified."

Byram slowly took a step to the side. His eyes were on
the open door and the big investigator at the same time.
"Mister, I really don't know what you're wanting—"

"I just told you, boy," Joey said, now lowering his voice
to hold Byram's attention in a different way. "I collect autographs. I got two presidents, a vice president, so many
movie and rock stars you almost can't count 'em all. Anybody's signature that might be worth a lot of money later
on. That is, if they're the real thing and I can prove it. I
certify 'em. You know how I do that? I do it with fingerprints. Fingerprints, you say . . ." Byram was edging farther
to the side, lining himself up better with the door and a
path past the big man, and Joey stepped to the same side,

blocking the way again. "Yeah, I said fingerprints, boy. You know even presidents got fingerprints. I hand 'em a big fat pen, been wiped clean. They use it to sign an autograph, and I snatch it back and I can lift their fingerprints off it and put 'em down on a card right next to those signatures. Rock stars are easier, they're always drinking or taking something. If you're around any place they're hanging out, it's easy to lift fingerprints off a glass or some kind of little spoon. You get my gist?"

Joey reached into his pocket now, and Byram's eyes narrowed as he watched the movement, then opened wide when a large roll of hundred-dollar bills was produced. Joey quickly counted off two bills and held them up in the air.

"I got old Alfred there's signature a couple of days ago, and his partner's, too—you know they're the biggest entrepreneurs in this town with their computer factories all over everywhere and that plant out in Clinton that makes that genetic rearranged seed and stuff. Going to save the world from starvation, they said. Their latest project. Might do it. If they do, they'll go down in the history books."

As Joey paused, he nodded slowly. "Down in the history books," he repeated, "and I have their autographs—certified. Except for that one." He nodded toward Wynn's body. "Made off with my pen, he did, before I could snatch it back. But the good Lord's provided me another avenue now."

He smiled and nodded in satisfaction, then held up the two bills. "All you gotta do is let me take his fingerprints. No harm done to anybody—wipe off the black smudge when I'm through."

Byram didn't raise his hand to receive the money. Joey leaned forward and stuffed them down in the young man's jeans' waistband, the sudden reach causing Byram to flinch. "No harm at all to it," Joey said. He held his finger in the air as if to get Byram's particular attention.

"And here's the kicker, boy. You don't tell nobody I was here getting these prints. You know, so nobody else can get the same idea and try to get one of those duplicate machines to print 'em out a few names and stick finger-prints on them. . . . You do that, not say anything, and I don't hear nothing getting around about what I'm doing, and I'll visit you again in a month or two and give you five hundred more. How's that for a man-to-man fair deal?"

Spence stared a moment longer at the tall wall of body drawers rising nearly to the ceiling. He walked to his right and looked around the corner of the drawers at the washing table and the porcelain sink. He looked back at the morgue door that had been held open by the gurney carrying Dr. Lambert's body. *Nothing,* he thought. Nothing made any sense. Dr. Lambert wouldn't have had anything on him of interest to anyone. *But they went through his pockets.* He looked back at the metal drawers and walked to them.

It took him a few seconds to find Tommy Small's body. It lay in the fourth drawer up from the floor in one of the center sections. Holding the drawer open, Spence stared at the tag on Small's big toe. A murderer. Gang affiliation, maybe? Some kind of note or message he had on him con-taining information that someone didn't want the police to see?

But that sounded like a B-movie plot. The police would have searched the body at the scene of the shooting. The nurses in the emergency department would have gone through Small's pockets to see if there were any personal effects before he was sent to the morgue. The same as they had done with Alfred Wynn.

Nothing made any sense.

He looked once again at the washing table. The instru-ment cart sat next to the sink. The section of metal that had been driven deep into Alfred Wynn's forehead still lay on the cart. The telephone rang.

He walked to the small table and lifted the receiver to his ear.

It was Flo. "Spence, the funeral home said someone will have to come down and sign the papers authorizing the

embalming. I told them there wasn't anyone in the area."
He could hear the compassion in her voice.

But someone has to do more than simply have compassion, he thought. There has to be a resolution to this. A murder can't be committed in the middle of the day in a hospital swarming with people and the perpetrators get away.

"Spence," Flo questioned.

"Tell them I'll sign," he said.

"I don't mind making the arrangements," Flo added, "if you could give me an idea of what you think Dr. Lambert might have wanted."

"Thanks, but I'll handle it."

"I really don't mind."

"I appreciate it, but I'll do it," Spence repeated.

As he replaced the telephone receiver in its cradle, he noticed the cigar ashes in the metal cup on the table. He thought of Dr. Chokchai and the tear seeping down the man's face as he walked past Lambert's body. Two old men and now only the one left. How often they had eaten in the cafeteria together, and now that gone. He decided he should ask Dr. Chokchai if he wanted to help in making the arrangements. He lifted the cup into his hand, stared at the ashes for a moment, then tilted it to dump the ashes into the small box-shaped, biohazard disposal container next to the table. He saw the tiny piece of metal. It had a speck of blood, now turned black on its side. A fragment of brain matter was imbedded in the blood. He looked back at the large section of metal lying on the instrument cart and thought of the tremendous force that must have been exerted during the accident. Then he dumped the ashes and the piece of metal into the container.

The little square made a light clinking sound as it landed next to a pair of latex gloves and bounced under a crumpled, blood-stained paper towel.

Joey sat in the Elite, a restaurant that had been a fixture on Capitol Street in downtown Jackson for as long as he could remember. He had ordered the chicken-fried veal with white gravy, his favorite, but had taken only a couple bites from the plate. Sitting at a table close enough to the narrow front of the building that he could see through the plate glass windows to each side of the entrance, he saw the stocky shape of Bob Kennedy when the FBI agent stepped off the curb on the far side of the street and walked across the pavement toward the restaurant. He was dressed in a beige suit, with his coat open, his collar unbuttoned, and his tie loosened around his thick neck. When he stepped inside the Elite their eyes met. He came toward the table.

"How's ridding the world of criminals going?" Joey asked as Kennedy pulled back a chair on the other side of the table and sat down.

"Just trying to put up with the bureaucrats long enough to get my retirement in. You're looking good."

Joey frowned. "I wonder if that's what recovering alcoholics have to put up with: You're looking good; don't see any red eyes or haggard look today. Anybody pissed on you lately, Joey? You pissed on anybody?"

Joey hadn't tried to keep his voice low, and an older couple at a booth off to his left looked his way.

"Yeah," Kennedy said, "you're looking good and starting to sound like your old self again."

"Like you didn't already know?"

"I ask about you from time to time."

"And the birthday present you brought over. I told Pat that was to get a closer look."

"The only way I can with you not into hanging out."

"Dr. Bower said no old friends for two years. Got six more months to go."

"Yeah," Kennedy said, nodding, "I know. So, assuming I still count as a friend, why the phone call?" He reached his big arm across the table, lifted a french fry from Joey's plate, and deposited it into his mouth.

Joey held the fingerprint cards across the table.

"One's Tommy Small—former thug the cops took out. The other's Alfred Wynn—car accident."

Kennedy nodded as he took the cards into his hand. "Heard about Wynn on the radio—one of the executives at Computer Resources."

"I want to know everything there is to know about them. I mean every last detail. Do whatever you have to do."

A waitress holding a menu out interrupted them, and Kennedy looked up at the woman, smiled politely, and shook his head no.

She returned the smile and walked away. Kennedy looked back across the table. "That's what you always used to say, Joey—do whatever you have to do. The last thing, each time, just before we went out."

When Joey didn't respond, Kennedy added, "I had a nightmare last month. First time in a long time. Nearly scared my wife to death—dove off the bed onto the floor."

Joey nodded, again without speaking, and Kennedy added, "Thought I'd tell you so you didn't feel like the lonesome duckling. We all have more memories than we want."

As Kennedy paused, he grinned, and slid his coat sleeve up his forearm. He unbuttoned his shirt sleeve and pulled it up. At the center of his wide forearm was the tattoo of a snake coiled around a skull, with the reptile's head raised above the skull and its fangs bared. "Wife wanted me to get this taken off," he said.

He looked at Joey's arm. "Judy said she heard Dr. Bower talked you into having yours removed."

Joey unbuttoned his sleeve and pulled it up his arm, displaying an identical tattoo.

"I didn't think so," Kennedy said.

He grinned again. "Twelve reasons why I didn't think so."

"And six of us to go," Joey said.

Kennedy nodded. "And the last man standing to be the one to take his off."

"And drink eighteen beers for all of us," Joey came back.

Both men clenched their fists where they lay and kept

them balled as they stared into each other's eyes.

To the old man sitting next to his wife in a booth a few feet away from them, it was as if he were witnessing a pair of aging college graduates, refusing to grow up, exchanging some kind of fraternity recognition symbol. He shook his head and smiled at the silliness of it all. But his smile faded when he looked at their expressions and realized how serious they were.

"Damn," Kennedy said in a low voice. "They should have put us all away."

٩

BY THAT NIGHT, the last of the clouds trailing the storm front had moved north out of sight, and the faint light of a half-moon bathed the darkened funeral home in its glow. The structure had been remodeled several times during its long existence, and what little remained of its original columns and bricks was obviously worn, giving it at the same time both a forlorn look and an air of quiet dignity. The embalming area was at the very rear of the narrow structure.

In that area, the glow from a solitary night-light cast the man's wide shadow against the wall as he leaned over Alfred's body. Naked, it rested on its back in a long porcelain sink with drains at each end.

The man held what resembled a small video camera above Alfred's forehead. The rear of the device was the viewing screen. It glowed a dim hue of white.

As the device was lowered closer to Alfred's forehead, the glow changed to an outline of his skull. The view was penetrating, with the brain mass outlined in a light blue-gray. The deep wound to one side of the forehead appeared as a dark tunnel on the screen. A tiny square embedded in the brain mass beneath the other side of the forehead glowed as if it were reflecting the device's light.

The low hum of a drill beginning to run sounded much louder than it really was in the otherwise total quiet of the room.

The hum shifted to a deeper, lower-pitched sound as the bit passed through the skin across the forehead and dug into bone.

A moment later it cut into the brain matter.

In the viewing screen, the tip of the bit neared the square, nudged it, and was withdrawn.

The man inserted a thin pair of forceps inside the hole, caught the chip, and carefully pulled it from the brain.

It wasn't any larger than a pencil eraser, and it had a hairlike projection resembling an antenna rising from its center. He slipped it into his trouser pocket.

Now he clasped Alfred's far side, turned his body over on its stomach, and pulled on the shoulders, sliding the head and the shoulders to where they hung off the sink with the face and the hole drilled in the forehead facing downward toward the floor.

A metal gallon pail resembling a paint can already sat directly under the head. It was filled with a clear liquid.

The man stepped back.

A match flared.

The man pitched the flaming match into the liquid.

It made a popping sound, and flames jumped up toward Alfred's face.

In moments the head was completely engulfed in the bright yellow flames and beginning to char. Flaming hair fell to the floor. The skin turned black, began to bubble and swell.

The man retreated a step but kept watching, witnessing the flames beginning to burn the flesh away, exposing parts of the facial bones, which, in turn, became black and began to sizzle.

Outside the funeral home, a police car, its accelerator barely depressed, crept slowly up the otherwise deserted street in front of the aging structure. It came to a stop in front of a line of tall bushes along the sidewalk, but its motor kept running.

The blocky figure inside the car alternated his gaze between the rearview mirror and the pavement ahead of him.

A minute passed. Then another.

Suddenly the man who had been inside the funeral home hurried from the bushes, swung open the passenger door, and slipped inside the car. It started moving again.

A few seconds later, its headlights swinging to the right, the car turned off the street and disappeared down another narrow thoroughfare.

Back at the funeral home, a faint yellow glow reflected off an open window at the rear of the structure.

Seconds later a tongue of flame leaped out the window and curled up the brick wall. In minutes, the entire back of the aging building was enveloped in flames. It was a full five minutes before the first siren was heard.

Spence was in the shower when he thought he heard the sound of the doorbell above the noise of the rushing water. He listened more closely. He heard it again. He quickly rinsed the shampoo out of his hair, grabbed the towel off the lavatory, and, drying off as he walked, moved out of the bathroom through the bedroom into the apartment's small living room.

The doorbell rang again as he neared the door, then quickly rang once more. He pulled the towel around his hips and knotted it at his waist, brushed his hair back from his forehead, and opened the door.

Christen Dantonio, standing in the glow of the light fixture outside the door, looked him up and down. A small smile crossed her face. "If your Bronco hadn't been in the drive I would have missed this," she said. "I should have brought a photographer with me so I'd have a keepsake."

"I have a photograph inside you can have," he came back.

She held out two letter-size sheets of paper stapled together. "I told you I would let you read the article before it came out."

As he took the sheets into his hand, she walked past him into the apartment. She wore baggy shorts and sandals, with much of her slim figure swallowed in an oversized sweat-shirt that hung below her hips, giving her the appearance of someone even younger than the mid-twenties he had guessed when he first saw her in his office. Dressed as she was, he could imagine her being carded at a bar. He looked at the big octagonal clock on the wall above the TV. It was nearly ten. "What time is your deadline?" he asked.

"Passed. I already turned the article in."

He glanced at the sheets. "What good does it do for me to read this then?"

"I don't know. I just told you I would let you before it came out." She looked back across her shoulder as she walked toward the kitchen. "I hope you didn't think I would let you censor it."

He looked at the first line. It said, "If scientists are on the threshold of implanting artificial sight into the brains of the blind, how far away from implanting thoughts can they be—even intelligence."

He felt a little irritation. "I thought that kind of specu-lation was going to be off the record."

"It's not you speculating," Christen called from the kitchen. "It's me. Read the article." He heard the refriger-ator door open.

The columns and front two-thirds of the old funeral home had been saved. The hands on the steeple clock still moved. The rear section of the narrow structure was a total loss. The last few feet at the rear, where the embalming room had been, were totally gone except for a partial section of one charred wall still standing.

One of the firemen spraying water onto a pile of smol-dering brick and timbers, shook his head. "His head and shoulders nearly completely burned away," he said to the police officer standing next to him. "Just part of the charred skull left. The chemicals in there burned hotter than gaso-line."

He shook his head again. "What do you tell the family—

hand them an urn and say we think these ashes are from the head, or maybe from the roof?"

The officer didn't say anything. Just nodded.

Standing in the wet ashes covering the foundation at the rear of the building, the owner, a short overweight man with his gray hair cut in a fifties-fashion flattop, stared at the body bag being carried out of the ruins by two officers. It was filled with something much more shriveled than a man's body should be.

The owner looked back at the only recognizable object left in the embalming area, the long porcelain sink, charred but still standing. A puzzled expression crossed his face. He shook his head.

"I would have thought the sink would have at least protected the body from being cremated to that degree," he said. "How did he end up on the floor?"

Police chief Carlos Solomon, a black man in his mid-forties with the size and build of a professional football tackle, nodded his understanding of what happened. "In a hot-burning fire like that, strong gusts are created—one just sucked him out of the sink. Or maybe some of those chemicals exploding jolted him out."

The owner looked up at the chief, then nodded himself. "Yeah, I guess," he said. If anybody would know what could happen in a fire, he knew, it would be the chief. Solomon in fact had been a state arson investigator years before, until after a remarkable series of successful local investigations he had caught the attention of both the public and the Jackson City Council. He had been offered a high-ranking job with the police department, and within three years he was named to the top post of the department when he uncovered a kickback scheme involving the then chief of police, a council member, and the head of the streets maintenance department. All three had decided to plea-bargain when shown the mountain of evidence Solomon had secured almost completely on his own. Few if any former Jackson police chiefs had ever been as popular—or considered as smart. And nobody was as interesting a public speaker. Whether at a gathering of senior citizens or in a junior high school assembly, he seemed to always know just exactly what to say to draw the audience to him. There was even talk now of a mayoral race, with community leaders across racial lines and from all levels and positions in the city saying they would back him. Yeah, the owner thought, if anyone could guess the cause of this happening and guess correctly, it was Solomon.

"If there's anything my department can do to make your cleanup task easier . . . ," the chief now said. "Setting up construction barriers, directing traffic . . . I don't know if you're fully covered with the insurance . . . maybe you'd want to build back more than you had. I've made some friends within the construction business in the city. I think for a building like this I could get you some real good deals with contractors who would like the publicity of being part of restoring a historic landmark."

Then police chief Carlos Solomon shook the owner's hand warmly. "If you need me just call on me," he added, and turned away toward his car.

As he reached the fireman and police officer standing near the curb, he stopped, shook each of their hands in turn, commended them on the good job they were doing, then walked toward his car parked at the curb.

"Uncle Dutt."

The owner of the funeral home, hearing his name, looked across his shoulder at his nephew crossing the matted grass, wet from the tons of water the fire hoses had sprayed into the building.

"Uncle Dutt," the red-haired boy repeated, his long ponytail swinging behind his back as he hurried to his uncle and stopped next to him. "I've got something that might be real important to tell you."

"Well?"

"Uncle Dutt, there was a man here asking for fingerprints. I—"

"Fingerprints?"

The redhead began to explain about the visit, beginning

with how obviously crazy the large man was.

He wasn't halfway into the explanation when his uncle looked across his shoulder to see if the police chief had driven away yet—and saw Solomon standing only a few feet away, listening.

"You heard what my nephew said? Would the crazy bastard have burned it so nobody else could get the prints?"

Solomon walked closer. "Fingerprints?"

Byram nodded.

"A large man?"

"Six-one or -two. Heavily built."

"What was his name?"

"He said, uh . . . Boyd, Jack Boyd."

"Might not have been his real name," the owner said. He looked at the charred remains of the funeral home. "If he had anything to do with this . . ."

"Maybe the name wasn't real," Byram said, "but the scar on his face was sure enough. Ran from his nose up into his hair. Looked like hell."

Then Byram began to give the rest of Joey's physical description and described the kind of clothes the large man wore.

Chief Solomon listened closely but didn't make any move to take notes. He never took notes and never seemed to forget anything.

His mind was obviously his strong point.

Spence had hurriedly finished his shower, then read Christen's article while he had dressed in the bedroom. He liked it. It had quoted him in such a way as to make him sound confident that his team's method of research would eventually come to a successful conclusion, but it didn't make him sound overconfident. Christen had done a superb job of filling in around his words with her speculation that much good could come from the research as he now had it structured—even peripheral good. "Like the unforeseen beneficial spinoffs that had come from NASA's research originally designed solely for space exploration . . . ," she had written.

That was good. A good line to take to relieve some of the pressure. For there was pressure at UMC. Enormous pressure. The center had been the first medical complex in the world where a heart transplant had been performed, and, now, along with Harvard and Stanford Universities' medical centers, it was one of only three test sites in the nation working with the twin-magnet interventional MRI in curing kidney cancers by freezing them—another medical breakthrough. And that brought pressure to do even more. To be among the elite once again, first in making another breakthrough if at all possible. Maybe, with the help of Christen's article, it would appear foolish for anyone to interfere with the direction of his research as he now had it aligned. At least for a while. Give his program a little more breathing room. He liked it.

Now, dressed in jeans, tennis shoes, and a short-sleeve pullover, he sat in the apartment's small living room in an armchair across a coffee table from Christen, who was sitting on the couch. "I hope all of the board members read," he said.

Christen, one of her bare legs crossed over the other, a sandal hanging loosely from one small foot, set the beer she had gotten out of the refrigerator on the table. "I love your enthusiasm," she said. "I hope you are successful. My little brother was born blind."

"I'm sorry," he said.

"He acts like it's only a minor irritation that sometimes slows him down. He's in his final year of a psychiatry residency in Florida. He says I'm going to be his first case." She smiled, but only a small smile, and it didn't last but a moment. Her tone became more subdued now. "He says he wants to teach. I see that as a chink in his armor. I know he would really like to go into private practice, but he's not certain he can handle it being blind—first time I've ever seen him back off of something."

She looked down at the beer, lifted it into her hand, then

set it back down on the table. The light clinking sound the
can made told him it was empty.

"Would you like another one?"

"You only have one left. I was doing my best to be
polite. I have to get on home anyway, I have an early interview with the chief of police in the morning for another
feature I'm doing—crime in the city. Apropos with what
happened to Dr. Lambert, huh?" she added, and shrugged.

She came to her feet, glanced at her watch, then toward
the kitchen. "Well . . . it is still early." Her grin came back
again. "I'll split it with you."

As he stood she said, "Unless I'm making a nuisance of
myself."

"Not at all," he said.

She smiled again. She had an easy smile. And somehow,
in her casual attire she seemed even more attractive than
she had when he had first seen her in his office.

She walked toward the kitchen and he watched her go.
It was hard not to stare at her tight legs and the movement
of her perfectly rounded hips under the oversized sweatshirt. What he had thought of as pushy in his office, now
seemed more like an easy confidence she possessed.

Beautiful. Intelligent. Confident. Independent. It was a
combination not seen very often.

"Whoops, this is a bottle of root beer," she said from
the kitchen. "But you do have orange juice and lemon
juice." He heard a bottle clank against another and the refrigerator door close.

"You ever drink spiced orange juice?" she called. "You
mix a cup of orange juice with a teaspoon of lemon juice
and a teaspoon of honey, and heat it to the temperature you
like your coffee. My mother used to make it all the time
when I was a little girl."

He heard cabinet doors being opened.

"Do you have any honey?"

Police chief Solomon moved his hand slowly across the
instruments on the stainless steel cart, separating each in-

strument from the other with his fingers, feeling along the cold hard surface with his fingertips.

A few seconds later he dropped his hand back to his side. He looked at the porcelain sink and the washing table. He ran his gaze across the tile floor.

Then he moved to the small table and telephone sitting against the morgue's front wall.

He saw the stainless steel cup and reached for it.

In his bedroom, Walter Quinlan stared blankly at the wall. What he saw in his mind was Solomon's hand close around the small stainless steel cup and tilt it toward him, his view was down inside the container's interior.

The cup was replaced on the table.

The view went to the small biohazard disposal container sitting on the floor next to the table.

It contained a crumpled, blood-stained paper towel, a pair of latex gloves, and a dusting of cigar ashes.

Now Solomon was slipping something out from under his coat. It resembled a small video camera. The rear of the device glowed a dim hue of white. Solomon was beginning to turn slowly in a circle. The viewing screen continued to glow white. He turned nearly back to where he started his rotation. A brighter, almost dazzling, small white spot appeared in the middle of the screen.

The device was tilted toward the floor.

It moved over the biohazard disposal container.

Solomon's hand was reaching down into the container. He quickly moved his fingers against the crumpled paper towel, moved it away from the gloves, felt . . .

He lifted his hand with the small chip clutched securely in his fingertips.

Quinlan smiled his satisfaction.

The view suddenly swung to the morgue door as it opened.

A tall black orderly pushed a gurney carrying a sheet-covered body inside.

"Oh, excuse me, sir," the man said, halting the gurney.

"That's fine, I don't want to be in your way," Solomon said politely, his tone soft and friendly, more like that of a politician soliciting votes than of a cop. "I'm through anyway." He held the small device down at his side as he walked toward the doorway.

Quinlan, no longer interested in the image, clicked it off.

In its place another picture appeared, this one of Dr. Spence Stevens, standing on the sidewalk in front of his open apartment door, looking out into the night, watching a shiny black Lexus drive away.

10

"SMALL WAS A thug with a record going back to when he was twelve years old," FBI special agent Bob Kennedy said. "But always individual stuff—didn't have any gang affiliation as far as I can tell."

Joey was listening intently to every word that was being said to him over the telephone, though he cradled the receiver casually against his shoulder as he stared out his office window at the traffic passing by in the sun shining down on the narrow blacktop outside the building. No gang affiliation by Tommy Small meant that it was unlikely that Dr. Lambert's death had anything to do with him. No debt the old pathologist might have gotten into and been unable to repay. No quid pro quo he owed and failed to perform. A simple thug like Small would have very little chance to have even met the doctor. And nothing Small would have been carrying that two gang members would have been coming to the hospital to retrieve before the police found it.

"Mr. Wynn's prints ran through as pretty as you please," Kennedy continued, using the title *Mister* rather than only the last name, as he had done in Small's case, out of respect for the more prominent of the two men brought to the hospital morgue that day. "No matches showing him ever printed for anything. Evidently not a blemish on his record. Only thing is," Kennedy added, "he was a nonentity for several years."

Joey watched a big Waste Management truck drive by as he continued to listen.

"He was born in a private hospital in southeast Missouri. I got that information straight out of newspaper archives. It was in a feature article done about the executives at Computer Resources. His family moved a hundred miles south to West Memphis when he was in his teens. There wasn't any more I could get from the article, but there's a couple of income tax returns on file when he had a job in West Memphis—he worked for a car dealership. After that, there's a big blank—nothing. Then suddenly Mr. Wynn, without anything to show he's even been alive for a period of ten years, shows up here and takes a job with Computer Resources. That was eight years ago. Then the truck ends that today."

Kennedy paused for a moment. "Again, everything clean as a whistle as far as the information available. But the long gap is a little strange."

Kennedy ended his report by saying, "One more little thing. I called Jefferson City, Missouri, and there's no record there of Mr. Wynn ever living in the state.

"I mean his birth certificate isn't even on record."

"Did you hear about the body burned in the funeral home fire last night?" the city editor asked. Attractive in a plaid skirt and matching jacket over a white blouse, she was in her late forties. She laid a sheet of paper on Christen's desk. "I scribbled out a few details that were on TV this morning," the woman added. "Probably just need something short on it."

Short? Christen thought. To go with the short article on MCI WorldCom. And the longer article on the mayor-councilmen dispute. She had just put the finishing touches on those. And she still had material she had to collect for her crime series. She looked out across the spacious open area on the second floor of *The Clarion Ledger*. Reporters sitting in their small individual cubicles arranged side by side in long lines, busily typed on their computers or hurriedly thumbed through material or spoke on the telephone, trying to run down information for their stories. She looked up at the editor and wanted to say, "Why didn't you give this to me when you heard about it this morning—so I'd have more time on it?" But she didn't. Instead she asked, "How many inches?"

"Eight to ten," the editor said, and turned away from the desk.

Christen watched the woman walk toward another reporter at work on his computer. The woman looked down at him, said something, and handed him a sheet of paper. The reporter looked at what she had given him and shook his head wearily.

Why in hell don't you do it yourself? Christen thought, still staring at the editor.

Frowning, she dropped her gaze back to the sheet the editor had laid on her desk, stared at the woman's scribbling for a moment, then reached to the telephone, punched a number in, and lifted the receiver to her ear.

A male voice answered.

"Is Dr. Stevens in?" she asked.

The voice said, "Yes," and she replaced the receiver without saying anything more.

Then she stood. She glanced toward the clock on the far wall, reached back to the desk, slipped her tape recorder inside her purse, and lifted a small notebook into her hand.

With a last frown directed toward the city editor, she walked toward the exit from the big room.

Though it was barely two o'clock in the afternoon, Freddie had begun yawning repeatedly. "Women and work don't go together," he said.

"Hot date last night?" Spence asked.

Flo rolled her eyes. When she looked back down at the nerve tissue sample she was working with, Freddie grinned. Spence lowered his eyes back to the double-barrel microscope.

"Spence," Joey said from the doorway.

Freddie smiled at the big investigator. He had met him before. Flo stared at the man. It was the first time she had ever seen him. Spence walked across the floor to shake hands.

"You have a minute?" Joey asked.

They went into the office.

Stopping just inside its open door Joey said, "I had an FBI friend of mine do some checking. I've mentioned him to you before. Bob Kennedy, one of my . . . my group in the past. He says that Small and Wynn read like you would have expected them to. I still have a few things I want to check out. For one, Wynn has a couple of gaps in his life. Nothing big. But they're there."

"Gaps?"

"He was born in Missouri, but there's no record of a birth certificate there. There might be a reason for it. He was born at a private hospital that went out of business soon afterward—don't know what kind of financial condition they were in or if they were keeping up with records very good near the end. But the gap's there. There are a couple of years of income tax returns after he moved to Arkansas. He worked for a car dealership. Then there's nothing else until he shows up here and goes to work for Computer Resources eight years ago. From a car salesman to the senior vice president of the largest company in the state. Bill Gates worked out of his garage. Computer types don't always come up the same way as others. Still, it's interesting."

"I appreciate it, Joey."

"I'm not through checking yet."

"Again, I appreciate it. But there's probably no way either of the bodies would have had anything to do with this. Maybe the police will figure it out."

"West Memphis is only an hour's flight away. I'm going to see if I can find anybody who knew Mr. Wynn back then."

"Why?"

"To see if I can find out where he went when he left

there, what he did for the next few years, who his friends were—back then. There's been bigger people than Alfred Wynn involved in something that turns out surprising. You never know. Sometimes you have to start at the beginning to get to the end."

"Joey, I—"

The big detective holding his hand up in front of him, silenced Spence.

"Besides, it's like reading a good mystery and halfway through the book there aren't any more pages. I don't like gaps."

When Spence didn't immediately say anything, Joey said, "You don't think of me as the curious type? It's what I was trained to be. It's ingrained now. Don't worry about the bill. I wasn't going to charge you anyway."

"Yeah, you are. If you go any farther."

"Okay, so a trip to Memphis will cost you a couple of hundred."

"That wouldn't even cover—"

"Plus the ticket," Joey said.

Spence smiled. "You are crazy."

"Tell me about it, Doc."

"I'll go with you."

"What?"

"I haven't had a day off in months. So I'll take a vacation."

"You don't want someone to get away with this, do you?" Joey said.

"No, I don't."

"Multiply that times twelve good friends, the best you've ever known, and imagine yourself responsible for what happened to them—and you get more of an idea what started me down a dead-end road."

"I didn't want you to start thinking about that again."

"I'm not thinking about it. It's just a fact. Okay, so both of us will take a short flight."

Spence caught the movement out of the corner of his eye.

Christen Dantonio had moved up beside the open doorway. Her slim figure clad in a short skirt and blouse, she
held her purse and a small notebook in her hands.

"Afternoon, Doctor," she said, and smiled politely.

He nodded his greeting.

She looked at Joey.

Spence said, "This is a friend of mine, Joey McDonald."

She smiled at the investigator, and Joey nodded, and
then Spence saw her eyes come back to his. "I told you I
was doing a series on crime."

"Excuse me," Joey said. "I'll find out about the next
available flight and call you."

Spence nodded, and Joey stepped past Christen into the
laboratory and walked toward the door. She looked after
him for a moment, then brought her eyes back around. "I
know you don't want to talk about Dr. Lambert," she said,
"but I'd like to get some details about the murder so I can
mention it in the series. I've heard they wore surgical
scrubs and left them in the parking garage. Maybe someone
saw them and didn't watch the news last night or read the
paper this morning. Maybe someone like that would have
just assumed it was a couple of doctors in a hurry to get
somewhere. If I mention it again maybe they'll read the
paper and notice it this time. They might have a description."

"I appreciate that," he said.

Christen looked into the laboratory at Flo, down on one
knee and holding a bright-yellow bowl out in front of her.
A few feet away, the black potbellied pig with his white
feet braced wide on the floor, faced in her general direction.
Between them was a pair of two-foot-high walls of cardboard, painted a dark brown. Each ran twenty feet out to
the sides. The one nearest the pig had an opening a few
feet out to his right. He moved forward, stopped, and
moved his head slowly from side to side.

Spence came around his desk to join Christen, now
standing in the door staring at the plump animal. "That's

Tank," he said. "He's trying to find the openings in the cardboard."

The pig's head continued to move back and forth. Then it stopped its movement and tilted to the side, the snout facing the opening in the first wall. He slowly came forward, then increased his pace as he neared the opening and hurried through it.

He stopped again, standing between the two walls now.

His head moved slowly back and forth once more, then stopped, tilted to the side, and then he hurried toward the next opening. Passing through it, he began to trot toward Flo.

Spence nodded toward the bowl. "His favorite," he said. "Corn chowder."

"He's almost blind?" Christen said with a questioning tone in her voice.

"Totally blind since birth," Spence answered. "His right eye is actually a minicamera. It's wired around the retina into the occipital lobe. When we first started he could only distinguish between total dark and bright light. Now he can differentiate some subtleties—the difference in the dark cardboard and the openings. We haven't been able to obtain the same results with the human eye, yet. But it's promising."

"Can't he smell the food?"

Her question was an intelligent one. Pigs had one of the keenest olfactory systems in the animal world. A pig could navigate in total darkness through almost any winding barrier, solely by following a smell of something he sought.

Flo pulled a tight, clear plastic wrap off the bowl and sat it on the floor. Tank dug his snout into the chowder and began eating it noisily. Flo stood and looked across the floor. "I think I'll rearrange the panels," she said. "He might be starting to memorize the openings."

Spence nodded. "I have to leave, and I might not make it back by tomorrow. So you handle anything that comes up."

"Might not make it back?"

"If anyone's looking for me tell them I'm taking a . . ." He had started to make the same lighthearted comment about "a quick vacation" that he had made to Joey. But that wouldn't go over well with someone like Brimston, if he thought to inquire. "If anyone wonders where I am tell them that I've run down to Tulane to check on their research progress."

"Is he with the police?" Christen asked.

"Excuse me?" he said, looking back at her.

She was looking toward the door where Joey had exited the laboratory.

"Oh, Joey, no, why?"

"I overheard you saying something about checking on Dr. Lambert. I assume something to do with his murder."

"He's just a friend. Not a policeman."

"But he is doing some checking for you—about Dr. Lambert's murder?"

"Yes."

"That's sweet," she said.

11

As the tarmac at the Jackson International Airport dropped away beneath the Northwest Airlines jet, Spence looked out his window behind the port wing. The dual ribbons of Highway 80 passed beneath the steeply angled craft, then the wider lanes of Interstate 20. In seconds the landscape below turned from closely spaced commercial buildings to subdivision homes to a more rural scene of open fields and trees. With the airliner yet to pass into the thin overlying clouds, he saw the sprawling complex making up the state mental hospital at Whitfield and, not far from it, the blocky buildings of the state correctional facility, surrounded by tall fences tipped with razor wire.

Looking from the seat next to him, Joey stared at the wire. Joey suddenly felt the sensation coming and looked away from the fence. But it did no good. He was back in Nicaragua.

The layers of razor wire topped the fence surrounding the complex there. A much filthier complex infused with the odor of urine and feces. And blood. The blood pouring down his cheeks from the thin iron rod that had been slashed into his face like a whip by the scrawny little guard with the straight black hair hanging across his forehead. Nobody will come for you, the man had said. Nicaragua and the United States have a sound relationship now. Nobody will ever admit you were here. The man was right. Not the U.S. authorities—they wouldn't want the embarrassment of an American eradication force. The U.S. Congress had laws against assassination. And certainly the local Nicaraguan authorities weren't going to say anything—they were too busy posing for photographs in front of the water plants and electric power stations being built with the funds they had received from America, and smiling and receiving congratulatory handshakes from members of the U.S. State Department, who were putting on a show themselves.

You have no country, the guard said. Whatever we do to you is only for our knowledge.

Not quite, he knew at the time. If it was that simple, he and the rest of his team would have simply been shot and dumped in a shallow grave. Reports of their torture were indeed meant to slip back to the United States in small snippets over the weeks it was to continue. It was a warning to the special units command, or the CIA or army intelligence for that matter. You could never stop this, were the words the daily torture was meant to convey back home. The torture would go on for as long as possible, stopping only when the human body was ready to die no matter how careful the tormentors were. And then it would start again the moment the body and soul had rested enough to withstand it once again without dying. Which group of Yankees do you wish to send here the next time to face this? was the message. And the message would go no farther than the State Department. For if it did, it would not be those administering the torture who would be branded evil so much as the authority who okayed the eradication program in the first place. The guard was smiling. "You don't exist, yes?" he said. "Much bigger lies have been swallowed, no?" he asked. Yes, Joey knew, and felt the thin iron rod come down once again, cutting deeply into his face.

"Joey?"
The voice pulled him out of his thoughts.

"Joey," Spence said again.

The big detective's eyes came around.

"Joey, what's—"

"Nothing," Joey said in a sharp tone. Then he swallowed and lowered his voice. "Nothing. It happens sometimes, but then it goes away."

Before Spence could say anything else, Joey said, "Okay?"

Spence turned his face back toward the seat in front of him.

Several seats toward the rear of the airliner, a large man with thick dark hair focused on Joey's big hand, squeezing his armrest hard for support.

In Jackson, Genowski and John watched Joey's hand clasping the armrest. Walter Quinlan saw the same picture.

"I'll be interested to see if they can find out anything," Quinlan said. He was smart enough to know that he could never be too smart. There could always be something he hadn't thought to erase in the long trail that extended back a lifetime.

"I would like to know," he repeated.

John and Genowski had the same thought, they wanted to know the answer, too, the same answer that four of them would like to know. Four of them left in total, now that Alfred was gone. Beyond the four, the others didn't matter. The new ones. Their thoughts were directed toward matters quite different in nature.

They rented a car at the Memphis International Airport and drove over the old I-55 bridge to West Memphis. As they turned into the car dealership's wide lot, Joey looked up at the sign as large as a billboard overhanging the entrance. "Same dealership, same address, same owner," he said, and looked down at the notepad containing the information gleaned from Alfred Wynn's twenty-five-year-old tax return. "Now we find out if anybody still remembers Wynn.

Don't count on it. Car salesmen come and go like migrating ducks."

The dealership manager couldn't have been older than thirty-five. He obviously hadn't been there when the young Alfred Wynn had been employed as a salesman. Spence didn't have to be a detective to know that investigating was five percent getting somewhere and ninety-five percent frustration. The dealership was going to be a dead end.

But he found out he was wrong.

"Aubry Cook," the young manager had said. "He was the top salesman here for three decades. Retired last year. He can recall every customer he ever sold a car to and every salesman who ever worked here. The man's a genius. No telling what he could have been if he'd just had the money to get an education—he'll remember your Mr. Wynn."

Aubry Cook lived in a moderate-income subdivision on the outskirts of West Memphis. His wife was a short, heavyset woman with her once dark hair now mostly gray. Aubry, a tall, thin gray-haired man dressed in blue coveralls, was setting out tomato plants against the chain-link fence that separated his property from that of the neighbor's behind him. He smiled pleasantly at Spence and Joey as they walked toward him.

"Getting them out later than I like, too," he said, "but they're going to taste just as good when they're grown. Come back in a couple of months and I'll give you all you can eat in one sitting," he said. "Or if you fancy fried green tomatoes, in about six weeks. What can I do for you?"

Joey was the one who spoke as they stopped in front of Aubry. "We're trying to get some information on a young man who worked at the dealership some twenty-five years ago. His name is Alfred Wynn. The manager said you would remember him."

Aubry was nodding. "Yeah. Remember him well. He done something wrong?"

"We're not sure," Joey said.

"You police? You look like police."

When Joey didn't answer, the old man sighed. "Well," he said, "anything to help the authorities. He was just a kid. Not more than sixteen when he first went to work there. Never was in any trouble I ever heard about."

"What do you know about his family or any friends he might have hung around with?"

"Friends?" the old man questioned. "You're with the army, aren't you?"

"Why do you think that?"

"Randle."

"Randle?"

The old man nodded.

"What do you know about Randle?" Joey asked.

"Same thing you do, I'm guessing," the old man said. "Alfred wasn't ever like that. It wasn't in him. Though I'll have to admit, even though I knew Randle was headed down the wrong path, I would have never guessed he had something like that in him either."

"What did Randle do?"

When the old man didn't answer, Joey said, "I'm asking you what *you* know about it."

"Raped and killed that girl in Singapore." A questioning expression crossed the old man's face now. "You all thinking about paroling him now?"

"You know where Wynn went after he left the dealership?" Joey asked.

The questioning expression on Aubry's face remained for a moment more, then he erased it and said, "Down into Mississippi. Heard a few years later he was working as a tractor driver on a farm."

"Where?"

"Somewhere around the Tupelo area. Don't rightly know just where."

"What else do you know about him?"

"That's the whole of it."

"Did you know his parents?"

"Good people," Aubry said. "Killed in a house fire the

last year Alfred worked here. Not burnt up—suffocated from the smoke."

"Do you know of any other relatives?"

"No. The Wynns moved here from Missouri the year before Alfred went to work at the dealership."

"Any close friends still around here? Anybody who might know more about Mr. Wynn?"

"Alfred was a good boy," Aubry answered. "But he was sort of a loner at the same time. Especially after his parents died. I mean he was polite enough when you spoke to him, but he just didn't have much to say unless you straight out asked him something." The old man clasped his jaw in his fingers and thought for a moment. "I can't rightly say I even recall him ever dating a girl. Least one I heard him talk about. Course then, I'm a good twenty-five years older. He might have thought it was none of my business."

"Is there just one high school here?"

"High school?" the old man questioned. "So maybe you can pick some of his classmates out of a yearbook to talk to?" He smiled. "Not about Alfred, you won't. He didn't have any more education than I got. Maybe less. Like I said, though he was only around sixteen or seventeen when he first came to work at the dealership, he didn't attend no kind of school while he was here. Never talked about one he attended in Missouri. That might be partly why he was such a loner—embarrassed at his lack of education. Though he talked well enough. Good as I do, anyway. Just Randle, that was the only one I know he ever made up to."

When Joey didn't ask another question right away, the old man said, "He was really a good-looking boy. Damn shame he didn't try to find some girl to spend his time with. I 'magine there were plenty that wouldn't have paid no mind to his lack of education once they saw how good-looking he was. I got a picture of him if you want to see what I'm talking about. Regular movie-star-type looks— reminded me of James Dean. You know how he looked in *Rebel Without a Cause*? Wore his hair that way, too. You know, slopped over to the side of his forehead."

"I'd like to see the picture," Joey said.

It was stuffed in among a hundred other old photographs and keepsakes stored in a wooden trunk at the foot of the old man's bed. It took Aubry several seconds of sorting through the photographs before he found the one he was looking for. It was a faded original of a publicity photograph for the dealership. The employees stood in a line three deep, with Aubry in the front line and waving. He pointed his long finger toward a boyish face in the second row.

"That's Alfred," he said.

He pointed to another young face next to Alfred's. "That's Randle. But I guess you already know that. They look a lot alike, don't they, except for the height. Could almost pass for brothers. Maybe that was one of the reasons they took to each other."

"See," Aubry said, holding the photograph out.

Spence looked at the photograph. But he wasn't looking at either of the boys' faces. He was looking at the difference in height Aubry had mentioned. The boy that Aubry had pointed to as Randle was as tall as Aubry in the photo, a good six-foot-three. The boy he had identified as Alfred was much shorter, several inches shorter. Spence could only go by what he remembered of Alfred's height as his body had lain on the gurney in the morgue. But he *definitely* was well over six feet.

Spence wanted to make absolutely certain he hadn't made a mistake in which boy Aubry had identified as Alfred, and he pointed at Alfred's face.

"You said this is Alfred?"

Aubry nodded.

Spence looked at Joey. "The body in the morgue was nearer six-foot-three, maybe six-four."

"The morgue?" Aubry questioned.

"How tall was Alfred?" Joey asked.

"Maybe five-eight or five-nine," the old man answered.

"You're positive that's Alfred?" Joey asked, now placing the tip of his finger against the boy's face.

"Course I'm sure," the old man said. "What do you mean, the morgue?"

"You said Randle was in the army?" Joey asked.

"Yes, went in right from here."

"And he was court-martialed for killing and raping a girl?"

The old man's answer was slow coming. "You knew that," he said, "didn't you?"

"How old was he when he worked here?"

"Uh, a year or two older than Alfred."

"Could I borrow that photo?"

"Borrow? Well, I . . . Yeah." The old man held it out.

Joey said, "Thank you for your help," and turned away toward their car parked in front of the house.

Spence nodded their thanks back at the old man, then hurried after Joey.

As he caught up to him he said, "Joey, they were kids when the photograph was taken. He could have taken a growing spurt." He in fact had known a boy who had been a great high school basketball player, but with him only standing five-eight as a junior, few colleges had shown much interest. Then over the summer and fall of his senior year he had grown to six-two and became one of the top guard prospects in the state. Not to mention David Robinson growing from a player of moderate height in high school to one tall enough to dominate in the NBA by the time he had graduated from the naval academy. Late growing surges happened all the time.

"It's possible," Joey said. "But it's interesting that the one Aubry pointed out as Randle was as tall then as you say Alfred is now."

Spence glanced back at the old man again. He had returned to working with his tomato plants. "You think he has them mixed up? It's been twenty-five years."

"It's going to be easy enough to find out," Joey said. "I have Alfred's fingerprints."

"Fingerprints?"

"Yeah. But what I'm going to do next, I have to do alone."

12

CROSSING THE MEMORIAL Bridge spanning the Potomac River, Joey stared ahead through the taxi windshield at Arlington National Cemetery. He thought of the men from his past teams buried in that hallowed ground—one from a sortie into Lebanon; two from Libya, those two from a damned accident, a helicopter going out of control in a dust storm near Al Jawf. But at least the three from those missions had been buried in the cemetery. The two from South Africa hadn't. Their bodies had never come home to be buried, the real reason for their deaths never even recognized—the story their parents were told had been one of a helicopter crash in the Pacific, with the bodies never recovered. The deaths in Nicaragua hadn't produced any flag-draped coffins for burial either. He never knew what their families were told. He hadn't been in any condition to know if he had been told. Theirs had been the last deaths. By direct order, neither he nor any other of the surviving six team members had been allowed contact with any of the families. But that had been nothing new, as none of the team members had ever been allowed contact with any other team member's family since their training had first begun. He kept staring at the cemetery. He thought the longest of the seven who had died in Nicaragua. They had not just died, they had been slowly murdered. And his last thought as the cemetery passed from view was of the two of the six survivors who were still in hospitals. Mental hospitals. That is what Kennedy had meant when he said, "They should have put us all away."

At the Pentagon, he was met by a guard armed with a holstered automatic. Other men with heavier arms were encountered as he passed through metal-detector gates on the way into the inner passages of the massive structure. Colonel Michael Weaver was dressed in civilian attire, a moderately priced business suit no different than that worn by any of the minor-level bureaucrats swarming Washington. He came out of the chair behind his desk and they hugged like close brothers, not of blood but of bloodletting, and that bond closer than all but the closest of family ties.

"Were you able to help me, Michael?"

"They did a job on us the last time, didn't they?" Weaver said.

"It wasn't just the last time," Joey answered. "It was all of the jobs piling up on us. All of the deaths. Each time I swore I was going to figure out a way to keep it from happening again . . . it happened again."

"You were no more responsible for them than I was," the colonel said.

"I was in charge."

"The best commander I ever had," Weaver said. "The best ever."

"Did you get me the information?"

"You're not working for them again, are you?"

"You know better than that, Michael."

"It's because this sounds like something they would have been involved in. I say that because I couldn't scare up a set of fingerprints on Randle. There's plenty about him being court-martialed and sentenced to life. The photo you faxed me and his old photos are the same. I even cross-indexed to old newspaper articles and found the same story. But no prints on record anywhere. The records say he ended up committing suicide at Leavenworth."

Joey waited.

"But if you want to take it to another level," Weaver started, "right after I came back into the real world there was talk of a group that had volunteered for experiments a few years before. All of them supposedly straight out of Leavenworth after being sentenced to life. One was an army corporal sentenced for rape and murder. No name that I ever heard mentioned. No particular place where it happened like Singapore. The dates tie to when Randle would have been about the right age—it could be him. The experiments lasted for about three years, evidently without much success. Then there was an accident at the site. All of them were killed. The volunteers, the scientists, the entire team. Some kind of explosion—about ten years ago. With the project ended, I imagine that's why some of the old hands talked about it in bits and snippets. One of their war stories."

"What kind of experiments?"

"From what I gathered, it had to do with neurotechnology. If not exactly that, at least something to do with brain waves."

The telephone on the desk rang, and Weaver lifted the receiver. "Yes?"

Neurotechnology, Joey thought, the attempts at trying to link human brain waves with computers, either in an effort to aid those computers or attack them. Despite the secrecy surrounding such programs, there were few in any branch of intelligence that weren't aware that both the United States and the Soviet Union, before the breakdown of that empire, were heavily involved in such experiments.

Sometimes the "rumors" of such experiments became so widespread the military officially announced them, as a way to formally bring them to light before saying that they were being discontinued, and end the rumors.

It was in this manner that the army's experiments aimed at controlling computers in missiles with brain waves had been discontinued more than a decade before—though Joey knew in fact that such experiments were ongoing right up until the time he had returned to civilian life. And pure brain wave experiments ranging from "remote viewing," in which subjects said to have psychic ability tried to concentrate hard enough to see what was happening far from them, to "long-distance assassination" had been rumored for as far back as he could remember.

Some experiments had left the stage of "rumor" and had now become fact, such as the navy's success in using computer-enhanced, biofeedback–sensory wave techniques to improve the physical and mental quickness of U.S. Navy Seals. And he knew that scientists at Wright-Patterson Air Force Base had met with success in experiments aimed at using pilots' brain waves to manipulate the instrumentation of a combat jet during the high-G stress maneuvers that left a pilot nearly physically frozen. In fact, he had read only weeks before that now even civilian scientists at the University of Tübingen in Germany and elsewhere had similar success, developing a technique that allowed paralyzed patients to use their brain waves to spell out messages on a computer screen.

Then Weaver, replacing the telephone receiver and speaking to him again, pulled him out of his thoughts. "Six of them volunteered in all," Weaver said, continuing speaking about the experiment that had ended in an explosion killing all of those involved. "I heard that number from more than one source."

He paused and then added, "I put in some calls. Nobody anywhere could tell me where Randle's body is buried. So no fingerprints on record. No record of burial. One of the volunteers young enough to be the age Randle would be now. It could be the same guy. But he's dead—officially."

"Unless it is *them*."

Weaver nodded. "I don't know of anyone else who could cover up something like that. But something would have had to happen to remove the original Alfred if there was a switch. Something natural. Even *they* wouldn't have taken him off the map, not a U.S. citizen uninvolved in any way. This is all for a doctor? If it was for one of us, I'd understand better."

"I'm probably standing here because of that doctor," Joey said. "Dr. Spence Stevens. When he came down the

street all he saw was a bearded, dirty, doped-up slob standing there with a broken beer bottle in his hand threatening
the cops. They would have already shot me if there hadn't
been so many witnesses around. He later said he saw me
tremble. He knew I wanted to quit, he said, but he told me
he recognized I couldn't. He didn't have to do anything.
Under the same circumstances I wouldn't have. Especially
as green as he was—he was just starting his residency and
probably never saw anything like me before. But he came
right by the cops with them yelling for him to stop. Later
they tried to get the DA to charge him with interfering with
police officers. Bastards were pissed off because they didn't
get to shoot me, is what it amounted to. He's the one who
got Dr. Bower to work with me. Nobody has ever been
able to control my mind but me—and I'd been taking myself down deeper every year. But Bower did. I owe him.
And I would have never met him if it wasn't for Spence
Stevens."

"You going further on this?"

Joey nodded.

"I figured you were," Weaver said. He pulled a folded
map from his inside coat pocket and handed it over. It was
a standard civilian state highway map of Montana. "I circled the property where the site had to be," he said. "The
cover was an ordnance testing ground. Closed down now.
It was in cold-weather country—I heard that much. No
other government property fits."

As Joey slipped the map inside his coat, Weaver said,
"I don't have to remind you that the military has plastic
surgeons—a little cut here, a little nip there and he *would*
look like Alfred. Maybe the experiment wasn't a complete
failure. Even the old hands might not have known that.
Much of the information could have been contained with
the operation officers at the site, and maybe one or two
more back here. Maybe it's an ongoing project. If that's
true, maybe you don't want to go any further."

Joey said, "With Computer Resources part of it."

"Possibly. A little hidden government funding on something the company was interested in. A favor returned in the company putting someone on their payroll, maybe for the government to keep an eye on what's going on with their money, maybe to hide someone that needs hiding. Or maybe it's just nothing. Maybe Randle committed suicide, a snafu sapped the fingerprint records, and your Alfred is Alfred."

Joey nodded.

Weaver was silent for a moment. "I'm starting leave day after tomorrow. Have a couple of weeks saved up. I can stretch it into more if I have to. I was planning on just taking it easy and working with my roses. But if you think you might be getting into something you'll need help on . . ." He smiled a little. "I mean, why shouldn't I go ahead and jump in head first, I've already given you enough classified information to get brought up on charges."

"I appreciate it, Michael, but you enjoy your gardening."

"Seriously, Joey, don't get your ass in a crack. Not now. Not after everything that's behind you. Not after everything you've *put* behind you."

"I'm not going to get anything in a crack."

"At the risk of sounding like a nervous old has-been, why don't you give me your word you'll call me in a day or two—let me know everything worked out alright."

"It's a deal."

The corner of Weaver's mouth rose in a half-smile. "Those were the days, weren't they? Remember when I was in the hospital after we went after Mendez? I actually considered slitting the throat of a loudmouth navy asshole in the bed next to me. You think Dr. Hindman—you remember him—you think he would have thought I really was crazy if he came into the ward one morning and saw that loudmouth hanging by his ankles from the ceiling? I mean I actually thought about doing that."

Joey smiled.

"I hope we did some good," Weaver said.

"We did."

Weaver nodded. "Hope so," he repeated. "As I said, one

of the volunteers was the right age to be Randle. If you try to track any of this further, three of the others were a few years older according to the talk. A fifth one is who the old-timers talked about the most. Evidently he was a real wacko. A long-term sergeant, he was confined for killing a black officer. A hate crime. He was into it all; a Hitler fan, spouting off about the need for a new world order. Maybe with the experiments having to do with the brain, they were trying to change the way the volunteers thought. I guess he would have been a real test."

The last thing Weaver said was, "The sixth one was a female. Still in her teens, she came into the program just a few months before the accident. She had killed an instructor during basics—evidently they had something going and he got rougher than she liked. She was said to be a real knock-out."

Spence answered the telephone on the third ring.

"Dr. Stevens," the now familiar voice said.

"Hey, Christen."

"Dr. Stevens, do you . . . Spence, I'm going to be blunt. I'd like to go out with you. I have a notebook and pencil right here in my hand. If you say no, I can just scratch you off the list. So which is it?"

He could visualize her tight figure, her dark hair framing a face that was difficult not to stare at.

"I'm glad you called," he said.

Christen was silent for a moment. "And that means?"

"Where's your favorite place to eat?" he asked.

13

YOU HAVE TO know where the beginning is to be able to find the end, Joey thought as he looked down at the narrow runway seeming to come up unusually quickly toward the descending Learjet. *If you didn't get caught up in how difficult the puzzle is going to be. Just use common sense.*

He was as knowledgeable as Weaver about government properties, both military and so-called civilian; his job had once been to be familiar with the security surrounding the most sensitive of them all. And given that the experiments had taken place somewhere in the northernmost states, it wouldn't have been any harder for him to circle the most likely site on a map, as Weaver had done. None of the other properties were secure enough for something that would have been as highly classified, and all of them still had ongoing activity—an explosion hadn't shut them down.

The sleek craft bounced badly on touching down.

Joey looked across his seat at the pilot.

"Downdraft," the man said apologetically.

The cold was evident when Joey stepped to the tarmac. He slipped a jacket out of his duffle bag, pulled it on over the flannel shirt he already wore, lifted the bag, and walked toward the square concrete block building that served as a terminal at the small airport.

Thirty minutes later, a light layer of snow that had drifted across a section of the highway swirled and rose in the wake of his rented Camry as he sped along the narrow pavement toward the setting sun. To the Camry's sides, square-shaped hills with their tops swept flat by the wind ran in alternating series. Limestone outcroppings showed a dull gray-white in the fading sunlight. Few bushes and no trees marked the landscape. Only rock, and more rock.

It was dark by the time he reached his destination—a solitary stopover consisting of an aging service station and four small house trailers arranged in a half-circle facing the highway.

When he walked through the station's open door and stepped inside the old structure he saw a short, husky man with long white hair and matching beard, leaning back in a straight chair set near the far wall. Dressed in jeans and a plaid hunting jacket, he was reading a newspaper and didn't look up—as if it wasn't an unusual occurrence for someone to be entering the remote station. A half dozen empty beer cans lay on their sides on the floor beside the chair.

Joey walked to the worn wooden counter a few feet from the door. Behind the counter there was a doorway leading to a dimly lit room at the rear of the station.

But no one came through it.

"Gas pump's already on," the old man said from behind the newspaper.

"That's not what I'm here for," Joey said, turning to face the chair.

The paper came down slowly.

"You want some snacks, the price's already marked."

"I need a room for the night."

The old man's eyes narrowed.

Joey nodded back across his shoulder out the open door. "The sign outside says the trailers are for rent."

"Yeah, they are," the old man said. "By the week, day, or hour if you got someone with you and can't wait to get to a real motel. Even that don't happen very often." He reached to his side and lifted an aging, double-barrel shotgun from where it had been resting across the top of a cardboard packing case. Holding the weapon by its barrel and the newspaper in his other hand, he walked across the floor and behind the counter.

He was wearing only a stained T-shirt under the hunting jacket, and the jacket was gaped open with its top two buttons missing. "Where you from?" he asked, laying the newspaper on the counter.

"Jackson, Mississippi."

The man glanced through the smeared plate glass window at the front of the store toward the Camry. "What are you doing in the middle of nowhere?"

"I'm looking for an old military testing ground."

The man's eyes, never fully relaxed, tightened further. "You're a few states off the mark—the only testing ground I know about is in Nevada."

"There was one around here, once. Would have been a group of buildings somewhere on the property. Maybe more than one group. But definitely military."

"You don't say?"

"I imagine you've been around here long enough to remember it."

"You think so?"

"It would have had a lot of activity around it—you couldn't have missed that."

"Couldn't, huh?"

Joey reached toward his rear pocket for his wallet. The old man, never having let go of the barrel of the shotgun, raised the weapon higher and placed his other hand under the trigger guard.

"Wallet," Joey said, and pulled it from his jeans. He opened it and slid out a thin stack of fresh hundred-dollar bills.

"Let's start over," he said. "I'm looking for the site of an ordnance testing facility that was closed down around ten years ago. I know the property isn't far from here, but it has a lot of acreage. I want to know exactly where the buildings were. I'll pay you five hundred dollars if you tell me how to get to them." He counted out five of the bills, laying them one at a time, side by side on the counter.

"Who are you with?" the old man asked.

"I'm a private investigator doing a favor for an old friend."

The man stared for a long moment, his eyes narrowing once more under his thick eyebrows. He had a smudge of grit across his forehead. "Private investigator?"

Joey nodded.

"Could I see the ID in that billfold?"

Joey held the wallet out and the old man took it into his hand, flicked it open, and squinted at the driver's license encased in a plastic holder. "Says Jackson, Mississippi, alright."

He handed the wallet back, propped the shotgun against the back of the counter, slid the bills together, and lifted them into his hands. "Wasn't no group of buildings. Was an underground complex. Be an extra twenty for the trailer. Second one from the right's the only one's got gas if you're looking to cook anything or wanna stay warm. The site is about ten miles from here, down an old road that ain't all there anymore. For fifty more dollars I'll get you there in my Jeep. To the edge of the property, that is, and line you up where you can go look where the site is for yourself, if you want to. I'm not going in with you, though. It's abandoned alright, as far as anything still going on there, but it's still got guards around it."

The temperature dropped rapidly during the first part of the night, heading down into the twenties. The old man, still wearing nothing heavier than his plaid hunting jacket and jeans for protection against the cold, sat in a rickety straight chair outside the trailer. Joey, wearing a heavy coat now, sat in an identical chair across from him. A fire burned kindling in a bucket between them.

The old man pulled another Bud Light from the twelve-pack sitting on the ground. Four empty cans lay on their sides by his feet.

"You want another?" he asked, his breath condensing in a wispy vapor cloud in front of his face.

Joey shook his head. He still had half of his second one left.

"It's free," the old man said. "In trade for the good company."

His name was Jorgerson. Joey didn't know if that was his first name or last. It was all he had given. "No, thank you."

Jorgerson nodded, popped open a can, took a long drink out of it, then scratched his forefinger at something bothering him on one side of his face. "Don't get much of that out here," he said. "Company, that is. You married?"

"Yeah."

"I was. Mildred was her name. She's gone now. You have any kids?"

"No."

"I got one. He's a veterinarian in Butte. Jonathan Jorgerson, Junior. Doing me proud being so educated and such a big name in town. Not to mention he did it all on his own. I didn't have the money to send him to college. He went on the military's money—the marines. Wish he had located a bit closer, but he thought he could make a better living there. We get together here for some elk hunting though from time to time. He's a hell of a shot."

Joey slipped his cellular phone from the coat and punched in a number.

It rang several times without an answer, and he lowered it back to his lap. He looked in the direction Jorgerson had indicated they would be going. The full moon cast a bright light. Bare, gently undulating ground, broken here and there by an occasional wind-flattened bluff and a light scattering of snow, seemed to run forever.

"You won't think it's any more than what you're looking at now when I point it out to you," Jorgerson said. "That is, unless you were to go down inside it. They came in here about fifteen, sixteen years ago and worked for a full two years with big earth-moving equipment. When they were finished you couldn't tell a speck of difference in the lay of the ground, like it hadn't been touched a bit. All of it underground."

He took another long drink from the can. "The people staying there came and went by helicopters. But they weren't hiding they was there. Explosions went off now and then. Copters came in during the day as well as at night. They built a ten-foot-high fence all around it and had armed guards and some big dogs patrolling the fence around the clock. You sure you don't want another beer?"

"No."

Jorgerson shrugged, sipped the last drops from his can, and leaned over to slip another one from the pack. "About ten years ago they had a real big explosion and fire. I was a couple miles away at the time and actually felt the ground shake. For a few days there was a lot more helicopters coming in and out, then everybody left. Except the guards I told you about. They have a couple of house trailers sitting right in the middle of the property, in a depressed spot where part of the mountain collapsed in on itself after the explosion. They patrol the old fence every night. Signs saying you'll be shot if you enter the property are still up. Placards with the faces of mean-looking dogs with their mouths open tacked all along the fence. But you don't need to pay any attention to that; dogs aren't there anymore. There's nothing there but the old rooms underground, mostly all caved in, and they're still guarding it."

"You said 'mostly' all caved in."

"How many hundreds you got left, Mr. McDonald?"

Joey sat a moment, then pulled his wallet from his pocket and slipped a hundred out from among the remaining bills. He held it toward the old man. Jorgerson took the bill but kept his gaze on the wallet. "I know because I been down there—in the rooms."

He nodded at the wallet. "And I get the feeling that you'll part with that last few hundred if I showed you how to get down in there yourself."

*   *   *

Christen had picked Monte's, a cozy restaurant in the small
suburb of Ridgeland, joining Jackson on the northeast. She
had ordered the lasagna tastricoti while he had chosen the
seafood pasta. The bottle of wine was still a quarter full
when she held up her hand to keep him from pouring her
another glass. "I can drink beer all night, but just a little
bit of wine and I feel like I need to go to sleep," she said.
"Guess it shows the country girl in me. Tell me something
about yourself. I mean more than just the research part.
Your family?"

"My father's dead. My mother lives in Gulfport. That's
where I'm originally from. My older brother still lives
down there."

"I'm sorry about your father. That probably made you
closer to Dr. Lambert, didn't it?"

"I never thought of it that way."

"I could see it happening," she said. "I lost mother eight
years ago and I know I wondered who's going to advise
me now."

Her expression, serious as she spoke of her mother, now
lightened, and she spoke in a livelier tone. "I'm from Itta
Bena. Well, not even from that large of a town actually. I
grew up on a farm outside of Itta Bena. If you're bored for
conversation, ask me something about growing rice or raising catfish. If you can believe it, I have eight brothers and
sisters. Actually all of them are half-brothers and half-
sisters except for the one brother I told you about when I
brought the article over to your apartment. We were
mother's only children, but Daddy's third and fourth, on
his way to nine—from four marriages. He's on his fifth
now. You'd like him. He really is a great guy to talk to,
and generous to a fault." She held up her wrist, showing
him her diamond-studded bracelet, and smiled. "Probably
part generous and part feeling guilty for not being around
me much since I was a little girl, but I love him in any
case. He just can't seem to find who he's looking for. He
settles in, then before too long he sees someone else walk
by—and bam, he's breaking up one household to form a

new one. Everybody has always said I take after him.
Maybe that's why I haven't found anybody I want to take
a chance on yet."

He noticed her eyes weren't quite as open as they had
been when they started on the bottle of wine.

"You're looking at my eyes," she said, and grinned.
"They give me away, don't they? Coffee doesn't help either. Not after I've had enough wine. You want to go to
your apartment and just sit around? I'm not physically up
to much more."

"That'll be fine."

Her grin reappeared as she came to her feet. "I am forward," she said. "But I'm also old-fashioned. Actually
something of a prude. Probably has something to do with
rebelling against Daddy. Don't want you to get the wrong
idea about me going to your apartment."

"I think I can control myself," he said.

"Good," she said, and started toward the entrance.

He lifted the ticket the waitress had laid on the table,
and followed after Christen.

His apartment was only fifteen minutes away. Christen
was quiet for most of the ride, yawning twice, only remarking about the rock music playing on the Bronco's radio. "You like that stuff?" she had asked, and switched to
a station playing favorites of decades before. "I told you I
was a country girl," she said.

At the apartment, she found the same station on the radio
in the living room. "Would you like to dance?" she asked,
holding out her hands.

"The Great Pretender" was playing. As he took her hand
in his and slipped his other arm around her back, she said,
"I wish they still played music like that. I like dancing. But
not standing across from each other trying to see who can
look the most awkward jiggling to some crazed band playing. Do you know how to jitterbug? Granddaddy taught me
when I was a little girl."

The skin of her cheek was warm, her body soft, molded
loosely against his. Her perfume gave off a pleasant aroma

he couldn't quite place. "You dance pretty good," she said in a soft voice.

They continued slowly moving in time to the old tune.

But not for long. He felt her yawn. Then she shook her head, moved her face back from his and looked into his eyes. "I can't believe it," she said, "but I can hardly keep my eyes open. I'm going to have to rest for a minute."

As she stepped away from him, pulling him by the hand toward the couch, she added, "Hope that doesn't hurt your confidence—you are a good dancer."

"I've been put down worse."

She smiled, sat down on the couch and, still holding his hand, pulled him down beside her. "I'm sorry," she said.

She tucked her legs up under her and leaned her head against his shoulder. He felt her warm breath against his neck.

"I'll just rest my eyes," she said. "We can talk."

She was silent for several seconds.

Then she snuggled closer against him, and her breathing began to slow.

A moment later she muttered in a voice almost too low for him to hear:

"I'll say one thing for Daddy—he's certainly fertile."

Outside in the parking lot, Flo sat in her pickup staring at the lighted windows of the apartment.

She had been there for fifteen minutes, arriving shortly after Spence and Christen had.

Her hands nervously clasped and unclasped the steering wheel.

14

SPENCE LAID CHRISTEN gently back on the couch and slipped a sofa pillow under her head. He got a blanket from the closet in his bedroom and gently covered her.

He heard the soft knock.

He looked toward the front door.

It came again, a soft knock rather than the doorbell ringing.

He walked to the door and opened it.

Flo stood there. Her makeup perfectly applied, her tight figure clad in a loose dress closely molding her curves, she smiled softly at him.

"I know it's late," she said. "But I saw your lights on. I didn't want to ring the doorbell and wake you if you were asleep. I, uh . . . I felt like I haven't expressed how really sorry I was at Dr. Lambert's death. How sorry I feel for you. I know how much he meant to you. I get used to being so . . . so professional around you in the lab. I wanted to stop by and . . ."

She looked at Christen, asleep on the couch. She had moved since he had covered her, and a bare leg was exposed to above her knee.

Flo's eyes came back to his. She moved her hair back off her shoulder in a nervous gesture. "I'm sorry," she said. "I shouldn't have come by unannounced." She turned toward the parking spaces.

He caught her by the elbow and turned her back around.

"It's alright," he said. "I appreciate your coming by. That's Christen. She was, uh . . . tired."

"Tired?" Flo said.

"Uh-huh, she—"

"I need to go, Dr. Stevens," she said. She once again walked toward the parking spaces. He stared after her. Moments later she was driving away.

"Was that Flo?" Christen asked from behind him.

She had the blanket wrapped around her.

He looked back in the direction of Flo's pickup.

The old Jeep bounced through the night.

The rusty vehicle's headlights were so coated with grime that they cast only a dull glow a few feet out across the hard ground before their illumination was lost in the brighter light of the moon. Jorgerson wore glasses now. "Nearsighted," he had said as he slipped them on. He scratched the inside of his ear with the end of his little finger. "You'd think with this once being a high-tech laboratory that the guards left here would at least have some fancy surveillance equipment," he said. "But they don't. At least no more than night-vision goggles. I know that because they caught me driving inside the fence one night and the goggles was all I saw. I told them I was hunting. I was in there driving all over the place for an hour before they noticed me and came roaring out of the trailer area after me. Couldn't have much fancy equipment if it took them that long to notice me." He lifted a small silver flask from the canvas compartment of the Jeep's door and held it across the seat. "Ought to charge you for this," he said. "It's a lot more expensive than beer."

"No, thank you."

Jorgerson unscrewed the flask's top and took a long drink from the container, smiling and wiping his lips with the back of his hands when he lowered it to the steering wheel. A front tire bounced over a rock, causing the Jeep to tilt to the left, and Joey grabbed the dash for support.

Then he looked across the seats. "How do you know it was a laboratory?"

"Fancy bottles and glass tubing, scales, microscopes, other things I don't know what they are; the kind of stuff that goes in a laboratory. It's all over the place down there. I lied a little when I said they caught me driving all over the property. I did that, too—to check them out. But they couldn't catch me that night. The night they caught me I had parked the Jeep and was walking toward the air shaft I'm going to show you, and they came up on me before I knew it. They took me to the trailers, questioned me for a while. 'Course I didn't tell them what I'd been getting ready to do—going down there. You sure you don't want a drink?" Jorgerson held the flask out.

"No."

Jorgerson took a long drink from the container. "I guess you wonder what I go down there for?"

Joey looked across the seat.

The old man smiled. The liquor, and the cans of beer he had drunk before that, made the smile loose and wide. "That's for me to know and you to find out," he said, and chuckled to himself, then took another swig from the flask.

"Yeah, a high-tech place," he said, sticking the flask between his legs. "High-tech place, low-tech guards. When all the hype went out of the place with the fire, I imagine the military pretty much forgot about it—just assigned some half-trained MPs to look after it for a while. And probably forgot about them by now. They don't wear uniforms. They say they're government game managers, studying what happens when everybody's kept out of a place and it's let go back to the wildlife. What wildlife? A few rabbits and snakes maybe. You sure you don't care for none," he added, lifting the flask from between his thighs and holding it across the seat once more.

Joey shook his head no, lifted the cellular phone from his lap, punched in the number again, and waited. It rang several times, again with no answer. The Jeep tilted abruptly as its left wheels slid into an eroded trench. Jorgerson tugged the steering wheel hard to the right and the old vehicle tilted again and lurched back up onto level ground. He took another drink from the flask, recapped it, and placed it back between his legs once more. "Who you trying to call?"

"My wife."

Jorgerson nodded and turned his face back toward the Jeep's dusty windshield. "Just a li'l bit mooore," he said in a suddenly slurred voice. "Up over that next rise is the property lines. Line," he corrected himself. He looked down at the flask between his legs and chuckled. He stopped the Jeep.

"Just be a second," he said as he stepped from his seat to the ground.

A moment later he was relieving himself on a flat rock dusted with a thin coating of snow.

Joey stared across the ground ahead of the Jeep. To the left, a ridge ran a few feet tall for a while, then angled sharply up toward a high overhanging bluff. To the other side and in front of him was barren rock and more barren rock. He glanced back at Jorgerson. *A laboratory*, he had said. Weaver had said neurotechnology or brain wave experiments. There would have to be a laboratory—and a whole lot more. He wondered how much he was really going to get to see.

"I feel better," Jorgerson said, climbing back into the Jeep. "Lot better. You know what I mean?" He wiped the lenses of his glasses against his jacket and slipped them back on. They started forward once more, the old vehicle beginning to bounce again as he ran it up to the ten to fifteen miles an hour that he had held it at since they cut off the old county road and started cross-country.

Joey lifted the cellular phone once more. It was a satellite cellular. No matter the part of the world he might be in there was always a satellite overhead that would transmit his call to its intended destination. But it didn't work underground.

He punched in the number as Jorgerson watched.

"Really a lot of alligators in Mississippi?" the old man asked.

"Lots," Joey said as he lifted the phone to his ear.

Christen's eyes opened. She stretched her arms and looked across the living room. Spence looked back at her from across the small table in the dining area. "How long have I been asleep?" she asked in a soft voice.

"About an hour."

"Sorry." She swung her legs to the floor.

"It gave me time to catch up on some book work," he said, laying his pen down next to the papers he had been working on and coming to his feet.

"I went back to sleep right after Flo left, didn't I?" Christen asked as he walked up to the couch. "Hope I didn't mess something up you had going."

"With Flo? There was something wrong with her. But jealous? Not a chance in the world?"

"You think I'm blind?" Christen said. "Or maybe you are. She comes by here this time of night just to tell you she feels bad about Dr. Lambert. Spare me." She stood. "I need something to drink—and I don't mean with alcohol in it. I'm never going to drink wine again. It's your fault, you know."

"Mine?"

"You ordered the wine."

"You should have told me."

"I wasn't going to drink very much—but you kept re-filling my glass." She laid her hands on his forearm, came up on the toes of her shoes and kissed him on the cheek. "Your fault," she said softly.

She remained standing close, her body gently touching his. "Accept your responsibility like a gentleman," she added.

Her perfume gave off a pleasant scent. "If I have to," he said. He moved his hands to her small waist.

"Have I kissed you yet?" she asked, her voice still soft. "Sometimes wine makes me forgetful, too."

"Kissed me a lot," he said.

"Really?"

"Uh-huh." He slipped his arms around her waist.

Her face came closer, looking up into his. "You know I said I was old-fashioned."

"You're still relatively safe."

"From you?" she asked. "What about from me?" She clasped the back of his neck with her hands and ran her thumb nails along the skin. She came up on her toes again, and kissed him gently on the lips.

The telephone rang.

He returned her kiss, as gentle with his lips as she had been with hers. Then he smiled at her and leaned down to the coffee table to lift the telephone receiver. She remained close against him.

"Hello."

"Spence, I need you to do me a favor."

"Hey, Joey. Sure."

"Pat is driving back up from visiting her mother on the coast. I've tried her twice, but she's not back yet. For some reason the answering machine isn't working. I'm getting ready to go where my phone won't work. If she tries to call me and doesn't get an answer she's going to worry. It's the way things were. You know. If I don't call her, she calls me—every night. She should be home any minute. If you could call every once in a while and when you get her, tell her I'll be calling as soon as I can. . . ."

"Sure, Joey."

"Tell her I'm taking care of him," a faint voice said in the background.

"Who's that?"

"That's Jorgerson."

"Who?"

"The last of the mountain men," Joey said.

The other voice spoke loudly now. "Jonathan Jorgerson the first. King of the wild frontier."

Spence smiled. "You at a party?"

"Randle might have been involved in a government experiment."

"What do you mean?"

"This is as far as we can drive," Jorgerson said in the background. "It's about a quarter of a mile to the shaft."

"Where are you?" Spence asked.

"I'll catch you up on it later," Joey answered. "Don't forget to call Pat."

The line cut off, and Spence lowered the receiver. Christen was still close. "Joey?" she asked.

He nodded, leaned to replace the receiver in its cradle, and came back up softly against her. "Yeah." He raised his hands to the sides of her face, and clasped it softly.

"What's he doing?" she asked.

"I don't have the slightest idea."

"Still about Dr. Lambert?"

He nodded again. She stared into his eyes for a moment, then gently backed out of his arms. She left her palms placed against his chest. "You're going to have to help me remain old-fashioned," she said.

He held his hands up out to the sides of his shoulders.

She smiled and turned toward the kitchen. "I have to have a drink of water. Who did you say was with Joey?" she asked back across her shoulder.

They had parked the Jeep behind a rise and now walked across the rocky, moonlit ground. Jorgerson had a couple hundred feet of thin nylon rope coiled across his shoulder and carried a miner's lamp powered by a battery the size of a six-pack. Joey carried the thick leather gloves the old man had given him and wore tightly laced combat boots with his jeans stuffed into their tops.

"Actually we were driving inside the property for the last couple miles," Jorgerson said. "But they don't never patrol it. Only inside the fence around the old site."

It took several more minutes.

Jorgerson stopped in front of a section of the fence where the wire had come loose from its tall steel supporting poles and lay flat in a long line across the ground.

"They don't fix anything," he said. "Just let it lay where it falls. I guess to give the impression the military hasn't any more to do with it. Just the game management people," he added in an amused tone, and walked across the wire. It bounced against the ground, making a faint metallic sound.

Several hundred yards ahead of them, a mounded hill, thirty to forty acres in size, rose like a giant blister from the rocky ground.

"It's under there," Jorgerson said. "The trailers and the game management people are on the far slope."

Everything he said, he said in a normal voice, like they were in casual conversation walking down a city street. In the deathly quiet of the night, interrupted only occasionally by the whine of the wind coming and going in long, whipping gusts, he sounded like a loud radio. As they grew closer to the hill the moonlight seemed to fade, the night growing darker, even though Joey knew that wasn't the case. It was only him. His wanting to see better. See more than shadows behind every boulder and outcropping of rock. *See everything. Hear everything. Know everything.*

He was automatically reverting *back*. Each time Jorgerson took a step it sounded like the foot of a giant slamming down against the ground. Rocks turned under the old man's boot, sounding like the start of small avalanches. It took an effort not to grab Jorgerson's thick neck, gripping it in a way that left no doubt he shouldn't make another sound.

But this wasn't a mission.

This wasn't a place you could die if you were discovered.

Jorgerson stopped a third of the way up the slope. He squinted down at the ground, then took a couple steps to his right and leaned forward, digging his fingers in among the pebbles there.

When he pulled, a section of the ground came up. Dirt and small rocks slid off a crudely fashioned covering made of old boards with canvas stretched across their tops.

Jorgerson laid the cover to the side. "You're a pretty big guy, but not any bigger around than I am," he said, lowering his stocky body on one knee to the edge of the shaft and slipping the nylon rope off his shoulder. "A little longer, that's all—you'll fit through just fine." He began to tie an end of the nylon rope to a steel pen driven into the hard ground next to the opening.

Joey stepped to the opening and stared down into the shaft. The covering hadn't been more than three feet square. The opening didn't appear to be more than two feet in diameter. "It's not straight down, but angles," Jorgerson said. "You won't really need the rope until you near the bottom—shaft has fallen in there and left a wide drop on down into the rooms."

He finished tying the rope to the pin, pitched the remainder of the tight coil into the shaft, and came to his feet. "Private detective, huh?" he said. "Working for one of the family members, would be my best guess. Well, the bodies are still down there. The ones you can see anyway. They never brought in digging equipment after the explosion—just left them where they lay."

He held out the lamp. "You'll need this," he said.

Then he grinned. "Hope you don't tend toward claustrophobia."

Joey looked at the old man—an old man he had met only hours before. With the long white hair hanging down across his shoulders and a beard, he looked the part of who he appeared to be; a grizzled loner shunning society, maybe a prospector in his younger years. But in a mission done right, everyone looked the part. His beard gone and his hair trimmed short he could easily look the part of a military officer. Despite his overall slovenly appearance, there was a definite tightness to his muscles and an erectness to his posture. Maybe the unit guarding the site was not half-trained MPs after all.

He looked at the opening. An opening to a grave for the bodies Jorgerson talked about. Close the opening, and the shaft could be a new grave for anyone who might venture down there before it was closed.

"You're going with me."

Jorgerson's eyes narrowed behind the glasses. He scratched the back of his neck and shook his head a little. "Now that weren't the deal, mister. I've showed you how to get down in there. The rest is up to you."

Joey pulled his wallet out of his hip pocket, opened it, then dug a folded set of four one-hundred-dollar bills out of a narrow pocket.

He held the money out.

"Thought you gave me all you had before," Jorgerson said. He looked toward the hole and frowned.

"You know how much trouble getting up and down inside there is?" he said in an irritated tone.

Still frowning, he held his hand out for the money. As Joey handed it over, Jorgerson looked back toward the hole. "You go first," he said. "You're not familiar with the shaft and I don't want you fumbling around and knocking rocks down on my head."

"You go first," Joey said.

Jorgerson stared at him.

He returned the stare.

"Okay," the old man finally said, "if that's how you feel about it. But stay close. They didn't bother to case it when they drilled it. The rock wasn't going to move. But there are naturally fractured places—where loose rock can break apart. One bouncing down the shaft from a couple of feet hurts a lot less than one from several feet above."

He slipped off his glasses and put them in his jacket's breast pocket, then reached inside a side pocket and pulled out a pair of leather gloves. As he slipped them on, he sat down at the edge of the shaft. He looked back up over his shoulder.

"About a hundred feet to the bottom," he said. "But I promise you it will seem longer."

Then he lowered his feet into the hole and squirmed down inside it.

His wide shoulders seemed to catch at the sides of the opening for a moment. He looked like a thick cork in a bottle.

He squirmed and dropped lower. Only the top of his head, his white hair casting a light glow in the moonlight, remained in sight.

Then it dropped from view.

15

THE SHAFT SEEMED to grow more constricting to Joey the deeper he went. Even though he had left his heavy coat in the Jeep and wore only his jacket now, he still filled the passageway almost completely. Unyielding rock pressed against his sides and pulled against his stomach and chest as he half slid, half crawled backward down the shaft. He thought about how much more difficult the trip back up would be with the steep angle. Jorgerson not only didn't tend toward claustrophobia, he was in remarkable shape, a fitness more likely in a man who worked out daily rather than one who sat around and soaked up beer.

Then came the old man's voice saying, "Careful now. Fractured rock right here. *Don't* knock any down on me."

The sound of pebbles sliding down the shaft, then a thumping, bouncing, echoing sound growing rapidly fainter, passed up to Joey.

"See what I mean," Jorgerson mumbled.

Joey came slowly on down the incline. The area of fracture Jorgerson had passed through was loose and scaly, like limestone. Pebbles the size of marbles broke free and slid past Joey's boots despite his trying to squeeze through the area as gently as he could.

"Damn," Jorgerson cursed below him.

Then he said, "The shaft starts widening now. It's where the explosion brought it down. Hang onto the rope. You

slip and fall into me and we'll both end up splattered down
below."

Light suddenly glowed around Joey. Beneath his feet he
could see the bright illumination of the miner's lamp. That
he could lean his head to the side enough to look down at
all showed that the shaft was widening.

It rapidly widened even more. Jorgerson had his feet
spaced wide out to his sides, his hands clasping the rope
now. His boots made scuffling sounds as they gripped and
slid against the sides of the shaft.

Then he stopped, perched over an area that widened into
a dark void only dimly lit by the miner's lamp hanging
from a cord around his neck. "Okay," he said. "You have
to use the rope altogether the rest of the way."

The nylon bit into Joey's chest and pulled against his
leg as the old man's weight suddenly stretched it taut.

Jorgerson swung back and forth, then quickly lowered
himself into the void.

Joey slid down the rope behind him.

His feet landed roughly on a pile of rock mounded into
a small hill. Part of a fan blade as large as a boat paddle
stuck out of the rubble. It was the fan that had sucked air
down the shaft and had come down with the rock when the
explosion had occurred. Jorgerson slipped his glasses on,
then climbed down to a concrete floor and shined his light
ahead of him.

The concrete ran for thirty feet before ending abruptly
in a solid wall of wide, broken slabs of rock packed tightly
together.

The light swung back to the left, illuminating walls of
steel painted a light green, partially coated by soot. In spots,
mold covered the metal from top to bottom, but there was
no feel of dampness. The air carried a light scent of stale
dirt—and an odor of fire, which had lingered for ten years.
Joey now noticed a section of the steel that was not only
soot covered, but buckled from the intense heat that must
have played across it.

Jorgerson swung his light along the wall to another pile

of rock. This time the broken and cracked slabs were stacked only a few feet high, leaving an open space of several feet between their top and the jagged rock overhead.

"The only way is up and over," Jorgerson said. He started toward the pile.

"Wait a minute," Joey said. He had noted when they reached the bottom of the shaft that there hadn't even been a hint of sweat on Jorgerson's forehead despite the arduous strain of the journey.

"What?" Jorgerson said. He waited as Joey came to him. "What?" he said again.

"Hold your arms out to your sides."

The old man stared for a moment, then slowly lifted his hands up and out from his shoulders. Joey quickly felt around the hunting jacket and behind the old man's waist.

Then Joey stepped back. "Sorry," he said. "I had to be sure."

"Sure of what?" Jorgerson said in a low voice as he lowered his hands.

"It's a long story."

"I don't guess you want me to feel that bulge behind *your* back under your jacket," Jorgerson came back.

Joey smiled a little. "It's an automatic."

"I didn't know what kind it was," Jorgerson said, "but I knew it was there. Course I didn't notice it until we were in the Jeep, and it was too late then. I'd already left my shotgun back at the station." He glanced across his shoulder at the wide pile of rock. "So now if all this foolishness is over with, you ready to go on?"

Joey nodded.

Jorgerson walked to the rocks. He hung the lamp back around his neck, climbed onto the top of the barrier, and began crawling across the wildly uneven surface.

In seconds they were both in the next open area. Jorgerson, the lamp shining in front of him, walked through a far doorway.

It led into another big room. All its walls were in view, with only an occasional large rock spotted about the floor.

Six-foot-tall metal lockers lined one wall. Their doors stood open and their insides were bare. Every surface—the lockers, the steel walls, the relatively smooth rock ceiling overhead, the opening to another doorway a few feet away—was marred with thick streaks of soot. Holding the lamp in front of him, Jorgerson walked through the doorway.

Immediately past it, a pile of tightly packed large slabs of rock rose in a continuous mass to disappear into the darkness above.

Jorgerson dropped to his knees. His light showed a narrow triangular-shaped opening made where two wide slabs of rock had lodged together, keeping the debris above from coming all the way to the floor.

Before starting into the opening, Jorgerson said, "I guess with me going first you don't have much to worry about. But there was a big rattler in here once before. If you hear me scream, backtrack out of here quick unless you want to see if I can squeeze by you in a real hurry."

Joey followed the old man's slowly moving boots through the opening. It was obvious that Jorgerson was doing more than simply giving him a tour of the caved-in rooms. He was taking him somewhere in particular.

16

WHEN JOEY EMERGED from the narrow triangular-shaped tunnel running under the pile of rock that had blocked the way, Jorgerson already stood at a place where the open area they had entered ended in another solid wall of fractured slabs, this time great slabs of grayish-colored limestone. A steel wall to the side of the area showed an open doorway. But Jorgerson didn't walk toward it. Instead he shined his light on a wide pile of ashes mounded against the slabs.

"If you want to tell the families that something went on here that's not quite right, that might be your proof," he said, shining his light on the mound. "That is what you're here for, isn't it? The bodies were left in here. Some family member is upset. You're looking for proof of something to get an investigation started. Maybe force the government to come back in here and get the bodies out."

When Joey didn't say anything, Jorgerson said, "Well, here's you a little bit more for your investigation. Whatever was burned in this pile was done before the explosion. Had to be. See?" He moved the lamp's illumination to the rear of the mound. Crushed flat there, the ashes disappeared underneath the slabs. "The limestone came down on the pile after it was set afire. So obviously something was going on first."

Jorgerson leaned down and lifted a charred half of a notepad from next to the mound.

"It's all Greek to me," he said, scratching the back of

his head with the hand that held the lamp while he held the
pad out with his other.

As Joey took it into his hand, ashes flaked from its edges
and fell to the floor. The darkened half of the first page
contained line after line of numbers.

2	12	13	25	26	45	52	61
8	16	5	16	22	45	41	20
6	14	19	21	20	45	23	19
5	11	17	19	25	45	16	17
3	21	22	17	16	45	12	10
1	19	22	25	12	7	98	11
7	14	51	18	62	45	1	14

The next few pages held similar figures.

"The whole pad," Jorgerson said. "Not a word in it, just
numbers."

Joey slipped it into his jacket pocket and looked back at
the mound.

"Nothing more that's readable in there," Jorgerson said.
He scratched the back of his head again and said, "You
want another reason I know the military didn't burn this
when they came back to shut the place down?" He lowered
the lamp's beam to a line of boot prints coming and going
across the soot-covered floor. "All mine," he said. "The
layer of soot was as smooth as a baby's butt before I came
in here. Want to see the laboratory stuff?"

He turned toward the doorway to the side.

When they walked through it they emerged into a
fifteen-foot-wide corridor running at least a hundred feet to
another open doorway. As Jorgerson continued toward it,
the light from the lamp illuminated the sides of the corridor.
Every few feet, a perpendicular line of steel O-rings a couple of inches in diameter, lined one above the other and
attached to thick pins driven into the walls, ran from halfway up the floor to the smooth rock ceiling.

Nearing the doorway, Joey saw lines of thick rubber-coated cables that begin on each side of the corridor. All of the cables were threaded through the succeeding sets of O-rings that lined the walls.

He stopped where the cables began.

Their near ends had been sawed off cleanly, as if they had been severed with a hacksaw blade. Each cable had obviously originally run the full length of the corridor. Thick cores of copper surrounded by rubber coatings gleamed in the lamp's light.

Jorgerson had stopped, and he now stared at the cables. "You see why I been coming down here now?" he asked. "Came down here first time because I was curious—stumbled on the air shaft and wondered what it led to. But the copper is why I kept coming back."

For the first time, Joey was no longer wary of the old man.

"Why shouldn't I take it?" Jorgerson asked. "Salvaging something abandoned is not breaking the law. The way I see it, the only thing illegal is the trespassing I've done to get down in here. Now you've done that, too, haven't you? That's why I asked to see your ID. I didn't know if maybe you were some kind of government investigator come because you heard about me being out here. Yeah, I haul up as much cable as the Jeep will carry, burn the rubber off, and sell the copper. You'd be surprised how much I've made. Jonathan was. Jonathan, my son I told you about? He lectured me so bad after I told him about this that I had to promise him I would never go back down here again. 'Course I lied. There's enough left to last me for as many years as I'm able to haul it out and sell it.

As he paused, he shook his head. "Hell of it is getting it up to the surface. I cut it in long sections, tie the ends together, and tie a rope at the very end, take the rope back up the shaft with me . . . you couldn't just pull the cables up the incline—that long of a stretch of copper's too heavy. I have a pulley I rig up and then start hauling. It comes out like a long black snake full of shiny gold young 'uns."

As Jorgerson paused, he lifted a side of his mouth in a partial grin. "Now that I've come clean with you, what about you doing the same for me? Mister, what are you here for?"

Joey thought about the mound of ashes. Deliberately piled and burned before the explosion. Somebody had destroyed something. Records? Why? In anticipation of what? Knowing there was going to be an explosion? The destruction of the project?

Somebody knowing it was going to happen before it did?

"Well, guess you're not going to tell me, are you?" Jorgerson muttered. Without pressuring the point any further, he turned down the corridor toward the doorway at its far end.

He stopped just before he passed through it and shined the light up into the air. A wide grill, held by big bolts drilled into the rock ceiling, covered fan blades as large as those on the fan lying at the bottom of the first shaft. Rocks the size of watermelons lay across the grill.

"This shaft's caved in on itself up at the top," he said. "Not no way to get down here but the way we came."

He walked through the doorway.

It led into a room thirty- to thirty-five feet wide and forty to fifty feet deep before the way was again blocked by a solid mass of fallen rock. To the left, a stainless steel counter ran along the wall. Stools sat in front of a pair of microcentrifuges a foot in diameter. Glass beakers and test tubes of all sizes, some of them shattered, lay scattered along the counter. A water bath the size of a suitcase sat on a table at the center of the room. To the right, a half dozen binocular microscopes were spaced a few feet apart atop another long counter. Stools were neatly pushed under the counter directly in line with the microscopes.

Jorgerson shined his light against the wall of rock at the far end of the area. "You believe me now?" he asked. "Told you there was a laboratory, didn't I? And this is it. And this is also the end of the tour—rocks won't let you get into any of the rest of the place. Four rooms that aren't completely caved in, the corridor full of cables, a few microscopes and a pile of ashes. What you see is what you get."

As the lamp's light had flashed past the microscopes as Jorgerson talked, Joey had noticed something glint at the far end of the counter.

"Shine it back there," he said.

"Where?"

Joey held his hand out for the lamp, and Jorgerson handed it to him. Joey shined it toward the end of the counter and walked in that direction.

As he drew closer he saw the reflection had come from a stainless steel cart. Instruments wrapped in white cloth lay in neat, arranged lines across its top.

He lifted one of them and unwrapped it.

It was what he had thought it would be—a surgical instrument.

He unwrapped a scalpel, then a forceps, laid them back on the cart, and shined the light toward the microscopes. He walked to the nearest one.

It had a slide in place. A tiny, flat copper-colored square of metal less than half the width of a pencil eraser lay on the slide.

He held the flashlight where the beam shone directly on the slide and lowered his eyes to the double-barrel optics. Under the high magnification, the dark square looked like it was imprinted with a myriad of small raised highways, tightly grouped, and crossing each other repeatedly.

"A computer chip."

"What?" Jorgerson asked.

Joey raised his eyes from the microscope.

"What'd you say?" Jorgerson repeated.

Joey looked back at the cart of surgical instruments.

"I would have sold the microscopes," Jorgerson said, "but they all have serial numbers. I figured maybe that would make it illegal. What do you think?"

Joey pulled the slide from the microscope. He looked at

the chip for a moment, then slipped it off the slide and put it into his jacket pocket.

He moved slowly up the counter. None of the other microscopes had slides in place.

"Still not going to tell me what you're looking for?" Jorgerson asked.

"I don't know," Joey said.

"Don't know? Damn, you've gone to a lot of trouble to not even know what you're looking for. But, hell, it's your money."

Joey walked along the other counter, shining the lamp along the steel surface.

Jorgerson turned his head back in the direction they came. "Well, tour's over, Mister someone-who-don't-know-what-you're-looking-for. Unless you want to see the bodies. That's not it, is it? There's a couple of them buried under the rocks. Fact that place we crawled through has some bones from a hand, off to the side if I'd have thought to shown you. Found part of an arm bone, too. It was blackened, with part of it no more than ashes. You saw where heat buckled some of the steel walls. Must have been some of the chemicals down here, and air being sucked down the shafts like oxygen hoses feeding blowtorches. I imagine some of the bodies were cremated; I think that's why there's only an occasional bone here and there. I gave it a burial under some rocks the first time I came down. I think I remember where it is."

Joey looked back at the cart of surgical instruments. Bones weren't what he was thinking of now. Weaver had said he thought the experiments had to do with neurotechnology: "If not exactly that, at least something to do with brain waves."

Joey thought about the bodies that had come home from Vietnam with drugs sewn into their cavities. Could that have been the case with Wynn's body? Something *within* it? Something that was designed to affect brain waves? He felt inside his jacket pocket, running his fingers over the chip, and looked at the cart of surgical instruments.

An implant?

But not placed in the body after Wynn was dead.

Implanted, he thought again.

He turned and started back in the direction they had come.

"Hey, not so fast," Jorgerson said, scurrying along behind him. "Keep that lamp where I can see where I'm walking or you might end up with another body down here."

Then he added, "Sorry about getting a little bit tipsy back there in the Jeep. Had a little more than I thought I did. But you saw that when I take a leak it takes the load off the kidneys and they start working again—cleans the alcohol right on out of the system. Don't take no time until I'm back up and running in full gear again."

Behind him, Joey heard the top to the flask being unscrewed once more.

"You don't talk much, do you?" Jorgerson said.

It took them twice as long to go back up the shaft as it had to come down it. There was nearly complete silence, only the light sounds of their clothes brushing against the shaft as they crawled and the occasional sound of their boots pushing against rock to boost them forward. Joey used the silence to think.

They could have gotten the bodies out. They bored and blasted the rooms out once, they could have done it again, at least enough to recover the bodies that hadn't been cremated by the intense heat or mashed into nothing at the bottom of the largest piles of rock.

But there might have been only a few souls present when the explosion went off. Two or three scientists. Not many more support personnel and guards. As few as a dozen people in all in addition to the volunteers. If the project was deemed important enough, it was possible that those responsible for organizing it didn't want a cleanup team coming back in. Bulldozer drivers and crane operators weren't the types given high security clearances. One of them, just one of them, seeing something he wasn't supposed to see and later speaking about it could jeopardize a lot more than just one project. If it was important enough it could damage the nation's security. Maybe destroy its security. There had been projects that made that much difference. When the scientists toiled at Los Alamos during World War II, those in charge were well aware that Hitler's scientists were working toward the same goal. The implications of what would have happened if Nazi Germany had won the race were nearly unthinkable.

That thought had guided military scientists' thinking ever since. They couldn't afford to come in second in anything that could alter the balance of power.

So maybe no one who might talk would have been brought in. No cleanup crew. The families of the ones who perished and never came home could be handled. It had been done before.

The air shafts could have gone unreported for the same reasons. Few members of the military would have had the clearance to see the blueprints originally. A facility's overall size, the size of its rooms, and the size of its accompanying structure could go a long way in telling someone what it was designed for.

And to a normal crew arriving to seal the destroyed facility there wouldn't be any reason to assume air shafts had been needed for a site already exposed to more than enough life-giving air through its main entrance.

On top of that, they, whoever they were, had left guards remaining; no one would have the free run of the hilly site.

Anything was possible.

Even an implant.

Maybe one that worked.

But worked to do what?

And on criminals? Had somehow, for some reason, one of the volunteers been assigned out of the program before the explosion?

Still on that assignment ten years later?

Randle? Or Alfred Wynn, or whoever he was?

Joey shook his head with his thoughts. Would the chip

in his pocket lead to any answers—or more questions?

Above him, Jorgerson sighed in relief. He was just reaching the opening leading back out onto the side of the slope. As he squirmed out of the opening, tiny particles of rock and grit slid down the shaft, and Joey lifted his face until they stopped moving by him.

Then, hand over hand, partially crawling, partially pushing against the hard rock with the toes of his boots, he moved to the round opening, glowing with the moon's light.

When his head came up past the rim, the change from the near total blackness of the shaft made the side of the slope seem to glow as bright as daylight for an instant.

He felt the cold steel of the automatic press against his head.

Jorgerson stood a few feet away. He had a scared look on his face and his hands held high in the air. A large man in a long, dark coat held another pistol on him.

When Joey started to look up over his shoulder at the man behind him, the automatic pressed tighter against his scalp. He came on up out of the hole.

A hand came around him, patted the sides of his jacket, then felt along his waist. His automatic was found and taken from him.

Now the man came around in front of him. He was dressed in a long coat similar to the other man's but he was younger, in his middle to late thirties. Though as tall as the other man, he had a much leaner build. He motioned with the automatic, and Joey started down the hill.

Jorgerson was already walking ahead of the other man.

When Joey walked over the small rise, he saw a gray van parked beside the Jeep. Another man, tall and heavyset and dressed in jeans and jacket, waited next to it. He motioned with his pistol for them to come forward and opened one of the blocky vehicle's rear doors.

Jorgerson, his hands still in the air, went into the rear seat first. Joey followed him. Behind them, the man who had motioned them inside slipped onto the seat and closed the door behind him, keeping his pistol pointed in their direction.

The driver's door slammed, and the motor started.

The lean, young man climbed inside onto the front seat and pointed his weapon over its back.

The van slowly moved forward.

Joey saw in the rearview mirror that the Jeep was following them.

They rode for thirty minutes, no one speaking. Jorgerson's hands had started trembling in his lap. Joey caught the old man's eyes and tried to smile reassuringly.

The vehicle stopped.

Jorgerson took a deep breath.

Both back doors opened, and the men motioned them outside.

Jorgerson's hands were still trembling.

Then Joey saw the tire tool.

The man who held it stepped forward.

There wasn't anything else a tire tool could be used for, Joey knew.

Despite the overwhelming odds, he lunged at the man nearest him.

The man jumped to the side in a motion quicker than a man should be able to move; Joey only caught him a glancing blow with his shoulder but managed to wrap his arm around him driving him backward. Joey grabbed for the gun hand.

The tire tool slammed into the back of his head.

Joey tried to hang on, but his arms weakened.

The tire tool came down hard again.

Joey, still trying to hold the man, slid down his legs and rolled to his back.

"No," Jorgerson cried.

Through blurred vision, Joey saw the man with the tire tool now stepping toward the terrified old man. Another man grabbed Jorgerson's arms from behind him. Jorgerson tried to jerk loose, and his glasses fell off.

The tire tool rose in the air and came down hard.

Wind expelled from the old man's lungs.

The one holding him let him go, and he crumpled backward to the ground.

His vision still blurred, Joey saw the man with the tire tool straddle Jorgerson's limp form with his feet.

The tire tool was grasped in both hands.

It raised high in the air.

Then came down lightning fast.

The sound that came from the blow crashing into Jorgerson's head was like that of a coconut bursting.

The man held the blood-covered tire tool at his side, then turned.

Joey forced himself over onto his stomach and tried to push to his feet. His hands felt numb against the hard ground, and his arms trembled in their effort to lift him up.

He managed to get to his knees.

A pair of legs in jeans stopped beside him.

Now he felt a cool, wet mist hitting his face.

Across his shoulder, he saw the young man held a small spray can in his hand and was directing the mist downward.

Joey felt his breath suddenly leave him. A weakness flooded across his body. His arms collapsed underneath him, and he fell forward hard onto the ground.

Even as he rapidly grew weaker, he summoned the effort to roll to his back.

He stared up at the young man.

The spray can had now been exchanged for the tire tool.

It raised into the air.

Joey tried to lift his hands in front of him, but his muscles wouldn't respond, and his arms remained lying on the ground beside him.

And then the tire tool came down hard again.

And again.

And again.

Joey's foot kicked a last time.

The young man knelt and quickly started searching

Joey's pockets. The other men were going through Jorgerson's jacket.

The charred notepad was quickly found, then the chip. The young man came slowly to his feet, staring at the tiny piece of metal.

In Jackson, Quinlan had the same view of the chip. Genowski and John, standing next to him, did, too.

"I want the shafts searched for any more chips we might have left behind," Quinlan said. "Then I want it dynamited closed."

He wasn't speaking to Genowski and John, though they heard every word. He was speaking to the men in Montana, and it took only a couple of seconds for his voice to reach them. The transmission was done with the same basic technology that carried satellite telephone conversations. The four satellites capable of transmitting these beamed signals were all military satellites. The particular equipment used to relay Quinlan's and the others' voices was housed in a small container that took up only a minute part of each satellite's space. And its existence was unknown even to those who launched the satellites, nearly fifteen years before. The container had been there from the beginning. But the experiment that would make use of the equipment housed in it went bad, and the equipment was never activated.

But it was there ready for use if it was ever needed in the future. And, powered by solar panels, it would remain ready forever.

In Montana, the young man holding the computer chip had nodded at what was said as if Quinlan had been standing next to him waiting for a response. Then he had leaned over and slipped his hands under Joey's limp form. The big detective was heavy, but the young man had no trouble lifting him.

Now he turned toward the Jeep, its motor still running,

its dust-covered headlights casting a dim glow out across the hard ground.

In Washington, D.C., Colonel Michael Weaver, dressed in his bathrobe, his hair mussed from sleep, opened his condominium door and looked outside at the young, tanned face of Captain Blaine Walker, standing in the flickering glow of a gas lamp. Walker was dressed in a windbreaker over a pullover and jeans.

"Sir," he said. "You're wanted back at the office."

When Weaver took the time to look toward a car with its motor running sitting in the condominium's driveway, Walker said, "Immediately, sir."

Though young and only a captain, Walker had risen rapidly in prestige in the intelligence group where he and Weaver operated, especially in the last few years. He was not an errand boy; his coming personally to Weaver's home meant something very important was happening, or about to happen.

Weaver turned back into the condominium. He was moving faster now, loosening his robe as he strode toward his bedroom.

"It'll take me a minute to get dressed."

Behind Weaver, the young captain reached into his windbreaker pocket and lifted out a small spray can.

17

THE YOUNG CAPTAIN had carried Colonel Weaver's limp form from the condominium as easily as a man might carry a baby. Now he laid Weaver onto the backseat of the car that had been waiting in the drive and closed the door.

A moment later the captain slid into the front seat, and the driver began to back the car toward the street.

When they turned out onto the pavement they drove slowly, but not too slowly, being careful to maintain a speed that wouldn't attract any attention.

In a few seconds, they had turned onto another street, and the car's taillights began to be blocked by trees running alongside the pavement—and disappeared altogether.

After Christen had awakened on his couch, she wanted to see the paperwork he had been doing in the dining room while she slept. It was actually a summary of progress made in the conductivity of impulses into the occipital lobe, designed for Dr. Brimston's presentation to the board members. It was largely technical, but she quickly caught on to most of it. She had said wistfully, "But it takes so long for something to be approved for use even if you should make a breakthrough—if anybody makes a breakthrough." He had known she was thinking of her blind brother. And then she had glanced at her watch, sighed, and said she had a long day at the paper ahead of her. They had listened to old tunes on the Bronco's radio as he drove her back to her apartment.

Now, she stopped in front of her door and looked at the bright moon hanging to one side of the sky. "It's beautiful, isn't it?" she asked.

She came up onto her toes, kissed him softly on the lips, and drew her face back, looking into his eyes. "Really was a great night," she said. "Except I think I missed part of it. Sorry," she added, "but I obviously can't handle wine." She smiled softly.

He slipped his hands around her back, pulled her gently against him, and pressed his lips against hers.

She returned the kiss, then drew her face back a couple of inches from his. "Maybe I can stay awake the whole night next time. There is going to be a next time, isn't there?"

"How about in a couple of hours?" he asked and smiled.

She returned the smile, slipped her key from her purse, and turned toward the door.

When she opened it, she turned back around and said, "Oh, by the way . . . I told you I was old-fashioned, but I'm also only twenty-six and not dead yet. You might bear that in mind when I'm stretched out in front of you the next time."

She was teasing, and she was smiling again, and she was beautiful. Now she turned and stepped inside the apartment.

"Call me," she said, looking into his eyes until the door closed past her face.

He stood there for a moment.

A little too much teasing, he thought. But highly effective. Grinning, he turned away from the door and walked toward the Bronco.

But only a few steps later, and the grin went away as the limp form of Dr. Lambert lying on the gurney at the morgue door passed through his mind. He took a deep breath. At the Bronco, he opened the driver's door and slowly slid inside behind the steering wheel, still thinking.

He sat there for a moment, then glanced at his wristwatch. He sat there for another moment, then reached to the seat beside him, lifted his cellular phone, and pushed a memory button.

When his mother answered, her voice was both sleepy and filled with a nervousness at getting such a late-night call.

"Mother, I just wanted to know that you were okay," he said.

The section of desolate Montana highway had been built alongside a barren hill. To the left of the pavement, a sheer precipice dropped fifty feet to a pile of large fractured rock, boulders and limestone that had once been part of the hill. The Jeep lay upside down, crushed against the rock. Wispy tentacles of smoke from the still warm engine curled up into the cold night air to hang in a small cloud over the vehicle. Joey's limp form lay a few feet away. Jorgerson's body protruded from underneath the rear of the vehicle.

Above, standing at the edge of the precipice, the lean young man who had wielded the spray can and tire tool, stared down at the one dim headlight still casting its glow from the Jeep's front out into the dark night.

"Rhiner."

At his name being called from the edge of the highway behind him, the young man looked across his shoulder.

Past a long curve circling beyond the hill, a pair of headlights showed a vehicle speeding up the pavement.

"Rhiner," the man at the edge of the highway repeated. He stood next to the gray van.

Rhiner faced back to the empty air in front of the precipice. He stared out through the dark for a moment, then his gaze dropped once more to the Jeep on the rocks below.

His hands, hanging at his sides, suddenly trembled.

He closed his eyes.

"Rhiner."

The vehicle coming up the highway was traveling much

faster than it had first appeared. It was less than half a mile away now, and closing the distance fast.

Rhiner stared in the vehicle's direction, then reached into his coat pocket and lifted out Jorgerson's glasses. The thick lenses were cracked. The frame was bent. He stared at the glasses for a moment longer, then used a flick of his wrist to send them sailing out into the air toward the rocks below. Then he ran toward the van.

The other men were already inside it.

Rhiner threw open a side door and hurried into the blocky vehicle.

Its rear tires showered pebbles toward the edge of the precipice as it made a tight U-turn from the shoulder onto the pavement and, its headlights still off, sped away from the oncoming lights shining from the front of a shiny, new Ford Expedition racing up the highway.

In the Expedition, Donna Hardy frowned at the dashboard. The speedometer needle was past the hundred-mile-an-hour mark.

"You're going to burn it up before we've had it a week," she said.

Charles Hardy kept the accelerator pressed almost to the floor. He suddenly eased his foot up when he saw the van that had pulled out onto the highway a couple hundred yards ahead of him.

"What's that?" Donna asked.

"A Chevy van. The idiot doesn't even have his lights on."

"No, Charles, what's *that*?" She was looking off to the side of the pavement, where the precipice fell away to a large pile of rock beneath it.

She was staring at the dim glow of the Jeep's headlight.

In Jackson, Quinlan's view came from eyes staring out through the rear window of the gray van, speeding away from the Expedition that had quickly come up the highway. As the Expedition slowed and eased to the side of the pavement, his expression twisted into one of irritation.

Then a second box clicked on in his mind to go with
the view of the vehicle. This new image was of a tall,
handsome man in his late forties, dressed in a white bathrobe and leaning back in a chair on the porch of a log cabin
that looked as if it had come out of the pages of a history
book.

18

ALEXANDER "ALEX" RAYE leaned back in a chair on the porch of the aging log cabin. His long legs were extended out from his bathrobe, with his feet propped against one of the posts supporting the overhanging roof.

Now he leaned further back in the chair, stretched his arms out under the robe's sleeves, and inhaled deeply, enjoying the sweet scent of honeysuckle growing in the woods surrounding the cabin.

An entire week, he thought. An entire week of not being bothered with important meetings and important telephone calls and important constituents who wanted to be given a personal tour. An entire week of nothing but lazily fishing in the nearby marsh that was dotted with duck blinds. An entire week of privacy.

There was, of course, his cellular phone, by which his staff could contact him if some emergency threatened world stability. But short of that, they knew not to call him for any reason.

He smiled his satisfaction and moved his hands behind his head, staring at the peaceful sight of the moon casting its dim glow across the trees fifty feet in front of the cabin.

Then he heard the board creak.

He looked at the man stepping up onto the end of the porch. Alexander jumped to his feet and turned toward the cabin door. But another man was already inside, coming quickly through the rustic living area toward the door. A third man came up on the other side of the porch.

They all held small spray cans in their hands.

It had taken the Montana Highway Patrol a full twenty minutes to respond to Charles Hardy's cellular call made from the scene of the accident on the desolate stretch of highway. The Expedition and two patrol cruisers with their lights flashing, sat at the side of the pavement nearest the steep precipice. An officer was still down below with the bodies, searching them for identification. The other patrolman, an older veteran with many years' service in the area, stood in front of Donna Hardy.

"It was a Chevrolet extended van," she said. "It weaved out on the highway just before we got here. I'll bet it was a drunk. Ran the Jeep off the road." She nodded knowingly.

"It was an express van," Charles said, standing close to the edge of the steep drop-off, looking down at the other, younger patrolman starting up a narrow path that led past the precipice back up to the pavement.

His wife shook her head. "It was bigger than an express van, it was an extended express."

"Gray, anyway," he said.

"And a drunk," she added.

The officer in front of them raised a small two-way radio from his belt to his mouth, relayed the information that another vehicle might have been involved in the two-fatality accident, and gave the direction it was traveling on the highway. "A gray Chevrolet express or extended express van. Number of occupants unknown."

"An extended express," Donna said, "and a drunk."

The younger officer came up onto the bluff and walked to them. "The big guy didn't die instantly," he said. He opened the wallet he had brought up the path with him. "Joseph McDonald. From the marks on the ground it looks like he crawled a few feet trying to get to a cell phone. He almost made it."

*   *   *

Spence lay on his bed with his hands behind his head on the pillow. He could still smell the scent of Christen's perfume. She had only lightly pressed against him, and her soft kisses had been innocent, but they had stayed with him more than any other he could remember. He liked the sensation. Smiling, he reached to the nightstand and lifted the telephone receiver. He punched in Joey's home number.

He let it ring five times. But, again, Patricia didn't answer.

He replaced the receiver, glanced at his watch, and lay back into the pillow again.

Now Flo passed through his mind. *Jealous?* he thought. Impossible. She had not so much as given him a soft look in the months she had worked for him. At least not a soft look that could be construed as anything but friendly. Only friendly.

Nothing but friendly.

The ambulance was present now. Paramedics used a stretcher to carry Jorgerson's body up the steep path. The older highway patrol officer looked toward the crushed Jeep, lying upside down. Mr. Jorgerson's son, a veterinarian in Butte, had already been notified of the accident. Headquarters had tried Mr. McDonald's home number in Jackson, Mississippi, but hadn't been able to get any answer.

Flo wore a black, disposable surgical apron and had on latex gloves. She brushed a dark lock back from her forehead and looked at the clock on the far wall of the laboratory. It was 2:00 A.M.

She looked back at Tank. The potbellied pig lay on its side, sedated, breathing softly. Flo lifted an instrument that looked little different from a thin, stainless steel screwdriver from the instrument cart beside her and reached forward toward the plump animal's eyes.

*   *   *

The hearse sped south on I-55 toward Jackson. Alexander "Alex" Raye, still clad in the white bathrobe he had worn as he sat on the cabin porch, lay in a blue stainless steel coffin in the rear of the long vehicle.

But he wasn't dead. It would take an especially close examination to realize he was only in a deep comalike state with his breathing almost totally arrested.

On the one chance in a million that some highway patrol officer might go so far as to look inside the coffin to make certain the hearse wasn't actually a morbidly disguised drug runner on an interstate frequently used by drug traffickers coming south from Memphis toward Florida, Raye's looks had been drastically altered. His hair, normally puffed around his head and sprayed so stiffly in place that a gust of wind wouldn't ruffle it, had now been combed down around his ears. Its natural brown color flecked with gray, had now been dyed black. Glasses with thick lenses made his closed eyelids seem to fit over eyes much bigger and more rounded than Raye's had ever been.

But the biggest change was in the body itself. An injection with a solution containing a toxin much like the venom in a bee sting had enlarged his cheeks and neck, though they didn't appear to be swollen, only fat. The final disguising effect had been added when the face had been sprayed with a clear substance that gave the skin the characteristic plastic look of the dead after they have been prepared for burial. No one would recognize him.

Though a lot of people were well aware of who he was.

Spence tried Patricia's number again. This time she answered on the first ring.

"Patricia, this is Spence Stevens. Joey called and asked me to tell you that he was going to be where you couldn't reach him on his phone for a while. He said he'd call you as soon as he got a chance. He might have already tried— he said your answering machine wasn't working."

"The telephone was ringing when I came in a few minutes ago," Patricia said. "It was probably him. I had car trouble. You wouldn't believe. Thanks for calling, Doctor."

Spence replaced the receiver, turned off the lamp next to the bed, yawned, and lay back on his pillow.

In Montana, Tom Rhiner parked the gray Chevy van under his carport, stepped outside, and came around the rear of the van toward the steps leading up into his home.

It was a small ranch-style house, made bright in the moonlight by a fresh coat of paint. A hundred feet behind the house, a white fence fronted a barn. Behind and to the sides of that wide structure, grazing land spread out in all directions under the moonlight.

He came up the steps, sprinkled with a light dusting of snow. His wife looked toward him when he opened the door and stepped inside the house.

"Where have you been, honey?"

"I'm sorry. I started talking with some guys—let the time get away."

She came across the carpet. She was tall herself, at five-ten, but she had to arch up onto her toes to kiss him on the cheek. "Fine thing, you out at this time of night and me not knowing where you are. Fred Carroll called. I was embarrassed I couldn't tell him. I told him you were probably out drumming up support for the next election. Fine thing," she repeated, "having to tell a lie for the next congressman of this district."

She smiled as she stepped back, leaving her hands holding the sides of his arms. "Some would say that lying goes with being a politician. When you get to Washington I know you're going to help change that kind of thinking by the way you conduct yourself. And that makes me proud. Are you hungry?"

He shook his head.

"What's wrong?" she asked, her brow wrinkling.

He had been almost expressionless while she spoke, and he remained that way.

"Nothing," he said, "only tired."

"You want me to fix you a hot bath?"

"No, I think I'll watch television for a while."

"You said you were tired."

"I want to relax for a little while."

"I'll get you a glass of milk," she said, smiled, and walked toward the kitchen.

Rhiner stared after her for a moment. Then he took a deep breath. He thought about the tire tool, and the blood, and the murders, and what he had become.

He closed his eyes tightly, trying to drive the thoughts away, but it did no good. He rubbed his face briskly, and that did no good, either. Lowering his hands, he saw the speck of blood under the tip of his thumbnail and his eyes closed again and he began shaking his head back and forth.

Then he strode, almost ran, toward the bathroom.

"Tommy, Paul wants to tell you good night," his wife called from the kitchen. "He said to wake him up no matter what time you came in. I promised."

He closed the bathroom door behind him and spun the lavatory faucet wide open. He grabbed the big bar of soap sitting at the side of the lavatory and begun rubbing it hard into his hands.

Five minutes later, the speck of blood long gone, his hands turning red from repeated scrubbings, and he still couldn't stop washing them.

"Tommy," his wife said outside the door.

He looked into the mirror. His long face was twisted with his anguish. He closed his eyes, took a deep breath, then leaned forward and splashed water on his face.

Quickly drying it on a hand towel, he looked into the mirror again. Then he turned the faucet off and opened the door.

Paul slept in the bedroom down the hall to the right.

Tommy slowly entered the room and walked to the narrow bed. He stared down at the five-year-old for a moment, then eased down on the edge of the mattress.

"Paul," he said in a soft voice, "I'm home."

The boy's eyes slowly opened and he smiled softly. Tommy leaned forward to hug him where he lay, but Paul sat up in the bed. Tommy felt the little hands slip around his neck. "How have you been today?" he asked his son.

"Just fine," Paul said. "What have you been doing?"

Tommy couldn't keep his throat from tightening. He had to swallow before he could speak.

"Working."

"Are you still going to be a congressman?"

"I'm going to try, son."

"Mother said you were out meeting people to get them to like you when you tried."

"Yeah," Tommy said.

Paul slowly lay back on his pillow. "Good night, Dad."

Tommy stood. "Good night, Paul."

Then he turned toward the door.

"I said my prayers tonight all by myself," Paul said behind him. "I asked God especially to take care of you."

Tommy couldn't look back toward the bed. Tears had started running from his eyes.

Spence had just fallen asleep when the telephone rang. He reached to the bedside table and fumbled for the receiver.

"Hello."

"Oh, my God, Joey's dead," Patricia screamed.

Spence sat up and swung his feet to the floor.

"Oh, my God," Patricia screamed again.

"Patricia, what happened?"

"In a car accident. Dead. Oh, my God, he was killed in a car accident in Montana."

"Mont . . . I'll be right over."

"No, no. Mother's on the way. I don't want to see anybody. I don't mean you, Doctor. I just don't want to see anybody. I knew you would want to know. Joey thought so much of . . . He thought so . . ."

And then Patricia started sobbing so hard she couldn't continue.

A moment later, he heard her replace the receiver. He slowly replaced his and remained sitting on the edge of the bed. An accident.

The thought came again, but this time as a question. *An accident?*

Jorgerson. He remembered the name. He lifted the receiver back into his hands. He didn't know the number he wanted to call. The telephone directory was at the bottom of the bedside table.

It took him only a few moments to find the name.

If it was the correct Bob Kennedy?

He punched in the number.

It rang twice, then three times.

A sleepy voice said hello.

"Is this Bob Kennedy, the FBI agent?"

"Who is this?"

"Is this the residence of the FBI agent?"

At his raising his voice, there was a moment of silence on the line, then the man said, "Yes, I'm with the FBI."

"This is Spence Stevens. Dr. Spence Stevens. I know Joey's mentioned me."

"Yes, Doctor, what is it?"

"Joey's been killed. They say it was a car accident. I—"

"Where?"

"In Montana."

"Montana?"

"Yes. Patricia called. That's all she told me. But there was a man with Joey named Jorgerson. I don't know who he was, but they were together earlier tonight. It had to be only a short time before the accident. I'm not certain what Joey was doing there but we had been to—"

The agent didn't let him finish. "You at your house, Doctor?"

"Yes."

"Stay there, I'll be right over."

Kennedy sat on the edge of his bed for several seconds, stunned at what Spence had just told him. Then he lifted the telephone receiver and punched in Patricia's number.

When she answered, she was crying.

19

SPENCE HEARD THE tires on Kennedy's car squeal as the FBI agent braked to a stop in front of the apartment.

When Spence opened the door, Kennedy was crossing the sidewalk, taking long strides as he came toward him.

"I want to know everything Joey's told you," he said as he neared the doorway. Spence stepped aside, and the agent came inside the apartment and turned around to face him.

"You said Joey was with someone named Jorgerson?"

"Yes."

"How do you know?"

"Joey called on his cell phone and asked if I would call Patricia and tell her he was going to be where she couldn't reach him for a while. The man was with him then."

"Where Pat couldn't reach him for a while?"

Spence nodded.

"What was Joey doing in Montana?" Kennedy asked.

"I don't know."

"He was doing something that made you wonder if it was an accident. You don't think it was. That's why you called me. Was he still working on this Alfred Wynn thing? He told me about that."

"I don't know. We went to West Memphis together. A man there had a photograph of Wynn when he was a teenager. We weren't certain that it was the same man we knew as Wynn."

"Why?"

"The boy in the picture was a lot shorter than Wynn."

"Shorter?"

"Several inches. He could have grown since then, but there was another boy in the photo—a friend of Wynn's. He was as tall as Wynn is now. He was about the same age. We wondered if the man had them mixed up. We wondered . . . This sounds crazy."

"I don't care how it sounds," Kennedy said.

"The friend's name was Randle. He went into the military and was court-martialed. We wondered if somehow the man in the morgue known as Wynn was really Randle. Joey said he could find out. He said he had a set of Wynn's fingerprints. Then he told me to come on back here. I didn't know where he went."

"Do you know what Randle was court-martialed for?"

"Rape and murder—twenty, twenty-five years ago."

"He would still be in Leavenworth."

"I know."

"I know where Joey could have gone," Kennedy muttered. "Hell, where he *would* have gone first." He walked to the coffee table and punched a number into the telephone.

He held the receiver to his ear for several seconds, then slowly lowered it to its cradle and stared down at it.

Spence was slow in asking, his voice low. "Do you have reason to think it wasn't an accident?"

"Frankly, Doctor, I don't have the slightest idea. But I'm going to find out."

"You're going to Montana?"

"Where I'm going is not anybody's business," the agent said in a gruff voice.

"Yes, it is, it's mine. If he was working on that up there, I the same as sent him. I'm going to Montana tonight, and whether I go with you or by myself doesn't make a damn bit of difference."

Kennedy stared at him.

The silence between them grew into several seconds.

Finally the agent said, "I'll have a plane at the airport in two hours. Meet me there."

Then Spence remembered. Dr. Lambert's funeral—in the morning. He struggled a moment in his mind. But this was *for* Dr. Lambert. He glanced at his watch and walked to the telephone.

As he lifted the receiver Kennedy said, "Hey, hold on a minute. I don't want anyone knowing where we're going."

"They won't." Spence punched in Flo's number.

It rang several times without an answer.

He replaced the receiver. He glanced at his watch again. Where could she possibly be at this time of night? The professional girl wonder, always at the laboratory before anyone else arrived there in the morning, always wide awake and anxious to work. He raised his gaze to the agent's "I have something I have to do, but it won't take long. I'll be at the airport waiting when you get there."

"I meant what I said about not wanting anyone to know where we're going," Kennedy said. "I don't want anybody to know we're going anywhere."

"I told you, they won't." Then Spence suddenly remembered. "He said *shaft*."

"What?" Kennedy asked.

"Jorgerson. I could hear him speaking in the background when I was on the phone with Joey. He said, *'It's about a quarter of a mile to the shaft.'*"

Twenty minutes later, hurriedly dressed in sneakers, jeans, and a pullover, a hastily packed overnight bag sitting on the seat beside him, Spence parked the Bronco in front of his office. He glanced at the sheet of paper on which he had scribbled a message. It was a note to Flo telling her he wouldn't be at the funeral and that he would like for her to take care of anything that had to be taken care of. He couldn't help but feel guilty at knowing he wasn't going to be there when they laid to rest the nearest thing he had had in years to a father. But it was also Joey dead now, not only Dr. Lambert. My God, there was even the outside chance that Joey was dead because of what he was trying to find out about the body that had been brought into the morgue. Alfred, or maybe Randle. That possibility kept hanging in the back of his mind. He had to know, for Joey now as well as for Lambert. He took a deep breath, opened his door, stepped outside the vehicle, and walked to the building.

Seconds later, as he came down the hallway, he saw through the glass panes of the laboratory door that the lights were on. He opened the door.

Flo turned around to face him.

"What are you doing here?" he asked.

"You scared me," she said.

Off to her side, several two-foot-tall sections of the dark cardboard had been arranged into a maze with half a dozen openings instead of the normal two they used in their experiments with Tank. The plump pig, walking slowly, went through an opening at the center of the maze, hesitated for only a moment, and then headed directly for the next opening. As Spence stared, the animal navigated it easily and began to trot as he hurried to the last opening, leading to the bright yellow bowl full of corn chowder.

"He can focus well enough to differentiate an opening ten feet away now," Flo said. "Even different colors. You can close the openings with a piece of cardboard the same color as the bowl and he'll push through them."

At a loss for words, Spence looked back at the maze.

"It's the impulses focused on the nerves into the retina," Flo said. I've been working with the definition almost every night. I knew you couldn't change the direction of the research right in the middle of what you were doing. It would make Dr. Brimston wonder if you were certain what you were doing. I've been coming down here at night, keeping notes of my own. I could see Tank improving each time— the definition getting better. I didn't want to tell you until I was certain." She smiled proudly now. "This is a big step, isn't it?"

Almost stunned at what he had witnessed, Spence nodded slowly. "What you've done is amazing."

She shook her head quickly. "No, what *we've* done. I only built on what you had already accomplished. I didn't have to go any further than making the impulses stronger. You were already almost there and didn't know it. You were so focused on getting the impulses concentrated into the lobe that you were looking past what the concentration might do with healthy nerves behind the retina. What is that?"

She was looking at the sheet of paper he held down by his side. "It's a message to you—asking you if you will fill in for me at the funeral. I won't be here."

"Won't be here?"

"I have something important that's come up."

"It can't wait a day?"

When he didn't answer her, she said, "Nothing's wrong with your mother or brother?"

"No. It's just something that came up and I can't explain it right now."

"Can't explain it?"

"I'll tell you later."

"You're not . . . You're not having some kind of problem?"

"No. It's not that big of a deal. I just told somebody I'd keep it confidential until we're finished."

"Spence, I . . ." She was obviously no more satisfied with his answer than he would have been with hers were their situations reversed.

But she didn't press it any further. "Okay, I'll handle the funeral. When will you be back?"

"I'm not sure. A day or two probably."

He noticed her eyes staring into his. Of course there was still her confusion at his sudden announcement. But he was also reading something else in the stare. Despite everything else on his mind, Joey's death, the achievement he had just witnessed with Tank, Dr. Lambert's death, and now his funeral, despite everything, he couldn't help but wonder back to what Christen said. *I'm not blind.* Was he? Or with Christen's words on his mind was he only imagining something in Flo's stare now? He looked at Tank, now finished with the chowder, and walking in a straight line toward her. She dropped down on one knee to pat him on the head.

Spence stared at the animal. And now he had another thought crowding in among the others. He felt elation at the progress in Tank navigating the maze, felt proud for Flo. Yet at the same time he felt a certain disappointment that he hadn't thought of trying the newly concentrated impulses on the nerve endings. He had been so caught up in trying to wire the impulses into the lobe.

And then an even greater surge of guilt than had swept over him in the Bronco made its presence felt. Here he was letting his thoughts about what he had done or hadn't done with the impulses take precedence over the thoughts that there were now two men dead. What his mind should be filled with.

He closed his eyes briefly, then looked back at Tank.

At least Walter Quinlan would be happy.

Kennedy's wife was well thought of by everyone. Though she had put on a few pounds over the last decade, she still had a pleasing figure. Despite being in her fifties, she had yet to show a single wrinkle in her face. But what she was most renowned for was her personality—few people had ever seen anything but a pleasant expression across her face. But she was frowning now.

She stared at her husband as he stuffed a pair of khaki slacks and two extra shirts down in his overnight bag. "Is it happening again?" she asked.

He glanced back across his shoulder. "Of course not."

She wasn't satisfied. She had seen him like this before. The last time a long ten years before—but it seemed like only a few days ago.

"Is it?" she asked again.

Kennedy looked at the stapled sheets of thin paper lying on the bed. It was the additional information he had requested and had been faxed to him since last speaking with Joey. He couldn't leave it in the house. He stuffed the sheets into the bag, zipped it closed, and turned to face his wife.

"Is it *them*?" she asked once more.

He set the bag on the floor and walked to her, slipped his arms around her back, pulling her to him, "I promise it isn't," he said, holding her close. "You know how much Joey meant to me. I have to go see where he died."

When she didn't respond, he said, "I have to, Judy."

He felt her nod against his shoulder.

He hugged her tightly, kissed her on the side of the head, and turned back to his bag.

Picking it up, he started from the bedroom. She followed closely behind him.

At the door to the house, he turned and kissed her on the forehead.

As he stepped outside, she caught the door and held it open, staring at him as he walked toward his car.

"Bob?"

He turned around to face her.

"Please be honest with me," she said. "I deserve that. I deserve it for all the nights I sat up waiting for you. I deserve it because you're my husband and I'm your wife."

He waited a moment. Then he said it in a way in which she would believe him: "If Joey's death wasn't an accident, and if it is *them*, I'm not going to be on their side at this time."

20

IT WAS NEARLY dawn. They walked up the two steps into the small cabin area of the private jet. The pilot, a middle-aged, heavily muscled black man with what seemed like a permanent scowl etched across his face, pulled down the door behind them.

Kennedy buckled himself in, then looked across the seat. "I called Pat just before I left. She had spoken with the authorities in Montana again. The Jorgerson you mentioned who was with Joey . . . he was killed in the accident, too—it was his Jeep they were in. I haven't had time to find out anything about him."

Kennedy paused a moment. "But Pat did say that Joey had gone to Montana following up on Wynn, and the possible switch in identities with Randle. Why Joey told his wife, I don't know. I wouldn't have told mine anything. It would just worry her. But that was Joey and Pat—their deal since he . . . retired. You know what I'm talking about there."

"Retiring?"

"Yes."

"Joey told me what he did in the past—in general. I know it was intelligence work for the government and that people died—that's why he had his problems."

Kennedy nodded. "Even with him retired, he shouldn't have said anything. But I know it came out while he was being treated with drugs by Dr. Bower. Joey told me he came to you and asked if you would try to keep Dr. Bower from ever mentioning it to anyone. Why he trusted you that much, I don't know. To me, telling you just compounded the problem. But that's what he told me he did."

Spence nodded. "I went to Bower. But he wouldn't have said anything anyway. What he had learned was within the boundaries of a doctor-patient relationship. I told Joey that, but he asked me to go anyway, so I did."

Kennedy was silent for a moment. He started to speak once, then was silent again for a moment, obviously carefully weighing what he was about to say.

"Well, you know that, and so now you're going to know I worked for the same group—with Joey. We retired at about the same time—me just a little after him."

"Why are you telling me this? You just said Joey shouldn't have told—"

Kennedy interrupted him with, "I probably shouldn't be telling you. But you said you were going to Montana whether with me or without me. You know some things. You said you overheard the man with Joey say, 'It's about a quarter of a mile to the shaft.' "

Spence nodded.

"So what kind of shaft, Doctor? A mine shaft? I'm not familiar with any in the area. And I called a couple people while I was waiting for the plane. They weren't familiar with any mines in the area either—and they would know. So, again, what are we talking about?"

Before Spence could respond, Kennedy said, "But the main thing is you know just enough to maybe get yourself hurt."

"What do you mean? Are you saying Joey's death was—"

"Not saying anything, Doctor—not anything for certain. That's what I'm on my way out there for—to find out. But, in the meantime, chew on this: Joey was following up on Wynn. He thought that there was a good possibility of a switch between him and Randle. Somehow that led him to Montana—Pat doesn't even know the particulars, but she does know that's why he was there. Now he's dead. The man that was with him is dead. There's the possibility of a switch in identities with Alfred and Wynn. There's no fingerprints of Wynn's anywhere on record—and I mean anywhere."

"You think Joey was murdered."

"I told you I didn't know, Doctor. But there's enough surfaced to make me nervous. And since you're tagging along whether I like it or not, I have some other things I need to tell you. Not everything. Some things I can't tell you. But I'm going to tell you as much as I can. I have to tell you, because if the people I used to work for are behind this and they decide we shouldn't be involved, then we don't stand a chance. You deserve to know that's what you could be getting into."

Spence was confused. "The people you worked for. I don't understand. You and Joey . . . I mean, damn, why do you even think something like that? They would be involved in Joey's death?"

Kennedy shook his head. "I don't think so. I really don't think so. They did a lot of things that shocked me. I did a lot of things for them that shocked me. But they never did anything that disappointed me."

The Walter Quinlan Biogenetics Research Center was housed inside a twenty-acre complex dominated by a sprawling one-story steel building containing more than forty thousand square feet of laboratories and office space. Everyone in Clinton was well aware of the eight-foot-tall chain-link fence surrounding the property, and they knew that armed security personnel in brown uniforms constantly manned the brick guardhouse at the only gate into the complex and patrolled the perimeter fence with attack dogs. They were also aware that this level of security was little different from that at almost any of the major biogenetic research centers around the country. A breakthrough in a soybean that would grow twice as many bushels an acre or in a vegetable that would prove impervious to disease or insects was worth hundreds of millions of dollars. And even though Walter Quinlan funded the center generously with monies from his vast computer company fortune, and was known as a philanthropist, they understood he was also a businessman. He wanted to cure hunger around the world, but he also wanted to make a profit, and he didn't want any breakthroughs the center might make stolen from him.

It was at this plant that a blocky, dust-streaked chemical supply truck drove up to the gate and stopped just as the first rays of the morning sun were beginning to peep above the horizon. The guards only asked where the chemicals were to be delivered, and then pointed out the particular building where the truck should go. It wasn't traffic coming into the center that might compromise a secret, for all arriving drivers were required to remain inside their vehicles until they were unloaded and had passed back out the gate again.

The truck drove toward a concrete block building the size of a small house near the rear of the complex.

Two scientists not normally involved in unloading chemicals and other arriving supplies stepped from the steel door leading into the building and waited as the truck turned and backed toward them.

With its rear only a few feet from the door, the truck stopped, and the driver and his partner, obviously Quinlan employees, since they came outside the cab, hurried around to the vehicle's rear.

Its wide door was opened. The scientists glanced across the deserted grounds, then reached inside the bed and slid what appeared to be a canvas-draped packing case, about eight feet long and three feet wide, toward them.

Its contents didn't seem to be very heavy, for the four men carried it easily. As they passed into the building, the canvas draped across the container caught on a side of the doorway and was pulled sideways, exposing the polished end of a blue stainless steel coffin.

It was the eighth such arrival that week, some of them coming from as far away as China and Iran.

* * *

The flight didn't take any more hours than Spence had thought it would. But somehow it seemed as if it had taken longer. Partly because he spent much of the time thinking about the breakthrough Flo had made and feeling guilty that he felt a twinge of envy. And partly because he was anxious to know about what he would find in Montana.

He had to know.

As the jet touched down, bumping slightly, he looked at Kennedy, stirring and coming awake from a sound sleep that had lasted nearly the whole trip. That the agent could sleep soundly with what he had been through in his past amazed Spence. If Kennedy hadn't indeed told him everything he knew, then Spence was glad he hadn't heard the rest—he had heard more than he had ever expected to hear. From anybody. Much more.

The jet began to slow and turned toward the outline of the building that served as the terminal for the small private airport.

Kennedy was using his cellular telephone to make another call. He had done that twice in Jackson and once more before he had gone to sleep in his seat. He hadn't received an answer any of the times.

This time he didn't either. But this time he quit hitting redial and punched in another number.

This one answered.

"Connect me to Colonel Michael Weaver's office," he said.

A few seconds passed.

"I'm a friend of Colonel Weaver's. Bob Kennedy. Would you tell him I'm on the line?"

A moment later Kennedy said, "I see. Thank you."

As he lowered the telephone to his lap, he had a puzzled expression across his face. "He's on leave," he said, more thinking aloud than making a statement.

Thirty minutes later, they drove a rented Thunderbird to the front of a funeral home in a small, out-of-the-way town that consisted of less than a dozen businesses. Once inside the building, Kennedy hesitated a moment when the owner opened the door into the embalming room.

"If you don't mind, I'd like to be alone with him for a moment."

The stocky agent hadn't turned around as he spoke, but Spence knew the words were directed at him as much as to the owner.

"If you don't mind," Kennedy added in a voice not near so authoritative as it usually was. "If you want to go first, I can wait until you're through."

"You go ahead," Spence said.

As Spence watched Kennedy walk inside the room, the old agent's shoulders slumped, and he seemed to lose an inch or two in height.

The door closed behind him.

The owner spoke in the low, monotone voice common to many funeral home people.

"Would you like a cup of coffee, Doctor?"

"No, thank you."

The short man nodded and turned away, walking toward the light showing from his office door. The thick carpet under his shoes muted his steps to the point there was no sound at all.

Down the wide hall toward the rear of the building, a lean, tall erect man in his late thirties came slowly up the carpet.

Spence heard the owner call him, "Dr. Jorgerson."

The king of the wild frontier.

The man stopped next to the owner. The owner said something and nodded across his shoulder toward the embalming room. They talked in low voices for a minute more, and then the tall man came down the carpet.

"Dr. Stevens," he said as he drew close. "I'm Jonathan Jorgerson. It was my father who was with your friend." He extended his hand.

His grip was firm. The muscles that ran up the outside of his neck were taut. His dark hair was trimmed short.

"I'm sorry about your father."

"Thank you, Dr. Stevens."

"Please call me Spence."

Jorgerson nodded and smiled politely. "Personally, I'd like to take Dad back to Butte with me. But I know he'd want to be buried here, out in the wide open. To him, two was a crowd. Except for me. And sometimes I wondered about me. You're making arrangements to take your friend back to Mississippi?"

Before Spence could answer, the door to the embalming room opened, and Kennedy walked outside. His eyes were tinged with red, and a tear he had failed to wipe away perched at the top of his cheek. Tears coming from the wide tough man surprised Spence. The agent stopped beside him. Spence nodded toward the veterinarian.

"This is Dr. Jorgerson. It was his father who was with Joey."

"Jonathan," the man said, extending his hand toward Kennedy's.

"Do you know how your father and Joey got together?" Kennedy asked as they shook hands.

"I was about to ask you the same thing," Jonathan said.

Kennedy shook his head that he didn't know. Then he said, "What did your father do for a living?"

"He owned a service station."

"Had he been in the military?"

"His vision wasn't good enough."

When Kennedy didn't immediately ask another question, Jorgerson said, "Why are you asking?"

"Joey was in the military," Kennedy responded. "I thought he might be an old friend. Do you know where the accident happened?"

"Yes."

"I'd like to see the spot," Kennedy said.

"Who are these people?" Tommy's wife asked.

She stood on the snow-sprinkled steps at the front of their ranch-style home. Paul stood beside her, his small hand in hers, looking up at his father. The people she had spoken about had arrived in a rental car, parked it next to the gray van, and waited there until Tommy had slipped on a heavy jacket and stepped from the house.

Two of them were dressed in jeans, thick shirts, and heavy jackets, as if they belonged in the area. The third, a large, heavily built man, wore a business suit, as if he had just stepped out of an office in Butte.

Genowski stared toward the house.

Tommy looked back at him for a moment, then at his wife. "They're friends who are going to help me in the election." Knowing how Genowski, in his suit, stood out from the others, Tommy added. "One's a lawyer. He's an expert at campaign strategy."

Genowski slid back inside the rental car as Tommy walked toward it.

Moments later, the car drove out onto the narrow road leading from the house and accelerated at a rapid pace toward the highway in the distance.

Inside the car, Genowski handed the small video-camera-like viewing device across the back of the front seat to Tommy. Then he looked at the driver. "Do you have the dynamite?"

"It's in the trunk," the man answered.

Kennedy held Jorgerson's broken glasses. A flashlight in his other hand, he stood on a boulder protruding above the mass of rock and limestone that had collapsed from the side of the hill long ago. He looked at where the Jeep had come to rest. He had already searched the rocks several times in the last thirty minutes. Still staring at the spot, thinking, he slipped the glasses inside his coat.

Then he turned toward the young Dr. Jonathan Jorgerson, standing a few feet away. "You said your father operated a service station?"

The veterinarian nodded. "An old one, off the beaten path—not far from here."

"I was wondering . . . ," Kennedy started. "It might be that Joey left some of his personal effects there—if that's where they were coming from. We have imposed on you enough. But if you don't mind, if you could point the way, we might drive over there to see."

"Is there something I'm not aware of?" Jonathan asked. It was the first time he had spoken without being spoken to since Kennedy had started moving around on the rocks, shining his light down into the narrow cracks and depressions marking the rough surface, occasionally reaching down into them for a fragment of the wreckage—and had found the glasses.

"Excuse me?" Kennedy said.

"You said you wanted to see the spot where your friend died. You've done a lot more than that. You're investigators, aren't you?"

Kennedy didn't hesitate. "Yes, we are."

"But not from around here," the veterinarian said.

Spence was surprised at how quickly Kennedy's mind worked as the agent said, "We're military. I told you Joey was *in* the military. It's basically a routine accident investi—"

Before Kennedy could finish the veterinarian said, "Not two of you. The military doesn't send two people to investigate anything. I know. I was in the marines. There would be a half dozen of you. More. And the military doesn't investigate car accidents."

Kennedy's expression stayed unperturbed, and he spoke in a level voice. "I'm sorry, Dr. Jorgerson, but we do in this kind of situation. You said you were in the marines. So you would understand better than most people—Mr. McDonald was involved in sensitive work for the government. I can tell you that we have no reason to suspect this *was* anything but an accident. But when people involved in his line of work die in an accident, we have to conduct an investigation—no matter how routine it is. That's all I'm allowed to tell you."

"Bull," Jorgerson said. Simply that and no more.

The agent stared at him.

"You've been looking around," Jonathan added, "trying

to find something more than just routine. Now you want to go to Dad's station. You can't learn anything about the accident there. Unless it's something more you're looking for."

Kennedy had waited patiently for the young man to finish. Now the agent said, "If there is more, would you want us to find out?"

"What do you mean?"

"If this is more than an accident, would you want to know?"

"It was my father."

"And if someone caused his death, you wouldn't want them to get away with it, would you?"

Jonathan didn't answer. He was staring intently into the stocky agent's eyes now.

Kennedy said, "We are with the military. And maybe this is nothing more than an accident. I told you the truth when I said I had no reason to believe it isn't. But there are some other things I can check. To make certain it *was* only an accident."

As the veterinarian continued to stare, Kennedy said, "And I told you the truth when I said this was sensitive. I can't tell you enough to satisfy you, but I need some questions answered. And I need your word that you won't say anything about it. I mean even to your wife. To anyone. If you can accept those ground rules, then if it is more than an accident we'll have a good chance to find out. If you can't accept that, then maybe we're at a dead end right here. And if your father and Joey were murdered, neither you nor I nor anyone else is ever going to know."

"I want to go with you when you go to the station," Jorgerson said.

"No. You can't do that." Spence saw Kennedy glance at him, and the agent added, "I'm baby-sitting one fool now. I don't need another on my hands."

Jonathan's eyes came around, too, and then he looked back at the agent. "I told you I was in the marines. I can take care of myself."

Kennedy didn't make light of the young man's statement. "If I needed someone to charge up a hill with me,
then I'm certain I couldn't be in better company. But that's
not what I'm talking about. You can't even imagine. You'd
be a babe in the woods."

The look on Jonathan's face made it appear as if he were
going to start pleading. But, instead, he said, "I have a map
in the car. I can mark it for you. But I want to know what
you find there. It was my father."

Kennedy nodded and patted the veterinarian on the
shoulder. "Son, you're not only going to know, but I'm
certain we'll be back asking you more questions."

"I'll get the map," Jonathan said.

Kennedy started across the rocks with him. They headed
toward the narrow path that ran up the steep slope.

Reaching the car, Kennedy raised his cell phone and
punched in redial as Jonathan went around to the passenger
side to get the map out of the glove compartment.

There was still no answer.

When Jonathan came back around the rear of the car
and handed the map to Kennedy the agent said, "I have a
couple more questions. I told you I needed your word first."

Jonathan nodded.

Kennedy added, "You say something to somebody and
you not only might ruin the chance of us ever finding out
the truth, you might be putting who you tell in danger."

Jonathan nodded again.

"I mean it, son. I mean it like nobody who ever gave
you an order in the corps meant it. If this isn't an accident,
and you tell somebody—anybody—you could be handing
them their death sentence—and yours, too."

Jonathan didn't nod as quickly this time, but he did nod,
and said, "I understand." Spence saw the veterinarian
glance at him.

"Now," Kennedy said, "Joey called Spence on a cell
phone the night of the accident. Your father was with him.
Spence heard him say something in the background about

a shaft. His exact words were, 'It's about a quarter of a mile to the shaft.' "

Kennedy's eyes came around again, and Spence nodded.

As the agent looked back at Jonathan, the veterinarian said, "He was talking about a shaft leading down into an old military research center—it's underground."

21

GENOWSKI HAD CHANGED into a jacket with a wool lining and khaki pants with their cuffs tucked into a heavy pair of boots. Tommy and the other man lay on the hard ground beside him. They watched the game management Jeep move slowly along the perimeter fence. As it neared the section of wire lying on the ground, one of the two men in the vehicle pointed to it and said something. The other man laughed. Moving slowly, the Jeep turned away from the fence and circled back in the direction it had come.

Alexander "Alex" Raye's eyes opened. He still wore the white bathrobe he had on at the cabin. His mind hazy, he realized he was lying on something both hard and soft at the same time. Dizzy and confused, he struggled up onto one elbow. It was a steel bunk covered with a thin mattress and bolted against a concrete block wall.

His eyes focused on the round metal bars past his feet. They ran from a bare concrete floor up to a concrete ceiling eight or nine feet above him. He suddenly realized he was looking into a jail cell.

Then he realized that he was *in* a jail cell.

He sat up rapidly.

When he did, his head seemed to spin. His vision blurred worse. And he collapsed back onto the thin mattress.

"Mr. Raye."

The soft voice came from nearby.

He turned his face toward the front of the cell. His vision starting to refocus, he saw a man standing outside the bars. He was tall and thin and wore slacks and a short-sleeve shirt, exposing long tanned arms.

Raye said, "Whaa . . . ti . . . is."

Surprised at the unintelligible words that had come from his mouth, he tried to clear his throat. But it was almost impossible to swallow. He could only keep his head turned, staring toward the man. His vision clearing rapidly now, he saw the man's face was narrow, and flecks of gray spotted his dark hair. He appeared to be in his late fifties.

"I don't normally greet incoming guests in person," Walter Quinlan said, continuing to speak in a pleasant, low tone, "but we've never had a senator's administrative assistant here before. And one whom I understand is being groomed by the senator to succeed him. That's what attracted us to you. To have him so interested in your future welfare should make you proud."

"I . . ." Raye's throat was still tight. Fighting off the dizziness, moving slowly, he managed to move his feet off the mattress to the floor and slowly sat up on the edge of the bunk. He tried to speak the same way, slowly, forcing each word through his throat. "What . . . am . . . I . . . doing . . . here? What . . . are . . ." He remembered the board creaking and the men coming up onto the porch. Another one had come from inside the cabin. His dizziness starting to abate, his throat loosening, his thinking suddenly becoming clearer, too.

The man standing before him had said, "That's what attracted us to you."

"I've been kidnapped?"

His throat clear now, the unintelligible sound had been replaced by rising panic.

"You're here to join us," Quinlan said.

"Join?" Raye's legs felt stronger now, and he pushed his hands back against the bunk and stood up. He swayed and had to make an effort to keep from falling. He tried to stand erect, and he mustered all the authority he could in his voice.

"I demand you tell me what you are doing. Who are you?" He now noticed there were other cells across the floor from his. Two men stared back at him through the bars running up and down in front of their faces.

"I'm in jail?" he wondered again, this time aloud. He looked back at the man outside his cell.

A smile crossed the narrow face. "It's more of a hospital," Quinlan said.

A gurney rolled in through the doorway at the far end of the small building. A tall man in a white lab coat was pushing it. Behind it came a second gurney and two more men.

They stopped in front of the cells across the way.

They said something to the men inside the bars. Raye didn't quite hear it.

One of the men suddenly backed to the rear of his cell.

The other remained where he was.

The men in lab coats unlocked the cell of the one who had retreated from them. He now climbed onto his bunk and pressed his back against the wall.

"No!" he yelled.

One of the men stepped toward him, lifted a small spray can, and depressed the nozzle. Raye threw his hands over his face and jerked his head to the side.

A moment later, the hands trembled, and it looked like he was having trouble holding them up.

His forearms slowly lowered and then fell to his sides, and he took a wobbly step, pitching head first off the bunk.

The man who had wielded the can lunged forward as quickly as an Olympic sprinter coming out of the blocks and caught the man easily in his arms.

A gurney was pushed into the cell.

At the other cell, the door opened and the man inside it walked outside. He climbed up onto the gurney and lay back. Straps quickly secured his wrists to its sides. The man who had put them in place lifted a wider strap across the man's chest and buckled it.

The other gurney was coming out of the next cell. Its unconscious former occupant lay on his back, his open eyes staring blankly toward the ceiling.

Raye raised his now trembling hand to the side of his face. He noticed the bloated feel of his skin. He touched his hand to his neck and felt even more swelling there.

What in God's name?

The gurneys passed outside the door into bright sunlight. It was the next day . . . or some next day, Raye thought. "Please," he started, turning his face back toward the man outside his cell, "tell me what . . ."

But the man wasn't there. He was walking in the same direction the gurneys had gone.

"Please . . . ," Raye called after him.

The man passed out into the sunshine, and the door closed behind him.

A hospital? Raye thought.

The game management Jeep had passed out of sight. Tommy pushed up from the ground and, carrying the small device that resembled a video camera, hurried toward the wire.

"You have a gun?" Kennedy asked. Spence shook his head no.

The agent reached under his coat to the back of his waist and pulled a snub-nosed thirty-eight into view. Spence took it into his hand, stared at the heavy weapon for a moment, then raised his gaze.

"You're not worried about Jonathan because it was his father who was killed?"

"It's more like if we were going to find out anything from him we had to tell him why," Kennedy said. "But, yes, it was his father. The people I worked with were capable of just about anything—but not participating in the murder of their own family members. No, what I'm worried about is whether he can keep his mouth shut."

They were in a back room of Jorgerson's old service station. Kennedy had hurriedly gone through drawers in all the small rooms. He hadn't found anything that had caught his attention. Now he lifted a long coil of nylon rope from among several coils hanging on the wall in front of him. "You bring a flashlight?" he asked.

"No."

Kennedy walked to a worn wooden table. Two flashlights, with their long battery containers streaked with grime and rusting, lay on the table. He tried one. It didn't work. He tried the other. It cast a dim light. "You knew there was a shaft," he said, turning around and holding the flashlight out. "And yet you didn't think to bring a light?"

Spence took it into his hand. "I didn't know we'd be going down inside it."

"You didn't think," Kennedy said in a voice lower than the one he normally used. "You weren't prepared." It was like he was a Scout master softly lecturing one of his troop.

But the look of irritation on the agent's wide face wasn't the kind a Scout master would display. "Damn baby-sitting," he muttered as he started for the door.

Outside in the brisk, cool air, he looked in the direction Jonathan had drawn them on the map.

Then he walked toward the rental car.

The look of irritation he had continued to carry as he walked through the station faded into a reflective look. "I hope they're not capable of anything like that," he said in a low voice.

He wasn't smiling.

"You can't even imagine," he added, the same thing he had said to the veterinarian. "He might not even be the son. You can't imagine what they're able to set up and make you believe. The only thing you can be absolutely certain of is that what you think you know is never what you get— if they don't want you to get it. You can't even imagine," he repeated once more.

*   *   *

The doctor came across the concrete floor like a physician in any hospital, dressed in a white lab coat with a stethoscope hanging around his neck and a chart in his hand.

But this is not any hospital, Raye thought, *and I'm not a patient.*

"This is Dr. Sams," Quinlan said, nodding toward the physician. "He was one of the first to join us. You build an organization by putting together the best people you can get, then building on that. Dr. Sams is a highly skilled neurologist—one of the best in the country when he joined us. And, of course, he's much more capable now."

Dr. Sams smiled into the cell as he stopped in front of the bars.

Raye stared back at him.

"We'll want to get a medical history first," Dr. Sams said in a pleasant voice, "and do blood work. All the normal routine." He lifted the chart in front of him and pulled a pen from his lab coat pocket. "What is your age?"

Raye turned back toward his bunk and sat down on it without answering.

Quinlan stared through his bars. His usual pleasant expression was gone. In its place was not so much an angry look as a serious one. "We have ways of assuring full cooperation," he said. "But it's quite stressful on the patient. We had one—a minor politician from North Korea—whose heart couldn't take the stress. The little man probably wouldn't have risen very much higher in his government anyway, but there was a chance. And it's relatively hard to acquire a politician with almost any power from that country. The ruling clique is so small and tightly controlled."

"Your age?" the doctor asked again.

When Raye still didn't answer, the doctor said, "Are you allergic to any medications?"

"Okay," Raye said, bringing his gaze to Quinlan's, "I'll answer your questions. But first, I want you to tell me exactly what I'm . . . is in store for me." He had tried to make his words sound strong, but they hadn't.

"Certainly," Quinlan said. "It's a necessary part of the

procedure. We tell each patient everything in detail before we proceed." He held his hand out, palm up toward the doctor.

Sams reached into his pocket and pulled out something so small Raye couldn't see.

"A computer chip," Quinlan said, taking it into his fingers. "Would you like a closer look? It's very noninvasive—part of the way we keep the body from rejecting it."

Rejecting it? Raye thought.

"Of course the body will reject a foreign object even as small as a grain of sand if other measures aren't taken," Quinlan continued. "There are some things we do to help during the surgery—"

Surgery?

"—but of course we can't do everything ourselves. You will be on regimented antirejection medication for the rest of your life—the same as a transplant patient."

Raye felt his hand tremble.

Quinlan held the chip up again. Raye saw it was flat in shape, and maybe twice the size of a pencil eraser.

"There will be three implanted all together. One will contain nearly unlimited information from which you can draw. In fact your chip will contain many more megabytes of knowledge than ours do. Computer chips are constantly being developed to store more and more information. In that sense the ones implanted in me are quite inefficient in the amount of information they contain—"

In him? Raye thought.

"—but it is sufficient for my purposes. Now as to the chips you will have implanted, they will operate off your brain waves. Your senator is on the Select Intelligence Committee, so you might be familiar with the brain wave research being done by the military. It's been going on since shortly after World War II."

A corner of Quinlan's mouth raised in a small smile, as if he was thinking of something amusing. "I suppose that when the vast scientific infrastructure built up during the war was no longer needed, the military found themselves with a plethora of scientists on the payroll with nothing much to do. Over the years, brain wave experiments have dealt with everything from attempts at psychic viewing to person-to-person mind control. The technology I possess is not nearly so exotic. To explain it in a modern-day context, it is quite similar to what happens when someone on a computer visits a website on the Internet. That website, if equipped properly, can register where the visit came from and, if desired, send back an impulse that is capable of reading the material on the original sending computer or even transmitting a command that can make that computer act in a particular manner. The only difference in our abilities is that instead of manually typing in our commands, our brain waves manipulate the instrumentation in the chips. The chips then act as the website, either registering what we wish to see or hear or transmitting out messages to those who will be equipped like you.

"Regarding the vast knowledge that you will soon possess, all you will have to do is think of whatever you are inquiring about. Your brain waves will cue the storage banks in the chips, and you can then quickly search through any amount of information as rapidly as any search engine on the fastest of computers. You will find that awkward at first, but it grows easier every day you work with it. The second chip contains a transmitter. It transmits to me and a few more like me. As I said, as in the case of the website, anything you can see we can see, if we so desire. Anything you say, we can hear within the two or three seconds it takes to reflect off a satellite. But the seeing and the hearing is a one-way street. You will not have the ability to see or hear what we look at and say."

The more Quinlan had talked, the more Raye had trembled. He was reduced to quivering now.

"But . . ." Quinlan held up his finger to make a point, "you will be able to hear me when I choose for you to. Again, that is totally at my discretion. Totally at the individual discretion of four of us who can direct words to you. You will have knowledge of our identities as well as those of others like you as soon as the implants are complete."

He caught the chip from his palm and held it through the bars. "This particular chip—the largest of the three you will carry—has multiple purposes. First, it will be implanted nearest the surface of your brain where, from time to time, it can be withdrawn and a new one implanted. We do that to constantly upgrade your knowledge—and your physical abilities. For, yes, in addition to the knowledge, the chip will also expand your physical capabilities. There are constant impulses from this chip—twenty-four hours a day—that will be stimulating centers in your brain that will add measurably to your quickness and even increase your strength without noticeably adding to your muscle mass. You won't be Superman, but you will be far superior physically to any man your size. Of course, mentally, others won't be much more than mere insects when compared to you. You might find it comforting to know that you will still have all the faculties you currently possess. You won't find anything different or disturbing. You will be you—but mine and the others' to summon for our bidding at our will."

Quinlan paused a moment and then spoke in a slow voice. "And our will," he said, "is quite simple. We, and soon you, will be the most intelligent people ever known on this earth. What better service to the world could we then be than to begin to direct humankind into greatness? No more wars, no more problems of any kind."

He waited a moment. "You understand?" He smiled now, a small smile with only a corner of his mouth raising. "You do understand. But you also think me mad, don't you? But that is only because you don't yet know how really great your intelligence will be, how great *you* will be. But you will know soon. And, when you are with us, you *will* do exactly as we say in helping us pursue our goals."

He weaved his fingers back and forth, drawing attention to the chip.

"Your private thoughts will remain private. We cannot read those. But, should your thoughts make you consider questioning one of mine or the others' commands as we pursue those goals, there's one last function to this chip. One I think you will be most interested in." He carefully balanced the piece of metal on one of the round horizontal bars.

Then he looked back into the cell. "If you should ever not immediately follow any of our commands, then in the two to three seconds it takes for our disapproval to reflect back from a satellite, this will happen."

He lowered his gaze to the chip.

Without any change of expression, without any noticeable concentration on his part, it suddenly began to dissolve. A thin plume of smoke arose. The chip softened and bubbled and a drop from it ran around the side of the bar, then fell toward the floor where it hit and gave off a tiny puff of black smoke.

"By now you would be quite dead," Quinlan said, "the acid in this chip having burned away a significant part of your brain matter."

His gaze came back to Raye's. His last words were, "In the past, three poor souls hesitated to immediately do our bidding. They are dead now. Though the brain has no pain receptors as such, I can nevertheless assure you their deaths were quite painful."

Tommy moved the finding device slowly back and forth. The viewing screen glowed a light white. He had started in the lab, the most likely place to find any chips that had been left behind years before—like those Jorgerson and the big detective, Joey McDonald, had found.

He had moved the device over the counter and microscopes first and then he had started sweeping the rock-strewn floor, moving the device slowly. He was halfway back to the door when a dazzling, small white dot appeared in the middle of the screen.

He knelt on one knee and lowered the device almost to the floor to pinpoint the exact spot where the chip lay. Then he used his flashlight to find it. He lifted it from the soot and stared at it for a moment. It was a transmitting chip. There had been only two types back then, the knowledge chip and the transmitter chip. The much larger chip that carried the acid hadn't been in existence then. The military hadn't thought of it. They hadn't conceived of the need for a chip that would be a defensive device if their subjects ran amuck.

They hadn't counted on that.

They should have.

"Here's the turn," Spence said.

Kennedy slowed the rental car and turned it off the highway toward a smaller one.

Soon they were bumping over parts of the road where the top inch or two of pavement was missing in wide sections, as if it had melted away like ice on top of the ground in the spring.

The car bounced through a particularly deep pothole and Spence felt the sharp jab of the thirty-eight pressing through his sweatshirt against his spine.

He reached behind him and moved the weapon from the back of his waistband to the side of his jeans. Though the heavy revolver was not as uncomfortable there, he still felt its pressure. In a way it wasn't a strange feeling. He had handled weapons all his life, from hunting with his father as a young boy to target shooting. That had all ended a long time ago, but he still had his father's old rifle and pistol in the apartment. And he knew he could still hit what he was aiming at.

But he had never aimed at a human. Yet, if his worst fears were confirmed, that Joey had been murdered as well as Dr. Lambert and he found himself facing the ones responsible, he didn't believe he would have any trouble pulling the trigger.

Dr. Lambert. Joey. The old man Jorgerson. Three people dead. And maybe him the same as responsible for the latter two deaths. . . .

Their names kept going through his mind. Trying to

force his thoughts to something else, he looked out his window at the barren land passing out to the side of the car. The farther they had driven, the more bleak-looking it had become, even in the bright sunshine. He dropped his gaze back to the map in his lap.

"About a mile now. Then we start cross-country."

Kennedy nodded.

Spence's worry was that once they got on the property they wouldn't be able to find the opening to the shaft from the description Jorgerson's son had given. It was only a general description, about being near the bottom of a slope on a hill that mounded above the surrounding area like a wide blister. They were to walk straight past a section of fallen wire in the perimeter fence and go due north. That's all Jorgerson had told his son.

"I hope the hell we can find it."

"The opening to the shaft?" Kennedy questioned.

"Uh-huh."

"We'll find it," Kennedy said.

Raye sat on his bunk staring through the bars at the two empty cells across from his. He had thought they would have come after him by now. An hour before when the doctor had given him an injection, he expected it would knock him out. But it hadn't. Something in preparation for the operation. Like the blood tests had been. And the steroids they said he would receive. How long after he took them would it be until the actual surgery? Quinlan had said it didn't change what you were, how you thought, your conscious being. But after the operation you had no choice but to do what you were told to do.

And then a person became, though far from mindless, not much more than a zombie, existing only to obey Quinlan's wishes. There was no doubt that Quinlan was mad, but there was also no doubt that he could succeed in taking over a country, or countries, perhaps. Hitler, Lenin, they had started with mere hundreds of followers, and their followers only members of the masses with no power base from which to give their movement impetus. Quinlan's followers would be in key positions. *Like me,* Raye thought, *anointed to be a senator.* Even some of the larger countries could be in jeopardy, at least thrown into disorganization and weakened through someone answering to Quinlan gaining a high enough position—and then that country falling prey to others seeing the weakness. Quinlan's idea for the worldwide peace he had spoken of wasn't a blueprint for peace but instead guaranteed war.

"There are things about the implant you might like," he had added, explaining the carrot that went with the stick just before he had ended his words. "You will be a genius. Others will be like ants under your feet. Power and riches will be yours as we take control." The others had realized that, he explained, and many had come not only to accept their fate but to look forward to what it would eventually gain them, he said.

Like selling their soul to the devil, Raye thought.

Like he would be forced to do soon.

Selling his soul to the devil—with no choice in the matter.

But there *was* a choice. Ultimately there was a choice in anything. Quinlan had said that he and the others were able to see what those who were implanted saw. Able to hear what they heard. But he freely admitted he couldn't read their minds.

My thoughts will be private, Raye thought. He would think and plan and find a way. Some way to get a message out without Quinlan or any of the others being able to see it written. Some way to deliver it without them knowing it was being delivered. Some way they would never know it came from him. Some way.

But if bad came to worse, there was the two to three seconds Quinlan had told him about, the lag between the time words were spoken and the moment he heard them. Two to three seconds to get a message out that would be clear with no misunderstanding. Two or three seconds to let somebody know about the nightmare Quinlan planned for the world—and hope it could be stopped.

Two or three seconds until he would be dead.

He had decided that's what he would do.

And then God would let his soul rest, he hoped. He hadn't sold it to the devil.

22

KENNEDY STARED AT the thin nylon rope that had already been trailing down into the shaft when they came upon the small opening. He dropped to the ground the coil of rope he had been carrying looped over his shoulder. "Looks like the old man was planning on coming back," he said, "and maybe Joey—if that's why they were together."

Spence looked at the crudely fashioned covering lying to the side of the entrance. They had no trouble in finding the shaft. They had gone due north from the fence, just like the old man had told his son. Kennedy walked straight to the opening without having to angle his path so much as a step to one side or the other.

Slipping a pair of leather gloves over his thick hands, the agent now stepped closer to the small entrance. "I'll go first. And if my big butt doesn't get wedged in there, it'll be a breeze for you." He looked back across his shoulder. "And if I do get stuck," he added, "I'll have you behind me, where you can pull me out." He wasn't smiling. The opening *was* small. There was no way to know if it grew narrower the farther down it went.

Kennedy sat down on the hard ground and moved his legs over into the shaft, turned, and started backing down into the darkness. Only half of his body inside the shaft, he stopped and exhaled audibly. "So far so good," he said. He still wasn't smiling. He closed his eyes for a long moment, took another deep breath, and slipped lower.

In a moment his head disappeared from sight.

Spence slipped on his gloves, turned around, and started backing into the shaft. Just before his head went past the opening's rim, he heard the faint, rhythmic thumping sound of a helicopter's blades. He thought of the game management people and looked up into the sky. But despite the lack of clouds and the bright sun, he couldn't see the craft. Then he realized that the sound was coming from closer to the ground, and the craft hidden from sight by one of the bluffs rising in the distance. The sound was fading now, the helicopter moving away from him rather than coming in his direction. He lowered his head below the rim.

Kennedy had already progressed well down the constricting, slanted passageway, and Spence tilted his head as best he could to peer down at him. A thin circle of light glowed around the edges of the agent's stocky body from the flashlight he was carrying.

Minutes later, passing through an area of fractured rock, Spence felt pebbles break loose from the shaft and move in a small landslide toward Kennedy. Some of the larger ones began to bounce and fell against Kennedy's shoulders and tumbled past him, but the agent didn't say anything.

Then his voice: "It's widening." Spence tilted his head and saw that the circle of light around the agent had suddenly brightened.

"It's getting wide," Kennedy called. "I'm going to have to use the rope. Make sure it's not caught on you."

Before Spence could even check, he felt the rope tighten against his side. He looked down. Kennedy swung back and forth, lowering himself hand over hand toward the darkness below him.

Spence hesitated a moment, briefly wondering how much weight the taut line could hold, and then he moved on down to where the shaft widened, grabbed the rope, brought his feet close together, and began sliding toward a darkness that suddenly glowed bright as the agent switched his flashlight back on.

Spence landed on a mounded pile of broken rock.

Despite the cold, perspiration dotted Kennedy's forehead. "I'm getting too old for this," he said.

His flashlight illuminated steel walls painted a light green and covered with soot. Spence switched his flashlight on. It cast such a dim glow that its beam was completely lost in the brighter illumination of the agent's flashlight. Spence switched it off and slipped its long handle inside his jacket pocket.

"We go that way," Kennedy said, shining his flashlight above a wide stretch of fractured slabs of rock stacked a few feet high.

When they climbed down the barrier's far side and walked through a doorway, Kennedy's flashlight illuminated metal lockers against one wall. Their doors stood open. Their bare insides reflected the flashlight's beam. Kennedy walked through the next doorway.

Spence saw that any further progress was barred by tightly packed rock that rose in an unending wall to merge into solid rock above.

This is all there is? he thought. It can't be. Jonathan said his father hauled cables out of here to retrieve their copper. Where were the remaining cables?

Kennedy walked closer to the rock, shining his flashlight before him. Spence saw that the agent had his automatic in his hand. It was held down loosely at his side, but he was carrying it. And he was the experienced one. He had told Jonathan that he would be like a "babe in the woods" if people the agent knew were involved. "You wouldn't stand a chance." Spence pulled the revolver from his waistband.

But where were they going from here, with the solid wall of broken rock in front of them? He shined his light to the left and to the right.

Kennedy had already been playing the beam of his flashlight along the barrier. "Here we go," he suddenly said.

Spence saw the small opening. Illuminated by the agent's flashlight, it was near the center of the wall of rock. Stepping around the larger stones lying scattered across the concrete floor in his path, he walked to it.

Kennedy had dropped to one knee. Leaning his body into the triangular-shaped passageway, he shined his light inside it. "I can see an open area on the other side." He ducked into the opening and began crawling forward.

Thirty feet of moving on their hands and knees and they emerged into another room twenty feet deep before another mass of solid rock rising toward the ceiling blocked the way.

But there was a closed steel door to the left, about twenty feet from a wide pile of ashes mounded against the rock.

Kennedy opened the door.

It led to a wide corridor running at least a hundred feet before it ended in still another closed door. To their sides, perpendicular lines of steel O-rings rose toward the ceiling. Nearing the far door, rubber-coated cables began, each of them threaded through the O-rings. "Here's where he got his copper," Kennedy said, looking at the severed ends of the cables.

They passed under a wide grill bolted to the ceiling and walked into the next room.

It was thirty to thirty-five feet wide. Forty to fifty feet ahead of them the way was once again blocked by a massive wall of rock. The flashlight flashing across it showed no further openings of any size, with the far ends of two long stainless steel counters ending under the rock. Spence glanced at the microcentrifuges and beakers and test tubes scattered along the top of the counter to the left. A large water bath sat on a table at the center of the room. The counter along the right wall contained a half dozen binocular microscopes spaced a few feet apart.

"You're a doctor," Kennedy said. "Is there anything in the equipment here that tells you anything?"

The flashlight's beam illuminated a cart sitting near the end of the counter on the right. A stainless steel scalpel and forceps glinted the illumination.

Then Spence heard the sound.

Their faces turned at the same time, and Kennedy

flashed his light through the doorway down the long corridor.

The sound, though faint, had been clear. A small rock
had rolled down a slab somewhere and fallen to the concrete floor.

Spence had carried the revolver loosely since having
pulled it from his waistband. Now he held it rigidly pointed
into the corridor. Rocks didn't change position after lying
ten years in the same spot.

Kennedy spoke in a low voice. "We can sit here an hour
or a week. But in the long run that way is the only way
out. I'm going to turn the flashlight off—it makes too good
of a target. I'm going to move to the right. You try to
remember that if you have to shoot. If a light comes on
from the other end, you *do* shoot, and quick. Don't give
somebody the time to illuminate me as a target."

The flashlight went off.

They waited a moment to let their eyes acclimate to the
darkness. But it never happened. Spence couldn't see his
hand six inches in front of his face.

The sound again.

This time louder. Not a single rock. Several rocks. Sliding.

They kept sliding.

Kennedy's light flashed on. "He's trying to get away,"
he shouted, and dashed into the corridor.

Spence ran forward.

Kennedy stepped on a small rock, his foot sliding out to
the side, nearly causing him to fall. Spence raced past him.

At the end of the hall, he hesitated at the open doorway
into the next room, pulled his flashlight from his pocket,
switched it on, and grasping the revolver in one hand, the
light in the other he sprung through the doorway and landed
in a crouch, sweeping the dim beam of the light and the
weapon rapidly back and forth.

Kennedy came by him, dashing toward the triangular-
shaped opening in the rocks blocking their way. He dove

as much as leaned into the opening and scrambled on all
fours through the small tunnel.

Spence came out behind Kennedy's feet as they emerged
from the tunnel. They moved carefully into the next room,
past the lockers, and sweeping their lights back and forth
slowly through the next doorway. Ahead of them, with only
the five-foot-tall barrier of rocks separating them from the
room where they came down, there was total silence.

But that was the only place left where anybody could
be.

Spence looked back across his shoulder.

Kennedy angled to the left and began crawling up onto
the barrier. Spence angled to the right. Kennedy, his stomach now pressed as low against the top of the rocks as he
could get it and still move, wiggled toward the room.
Spence began crawling across the rocks on his side.

Kennedy's flashlight illuminated the tall mound of debris below the shaft, and the rope hanging down—and
slowly moving.

He sprang to the floor and ran toward the mound.
"We've got him."

As Spence started up the mound Kennedy said, "Careful.
He can shoot down."

Spence held the gun pointed up past his forehead, his
flashlight pressed against the weapon and mirroring its slow
movement forward. The beam from Kennedy's light joined
the dim illumination from his. Spence glanced at the agent,
and slowly stepped forward, tensing as he shined the light
up into the dark void left when the shaft had come crashing
down.

No one hung on the rope.

It had quit moving.

Kennedy twisted around and shined his light back the
way they had come. "He decided he couldn't make it. He
can't be far away."

Moving his automatic in sync with his flashlight, he
shined the bright beam right and left, then played it along

the uneven surface of the five-foot barrier leading back into
the open area they had just come from.

Spence shined his light up the steel walls to his left.
Above where the steel left off, the dark rock of the hill's
interior rose into an arched ceiling. The rock was jagged
and uneven, with large cavelike depressions in places and
dark voids that bent around corners in others.

He started the beam back down the wall.

Nearly in line with the five-foot barrier, he halted the
light on a horizontal slitlike opening maybe three feet from
top to bottom. It was close enough to the top of the barrier
that a tall man standing on a stone two or three feet thick
could manage to climb up and hide.

Spence moved to the barrier and climbed onto its top.
Keeping his light and revolver focused on the opening, he
slowly walked forward. In front of him at the far side of
the barrier, a pile of loose stones rose like a stepladder up
the side of the wall. He stepped up onto them.

Rocks turned beneath his feet and slid down the pile.

The sound was similar to the sound of sliding rocks they
had heard.

He stepped higher, slipped, and his light was thrown off
of the opening. Kennedy came up onto the barrier. Spence
regained his balance, shined the light against the opening,
and tried to climb higher. Rubble turned under the pressure
of his step and slid away again. He slowly reached out the
end of the flashlight and shined it into the opening. But he
was still too low to see into it. He switched off the flashlight, slipped it into his jacket pocket, and reached out with
his hand.

Arching up on his toes, he got a grip on the lip of the
opening.

A hand shot out, grabbed his wrist and jerked him up
off his feet all in the same motion. Kennedy fired. The slug
passed into the opening and ricocheted off the rock with a
loud zinging sound.

Spence, lifted to the edge of the opening, pushed his

revolver above the hand gripping his and squeezed the trigger.

As the shot fired, another hand came out of the opening and slapped the weapon from his grip. It fell toward the floor. Kennedy was right under him. Spence came face-to-face with the man pulling him up into the hole; a narrow, young face, not any older than his. He tried to grab the flashlight out of his pocket to use it as a weapon. A balled fist came forward and struck a hard blow, stunning him. He tried to pull back from the opening but was pulled up yet again. His chest pressed against the lip of the rock. Tommy jerked one last time, then caught Spence's chest and threw him backward, letting go of his hand at the same time.

Spence crashed into Kennedy. The agent was buckled forward by Spence's falling weight. The automatic and flashlight flew out to the sides.

Tommy leaped from the opening.

Landing on the barrier, his tall body crouched in the glow from the flashlight lying on the rocks, he pointed an automatic.

Spence tried to stand but slipped and dropped back to one knee. The automatic's barrel moved toward his face.

And then without the sudden loud noise of the shot he was expecting, the barrel slowly lowered.

Spence didn't move.

Kennedy pushed awkwardly to his feet.

The man was staring at the blood splattered on his hand when he had driven his fist into Spence's face.

Then he looked at his thumbnail.

He shook his head. Slowly at first and then going back and forth rapidly.

"Nooooo!"

The scream caused Spence to flinch. The man dropped the automatic and hurdled forward with a long leaping stride. Spence sprung to his feet, ready to ram his shoulder into the charging form, and the man stopped and thrust his hand forward and held it open.

A tiny, almost imperceptible bit of dark metal lay on his extended palm.

"Take them, they're in all of our . . . ," he started. His eyes widened and his face twisted, as if in sudden agony.

His hand came forward. Spence felt the fingers tear at his, felt the piece of metal press into his palm.

Kennedy tackled the man, knocking him backward. But instead of reaching behind him to break his fall against the rocks, the man grabbed his head in both hands and screamed.

He slammed into the rocks with Kennedy on top of him. He screamed again, a long, piercing scream, convulsed, and slapped his hands against the rock. And then he was still.

Kennedy didn't move at first.

He slowly lifted his weight.

He stared at the limp form, then moved his hand to the man's neck and pressed his fingers against the jugular vein. He shook his head and pressed his fingers harder into the skin.

"He's dead."

The metal, illuminated dimly in Spence's palm, was not the single piece he had thought it to be, but three tiny copper-colored squares.

He stared at them for a moment, then closed his hand around them and looked down at Kennedy, still leaning over the body. "Why didn't he shoot?" the agent asked in a low, questioning tone.

Kennedy knelt that way for a moment, without moving, then began searching the man's pockets.

A second later the agent straightened. "He doesn't have any ID," he said. He shook his head. "Why didn't he shoot? I didn't kill him," he added as he reached to close the man's wide, staring eyes. "Not me tackling him. Not the rocks. He didn't hit them that hard."

Spence felt a drop of moisture fall on his hand. He raised his fingers to his lip. They came away red with his own blood. Still on his knees, Kennedy reached to his hip pocket, pulled out his wallet, opened it, and reached for the man's limp hand. A moment later he was pressing the fingers against a plastic card holder in the wallet.

He stood, closed the wallet, and slipped it back inside his pocket.

Spence looked at the limp body. "Joey was murdered, wasn't he?" There was no question in his mind about that now. "Because he came down here."

He started to say, "Maybe it had something to do with these," and show the tiny squares he held in his hand to the agent. Because he realized now they must be computer chips, maybe containing something important. But a thought passed through his mind. What the man shouted: "They're in all of our . . ."

Now he was thinking of the tiny piece of metal he had seen in the cup in the morgue. A tiny copper-colored square.

Something new that had been in the morgue.

Again he started to voice his thought to Kennedy, but then he stopped once again when he felt a sudden nervousness. The reason seemed impossible. But Kennedy had already said it himself: *You can't imagine what they're able to set up and make you believe.* He looked at the stocky agent staring down at the body. The FBI agent who had worked with Joey in the past. Joey wasn't still working. Kennedy wasn't supposed to still be working either—not at what he used to work at. He had said he wasn't. He had said he had retired shortly after Joey had. But not all the way retired back into civilian life like Joey had been. He was still with the FBI—the government. Spence couldn't forget how the agent, following only the veterinarian's general directions, had walked straight to the entrance to the air shaft without angling a step one way or another in any other direction.

"There's not even a bump on the back of his head," Kennedy said. "He just died."

Spence couldn't take his eyes off Kennedy. The agent's words about the veterinarian came to mind again: *He might not even be the son. You can't imagine what they're able*

to set up and make you believe. The only thing you can be
absolutely certain of is that what you think you know is
never what you get—if they don't want you to get it.

Spence opened his fingers from around the pieces of
metal. He kept one for himself, slipping it quietly into his
jacket pocket, and held the other two out. "He gave me
these."

Kennedy came to his feet.

He picked the squares into his hand.

Spence said, "I think they're computer chips. I want to
x-ray his head."

"X-ray?"

Spence nodded.

"Because of these?"

Spence nodded again. Because of what the man had
screamed, and because of the surgical instruments, and,
more telling, the similar kind of chip that he had seen in
the morgue.

He hesitated a moment longer. But he had already gone
too far if he was wrong. If Kennedy was the wrong one to
be talking to. *If I can't even imagine.*

"Because I found a chip like these in the morgue. The
same color. The same size. It was bloodstained and it
looked like brain tissue might be embedded in it."

Kennedy's eyes narrowed. "And you've known this all
the time and didn't say anything about it?"

"I thought the tissue was there from the force of the
accident. Would you have connected the two before now?"

"Is it still there?"

Spence shook his head no. "I dumped it in a biohazard
receptacle. It would have been carried off that same day."

The agent looked back at the young man's body. "I
know places we can have him x-rayed. But it's been a long
time. I'm going to have to go slow, make certain of whom
I'm dealing with."

Spence nodded.

You can't even imagine.

23

SPENCE CAME OUT of the hole first and scooted back from the edge, sitting on the cold ground as Kennedy climbed out and came to his feet on the other side of the shaft. The agent looked at the two chips in his hand.

"I don't want the vet knowing," he said.

Spence nodded.

"No one but you and me," Kennedy added.

"Joey was murdered, wasn't he?"

"Murdered," Kennedy said. "Or the Jeep was run off the road by someone chasing him." He shook his head. "Or none of the above," he added. "But somebody didn't want us down there." He looked at the chips again.

Genowski crouched behind a small rise as he watched Spence and the FBI agent hurry toward their rental car. He had an automatic in his hand, but they each carried a pistol in theirs. The odds were good that with surprise he could force them to give up before they could raise their weapons. But, if one of them didn't acquiesce so easily . . .

Besides, two more bodies to dispose of wouldn't be good. Two more people from Mississippi dying in Montana wouldn't be good.

That's how he rationalized letting them pass, staying crouched where he was as they made their way across the hard ground.

*   *   *

In Jackson, Quinlan frowned. He was aware of the reasons Genowski let the two hurry past him, but he wasn't certain it was the correct thing to do—not with them carrying the chips that Tommy had thrust into Spence's hand.

Quinlan turned and paced by the conference table. John sat at the table without speaking.

Quinlan looked at his watch.

"We can send somebody to intercept them before they can get to the plane," he said.

"They can't," John said.

Quinlan already knew that. It was simple logic, not even worth thinking about. The agent and the doctor were only thirty minutes away from their plane. It would take better than an hour to get anyone there to cut them off. He had only been wishing aloud. It was that important that the chips were recovered.

"We can be ready here," John said.

Quinlan shook his head no. They didn't need any more murders here either. Especially not the murder of another doctor from the medical center.

"We'll wait and see which one has them. Whichever one it is, then we'll find a way to stop him that doesn't raise any questions."

"There is very little chance they'll be able to get to any-one who can read them," John said.

Kennedy would be the most logical one to have the chips, Quinlan thought, his conclusion based on the vast knowledge, tendencies, and percentages they had stored in their minds. But he was also able to think beyond purely abstract knowledge, and he felt there was more than just who might have the chips in their possession. It was a gut feel, from the part of his mind that was still totally his from the past; maybe the feeling could better be labeled intuition. For some reason he worried about Dr. Spence Stevens.

And what he might do.

They walked up the two steps to the small cabin area of the private jet. The pilot pulled down the door behind them.

Kennedy buckled himself in, then looked across the seat. "I'll get him x-rayed. In the meantime you're going to go back to saving people from disease, or whatever it is you do. You know not to mention this to anybody. Any part of it. I don't know who's behind this, but you're out."

"What are you—"

"Listen to me," Kennedy said. "I don't know if it's them. If it's not, it could be someone else just as dangerous. But it's something big. And involved. Leave this to me. I know what I'm doing. And I'm good at it."

The stocky agent paused a moment. His eyes took on an almost reflective look, unusual in his hard features. "Joey was, too," he said. "He was the best. Nobody could outwit him or act quicker than he could, but they did. It's that dangerous. And I don't want you stumbling around in this trying to do something that seems like a smart move to you, and getting us both killed."

"I don't understand why you don't just go to somebody."

"Somebody? What about Walter Quinlan? We could just ask him about his former employee Alfred Wynn. That would be logical, wouldn't it?" Kennedy reached inside his jacket and pulled out a folded set of fax sheets stapled together.

"You can read these, or I can tell you what's in them," he said.

Spence waited.

"It's some additional information I requested since last speaking with Joey, and bottom line is my people couldn't find any of Mr. Quinlan's prints on record anywhere."

"Quinlan's?"

Kennedy nodded. "I wondered if the gaps in Mr. Wynn's life might could be filled in by learning something about what he had done and where he had visited since he surfaced in Jackson and went to work for Computer Resources. Since the word is that Walter Quinlan had personally hired Wynn, I requested information on him, too, to see if there might be some obvious connection be-

tween him and Wynn in their earlier lives. Didn't find any.
What I did find was that when Quinlan was a young man
getting started in the timber business he got busted for possession. Only pot, but it got him a sentence with time suspended and parole. When he stayed clean, a judge
expunged his record. That isn't unusual. What is unusual
is there are no fingerprint records available in the police
records. My people can't find out where he was born either,
so I don't know if there's a birth certificate. But no prints
so far. Does that make you want to tell him what we
know?"

Spence tried to stay logical with his thoughts. "The
judge could have ordered all his arrest records destroyed."

"That's right, or the police could have just done it on
their own after getting the expungement order."

"If you haven't seen his birth certificate yet, then you
don't know there aren't any prints of record. Mine aren't
on record anywhere else either—I've never been arrested.
I didn't mean to tell someone like Quinlan anyway. I meant
the Justice Department. The FBI. Tell them about the man
down at the bottom of the shaft. Have them x-ray him."

"And what if he doesn't have an implant?" Kennedy
asked.

"We still tell them there's a connection."

The stocky FBI agent smiled out of the corner of his
mouth. "Like there's a connection between Roswell and the
reports people have been coming up with ever since? How
well are they listened to? Like there's a connection between
area fifty-one and aliens? Do you want to come off looking
like just another kook? And what do we have to tell them
anyway; that there was once a laboratory there, that you
saw a spot of blood and brain tissue on a similar-looking
piece of metal back in the morgue? A piece of metal you
can't produce now. Or are you going to tell them you came
up with the idea because the guy down there grabbed his
head?"

"He said, 'They're in all of our . . .' That's what he
could have meant."

"You've told me that three times, Doctor. So even if you're correct, do you think it's your everyday bunch of criminals behind it? Do you want to be dead? They don't have to put a bullet in your brain. There's car accidents, injections that can make you have a heart attack. You want to die of a stroke? You want to just pass away peacefully in your sleep and have everybody say it's a shame you died so young? Take your choice. They can arrange anything you want—if that's who we're dealing with."

"They're not going to do anything if we go to the Justice Department. The FBI. At the very least, even if no one believed us, the publicity would protect us."

"Who in the Justice Department do you want to go to, Doctor?"

"Hell, go to the attorney general. The head of the FBI. They're political appointees—they're not involved in anything like this."

"They're not?"

"Not both of them. Not all of them."

"And with what little we know now—unless the implants are there—we're still kooks. Right? And, if whoever is involved doesn't want us continuing to cause waves—even if we're laughed away—we could still end up dead."

"They?"

"They," the agent said. "Either on our side or somebody else's."

"On our side? And we're afraid they're going to kill us?"

"They look at the big picture."

Spence stared at the agent for a moment, then laid his head back against the seat.

A moment later Kennedy said, "You know, it wasn't just Joey who lost it when we got back after the last time."

He had a small grin on his face, the first time he had not looked serious since they had boarded the plane on the way to Montana.

"I lost it, too," he said. "Not for as long as Joey did, but maybe even more intense. They had me at a VA hospital for a week before they even felt safe enough to take the straitjacket off." He shook his head a little. "A former mental patient—I could have forgotten about ever getting a job back in the Bureau again. But that was one thing about working for the people I did. I knew the records would be erased. I knew I wouldn't even have to think about that when I reapplied. And I didn't."

24

SPENCE STOOD IN the dim moonlight. His lips were moving, but no sound came forth from his mouth. Now he raised his head. Before him, the fresh dirt of Dr. Lambert's grave was mounded into a small ridge several feet long. Flo had made certain there were plenty of flowers. They lined the grave on both sides. A large wreath sat tilted against the temporary marker.

"Say hello to Carol for me," he said, though he had never personally met Lambert's wife. Then he knelt, softly touched the dirt at the end of the grave, and turned and walked toward his car.

When he arrived at his apartment, he locked the door and went straight to the bedroom, pulling off his clothes and leaving them where they fell. He lay back in the bed, raising the chip on the tips of his fingers, looking up at it. And then he used the telephone on the bedside table to make a call.

"Hello."

"David, this is Spence Stevens."

"Computer's not messing up again?" David asked. "With the amount of money y'all spend over there, it looks like they could get you something other than a dinosaur for you to work on."

"No, it's working fine now. Thanks for your help. I've got a question."

"Shoot."

"If I had a computer chip. You know like one of the chips out of a hard drive. If I brought that chip in and laid it on a table in front of you, is there a way for you to tell me what's on it?"

There was a moment of silence on the other end of the line. "You mean a way to hook up something to it that can read it?"

"Uh-huh."

"I wouldn't doubt it, but . . . I've never thought about that."

"Would you try to find out if there is some way? I need somebody to read something off a chip for me. Just a single chip, detached by itself. It's important."

"Every time you call, Doctor, it's important. But, yeah, let me ask around and see. I'll get back to you."

"I need to know right away."

"Give me time to think of who I'm going to call first."

"Really, David, I need it done right away. Tonight if you can—whatever it costs."

"Whatever it costs? That could give me an incentive if I didn't mind sticking it to you. But you can forget me finding out tonight."

"As soon as possible then," Spence said, and replaced the receiver.

"He has them then?" John said.

The telephone tap had been easy to install.

Genowski wasn't sure. "He just wants to know if they can be read. Logic is still with Kennedy having them."

25

HE HAD SLEPT little and rose early. He entered the laboratory just as the sun was coming up. Glancing at his watch, he walked straight to his office.

Lowering himself into the big chair behind his desk, he began punching a number into the telephone.

The voice that answered sounded sleepy.

"Am I waking you?"

There were a few seconds of silence, then David said, "No, Doctor, I always get up before the sun's up. I also always jog a hundred and fifty miles a day, eat Wheaties at every meal, and average having sex thirty times a day. No, you didn't wake me up. Not at all."

"Sorry. Did you find anyone who could read the chip?"

"Hell, Doctor, I don't even know anyone who gets up this time of morning."

"You couldn't find anyone last night?"

"I tried. I really tried. But Bill Gates wasn't taking any calls at the time."

"Sorry, David. Please let me know as soon as you can."

"When I know, you'll know, Doctor."

Spence replaced the receiver, stood, and walked to the window at the side of the office. The sun was visible now. He looked through the glass toward Tank's pen, thinking of what Flo had accomplished, then glanced at his watch again and walked back to the desk to make another call.

The voice that answered this time didn't sound sleepy.

"Bob, this is Spence."

"Yeah," the FBI agent said. "And I thought I told you to go back to doing whatever it is you do and let me call you when I'm ready."

"Have you thought of anybody who can make the x-ray yet?"

"Yeah, I've thought of several who can do it. But not any I'm certain I want to call."

"Okay," Spence said, realizing his impatience. "I'll wait until you call."

"Fine," the agent said. "I do have somebody going after the body though. I'll let you know when I hear more."

In Montana, Tommy lay on his back, his eyes closed, his fingers spread wide and his hands up close to his shoulders, where they had fallen after he had grabbed his head.

The rattlesnake sat coiled on his chest.

Twenty feet away, the finding device lay hidden under a stone.

The reptile stirred, and its head raised.

Its tongue flicked the air.

Sensing the vibrations, it uncoiled and slithered in a hurried zigzag pattern across the rough rocks, where it entered a hole formed by two slabs of fractured rock butting together.

A moment later, there was the sound of small rocks being jostled and two men in jeans, shining flashlights before them, crawled up on the five-foot barrier and came to their feet. They stared at Tommy's body, then walked to it, knelt down, and began fashioning a harness under his arms and across his chest.

Seconds later, they were dragging his stiff form across the rough surface on the way to the shaft leading up out of the site.

Less than an hour later, Tommy's body carefully stored a quarter-mile away underneath stacks of packing cases in the rear of an aging truck with GOODWILL INDUSTRIES stenciled on its sides, they stood at the narrow entrance to the shaft.

One of the men watched. The other set the timer on a small bundle of dynamite tied to the end of a nylon rope and lifted it over into the opening. Two other ropes already trailed down inside the hole. The three charges were to go off at different levels, ensuring the shaft was never used again.

When he had tied the rope to the steel pin next to the hole, the man rose to his feet and headed toward the other, who turned and walked with him down the gradual slope in the direction of the truck.

Neither of them spoke.

Walter Quinlan viewed the ground the men saw in front of them as they walked away from the shaft. Then he clicked the image off and stared into the mirror covering the wall above an ornate lavatory complete with solid gold faucets. He was looking at his face.

He stood there for several seconds, staring intently, then reached to his head and jerked off the patch covering his sightless eye.

He continued to stare. Nothing marked the eye as unseeing, but it was.

It was, and he couldn't stand it.

His features beginning to twist with anger, he lifted the patch up in front of his good eye, looked at it for a moment, then flung it across his bathroom.

Kennedy, already fully dressed despite the early hour, sat on the small patio off the kitchen, drinking coffee, his portable telephone lying in his lap.

The telephone rang. He looked at it for a moment, wondering if it was Spence calling back again, then lifted it to his ear.

"Hello."

It wasn't Spence. It was the FBI agent to whom he had

faxed a copy of the prints he had lifted from the plastic card holder in his wallet.

"Got a positive match," the agent said. "Name's Tommy Rhiner."

And then he proceeded to tell Kennedy the county in Montana where Tommy Rhiner lived, that he had been born in the state, lived there all his life, and had no previous criminal record. From what could be found out on such short notice, he was well thought of in his home area, a prominent member of his church and active in the community. In fact, he was said to be contemplating a run for Congress in the next election with a good chance of capturing the post.

After Kennedy finished with the conversation, he sat thinking for a few seconds. What had been the man's connection to this? If there hadn't been any prints as with Alfred Wynn and maybe even Walter Quinlan to this point ... If there hadn't been any, maybe things would start tying together, at least start showing some type of pattern. But there were prints. Was there no connection? There had to be a connection. He reached to his hip pocket, feeling the wallet he was carrying there. The two computer chips were securely taped inside it. He had slept with the wallet lying on the bedside table next to him. Soon there would be somebody there to get them. He was surprised they hadn't already arrived.

And then something occurred to him. He raised the telephone again and hit redial.

He lifted it to his ear and waited.

"Hello," a female voice answered. She had a Jamaican accent.

"Polly," he said. "This is Bob Kennedy. I've been trying to reach Michael for two days."

"He's on leave, Mr. Kennedy. He left me a note that he was going to Virginia Beach for a few days."

"Did he say where he was staying or leave a number?"

"No. The note only said Virginia Beach."

"Thank you," Kennedy said. "I appreciate it."

As he replaced the receiver, his wife walked from the house. She was already fully dressed in a skirt and blouse and was brushing her hair. "You're worrying me, Bob."

He came up out of the rocking chair and turned toward her. Cupping his hands behind her waist, he pulled her against him, where the side of her face lay against his shoulder.

"Honey," he said, "it's my job. It's what's expected of me."

She nodded her head against his shoulder. "I know."

"I give you my word I'm not working with them again."

"I know that. It just worries me when . . . when secret things start happening again."

"You didn't worry about what I was doing for twenty-five years."

"Because I didn't know what you were doing," she said.

He caught her shoulders gently and moved her face back a few inches from his. "It's no big deal. Except some bureaucrat in Washington decided to label this hush-hush." He hated to lie, but even more he hated to see her worrying.

She nodded. "I have to get on. Mother is determined she's going to the mall. You know if I don't get there by the time she gets up she'll try to drive herself—and at her age . . ."

He kissed her on the forehead. "I'm tired. I think I'll stay here rather than go into the office. Maybe when you get back, we can go get some lunch together."

"I'd like that," she said.

As she walked back into the house, he glanced back at the sun, then followed after her. In the kitchen, he turned his back to the counter, leaning against it. He wondered if the body had been recovered yet. He walked to the refrigerator and opened it.

"You want me to fix you some breakfast before I run?" his wife asked behind him.

"No," he said, lifting half of a cantaloupe out. "Is this still good?"

"It's only two days old," she said.

He pulled the plastic wrap from it. "This will do fine then."

"Love you," she said.

"Love you. Be careful."

As he sat down at the end of the breakfast table and began to salt and pepper the melon, he heard the front door close.

Seconds later, his wife backed out of the driveway.

He twisted the end of a spoon down into the melon and lifted a plug of the sweet fruit into his mouth.

As he chewed, he kept waiting for someone to open the door and come inside for the chips. They would have seen she's gone. He glanced at his watch. He looked across his shoulder at the telephone on the counter and thought about using it, but knew he couldn't take the chance.

He would go to the office. The telephone lines there weren't secure, but there were literally scores of them leading to the thick cables that contained hundreds of other telephone lines in the Federal Building. Nobody was that good. Not that quick. Not with that many cables to sort through. The line in his office would be the one he would speak on.

He heard the hiss and felt the moist spray hit the side of his face at the same moment. He kicked his chair back from under him and whirled around. He threw up his hand to knock the can away and fired a looping overhand right at the big man's face. But his hand missed the can and his fist sailed harmlessly through the air as the man ducked quicker than he would have thought possible.

Then Kennedy felt the effects. He gasped, his eyes widening at how quickly it was happening, and he dropped to his knees and toppled forward to slam heavily to the floor.

Hands were going through his pants pocket before his arms quit moving against the tile. His wallet was slipped out.

There, in the middle of a plastic credit card holder, taped carefully shut so they couldn't fall out, were two tiny computer chips.

But only two.

The view through Tommy's eyes had shown him thrusting three into the young doctor's hands.

In Montana, three men had stepped from the old pickup parked next to a barren bluff. Dressed in jeans, heavy boots, and jackets common to the area, they laughed and gestured like any trio of friends until they neared the property line of the old ordnance testing ground. Then they stopped for a moment, surveyed the area around them, and, now silent, their eyes darting from side to side, hurried across the hard ground, finally breaking into a rapid trot.

That they weren't breathing hard when they reached the entrance to the shaft was a testimony to the shape they were in. The lead man, a strongly built six-footer with long hair bouncing against his shoulders, unbuttoned his coat and reached inside it without slowing his pace as he neared the opening.

A long coil of rope came out. The other two men angled out to his left and right. At the rhythmic *thump, thump, thump*, of helicopter blades they looked up. One of them, the largest of the three at over six-feet-four, cupped his hand over an earpiece attached to a wire running up from inside his coat.

He said something into a tiny mike pinned to his jacket lapel, then nodded at what came back through the earpiece, and looked toward the shaft. "Still clear," he said.

The man staring down into the shaft shook his head.

"It's been dynamited shut."

The large man spoke into his mike again. This time his words were louder. "Bastards closed it. We're going to need drilling equipment."

26

FREDDIE ARRIVED AT the lab a little more than two hours after Spence had telephoned Kennedy and David. Slipping on his lab coat and buttoning it as he walked into the office, the young lab assistant nodded and said, "Good morning."

Spence glanced at his watch and smiled. "You getting here this early?" he said. "Maybe we ought to record this on tape. You finally started feeling guilty about skipping out early every day?"

"Not guilty at all with what I get paid," Freddie said. "And if you ever want to see me here this early again, you better get it on film."

He walked to the chair in front of the desk and lowered his long body into it. "Flo said all the cultures *had* to be rotated at . . ." He looked at his watch. ". . . in exactly fifteen minutes, and she couldn't do it all by herself. I should have told her I would help her for a week's salary."

He stuffed his hands down inside his lab coat pockets and leaned back in the chair. "She told me about coming by your apartment," he said, a grin across his face. "She's embarrassed. Beats the hell out of me why, but she admires you. I mean, she's not only here all day working with you, but she takes your notes home and studies them like they're Nobel Prize material." He nodded. "Yeah, she admires you. But more than that she has a crush on you."

Spence looked toward the laboratory door.

"But she's a few years older," Freddie continued, "so

she assumes you wouldn't be interested." His grin widened. "Now if it was me she felt like that about, I'd jump on her like a big buck deer in rutting season."

"I'm certain that would thrill her, Freddie. Is she here yet?"

Freddie looked at his watch. "She has fourteen more minutes. She's probably seen the Bronco and is wandering around the hall trying to get up the courage to come in. She really doesn't want to face you after acting like she did at your apartment."

"She didn't act in any way. She just told me she was sorry for coming over and disturbing me when I had somebody there. Does she know you're telling me this?"

"Hell, no, she'd skin me alive. What gets me is you've never noticed the way she looks at you. I figured she'd make some kind of move before now. What happened to your lip?"

"Bumped it."

"Looks like a cat scratched it," Freddie said, pulling his body together and standing. "But I knew you didn't have a cat. Well, the messenger delivered the message about the forlorn and unloved Juliet and hasn't been put to the sword . . . at least on this end. If you tell her what I just said I will be—and she'll twist it as she rams it in."

As Freddie walked to the door and out of the office, Spence leaned back in his chair. Hell, he thought, Freddie says it now. Christen said it. Maybe he *was* blind. He glanced toward the door. If he was that blind, his main concern would be that he had hurt her feelings without even knowing it. That would make it hard for her to work with him. Why she was even working at the laboratory he didn't fully understand in the first place. She not only was one of the smartest people he had ever met, she had to have been one of the smartest students ever in the field not to have gone ahead and gotten her doctorate. She had said during her interview that she had to catch up on what she owed, first. With her parents dead since she was eighteen, she had footed the entire bill for her education and was burdened with student loans. But doctorate or not, she could have gotten a job anywhere, especially at some of the big company laboratories, where she would have made more of the money she needed, too. But she had told him she wanted to work where any discoveries would be made available to all other scientists in the field. The big private companies, while certainly paying more, were also the most insistent on secrecy. And that, very simply, was why she had asked to work with him.

Intelligent. Compassionate. Obviously not obsessed with how much money she could make. She would be a good catch for some man. He wondered why she had never appealed to him in that way? But she hadn't. It certainly hadn't been because of the difference in their ages. Maybe their relationship had been too professional, as she had said.

But, again, despite Christen's and Freddie's words, Flo had never given him the slightest indication that she might—

"Spence, where in the hell have you been?" The words pulling him out of his thoughts were spoken by Dr. Hal Gregory before he even came through the office doorway. "Have you forgotten—championship playoff. All the marbles. The big showdown. And you're the only guy we've got on the team who can dribble a basketball without kicking it out of bounds. You weren't here yesterday, and Flo said you might not be back. Do you have any idea what that did to my nerves, old buddy? Have your jock on in two hours, Spence. Early-morning Armageddon."

"Hal, I don't know."

The tall neurologist narrowed his eyes. "What do you mean, you don't know? Damn, you don't know about what?"

The last thing in the world Spence felt like doing was going to the gym and getting into the bumping, shoving, shouting matches that went on during their league basketball games. Joey's body would be arriving soon. His funeral would probably be the day it got back. He had to call Patricia—he hadn't even gone to see her yet. He kept seeing the body lying on a pile of rocks at the bottom of the shaft. He was waiting on David to get somebody to read the chip. Kennedy was trying to get somebody to read the chips. Basketball was the last thing on his mind.

"Listen, Spence," Hal said. "You're the one who talked me into playing on your team in the first place. I told you I didn't get enough sleep as it was."

Hal took a deep breath as he paused. "Tip-off's in one hour," he said. "I hope to hell you're there."

His last words had contained a genuine note of irritation. Spence had never heard that before, not directed at him. Hal's eyelids were drooped. He probably hadn't gotten enough sleep in days. Spence knew he wouldn't be a staff neurologist and have to face their hours for all the money in the world. He didn't know how any of them ever got through their residency with their marriages still intact.

"Okay," he said.

"Whew," Hal said, raising his arm and acting as if he were wiping perspiration off his forehead with the back of his hand.

Then he hurriedly sat down in the chair and leaned forward on the front of the desk. "Now how in the hell do we whip 'em with Dr. Jefferson playing for 'em? Short of me taking a shot at his cruciate ligament during warmups."

Spence smiled. As he did, Flo poked her head around the doorframe. "Good morning," she said, looking at each of them in turn.

"Good morning," they said.

She smiled and disappeared back inside the lab.

Spence stared at the doorway.

There hadn't been anything different about her expression. Nothing she might have been thinking of. Nothing that he had done to hurt her feelings, either before in the laboratory or the night she had come by his apartment.

The truck stopping at the gate leading into the Walter Quinlan Biogenetics Research Center had DEEP-SOUTH CHEMICALS printed in big block letters across its sides. A guard

stepped up beside the cab, said something to the driver,
then pointed across the grounds, and the truck drove toward
a concrete block building the size of a small house near the
rear of the complex.

Two men in white lab coats waited next to the building's
steel entry door as the truck turned around and backed toward them. When it stopped, the driver and the man who
had been riding in the passenger seat, came back to its rear
and opened its double doors.

A canvas-covered case several feet in length and two
feet wide was slid out, and the four men, two on each side,
carried it inside the building.

Inside the case, Kennedy, his eyes closed, stirred when
the case was set hard to the floor, and then he didn't move
again.

Dr. Jefferson was a gynecologist—a six-foot-eight giant of
a black man with huge hands that made the newborns he
delivered look like toys when he took them into his hands.
He was also a former Jackson State basketball star who
might have made it in the pros if he had gone the tryout
route rather than opt to go straight into medical school. He
was the only domineering player they had to face in the
championship game—but that was almost like saying a
modern combat jet was the *only* thing a bunch of World
War I bi-wing fighter planes had to face.

Spence's game plan was for his team to keep getting the
ball inside, letting whoever was in the center spot charge
willy-nilly under the goal and try to loop the ball up over
Jefferson. They wouldn't score often that way, but the hope
was that if they did that long enough that Jefferson would
get into foul trouble before he fouled their entire team out.

Meanwhile, Spence knew his job would be to get the
ball down the court and prevent the other team from doing
that often enough to get some easy fast-break points. He
did have quick hands. He could hit a punching bag a half
dozen times before most could hit it twice. He had made
Second Team All-Conference as a senior at Delta State

based nearly solely on those hands and his defensive ability down the court. The scoring would have to be up to Hal, the only other player on the team with any college experience, having once played at Hinds. The game plan almost worked. Jefferson fouled out in the third quarter, and they came back, finally losing by only three points.

As Spence walked toward midcourt to shake hands with the other team's players, he looked up into the stands. He had seen Flo, dressed in slacks and blouse, come in during the halftime break and take a seat. But she wasn't there now. A moment later, finished with the congratulatory handshakes, covered with perspiration, and glad he had gone ahead and played the game—it had completely taken his mind off everything for the time that it had lasted—he walked toward the showers.

"Spence," Flo said. She had come up behind him. He turned around and she held out one cola in a paper cup and took a sip from another.

"Thank you," he said as he took it into his hand.

Coming to a league game wasn't something she did, not on a day when there was work in the laboratory. Maybe she did have something to say about her feelings and how he had reacted. She hadn't wanted to say something in the lab in front of Freddie. That was why she was here?

But instead of what he was thinking, she had something entirely different on her mind. "Spence, you've been gone twice in the last few days. First time on the spur of the moment right after that investigator Joey was here. Then the next time bringing me a note in the middle of the night that says you're going to have to miss Dr. Lambert's funeral. What's happening? I would have asked you at the lab, but I had to pick up some supplies and you were gone by the time I got back."

He started to shake his head that it was nothing. But she was obviously too bright to accept that. Then he thought how he *really was* staring into the eyes of one of the smartest people he ever knew. He had asked David about the computer chip, yet here he was standing directly in front of someone who had fixed the computers more than once herself. She would have done it more often, but David serviced the UMC computers and her time had been better spent working in eye research. But maybe not this time.

"I'm going to tell you," he said. "Because I have something you might can help me with. But what I'm going to tell you is going to shock you."

Her eyes narrowed at that.

"And I have to have your word that until this is all over, you won't repeat a word of anything I tell you to anybody else," he added. "I mean anybody."

She nodded.

As they moved up into the stands, she glanced at his cut lip, but didn't say anything. He could tell that her thoughts at the moment were on what she was about to hear.

Kennedy forced himself out of his stupor, struggling to get off the bunk. It took several seconds to even sit up, but then his head began to clear. Still unsteady in his movement, he managed to stand and walk slowly to the bars fronting his cell.

Colonel Michael Weaver stared back at him from a cell across the floor.

"I thought you were dead for a while," Weaver said.

Kennedy was so shocked he could hardly find his tongue.

"Where are we?"

"I'm not sure you really want to know," Weaver said.

There was no levity in his tone.

Dr. Spence Stevens's apartment was in northern Hinds County just inside the Jackson City limits. It was on the ground floor of a block of twelve similar two-bedroom units. A little girl had ridden her bicycle back and forth in front of the apartment for several minutes, and a teenage girl, speaking on a cell phone at the second floor walkway rail, had remained there for the longest time.

But there was no one present now. The heavyset man

stepped from his car and walked down the sidewalk toward the apartment.

The lock on the door was no problem. It took him less time to unlock it than it would take most people with a key. He stepped inside the apartment and shut the door behind him.

Before starting about his work, he concentrated for a moment. A box clicked on in his mind. Dr. Spence Stevens and his chief lab assistant, Flo, sat close together in the stands of a gymnasium, deep in conversation.

He clicked off the box, and now only saw the apartment's small living room. He reached under his windbreaker and pulled out a small viewing device. He clicked it on and a screen lit up.

Logic told him that the first place to look for a computer chip was in the bedroom. In a dresser drawer.

He strode toward the room.

Seconds later, he was turning slowly, holding the device out in front of him, his gaze on the viewing screen as he turned.

Flo continued to stare at Spence after he had finished telling her his story. She was devoid of all expression, either trying to make sense of it all or perhaps in shock.

Then she looked toward the exit leading from the basketball court. Two men dressed in jeans and sweatshirts stood there looking back toward the stands. She continued to look at them.

Spence looked in the same direction. "What?" he asked.

She turned her face back to his. "What did you say?"

"Do you know them?" He had never seen them before.

She hesitated a minute, and seemed distracted. "I, uh . . . one of them looked familiar. Like somebody I knew a long time ago."

When Spence looked back toward the exit, the men were gone.

27

HE HAD TOLD her everything. And Flo had no more idea than David where to find someone who could read what was on an individual computer chip. And Freddie had been wrong. Christen had been wrong. *Or I'm totally lacking in the ability to size up a situation,* Spence thought. And he had made it a special point to hear beyond simply what Flo was saying when they sat in the stands. Her inflection. Her tone. How she looked at him as she spoke. The night he had brought the note to her in the laboratory, even he had thought for a moment that he recognized some special attraction—how she had looked softly at him. But she had been so proud of herself with what she had accomplished with Tank. That was all the look had been.

He found it cocky to say, but she did admire him—Freddie was correct in that. But that was part of the reason she had come to work for him in the first place, and it had nothing to do with romantic attraction, but that he was totally dedicated to a field in which she was interested. More than interested. His notes or not, she had seen the clue in what he had recorded and used her own mind to improve the definition and focus directed into the nerves behind Tank's retina.

Then he thought about the notes again, scribbled page after page in his terrible handwriting and sitting on a dresser in the extra bedroom he used for his work at home. He turned the Bronco off of the street that led to the laboratory and drove toward the ramp leading up onto I-55.

It took him twenty minutes. A little girl rode her bicycle past on the sidewalk as he pulled into the parking spot in front of his apartment. When he stepped outside the Bronco, the teenager, Marie Ann, spoke on her cell phone at her accustomed spot next to the walkway rail a few feet down from her parents' second-story apartment, far enough away that there was no chance they could overhear what she was saying to one of her boyfriends. And she seemed to have a lot of them, he thought, a different face and a different car there to pick her up almost every other night. She leaned way out over the rail and waved at him. "Hi, Dr. Stevens," she called in her high-pitched voice.

"Hi, Marie Ann."

Dressed in tight shorts, and a too-tight T-shirt that stretched across her budding chest, she turned to the side and bent one bare leg slightly, resting her foot against her other ankle. Posed that way, never stopping talking on the telephone, never taking her eyes off him, she smiled until he disappeared underneath her. He unlocked his door and stepped inside the apartment.

He walked toward the spare bedroom. Notebooks and folders containing loose pages were in two stacks a foot tall at the far end of the dresser.

Sorting through them, he quickly found the notebook he was looking for.

He lifted it in front of him and turned through the first few pages, stopping where he had been recording the complexity of the focus and definition apparent in the impulses after they had reached far enough to be centered on the optic nerve.

Then, over the top of the notebook, he saw in the corner of the dresser mirror a stocky man stepping silently out of the closet and coming quickly toward him.

He held a small can in his hand.

The word *Mace* appeared in Spence's mind even as he spun quickly and slapped the can from the man's hand and swung his balled fist hard at the square chin.

The punch hit home, and he had already drawn his hand part-way back and started to hit again by the time the notebook hit the floor. Stunned by the first blow, the man's knees buckled at the second punch, and he collapsed backward at the third punch of the lightning-fast series.

Spence spun back to the dresser and jerked its top drawer open. When he turned back around he held his thirty-eight in his hands.

The man had quickly regained his feet.

He stared at the revolver.

Then he suddenly dashed for the door.

Spence raised the weapon but didn't fire. He dashed after him.

They sprinted through the living room, the man throwing a chair back behind him and Spence hurdling over it. The man dashed into the kitchen and grabbed for the door to the patio, and Spence caught up to him and slammed the heavy weight of the revolver hard into the back of his head. Stunned, the man started to collapse, then whirled around, his thick balled fist striking out quicker than Spence could have expected.

Caught full in the face by the hard blow, he felt himself stumbling backward.

Where the man's suit coat had come open, Spence saw the shoulder holster. Even as he saw the butt of the automatic sticking from it, the man's hand reached for the weapon.

Spence fired.

The bullet caught the man in his broad shoulder, knocking him around into the door. He spun back around, leaning against the glass panels, his hand reaching for his weapon.

Spence cocked the revolver.

The hand stopped, moved to the wound, seeping blood and spreading a bright red across the man's white shirt.

He slowly sank down the wall to sit on the floor, his legs bent and his knees raised up in front of him.

Keeping the revolver pointed, Spence stepped backward

to the wall telephone, lifted the receiver, and used his thumb to punch in 911.

The police car couldn't have been more than a block from the apartment. The siren sounded immediately. In less than a minute, two uniformed officers were hurrying through the living room toward the kitchen. Their automatics were held at the ready out in front of them.

Spence had never taken his eyes off the butt of the automatic in the shoulder holster. "He has a weapon."

"Give me the revolver," the larger officer of the two said. As the other officer went to the man sitting against the bottom of the door, the larger one repeated, "Give me your pistol."

Spence loosened his grip around the revolver handle, turned the weapon in his hand and handed it over butt first. "He has a weapon under his coat," he said.

But the larger officer didn't even seem to hear the warning. "Turn around," he said.

Spence looked toward him and stared directly into the pointed automatic.

"Turn around, Doctor."

The smaller officer was helping the man at the door to his feet. The automatic in the shoulder holster remained in easy reach.

"Turn around, you bastard," the wounded man yelled, still holding his shoulder.

The officer beside Spence extended the barrel of the automatic until it was only a few inches away. "You're under arrest," he said. "Turn around and cross your wrists behind your back."

28

THE WOUNDED UNDERCOVER officer was lying propped
up on his elbow on the gurney inside the rear of the ambulance. The paramedics had temporarily bandaged the
shoulder, to stop any more blood from seeping from the
wound. "The son of a bitch said the coffee pot was on and
he wanted to turn it off before he came down to the precinct
with me," he said. "He grabbed the pistol out of the drawer
and shot me before I knew what was happening."

The older officer standing at the rear of the ambulance
nodded. He was a black man with sergeant's stripes across
his sleeves. The paramedic pulled the doors closed, blocking the gurney from view, and the sergeant turned to stare
back toward the apartment. He had a spider mike attached
to his shirt's lapel, but he lifted the handheld radio he had
been using instead and spoke into it. "Officer Jennings was
serving an arrest warrant for the traffic violations. The doctor went crazy and shot him. I guess it shocked him back
to his senses when he saw what he had done. His story is
that Jennings was already in the house and he thought he
was a burglar. He said a teenager on the balcony can verify
Jennings didn't come in after he did. She says she wasn't
paying any attention. She remembered the doctor coming
in but didn't notice if anybody else did or not. She couldn't
see down to the door anyway. She was on a balcony above
the apartment. He said there was a little girl on a bicycle
that saw him come in just before the shot. We can't find

her, and he says he doesn't know who she was. Probably something else he's making up."

Spence, sitting in the back of a police car, his hands cuffed behind him, watched the sergeant's eyes come around to him. One of the rear doors stood open and Spence could hear the words clearly.

"I want you to get to the judge before we go down there and make sure this bastard's not going to get out on bail. He meant to kill a police officer."

Spence had been almost too shocked to speak when he found he was under arrest. The undercover officer, Jennings, had started a story about knocking on the apartment door, showing a warrant, and being allowed inside the house. Spence remembered realizing how much trouble he was in when he started protesting and the officer arresting him told him to shut up, and he didn't, and he found his face being driven into the wall by a hard shove against the back of his head. It had caused the cut on his lip to open again. Blood had trickled down to drop off his chin and stain his shirt. The blood was now dried against his chin, but his mind hadn't quit racing since the shock of the blow and his realization that the wounded officer had to be one of them.

But he hadn't said anything. To do so would make him sound as crazy as the officer claimed he had been when he turned around with the revolver out of the kitchen drawer.

Especially when he saw the wounded officer hand a warrant to the sergeant. The bastard had come prepared, even to the point of having an actual warrant. *You can't even imagine,* Kennedy had said.

But more important to Spence now was what the sergeant had said about getting to the judge and making certain there was no bail. He had to make a phone call. He had to let Kennedy know what was happening. He couldn't call him directly though. He couldn't call anybody and say what he wanted to say. Who might be listening? He looked at the officer standing by the open door, then moved his gaze to the sergeant.

Flo. He could call her. He could call her and not say anything except that he was under arrest. She would come to where he was. If they allowed him to talk to her, he could think of some way to get the message across. *But would he be putting her in danger?*

No. The police wouldn't find anything unusual in a lab assistant and friend coming down to see about him. Freddie would probably come, too. And surely somebody in authority from the university, certainly not believing the officer's story that he had gone crazy. His gaze moved to his apartment as the large frame of police chief Carlos Solomon filled the doorway.

He had arrived at the scene only seconds after the second police car. He had told the other officers that they needed to be especially careful about preserving the evidence or they would never get a conviction against "somebody of a doctor's prestige." Solomon had gone into the apartment and ordered the officers already in there to step outside until the forensic people and photographers arrived, then had remained inside the apartment, closing the door behind him.

Now he stared toward the police car.

Spence watched him walk across the sidewalk toward him. When the police officer stepped aside and Solomon leaned down to look inside the rear of the car, he spoke in a soft voice that belied his great size. "Did the paramedics look at that lip?"

"It's okay." Spence wanted to say something else. Explain. But he was afraid to talk to anyone, even someone with Solomon's reputation. It would take more than an explanation to convince anyone he wasn't crazy. He had to get word to Kennedy.

The officer who had been standing outside the door was reaching inside it now. "Come on," the man said, cupping his hand toward him. Spence scooted across the seat and was assisted out of the car and on to his feet.

Solomon smiled politely. "You're going to ride with me," he said, "where we can talk."

A few minutes later, Solomon turned south on I-55, toward downtown. He looked back across the seat. There was no metal screen separating them. "You want to tell me your version of what happened?" he asked in a soft voice.

Spence knew there was nothing he could say that would be believed, so the only thing he said was what he had already told the other officers. "He was inside the house. He stepped out of my closet and came after me. I got the revolver out of the dresser drawer, not out of the kitchen drawer." Then he remembered that Hal knew he kept it in the dresser drawer. Hal had found it when he was going through the drawer looking for a dry T-shirt after they had returned from playing one-on-one at the gym. "It wasn't in the kitchen drawer," he repeated. "It was in the dresser drawer."

Solomon nodded. "And . . ."

There was nothing else to say.

Solomon waited a moment, then turned his face back toward the windshield.

Without looking back over the seat, he said, "I obviously have to rely on the word of my officers. I'm sure you can understand that. But, uh . . . you are making strong claims against him. I . . . uh, is there anyone who might vouch for how you were acting this morning? I mean anyone you've spoken with who could verify . . ." He looked back and smiled pleasantly again. ". . . that you were acting stable when they spoke with you? This morning, or even let's say from early last night . . . Anyone you might have spoken to? Another physician? A friend? One of your lab assistants maybe? Maybe you could even tell me what you discussed as you remember it."

Even as Spence stared into the dark face that held such a pleasant expression, he felt a sensation of uneasiness spread across him. The cop inside the house had obviously been one of them. Now Solomon the chief was asking questions that no one would be expected to answer until they had spoken with an attorney.

You can't even imagine.

"Anyone?" Solomon repeated. "Anything in particular you discussed."

When Spence didn't answer, Solomon turned back to the windshield again.

A moment later he was guiding his car off the interstate onto Fortification Street, not the normal way to get downtown.

A few hundred feet farther, he turned right onto Greymont Avenue, a wide two-lane that passed through an older quiet neighborhood spotted with hundred-year-old oaks as it ran toward Belhaven College. Solomon drove to the curb and stopped. Spence looked out the window and then back at the chief. Solomon had turned and held what looked like a small video camera back over the seat. The camera slowly swept up and down Spence's body, like he was being photographed.

Now Solomon was opening his door and stepping from the car. A Miskelly Furniture truck passed them on its way toward the college.

"Step outside," Solomon said. Spence glanced out the back window. There was no more traffic coming down the street. It was Memorial Day weekend. Everybody was already out of town or had arrived and were now relaxing in their backyards, barbecuing and swimming. The thought that was going through his mind was impossible. Chief Solomon?

No, he thought. He was letting his emotions run away with him. He was accusing a police officer of burglary. The chief was just trying to find out what happened. That had been all his questions meant. Spence scooted across the seat.

"Turn around," the chief said.

When Spence did he felt Solomon's fingers work at the handcuffs, and then they clicked and came off. He turned back around in the seat to face the big man.

Solomon nodded him out of the car.

When Spence stepped to the pavement, Solomon spoke in a low voice: "Where is the chip?"

The sudden shock that Spence felt was like a blow, causing his legs to weaken.

Solomon's expression didn't change; it was still pleasant, despite what he represented now. A pickup truck was passing by. Spence looked at the man driving it, but the man was looking straight ahead. He felt Solomon's big hand close around his forearm. The voice was cold now. "If you tell me where the chip is. Right now. You'll be okay. If you don't tell me. I'm going to kill you. Right here on the spot. I'll grab you, we'll be wrestling—you told me if I let you out of the car you would tell me what really happened when you shot the officer. I believed you. You went for my gun. You know I can get away with it. Where's the chip? Right now."

Spence swung hard. The fleeting change in Solomon's expression told that he was surprised at how quick the fist moved even as it caught him under his mouth. A second blow followed, a third started, and was stopped as Solomon, moving even quicker, grabbed Spence's forearm. But the blows had rocked the chief a partial step backward. Spence tore his forearm loose from the crushing grip and swung his other hand toward the jaw.

Solomon blocked that with a blurred move of his forearm. Spence butted his head into the thick chest, and Solomon rocked backward again. Spence dashed toward the rear of the car and started to turn toward the sidewalk beyond it, but seeing a pickup and two cars coming up the street, he sprinted toward them.

Solomon closed the gap quickly. Spence started to dash in front of the pickup. The driver slammed on his brakes. Spence darted past the side of the truck and raced behind it only an instant before the car following it crashed into the pickup's rear. Solomon, almost caught between the vehicles, had stopped and jumped backward at the last second. He was still so close that the front bumper of the car brushed against his uniform when it was jolted to the side by the collision.

The second car now slammed into the others. Spence

sprinted up the driveway between two houses across the street. Solomon came around the front of the pickup and raced after him. People were opening the doors of the cars. Solomon had his automatic in his hand. He sprinted toward the driveway. Spence was nearing its end and angled to his left, running between the rear of the house to that side and its detached guest house. He raced past a swimming pool behind the guest house, laid his hand on top of a four-foot privacy fence, and vaulted over it into the yard of the house backing up to the property.

Solomon had sprinted up the drive and stopped. He looked at the glassed-in sunporch at the rear of the house to his left. In front of him was a guest house with the same white clapboard exterior as the main house. To his right, thick trees dotted another backyard. He could see no one running.

Spence raced down the line of trees running along the backyards of one house after another. He was breathing heavily, but kept sprinting. A cyclone fence barred his path. A rottweiler jumped against the wire and barked. Spence angled toward the house's front yard. He slowed a moment as he neared the street in front of the house, looking to make certain no vehicles were in sight, and then sprinted across the pavement.

He glimpsed the start of commercial buildings, beginning one street over. A police car passing on that street caused him to stop abruptly, but the car sped on past.

Then he suddenly stopped.

Not even Kennedy knew about him keeping one of the chips when he had passed the other two over to the agent at the bottom of the underground site. But Solomon knew. He had said *the* chip. One chip. If Solomon knew that, then he knew where the other two were. Kennedy was in danger and didn't know. Spence turned down the edge of the pavement toward the commercial area.

Solomon drove his unmarked car slowly along the streets in the Belhaven area. Genowski mirrored him a few streets over, passing the tree-covered lots closer to the college.

A horn honked behind Genowski, and a car with a young blond-haired driver passed him and turned into the college.

In a wider circle spreading out around the area, several police cars slowly patrolled the streets. Three of them were driven by officers not normally slated for duty this day but volunteering to come in on this particular search.

Spence stopped at the edge of the pavement and caught his breath, then trotted across the street toward the two pay telephones at the back of an Ergon station. Reaching them, he called information for the FBI office's number, then fumbled in his jeans pocket until he found the proper coins and dropped them into the slot at the top of the telephone.

When a female voice answered, he said, "I would like to speak with Special Agent Bob Kennedy."

"I'm sorry," she said, "but he's not in yet. Would you like to leave a name and number?"

He replaced the receiver, then lifted it again, dropped in the coins, and touched in Kennedy's home number. He looked across his shoulder up and down the street. A man stepping out of the station glanced toward the telephones before he walked on to his car, sitting in front of one of the gas pumps.

Kennedy's number rang twice. Three times. Four times. Five times. He kept waiting.

Six times. Seven times. Eight times.

He closed his eyes in exasperation and replaced the receiver. His eyes still closed, a thought passed through his mind. When Solomon was questioning him in the car he asked for him to reconstruct the details of his whereabouts, including whom he had spoken with. *Even let's say from early last night.*

Early last night. When he had arrived back in the private jet with Kennedy. Solomon knew the exact time the jet had come back. He knew. How? He knew about the chips and who had how many. How? He knew everything.

And something else. Solomon had asked whom he might

have spoken with. Another physician? he had asked. A
friend? *One of your lab assistants maybe?* Flo.

He quickly reinserted the coins and rang the lab number.

He waited even longer than he had with Kennedy. Eight
rings. Nine rings. Ten rings. Eleven rings.

Nothing. He glanced at his watch.

Where in the hell were they?

And then he saw the police car coming slowly up the
street.

He turned and walked quickly toward the front of the
station and then began running again.

Colonel Michael Weaver, already intubated and under general anesthesia, remained motionless as the tip of the steel
bit was pressed against his forehead. The motor hummed,
the bit spun, blurring the channels that ran down its length.
Bone chips piled up like sawdust around the small hole.

The tip of the bit stopped just before it entered the brain
matter.

A second doctor leaned across the table.

The tip of a scalpel was inserted in the hole and a tiny
incision was made through the layered membrane covering
the brain.

Now the doctor's gloved fingers held a wire not much
thicker than a human hair. At its end was a tiny copper-
colored microchip.

The chip was inserted into the furrow of a sulcus, and
pressed slowly through the incision into the tissue.

Perspiration broke out across the doctor's forehead. A
nurse standing next to him patted it away with a gauze pad.

29

SPENCE STEPPED FROM the bushes. He waited until the police car that had just passed along the street had driven out of sight and then he hurried to the block of pay telephones at the side of another service station. He dropped coins into one and touched in the lab number once more.

It rang once, then twice, then three times, then four times . . . He closed his eyes in exasperation.

Then he realized what had happened. Word had gotten to Flo about his arrest. To Freddie. To everyone at the medical center by now. She wouldn't be working in the lab as if nothing had happened.

He called her apartment number.

She answered on the first ring.

"Flo, I want you to—"

"Spence, where are you? Everybody is saying—"

"Flo, *shut up!*"

There was a stunned silence on the other end of the line. Now she probably thought he was as crazy as the police were saying he was. "Flo, what I told you in the gym. That's what's happening to me now."

"Happening to you?"

"Listen. It's . . . It's whoever they are. They're framing me. I don't have time to explain. Just don't believe anything you're hearing. But, Flo, the most important thing is not to tell anyone what I told you today. Don't tell anyone anything. Don't even say I spoke with you at all. Nobody knows."

"Spence, please, what is—"

"Flo, if you trust me at all, please do as I tell you. If you tell anybody . . . Say anything at all about what I told you, you could be putting your life in jeopardy. You know what happened in Montana. Please believe me, and don't say anything to anyone."

There was silence, again, and then she said, "I won't, Spence. How can I help you?"

He thought about Kennedy. He thought about asking her to try and contact the agent for him. But he had put her in too much danger already. Why in hell had he told her anything about what had happened in Montana? About any of this?

"Spence?"

"Flo, I have to go now."

"Spence, please."

"I have to go. I'll call back. But don't say anything to . . ."

He looked at the police car coming slowly up the street toward him.

He missed the cradle when he hurriedly hung the receiver up, and left it dangling on its cord behind him as he walked quickly past the front of the station and started moving down the sidewalk. He kept looking over his shoulder. The police car stopped at the intersection behind him, then turned, going in the opposite direction.

He slowed his pace and took a deep breath. He looked down at his jeans. They were spotted at the knees with dirt where he had knelt hiding in a yard. The front of his shirt was stained with the drops of blood that had fallen from his lip, and his sleeve had a streak of grime running from the wrist to the elbow.

He did the best he could to rub the marks away.

He kept walking.

There was still Kennedy.

He stopped at the next set of pay phones and quickly

touched the FBI office number in again. Kennedy still hadn't arrived for work. He tried the residence number again.

Once more it rang and rang with no answer.

He replaced the receiver. He caught his lip in his teeth. Then he called information, asked for *The Clarion Ledger*'s number, and called it.

"I'm sorry," said the woman who answered at the paper, "but Christen said she wouldn't be coming in today. Would you like her voice mail?"

He replaced the receiver and looked at the slot under the telephone for a directory. There was none there. He went to the next telephone. The third one had a worn copy, with its front cover missing. He quickly thumbed through it to the D's. He ran his finger down a page. DA . . . He turned the page. DANN . . . DANS . . . DANT . . . There was a number listed as C. Dantonio.

He tried it.

She answered on the first ring.

"Christen, this is Spence."

"My God, Spence, where have you been? They had a news break . . . They said the police were looking for you. What happened? Where are you?"

"Christen, I swear to God that cop was inside my house when I got there. He came out of the closet with a can of Mace. He was coming up behind me. I can't explain what's going on, but I swear I didn't do anything they're saying. It's . . ." He had started to say them. Who in the hell would Christen think *them* was?

"All I can do is ask you to believe me."

"I do. Where are you?"

"I need you to make a call for me." Nobody would think of her. Not even them. "There's an FBI agent named Bob Kennedy. I tried him, but I can't get an answer at his number. I need you to keep calling for me. I—"

"Spence, where are you? They're looking for you everywhere."

"Christen, listen. Will you do what I say?"

"Of course."

"Don't call from your house. It would be too dangerous for you."

"For me?"

"Just listen. Go to a pay telephone. Don't give Kennedy your name when he answers. Just tell him you're a friend of mine I told to call. Tell him to stay home once he gets there. Tell him he could be in danger. He'll know what you mean. Tell him I'm going to try to reach him."

"Are you going over there?"

"I'm going to contact him. Be sure and tell him to stay by the phone."

"Spence, I know you. We only met days ago—but I know you. I know you didn't do this, but they're looking for you. You need some time until this gets straightened out. Let me come and pick you up and I can take you somewhere safe."

"No."

"Please, Spence. For yourself, but for me, too. I'm so scared something might happen. They . . . they said you tried to take the chief's gun away from him and he said he knew you were going to shoot him. They're saying you're armed and dangerous. They might shoot you when they see you without even giving you a chance. Let me come after you and take you somewhere. Please?"

"No, I don't want you involved."

"I want to be involved."

"No."

"Spence, they're going to catch you. At least let me bring you a car so you can get out of the city."

"No."

"Spence, you know where my apartment is. You know what car I drive. It would sound logical to the police that you came over here meaning to speak to me and instead got cold feet and stole it. You can hot-wire it so it looks like I'm not involved at all. If you don't know how, I do. Please, just let me do something, please."

"Christen, this is too dangerous for you to—"

"Just let me leave a car for you somewhere. I can get back home without anybody knowing. If you just keep walking around, someone is going to see you."

"Christen, Dr. Lambert and Joey have already been murdered. I know both of them were killed over this."

She didn't say anything for a long moment. And then her voice again, lower now. "Spence, I know you're not crazy, and I . . . I don't know what's going on, but I believe you no matter how it sounds. Let me at least drop the car off. Leave it somewhere for you. Then I'll come back here and wait until morning to call the police. That'll give you time to get where you're going."

He waited a moment. Maybe if she didn't become any more involved than leaving the car. "Wait until dark. I want you to be able to tell the police you went to bed without noticing whether your car was still there or not."

"Okay," she said. "Where do you want me to bring it?"

He told her.

Then he made one more call.

"David, this is Spence."

He waited for the reaction he knew was coming if David had seen the news on television or heard it on the radio.

But there was none.

"I did find a guy who thinks he knows somebody who might can read a chip," David said. "He said he'd call me back in the morning—but that doesn't mean before the sun comes up."

"Okay, I appreciate it."

"When I hear, I'll call you. What time do you get to the lab?"

"I, uh, I'm not going to be in the office in the morning, David."

"I can leave a message on your answering machine at home."

"No," Spence said in a tone that came out too sharply. "No, it's not working right. Let me call you."

"Whatever you desire, Doctor."

As Spence replaced the receiver he knew David

wouldn't be making a call in the morning. David obviously hadn't seen the news yet. But he surely would by the next day. It would be in the paper by then, too.

He reached into his hip pocket and pulled out his wallet, opened it, and slid his finger down inside the little slot next to the plastic card holders. He lifted the chip out. He had wrapped it in tissue paper and then put a piece of foil from a gum wrapper around that to protect it. He stared at it a moment and then slipped it back into its slot and replaced the wallet in his pocket.

A police car was at the far end of the street and coming slowly his way.

He started walking again.

30

THE HEADLIGHTS CAME first. The car pulled slowly into the service station. It was Christen's black Lexus. She drove it by the pumps, as he had told her to do, then turned back out onto the street and drove toward the next intersection, a hundred yards away.

Seconds later, it turned east, and its taillights disappeared behind a line of trees and homes.

He gave her five minutes, more than enough time to get out of the car and walk out of sight, then he stepped out of the bushes and hurried along the dark sidewalk toward the intersection.

She had parked the Lexus against the curb. He closed his eyes in irritation. He had told her to leave it in the gravel driveway of the small home another hundred yards up the street. There was a FOR SALE sign on the house and no curtains in the windows; no one lived there at the moment.

But to park against the curb . . . If a police car happened by, it would certainly stop.

Glancing up and down the street, he began trotting toward the car.

A pair of headlights turning onto the street from a far intersection caused him to almost hurry off the sidewalk into a line of tall bushes to his side. But he saw by the running lights on the cab that it was only a big truck coming toward him. He began trotting faster.

Seconds later, he threw open the car's driver's door and
slipped in behind the steering wheel.

The keys were in the ignition.

Christen raised up from the rear floorboard, startling
him.

"*Damn*, what are you doing here? I told you—"

"Shhhh," she whispered, placing her forefinger over her
lips. "Yelling doesn't help."

"Dammit, Christen."

"Your vocabulary is getting rather limited, Spence."

He saw in the rearview mirror the headlights coming up
the pavement behind him. He turned the key, put the Lexus
in gear and guided it out away from the curb. The truck
behind him turned off at an intersection. Christen climbed
over the seat and plopped down beside him in a pair of
shorts and oversized sweatshirt. "Now," she said, "tell me
what is going on. I might get the Pulitzer out of this—if I
don't go to the penitentiary first."

He turned the car in the direction of her apartment.

"Spence." Her tone was serious now. "Will you *please*
tell me what's going on?"

"I can't."

"What do you mean, you can't? I'm doing this for you.
Why was the cop inside your apartment?"

"He was looking for something."

"What?"

He shook his head no.

"What, Spence?"

"I don't want you involved."

"I am involved, you nut. This is my car you're driving.
So, please, tell me now. What was he looking for?"

When he didn't say anything, she said, "Spence, why
did you ask me to bring you a car if you don't trust me?"

"I didn't ask you to. You're the one who suggested the
car."

"Whatever you called me for . . ." She placed her hand
softly on his shoulder. "Please, trust me, and tell me what's
happening before I go crazy."

He looked across the seat at her.

"Spence, I told you I know you didn't do anything wrong. But faith can carry a person only so far. Explain it to me. What was the cop after?"

"A computer chip." She *was* going to think he was crazy. "And Chief Solomon is involved. He's looking for it, too. That's why I can't turn myself in to the police."

Her brow wrinkled. "Chief Solomon?"

"And I don't know who else. But they're looking for it."

"A computer chip?"

He nodded.

"Where is it?" she asked.

"I've already told you more than I should have. I'm not going to tell you any more."

"Spence!" she exclaimed in exasperation. And then she spoke in a low voice. "You said Joey was murdered."

"Yes, and I don't want you to get hurt. Don't tell any-body—I mean anybody—that you helped me tonight."

"Do I look like somebody who wants to go to jail?" She was smiling again. And her voice was low, sweet. Her question and the smile almost made it look as if she was trying to be cute again. She still had her hand on his shoul-der. She raised it to his neck and gently massaged its side.

"Spence, if what you're saying really is true, they're going to find it. They've searched your apartment. You know they'll search the laboratory. They'll eventually . . ." She looked at his shirt and then his jeans. "You don't have it with you, do you?"

He didn't answer this time because he was staring into the rearview mirror. When he turned off the street in the direction of her apartment, he had noticed headlights turn behind him. He had made a second turn as they talked, and now he had just noticed the headlights swing in his direc-tion again. He pressed on the accelerator.

Responding to its powerful motor, the Lexus quickly increased its speed. He looked at the headlights. They were dropping farther behind.

"What?" Christen asked.

He watched the lights become dimmer. "Nothing," h
said.

"Spence, do you have it on you?"

The headlights turned off on another street now, ar
disappeared.

He breathed a sigh of relief, dropped his gaze bac
through the windshield, and eased the pressure on the ac
celerator.

"Spence?"

When he looked at her, she said, "Give it to me an
they'll never know."

"You're out of your mind. I told you Joey was dead–
murdered."

"They wouldn't know, Spence."

"No."

"You do have it on you, don't you?"

He saw the car then. It had its headlights off and it wa
a couple of hundred yards back. He would have never no
ticed it if it hadn't been passing directly under a street lam
as he glanced into the rearview mirror.

He stomped on the accelerator.

The Lexus jumped forward, its tires squealing.

"Spence."

She saw him glance in the mirror again, and she looke
back across the seat through the rear windshield.

"I'm going to turn right at the next street," he said.
was a street he had traveled often in a shortcut toward D
Heath's house. It was an old neighborhood, lined with sma
houses that rented cheaply, and old trees and shrubs tha
made some yards a veritable jungle. "When I stop I war
you to run into the bushes."

She braced her hands against the dash as they continue
to gain speed. He said, "That car's been trailing us with i
lights off." He looked in the rearview mirror and saw
pass under another streetlight. She was looking out the rea
windshield again. The car was gaining on them. He looke

at the speedometer. It read eighty miles an hour. He pressed the accelerator nearer the floor.

"You're going to get us killed," Christen said, reaching for her seat belt.

The intersection was directly ahead. "Hang on," he said loudly and jammed on the brakes. The front of the Lexus nosed down, and it began to slide sideways. He spun the wheel, and the rear of the car came around. He pressed the accelerator to the floor again, and the Lexus jumped forward down the intersecting street with a fresh squeal of rubber.

"Spence, my God, you're going to kill us!"

A yard thickly covered with bushes was just ahead on his right. Two more thickly grown yards sat down the sidewalk from it. He jammed on the brakes.

"Spence!"

The car slid to a stop.

"Get out."

Christen didn't move.

"Get out!" he shouted.

He glanced into the rearview mirror. The car behind them hadn't made the turn yet.

"Damn it, Christen, get out!"

"I'm staying with you."

The car behind them made the turn. Its headlights flashed on. He jammed the accelerator all the way to the floor.

With another piercing squeal, the Lexus leaped forward. Still gaining speed, he spun the steering wheel hard to the left. The car's rear slid around in the opposite direction, and he faced down a narrow blacktop as they lurched forward again.

Headlights swung around the corner behind him. Christen's purse had fallen out of the seat and lay against his foot on the accelerator. He reached for it and felt the heavy object inside it.

Looking in the rearview mirror and fumbling at her purse with his free hand, he opened it and felt inside. His

fingers touched the cold steel. He caught the handle a
lifted out a small thirty-two-caliber automatic.

She said, "I get nervous being alone at night."

Nothing else. Only that. As if there wasn't a car chasi
them. As if she might not be in a wreck and get killed
any minute now. He stuffed the revolver inside his wai
band.

"Give me the chip," she said, "and I'll get out. I'll ta
it to a ... I can't take it to the police, can I?" she said
a questioning tone.

"Hang on."

As they slid sideways again into another side street, t
bright headlights of the car behind him were right in l
face, so close he was surprised that the car's bumper had
clipped the Lexus's rear.

Christen was staring over the seat out the rear windo
"You can't stop now, can you?" she said.

"Bright observation," he said. She still showed no si
of panic. She had almost sounded like she was irritat
rather than scared when she had yelled at him about l
driving. She was incredible. Or she was crazy.

They were doing over a hundred. If any car pulled c
of a drive or street in front of him ... If anybody was jc
ging at night ... The headlights behind him began to p
out to the left of his taillights.

As they moved up beside the rear door, he wonder
why his stomach wasn't tight with fear, and then he realiz
it was. Everything had been happening so fast, he ju
hadn't had time to realize it. No time to think of anythi
A few blocks ahead of them a stoplight was turning aml
on its way to red. Two cars, side by side, were stopping
yield the right of way. He was going to have to stop.

And then he knew what he was going to do. His han
tightened on the steering wheel. Out of the corner of l
eye he watched the headlights coming up beside his do
A fleeting thought passed through his mind: *If those a
cops in an unmarked car pulling up beside me—innoce
cops who are only chasing a dangerous suspect...*

Then he saw the car was a new Lincoln.

Undercover cops didn't drive new Lincolns.

He saw in his side mirror the thick, chiseled face staring toward him. He jerked the steering wheel to the left, then back to the right in the next instant.

The Lexus had swerved only a couple of feet before straightening out again.

But it was enough. The other car's fender had been nudged by the Lexus's side. At the speed they were traveling it was almost as if the Lincoln was already riding on a cushion of air rather than holding traction on its wheels. The nudge had knocked it angling to the left. The headlights came back to the right again as the driver tried to pull it back in line, and then its rear started around. There was a bright glow of red at the Lincoln's tail as the brakes locked. The tires squealed. The car suddenly spun like a top propelled by the rapid twist of a child's finger. Three times. Four times it went around in the middle of the street, its momentum still carrying it forward. It quit spinning but was angled backward now, with its taillights showing and its headlights shining in the yards to one side of the street. Its wheels caught the curb, and it suddenly flipped, bounced up into the air, and crashed sideways into a big oak, wrapping around the tree.

A hubcap rolled in the opposite direction the Lincoln had gone, and the disk, shiny in the illumination of a streetlight, hit the opposite curb, bounced into the air, and disappeared into the bushes there.

Spence had his foot jammed as hard on the brake as it would go. The Lexus's nose started easing to the left, and he compensated carefully with a gentle turn of the wheel. The nose came back around, and the wheels, still squealing, angled in the opposite direction. They slid sideways to an abrupt stop. Two cars fifteen feet in front of him started through the light, now changed to green.

Christen's face was pale as she stared over the back of the seat. "You killed them," she said.

31

IT WAS INCREDIBLE good luck that the driver of the Lin
coln wrapped around the trunk of the oak tree had escape
with only a head laceration, the officer thought. The pas
senger had been even luckier. He only had the win
knocked from him. That they were even alive spoke won
ders for what front and side airbags did for safety. And th
strength of the Lincoln's construction. "They were in
black Lexus," the driver said, holding a handkerchief at h
forehead, trying to stem the bleeding from the gash ther
"When they drove past us, I recognized the doctor from th
photograph they showed on TV. I didn't get a good glimps
of the passenger. But there were two of them."

The officer looked back at the other officer repeating th
report they had called in a few minutes before. Patrol ca
were already speeding toward the area, all on the looko
for the Lexus. Chief Solomon, who had been out drivin
nearby on his way to a restaurant, had stopped by the scer
of the accident and then sped down the pavement in th
hope that he might aid in the search for a crazed man wh
had tried to kill a police officer and then tried to kill tw
citizens who had tried to stop him.

They were parked behind a clump of thick bushes along
service road leading into a new subdivision being bui
close to the reservoir.

"We must be in Paradise," Christen said, looking arou

at the newspapers and cans and paper bags from fast-food restaurants scattered along the side of the road. "Can't be hell or all that trash would already be burned up."

He stared at her in a mixture of disbelief and amazement. "Thirty minutes ago we could have been killed—and you're cracking jokes."

"What else is there to do? You rather hear me cry for mommy?"

"I'd think you were more normal."

"Me. You're the one who the cops say is crazy. And I don't know if I'm not starting to believe them. We're like Bonnie and Clyde now—I was with you when you ran that Lincoln into a tree."

Her voice lowered. "I hope to God, somehow, you didn't kill anybody."

"I hope not, too. But the way for you to get out of all this is let me drop you off and you don't say anything about being with me."

"It's my car."

"I stole it, remember?"

"If those people in the Lincoln didn't get killed, they've already told the police I'm with you."

"They wouldn't have been able to see you well enough to get a description."

"You don't know that. They could have. I could be involved now in something you say could get me killed—I could have been killed then. I'm . . ." Then her voice sank lower again. "I am scared. I'm trying to sound like I'm not, but I am. And I'm most scared because you won't be up-front with me. You say for me not to call from my apartment. You say that Chief Solomon is involved in something so I can't trust the police. Now maybe somebody is looking for me, and I don't even know why. I don't know what to be scared of, and that scares me even more." She stared directly into his eyes. "Don't you think I deserve to know now?"

"I really don't know for certain myself, Christen. I just know there are other people like the chief involved. People you would never think would be involved in anything. That's why it's so dangerous. . . ." He stared at her for a moment. "And that's why I should have never let you bring me the car." He reached for the ignition. "I'm going to take you out to the highway where you can call a taxi."

She laid her hand on his forearm, stopping him.

"So somebody can be waiting at my apartment for me?" she asked.

He laid his head back against the seat. "Damn, Christen."

"Your vocabulary is regressing again," she said, and smiled her smile that was more of a grin—her attempt at not giving in to her fear. She did deserve to know more.

"The military conducted some kind of experiment. It had to do with working with brain waves. There's somebody— a bunch of them evidently—trying to keep anything from getting out about the experiment." He shook his head a little then. "And I'm not certain about this, but I think that maybe some of the subjects of the experiment are . . . I think it worked, and some of the subjects are out there right now, walking around like you and me, maybe with computer chips implanted in their brains."

Christen shook her head in disbelief. "Spence, I—"

"Maybe I am crazy, Christen," he said before she could say anything more. "But if I am, so was Joey. And so is Kennedy."

She sat there a moment without speaking, as shocked as he had expected her to be. Finally, she said, "Did you get him on the phone?"

He shook his head. "Nor his wife."

"You think somebody . . ."

"I don't know."

"What are you going to do now?"

"I'm going to try to get a plane out to . . ."

When he didn't finish, she said, "Damn, Spence, why do you keep holding back? As crazy as all this sounds . . . As crazy as you sound . . . Still, if I wasn't on your side, all I would have to do is take you up on putting me out to call a taxi and call the police instead. But, hell, don't tell me. Let's just go get a plane out. To wherever in hell."

To Montana and get the body out of the shaft and—somehow—get the head x-rayed. It was his only chance. And then pray to God there was an implant. "Not in this car," he said. "Every cop in the state has its description by now." He glanced across his shoulder out the rear windshield.

"So what are we going to do?" Christen asked.

"What I'd like to do is get you out of here to a taxi. But if you won't do that, then I'm going to sit here until it gets late enough that there's not much traffic, and then I'm going to get another ride."

"Steal one?"

"Sort of."

"Why don't you let *me* take the plane out?" she asked. "The chip's the key to proving everything, isn't it? I could take it where you want it taken. I could take the taxi you were talking about. We could both take taxis. You . . ." She thought for a moment. "You tell me where it needs to go. If somehow you do get recognized, I'll get it there. If you make it to the plane, I'll give it back to you then."

"I'm not getting you involved."

"Damn it, Spence, I've told you, I'm *already* involved. You do have it on you, don't you?"

When he didn't say anything, she said, "Yeah, you do have it, and you're going to keep on not listening to me until you get caught and it's gone." She shook her head, sighed audibly, and then looked out her window. "The scenery is not so bad if you concentrate on the moonlight and overlook the garbage," she said in a deadpan tone.

Then she looked at him, stared for a moment, and slid across the seat toward him, facing him from only a few inches away. She moved her face closer and kissed him gently on the cheek. "You're an idiot for not listening to me," she said. "But why should I expect you to be different from any other man? The stakes are on the poker table and your male machismo rises to the top—don't want any dippy little woman getting in your masculine way. Okay, I'll just lie on your shoulder and be the good little female until they take you away." Her face came around in front of his. "What's wrong with your lip?" she asked.

"Somebody hit me."

She shook her head again. "You do live a wild life," she said, and grinned. She pressed her lips gently against the small laceration. "Does that make it all better?" she asked. "Now that the gentle little female has kissed it? That's what I'm good for, isn't it?"

He didn't answer her. She stared at him for a moment and then pressed her lips to the spot again, then slid her mouth over his, and kissed him again, her lips pressing harder now. Her hand touched the flat of his stomach. Her eyes stared into his. Her hand remained where it was, not moving, as he looked back into her eyes. He noticed her perfume for the first time that night. Her face came forward again, and she kissed him again, this time with her lips parted wider than before, and he responded with the same kind of kiss. Her hand moved against his stomach again, her palm pressing softly, moving from side to side, and lower. Despite all that had happened, despite his nervousness, he felt his pulse quicken. It didn't make sense. But what had made sense in the last few days? Her hand pressed against the automatic.

She started to pull it from his waistband, and he took it and slipped it down in the opening between the seat and the door next to him and turned her back against the seat in his arms, and kissed her harder.

And she leaned back toward her side of the seat, pulling him down on top of her.

32

SPENCE HAD FELT Christen's hand slip his wallet out of his hip pocket and pitch it onto the floorboard, as if it were in the way of her hands pulling against his clothes as she pressed up against him minutes before. Now, as she brushed her hair, she reached down and lifted the wallet into her hand.

"Family pictures?" she said, opening it and thumbing through the credit cards and license he had in the plastic holders.

"No family pictures?" she said. "What would your mother think about being treated like that?" She smiled softly at him. When her fingers started down in the long money pouch, he pulled the wallet from her hand and slipped it back inside his pocket.

"You're nosy enough," he said.

She came up on her knees and leaned forward, caught his chin in her hand, pushed his head back against the seat, and kissed him hard again.

He pushed her back this time.

"So who's the weak little wimp now?" she asked, and grinned down at him. "But you weren't too bad. When everything is said and done, I might just keep you in my harem. I might." She kissed him on his forehead, his nose, his cheek, and then his lips again, once more her mouth opening warm and moist against his and her hands clasping the back of his neck and pressing his face hard into hers.

Then she was running her lips around his ear. He felt the dart of her tongue. "Does that tickle?" she asked.

"Mr. Macho," she added, and looked into the rearview mirror. He turned his head quickly and looked in the same direction. The road was still empty in the dim moonlight.

She turned back away from him and sat down in the seat. "It is bad, isn't it?" she said, her tone no longer playful.

He looked at his watch. "I'm going after that other ride now. If you have any sense at all you'll let me put you out somewhere."

She answered by saying, "You mean *we're* going to get that other ride now."

He drove to within a hundred yards of the highway, leaving the Lexus hidden behind a thick clump of bushes. Then they walked to a service station and called a taxi.

It took the driver thirty minutes to arrive. They came around the side of the service station. Spence made it a point to walk slightly ahead of Christen, speaking with her so as to keep his head turned slightly away from the driver's view. But the man never looked anyway except to glance at Christen's bare legs beneath her shorts. Spence went around to the far side of the taxi while she went to the door directly behind the driver.

After they were inside and Christen told the driver where they wanted to go, he never looked back at them. But Spence kept watching him, waiting for any sign he might suddenly recognize one of his passengers.

But nothing happened, and after another thirty minutes of slow driving the taxi turned into the main entrance to the Medical Center. Spence sunk lower in the seat as they passed under bright lights. In a few seconds, most of the lights were behind them, and they followed a narrow street running toward the back of the center. They passed an empty parking lot, then passed a mobile x-ray unit parked off to the side and turned down the final street, which ended at the clump of buildings housing the research labs at the center.

As the taxi drove off, Spence looked around the dark-ened parking areas surrounding the buildings and didn't see anyone, or a vehicle he didn't recognize. But he still said, "You wait here. There's a chance the cops have someone checking to see if I might come back here. If someone's inside I don't want to have to worry about you getting shot." He handed Christen her small automatic. "You said you get nervous being alone at night."

She smiled her cute grin. "I'll try not to shoot anybody until you get back." She walked toward the shadow cast by a large shrub as he hurried toward the building.

He passed the white van he was there to pick up, sitting by itself in the last parking space to the right. It had the University Medical Center name and logo scripted on its side.

A hall light illuminated the glass-paneled doors at the front of the building, and he didn't want to have to pass through its glow. He went around to the side. When he reached the windows to the laboratory, Tank stepped out of his doghouse and looked through the wire. He tried the first window, and it was unlocked. He raised it, being care-ful not to make any sound even though he was hundreds of feet from where anyone could possibly be.

Quinlan, Genowski, and John all had the same box opened in their minds. They watched as Spence Stevens crawled inside the window at the back of the laboratory. As the doctor's feet disappeared into the darkness inside the build-ing, Quinlan looked at John.

Without a word, the big man turned and walked toward the door.

He was within fifteen minutes of the center.

As the door closed behind John and he hurried to his car parked outside the Biogenetics Center, Quinlan sent two others a command that would immediately be heeded.

They were uniformed police officers, currently on foot, chasing a burglary suspect down an alley in a southwest section of the city. It would take them approximately ten or fifteen minutes longer than John to arrive at the center.

Chief Solomon was the next one to receive the command. It woke him. He began quickly dressing as his wife stared from their bed.

"What are you doing, Carlos?"

He smiled back at her. "Little problem downtown," he answered.

"The president's in town," she said, "and somebody has taken him hostage?"

He smiled. "Not that bad."

"Well get your big tail back in bed," she said.

"I can't, honey."

The keys to the van were supposed to be in the upper-right-hand drawer of his desk. But when Spence moved into the office, opened the drawer, and felt for the key, it wasn't there. Passing out of his office and back through the shadows formed by the moonlight streaming through the laboratory windows, he walked to Freddie's drawer.

The key wasn't there either.

At Flo's drawer he found it, lying to one side of the other perfectly arranged items she had stored there. As he clasped it, he heard the door open behind him.

He whirled around.

The overhead lights flashed on.

Flo stared across the room.

"My God, Spence, where have you been?"

The words were the same as the words Christen had muttered when he first talked to her on the phone that day.

"Spence, they said on television that the officer came to arrest you on traffic violations. I knew that wasn't true. After Freddie got his second ticket, you told him if he got another he was going to see a jump in his insurance. You said you hadn't received a ticket since you finished your residency. I was so upset I—"

He had held his finger up to stop her. "Do you mind turning off the lights?" he asked.

She did as he requested, then closed the door and came

across the floor toward him. "Spence, I was so upset I called the police and told them there had to be a mistake. I . . . the officer who answered—she was a lady—she was nice. She almost sounded like she might believe me. But . . ." She shook her head. "When she checked the computer she said it showed you had a dozen traffic citations outstanding."

A dozen? How could . . . *Them.* It was like he was lost in some damn nightmare—not of his making—but of theirs.

"It's the people you talked about in the gym, isn't it?" Flo questioned. "It sounded so crazy. Did you go to West Memphis that day you said you were going to Tulane to check on their research progress?"

"What?"

"Did you?"

"Yes."

"The police know that. They said you had been acting erratic, lying to your staff, taking off suddenly. If I didn't know you, I would think something was wrong with you. You have to do something. They're saying you're armed and dangerous, someone who has now shot a police officer."

They were setting him up to kill him. A crazy man running the streets. "You better get out of here," he said.

"Let's go to a television station."

"Television station?" Then he understood what she meant. "So I can broadcast to the whole world what's happening. So I won't be in any more danger, because there's no need for anybody to do anything to me once I tell everything I know."

She nodded.

He had suggested almost the same thing to Kennedy. Except it wasn't a TV station he had mentioned but rather the Justice Department, the FBI. He shook his head no. "You know why? Because I'd be just as crazy when it was all over. In fact, after I told everything, I would have accomplished nothing but to verify the word of that cop I shot. You want everybody to believe his story?"

"They do now," Flo said. Her fingers touched his fore-arm. They were trembling. He caught them in his hand.

"I'm going to think of something. I . . ." He glanced at his watch and then turned and strode toward his office.

"Spence," she said as she caught up to him. "What are you doing?"

"I'm going to call a friend who I hope can get me out of all this." He thought about the wrecked Lincoln. "If any-body can get me out of this," he added.

"A friend?"

"An FBI agent."

"What's his name?" Flo asked.

"What?"

"What's his name, Spence?"

"Bob Kennedy."

Her hand came to her mouth. "Spence," she said in a low voice. "It was on the ten o'clock news. You hadn't told me his name, but it caught my attention because you said an FBI agent went with you to Montana. He's missing."

Spence hadn't thought there was anything that could make him any more scared than he already was, but Flo's words had. Kennedy was missing. Kennedy who was going to handle everything. Kennedy who would have been es-pecially careful.

"A spokesman for the FBI said they would make no comment other than he hadn't come in to the office, and his wife said he never came back to the house," Flo said. "But a reporter asked if he hadn't done this before. She said right after he retired from the military and came back to work for the FBI—he was in the Gulf Coast office then—he took off for a month and nobody knew where he was. She said it was post-traumatic stress from his stint in the military and the VA hospital had records verifying that."

It was the time Kennedy had mentioned in the jet coming back from Montana, when he said he went to pieces for a few weeks right after he returned to civilian life.

How did the reporter know? Kennedy said the good thing about working for these people was that the records of his stay at the VA hospital would be erased. Nobody would ever know about the condition he had suffered. Now the records had magically resurfaced to give reason for his disappearance. Kennedy would never be back.

"You're taking the van?" Flo questioned, looking at the key he held. "Freddie will notice it's gone. He'll guess who took it."

"And he'll say something about it?"

"Either that or go all to pieces thinking about it."

"I'll be through with it by then."

"Where are you going?"

He shook his head. "Flo, you really need to go on."

"Spence, for God's sake, don't you trust me?"

"I do, Spence," Christen said from the doorway.

She had opened it so quietly it hadn't made a sound.

Flo stared at her. Standing in the doorway she was only a shadowy figure. She walked toward them. She was carrying her purse in one hand and her small automatic in the other, hanging down by her side.

Flo glanced at the gun and then looked at him. When he didn't show any sign of nervousness at Christen coming toward him, Flo said, "She's with you?"

He nodded.

As Christen stopped in front of them, she looked directly at Flo and said, "The only thing I *would* wonder is why you're down here this time of night?"

Flo said, "What business is that of yours?"

Spence reached to Christen's hand and took the automatic. Flo was still staring at her.

Christen's gaze moved to his. "You said there were a lot of people involved," she said.

Flo didn't know what Christen meant.

He shook his head. "Forget it, Christen."

Flo's eyes turned back to his now. "Forget what?" she asked.

"Don't worry about it," he said.

"What do you mean, don't worry about it? What is she talking about?"

"Hadn't we better go?" Christen asked.

Flo looked back at her again. "What did you mean?"

"I don't think Spence wants you to know," Christen said.

Flo's eyes turned toward his again.

"Dammit, Christen," he said.

Flo was still staring at him. "Is she talking about what you and I . . ." She stopped in midsentence. He had told her no one was to know what they talked about in the stands, and she was honoring that.

"Okay," she said. "It doesn't matter. I'm going now. If . . ." She glanced at Christen and then back at him. "If you need me, Spence, I'll be at home." She walked toward the door.

"Flo," he said. "She knows."

Flo stopped and turned back to face him.

Christen was looking at him now. "You told her, too?"

"She knew everything earlier today. She didn't know what was about to happen. But she knows about Montana."

"Montana?" Christen said.

"It's where the experiments took place," he said.

Instead of responding to what he said, Christen looked toward the door and said in a low voice, "Did you hear that?"

He had. The faint almost imperceptible sound of the front door of the building closing had traveled to him through the partially cracked lab door. He walked quickly toward it.

Christen hurried along behind him. As he stopped at the door, she peered across his shoulder through the crack left at the back of the door where it was hinged to the doorframe.

Flo remained at the center of the lab.

John had stopped abruptly when the door latch had clicked loudly behind him. He held an automatic leveled in front of him. He waited a moment, then slowly started toward the laboratory door. Passing through the bright glow of the overhead light, he was blinded to the point that he couldn't see with his eyes that the lab door was cracked partially open, but he already knew it was. He knew who was in the laboratory, and the box in his mind showed Spence standing just inside the door. He held Christen's small automatic in his hand. It was ready, too.

But John kept walking. He knew he wasn't in any danger. He knew what was about to happen. He was totally surprised when the image clicked off in his mind, and then Spence leaned out in the hallway and raised the small automatic. John fired quickly, the loud sound of his weapon reverberating down the hallway.

Spence fired twice, the small-caliber thirty-two making more of a popping sound than blasts. One shot tore into John's arm, the other his shoulder. He fired again. Spence's return shot hit him in the head, and he flew backward to crash against the floor. Spence came out of the laboratory running, his weapon pointed at the limp form sprawled under the light.

Quinlan's face was twisted with rage. He had viewed the same thing as John had viewed, the image of Spence standing just inside the laboratory door. And then that image had suddenly clicked off, and the only image left had been that from John's perspective as Spence had leaned out from the doorway and returned John's fire.

On Spence's third shot, the box being transmitted from John's mind had vanished, too.

"He killed him," Quinlan roared. "Why did the bitch click her image off?"

Spence knelt beside John's limp form. Christen stood above him. Flo still stood in the laboratory doorway up the hall.

"He's not dead," Christen said.

The first two shots from the small thirty-two-caliber weapon had caused only flesh wounds. The third shot had caught him on the side of his forehead, penetrating the skin and ricocheting off the skull, leaving a furrow under the skin and an exit wound at the side of his scalp. He was only knocked unconscious.

"He was in the office all the time I was interviewing Solomon," Christen said. "I knew they were close."

Spence stood. His hands trembled. She had warned him when she saw who was coming down the hallway, but just because the man had been in the chief's office during the interview didn't mean he was one of them. But then the man had raised his automatic and fired and he had fired back as much out of instinct for survival as anything. If the man was only an honest cop who had been staked out at the building . . .

My God, when am I going to wake up? he thought. He was like an innocent man wrongly sentenced to life imprisonment. And everything he did to escape could now be real crimes. There was no way out. He felt trapped beyond belief. He looked at the small automatic in his hand. He had an urge to throw it away and not shoot again no matter what he faced. He took a deep breath to try and steel his nerves.

And then Christen said, "You said an implant."

He looked at her.

She was staring down at the man.

"The mobile x-ray unit we passed?" she asked. "It has its own power supply, doesn't it?"

He nodded. It was designed to operate completely independent of any other source of power as it visited rural areas screening for tuberculosis and any other diseases that could be captured on film.

He looked down at the limp form again. If he wasn't an innocent cop, was it possible that the man might have something implanted in his head?

"He's big though," Christen said. "We need to find something to tie him up with before he wakes." She glanced back toward the lab. "Or do you have something in there you know will keep him out?"

He looked back at Flo, still standing in the laboratory doorway. "Have her show you."

"Now we, like all animals, carry with us vestigial traces of our past ancestry, not least in our mental processes. To develop psychologically we must understand ourselves, and it should help us to do so if we can find ways to investigate those hidden depths in our minds from which we draw our impulses."

SIR WALTER LANGDON-BROWN

33

THEY HAD PUSHED the gurney with the man strapped on top of it into the rear of the UMC van. He hadn't moved, deeply sedated with the injection they had administered at the laboratory. Spence had driven slowly to the mobile x-ray unit and parked in front of the big vehicle's cab. The doors on the side of the unit weren't locked, and he hurried back to the van, looked up and down the dimly lit street, and pulled the gurney outside. Flo caught it on one side, Christen the other, and they half lowered it, half dropped it against the pavement with a bump.

As they pushed it toward the mobile unit, Flo said, "I'm sorry for not helping back there. When I got to the door and saw him lying there . . . I thought you had killed him. My legs were too weak to move."

He nodded as they lined the gurney up with the door.

"Ready?" he said.

The three of them strained as they lifted the weight of the gurney and the heavy body up into the unit.

Then they quickly climbed inside the truck, and Spence closed the doors behind them.

The x-ray equipment was generator-run. Spence flicked on the power switch.

Nothing happened.

Flo, obviously the most nervous from the expression on her face, was looking for where the film was stored.

He tried the switch again.

Again the generator failed to come on.

The two police officers, their pistols extended out in front of them, came slowly down the sides of the hall toward the laboratory. Just before they reached the open door, the officer nearest it crouched, looked across at his partner, then raised a flashlight and held it against his automatic.

Then he leaped through the doorway at the same time as he switched on the flashlight, sweeping it and his weapon rapidly back and forth. The other officer came in behind him, also crouched, swinging the beam of his flashlight and weapon across the other end of the lab.

Quinlan's face twisted with his rage. "Where are you, bitch?"

Genowski said, "Maybe she's making certain he has the chip first."

"He does," Quinlan growled. "That's obvious even to an idiot. The crazy bitch; she can have all the intelligence in the world and she's still a damn ignorant woman. We should have left her back at the site in the beginning."

As he spoke, his rage built, and his face became redder and redder.

Spence tried the generator switch once more. He shook his head. "I don't know what's wrong with it."

The man stirred. Flo looked at him. It was only the movement of a body heavily sedated but still alive with subconscious actions of its own.

"He never spoke all the time I was in the chief's office conducting the interview," Christen said. "He never smiled either. I remember that." She stared at the limp form for a moment, then stepped to the gurney and ran her hand under his hips.

She pulled out his wallet.

"Twice tonight," she said, and smiled in Spence's direction.

When Flo looked at her, Christen said, "That I've been nosy. It's a Dantonio genetic problem."

She opened the wallet and looked at the cards inside it. Her eyes narrowed. "Damn," she said.

When her face came up she said, "The executive vice president and chief financial officer of Biogenetics. What was he doing listening in on an interview about crime in the city?"

She looked at the limp form. "John Holliday."

She continued to stare at him and then shook her head. "What better place to experiment with brain implants?" she muttered, as much to herself as to them. "Probably the most state-of-the-art laboratory in the country." Her eyes came up to Spence's.

He stepped forward, took the wallet into his hand, and stared down at the business card in the plastic holder.

He remembered when he was in the jet coming back from Montana and Kennedy had asked him if he would like to call up Walter Quinlan and ask him about his former employee, Alfred Wynn. *Or would you think better of that if I told you that I was also unable to find any trace of Mr. Quinlan's prints on record?* Kennedy had said.

"I interviewed the president of Biogenetics," Christen said. "William Genowski. He gave me a tour of the plant. All except one room. It was really more than just a room. It was half the main building. He said the secrets were of such import that they didn't allow any outsiders inside."

She paused a moment. "I wonder if the secrets really are that unusual."

Spence looked at the big man's form again.

"No, Spence," Flo said. "Not any more. You're going to get killed."

"Not out at the plant at night," Christen said. "It almost completely shuts down. There are only the guards on the gate and one that patrols inside the fence."

"How do you know?" Flo asked.

"I told you I did an interview," Christen answered. "Mr.

Genowski said they closed down at night like any other business. In fact, Miss Flo . . ."

Christen waited for a last name, and Flo didn't give her one.

Christen said, "In fact, *Flo*, he made a joke about if he was going to break into their center he'd do it at night—and told me not to put that in the story." She was staring at Flo. "He thought I was cute," she added. "You can get a lot that way. But I guess you first have to have the credentials," she added, and smiled.

"Dammit, Christen," Spence said.

She looked at him. "The room would just be sitting there waiting for us to look at," she said.

He nodded.

She smiled. "Maybe I really am going to get my Pulitzer after all."

Then she looked back at John. "He's going to wake up eventually. We need to tie him up or something." She looked at a metal cabinet against the wall. It was marked with a red cross. She walked to it and opened its door.

"This will do," she said, turning around with a thick roll of white surgical tape in her hand.

Then she looked at Flo and said, "That big white van with University Medical Center on its side is not exactly the most subtle thing we could drive. If we could use your car it would be a lot less noticeable. You could wait here."

Flo stared back at her. "It's not a car, it's a pickup. And if it goes anywhere, I'm going with it."

Christen looked toward the closed door at the side of the unit, held her stare for a moment, and then nodded toward the door. "You go get it then," she said.

Flo stared back across the unit. It was obvious she didn't like taking orders.

The two officers had searched every laboratory in the building, and now emerged into the dim moonlight bathing the parking area.

"If she's with them, kill her, too," Walter Quinlan said.

"I'm tired of the bitch trying to run things her way."

The two officers stared at each other after the transmission. The reason Quinlan wanted her dead wasn't important to them. That he had ordered it was. The fear showed on their faces. She had the ability to stop them as quickly as Quinlan or Genowski or John could. They would have to be quick, before she realized their intentions, and shoot accurately so that she didn't even have time to concentrate as she fell.

Genowski was shocked at Quinlan's order, too. But he didn't allow any expression to show. He didn't know how Quinlan might interpret it. They were equals; all five of them had been equals in the beginning, but there had to be one to make the final decisions. Quinlan had taken over that task when they decided to destroy the laboratory and leave. He had held that position ever since. She was the only one who had ever voiced any objection to anything Quinlan had ever decided, and it was obvious that bad blood had formed between them. But not bad enough to reach this point. Not for her to die simply because she was going after what they wanted in a different manner than Quinlan had decided.

But, again, he showed no expression.

Only one could rule.

A superior among equals.

Inside the mobile x-ray unit, Spence finished wrapping another roll of tape around John and the gurney, tightly securing him in place. Christen had slipped a wad of gauze pads into John's mouth and placed a strip of tape across that. Now she ran another strip across his mouth. Spence watched to make sure the large man's nostrils stayed clear, where he wouldn't suffocate.

Flo drove her pickup next to the doors of the unit.

Spence opened the doors, and Christen jumped outside. He followed her to the ground, then turned around and closed the doors.

Flo pushed the pickup's passenger door open.

Spence stepped to it and waited for Christen.

"Christ," she grumbled. "Forgot my purse."

She turned and opened one of the doors, then scrambled up into the unit. A few seconds later she reappeared, jumped to the ground and turned to shut the doors.

That was when she saw the two officers.

"Spence," she said.

The officers started running toward the unit.

Christen sprung past Spence into the pickup. He jumped in behind her. Flo dropped the truck into gear and pressed on the accelerator.

The officers were only fifty feet away and pulling their automatics from their holsters when the pickup jumped forward.

"Duck!" Spence yelled, lowering his head below the rear window.

Christen sunk down in the seat. Flo ducked her head and looked in the side mirror. The officers aimed their automatics. Flo ducked lower.

Suddenly one of the men dropped his gun and grabbed his head. The other one screamed loudly. The first one took a step forward, screamed in a high-pitched voice, and toppled forward on his face. The other one, holding his head now, crumpled backward to the ground, his legs kicking wildly out in front of him.

The pickup, nothing but the top of Flo's head showing, raced down the street.

Seconds later, Spence raised up and looked through the rear window. But it was too dark to see back down the street and know what the officers were doing.

"They'll have these license plates, now," he said.

"We don't have any other choice but to keep going," Christen said.

Flo nodded.

Spence looked behind them again, waiting for the flashing lights of a patrol car to come racing after them.

*   *   *

At the Biogenetics plant, Quinlan and Genowski had watched through the eyes of the two officers as they ran toward the pickup truck.

The officers had nearly reached the big vehicle when suddenly the picture bounced, spun, with the image of the dimly lit sky and stars and the tops of buildings at the center passing rapidly by, blurred, and abruptly disappeared from view.

The screams came two seconds later.

"That bitch," Quinlan said.

Genowski felt the first real worry he had experienced in ten years sweep over him.

Solomon had nearly driven over the bodies of the two officers lying sprawled on the street close to the mobile x-ray unit. A hundred yards away, he had leaned his head out the window of his car to question a maintenance man standing on the sidewalk, looking back in the direction of the unit.

He had heard screams. "A pickup came by right afterward," he said. "It had three people in it, driving kinda fast."

And then Solomon heard the command from Quinlan. *She was to be stopped.*

Solomon felt the perspiration break out across his forehead. His private thoughts were of running himself, but there was no place to run to.

As the description of the pickup and its occupants was transmitted to him by Quinlan, Solomon reached to the mike on his dashboard to call the dispatcher.

It was less than thirty minutes later when a Hinds County deputy sheriff called in to report that he remembered seeing a vehicle and occupants matching the description speeding along a back road leading to Clinton.

34

AN EIGHT-FOOT-TALL CHAIN-LINK fence surrounded the grounds. The dominant building at the center of the complex was almost square in design, 180 to 190 feet wide, and a little more than 200 feet deep. Steel panels covered its exterior. Though a one-story, it was unusually tall, its roof constructed like the rounded, tall roof of a giant airplane hangar. Spence could see two men in brown uniforms through the wide Plexiglas window at the side of the gatehouse. He hadn't yet spotted the guard and attack dog that Christen had told him patrolled within the fence. But the grounds were only dimly lit from the one large light on a post above the guardhouse, and another one above the fence at the rear of the complex. They had been there waiting for several minutes.

"Maybe there's not a guard dog tonight," Christen said. "Who would try to break into a biogenetics plant anyway? I imagine the average local would worry about getting contaminated with something."

Flo rolled her eyes. Christen saw the gesture and frowned. Spence kept staring intently at the grounds, trying to see into the dark shadows alongside the building. But he still didn't see a uniformed man or dog.

"Well," Christen said impatiently.

"Spence, I wish you wouldn't," Flo said.

He stood. The heavy woods they were in prevented any of the dim moonlight from shining down on them and shielded them from anybody without night-vision binoculars.

"Spence?" Flo said again.

"We've already settled it," he said. "I'm going in."

They came with him, Flo on one side and Christen the other. The moonlight *was* dim. The wide building at the center of the complex hid their movements from any glance from the guardhouse on the far side of the grounds. They would have to be unlucky enough for the guard who patrolled inside the fence with the attack dog to see them if they were going to be spotted. He looked at Holliday's big automatic. He carried it now while Christen carried her smaller weapon. If he had to shoot again . . . Even an attack dog . . . He didn't know if he could pull the trigger again. They stopped at the fence.

It was easy to climb. They went over it all at the same time. He landed on the ground on the other side of the barrier just before Christen's and Flo's feet touched down. They raced toward the rear of the large building. There was no guard or attack dog yet. Maybe Christen was right. Maybe there was just nobody patrolling the fences tonight.

Two hundred yards away from the far front corner of the building, a guard in a brown uniform lay face-down on the ground. The shadows were especially dark at the particular spot with a pair of tall hundred-year-old oaks spreading their thick limbs out over the fence. The attack dog strained at his leash, wrapped around the guard's wrist. The dog, smelling the intruders on the wind blown his way, continued to tug at the leash. The tugging stretched the man's limp arm out straight. His other hand still cupped a side of his head, the position both hands had been in as he had died in terrible pain.

The dog continued pulling on its leash, the animal's teeth bared and its eyes staring toward the far side of the large building at the center of the complex. But the animal didn't bark. It had been trained not to, its handlers preferring it remain silent until it pounced, in the hope that such

an attack would give the dog a better chance against a man
with a gun.

"Look," Christen said.

Spence and Flo stared at the wide steel steps erected like
a scaffolding rising up the side of the building. The steps
ended at a door built into the side of the roof as it angled
steeply upward before rounding into a gently mounded top.
They hurried silently toward the steps.

When they reached the door at the top of the steps, it
swung back easily.

They stared into a dark attic extending back over the
entire building.

Spence hadn't thought of any need to bring a flashlight.
He would have thought he wouldn't want a beam shining
out in front of him, illuminating their approach.

Christen stepped inside first. Spence went in to stand
beside her and stare into the blackness. Flo, lighting a
match behind them, startled him.

He stared back at her.

"Freddie's," she said in a low voice. "He lost the striker
to the Bunsen burner and gave me these." It was a small
paper folder of matches. She stepped forward and held the
lit match up in the air out in front of her.

Around them, small stainless steel pipes and larger ones
wrapped in insulation snaked back and forth across the attic. There were electrical cables too, thick ones, thin ones,
again running in every direction across the flooring. The
light flickered out, and Flo struck another match.

As they went forward, they began to hear the low hum
of motors. A louder noise suddenly clicking on, startled
them. It was from an air-conditioner compressor.

Flo took an audible breath.

They walked slowly forward, being careful not to trip
over anything.

The match went out.

Flo lit another one.

They continued their slow progress.

The third match went out.

It took Flo longer this time, and Spence was just glancing back over his shoulder at her when the match flared into a small flame.

"Look," Christen said.

Ahead of them, past the limits of the glow of the match, in the blackness over the center of the building, thin rays of light shone up through some kind of grill.

They moved in its direction.

It was an air-conditioner vent. But no pipe connected to it. A few feet away, a pipe about two feet in diameter showed where the cool air had once traveled to the vent. Despite the sound of the motor to the air-conditioner compressor, no air came from it now. The pipe had to be disconnected from its source somewhere back in the darkness of the attic.

Christen had dropped to one knee and was staring down into the brightly lit space below. Flo knelt beside her. What Spence saw left him speechless.

A dozen beds spread out over an area that resembled a hospital ward. Three of them were occupied. A doctor in cap, lab coat, and latex gloves stood over one, adjusting an IV running into the arm of a man lying there with his eyes closed, his face clearly visible through the grill.

It was FBI agent Bob Kennedy.

"That's him," Flo said in a whisper. "The one the spokesman said was . . ." She shook her head. "My God, what are they doing?"

"Implanting computer chips," Christen said.

Spence was looking in every direction in the attic.

"We have to get in there."

Christen looked across the attic.

Flo, still staring down through the grill, slowly stood. She couldn't take her eyes off the agent. Then she raised her face and looked out into the blackness. "There," she said.

A faint ray of light filtered up into air fifty feet away. As they neared it, they saw the particles of dust floating suspended in the beam. It was another grill. But this time connected to a pipe. The thin ray of light streaked up through a connection that was partially loose.

Spence scanned the attic again.

But no more light showed.

"We can't use the front entrance," Christen said. "They could see us from the gatehouse. I don't know if there's another entrance or not. There should be—even Mr. Quinlan would have had to follow the fire code."

Quinlan sat in the chair behind his desk. The door to the office was locked and bolted. But neither that fact nor the fact that an automatic lay ready under his hand on the desk, had kept perspiration from beading on his forehead.

It hadn't kept John from staring toward the door either. He sat in a chair off to the side of the room, out of a direct angle of anyone suddenly bursting into the office. His automatic was clasped in his sweaty palm.

She was on equal footing with them. One possessed of knowledge about everything. A locked, even bolted, door wouldn't hold her at bay for long if she decided to come through it.

But she wouldn't, they knew. At least not in the way they were thinking. For she had the same knowledge they did and the same way of assimilating it. She would *know* they waited there ready for her.

How would she come after them? They knew without doubt she was coming. And that she was likely on her way now. That would be the most logical move for her to make. But how would she make it?

In their minds they were playing a game of chess against a computer. The one which basically she was. Their move had been to sit and wait. What would her next move be? It wasn't the kind of game they had been used to for ten years, not a game of men against mere insects, not a game of sheer genius against the common mind. But now a game against someone who was all they were.

Equals against equals.

*   *   *

There *was* another entrance.

A single steel door about a hundred feet down the building from the scaffoldlike steps they had come down.

Spence stepped up onto the concrete stoop and tried the doorknob. The door was locked.

"Let me try," Christen said. She looked at him as she stepped up beside him. "Crime in Jackson, remember—the cops gave me a demonstration." Then she frowned. "But I don't have anything," she said, feeling in her shorts pockets. "I had a nail file in my purse." She looked in the direction of the pickup parked in the trees.

Flo held out a safety pin, and as Spence took it in his hands and opened it, she fumbled back inside her slacks pockets again. She produced the stub of a pencil, then a small notepad and a few coins.

Christen tried the pin in the lock.

Spence felt in his pockets. But he knew nothing was there.

Flo was fumbling again. "Dammit," she said.

Christen, still working with the pin in the lock and not looking back at Flo, said, "I see we have another limited vocabulary."

"What?" Flo whispered.

"Nothing," Spence said. He was looking for the guard and the attack dog. Christen and Flo seemed like they had forgotten about the animal.

Flo was suddenly walking down the side of the building.

A round trash can sat in front of her.

She stopped in front of it. Her back to them, she started rummaging through its contents. Spence saw the glow when she lit a match. He looked toward the far corner of the building and then back across his shoulder. Flo was hurrying back toward them.

"Here," she said. She was holding out a length of stiff wire curved into a partial circle, like it had been wrapped as a binder around a large box.

Christen took it and turned back to the door.

"Voilà," she said a moment later.

Spence lifted John's automatic in front of him.

Christen cracked the door open.

It led to a darkened room.

He stepped inside ahead of her, then she came in, with Flo bringing up the rear. Across the room, a faint thin line of light glowed at the top of a door.

They quickly crossed the room.

The door wasn't locked.

Spence slowly opened it and peered into a brightly lit hallway. Down the corridor, a double door stood open, its sides propped back into the area it led into.

He took a deep breath, heard Flo take one behind him, and stepped into the hallway.

Christen had her small automatic raised and ready now.

At the double doors, Spence stopped and leaned slowly forward to peer through the crack left where the door to that side was folded back.

The beds lay before him.

35

SPENCE STARTED THROUGH the crack in the rear of the doorway. IV bottles mounted on tall, movable racks sat about the room. There were stainless steel instrument carts, cardiac monitors, and other medical equipment, all mounted on carrying racks with small wheels, scattered about the area. Kennedy lay in a bed about fifty feet from the door. The doctor was at a bed twenty feet farther over, leaning over the man lying there. The third man lay quietly on his back, his arms along his sides, breathing slowly, as if he were sedated.

"What do we do now?" Christen asked.

"Get out of here and call the police," Flo said.

Kennedy's arms moved, and he came up into a sitting position. The doctor walked toward the bed as Kennedy lifted his sheet back and dangled his legs off the side of the mattress.

The doctor stopped in front of him, nodded, and said something.

Two guards at the gate, Spence thought. *Maybe one with a dog outside on the grounds. The doctor . . . and maybe one or two more support personnel somewhere. But I've got a gun.* He stepped around the door and walked into the brightly lit room.

Kennedy saw him first. The stocky agent said something to the doctor, who turned around and stared toward the doorway.

Spence raised the automatic. Flo walked behind him.

The doctor moved toward the foot of the bed, then turned around and faced them again. Kennedy didn't move.

As Spence neared the bed, he ran his gaze around the wide area. There were two doors at the far side. He glanced behind him. Only Flo was there.

"Where's Christen?" he asked.

"She's covering our rear."

He looked back at the doctor. The man hadn't moved again—nor had he shown any expression of surprise or anything else.

"You okay?" Spence asked Kennedy as he stopped close to the bed. Kennedy didn't say anything. He hadn't shown any expression either. Spence looked at the red, swollen places on the skin to either side of Kennedy's forehead. Black stitches showed.

Kennedy lunged off the bed into him.

Stumbling backward, Spence wrestled against the agent's sudden charge. The doctor came in from the other side, reaching for the hand that held the automatic. Being spun to the side by Kennedy, Spence kept the weapon out of the doctor's reach. But now the man was reaching inside his lab coat, and Spence saw the shoulder holster and the automatic that was being pulled from it. With a lightning move of his hand, Spence swung his weapon over Kennedy's head into the doctor's face.

The man stumbled backward. A wide gash across his forehead poured blood into his eyes, partially blinding him. He reached his hands to his face. Spence, pushing with one arm against Kennedy's grip, swung his heavy weapon into the doctor's head. The man's legs buckled, his weapon fell to the floor. Flo smashed into him from the side, making as clean a tackle as a football player and driving him back onto the bed.

Kennedy pulled on the gun Spence held, trying to take it, but Spence jerked it out of the agent's grasp, raised it, and brought it down hard across Kennedy's head. Kennedy's eyes blinked. Spence hit him again, and then again.

He felt Kennedy's knees buckle against him, and Spence raised the automatic once more and came down as hard he could with it.

Flo, scratching like a silent enraged cat, was hurled backward off the bed by the doctor and went sprawling to the floor on her back with her hands splayed out to the sides. Kennedy crumpled to the tile. The doctor came forward and Spence hit him with a left, then slapped him hard in the side of the forehead with a roundhouse swing of the automatic, and the man's legs weakened underneath him. He twisted in a partial circle and fell across the bed.

Flo was on him immediately but stopped when she saw he was unconscious. Her dark hair mussed, strands hanging across her face, she turned and looked at Spence.

"We have to get out of here," she said.

As he stared down at the limp body of the agent, she said, "You're going to take him with us, aren't you?"

Spence nodded.

Flo turned her gaze toward three small tanks the size of scuba tanks on a rack at the head of a bed twenty feet away. "I think those are anesthesia and oxygen bottles," she said. "We don't want him waking up while we're moving him."

Spence nodded.

She hurried toward the tanks.

Outside the building, the attack dog gave a last tug on his leash, then sat backward onto the ground and howled.

The guards had come out of the enclosed gatehouse for a breath of fresh air despite the air-conditioning running full blast in the small structure. The loud sound of its compressor had kept them from hearing the dog's first howl, but they heard one now.

Their faces swung in the direction of the haunting sound.

"What in the hell?" one of them said.

He started walking in the direction of the sound.

The other guard looked back at the gate, and then hurried after his companion.

They stopped on the command, listened for a moment,

though no words could be heard coming through the air, and then they turned and hurried toward the main building, jerking their automatics from their holsters as they ran.

Quinlan watched the main building nearing through the guard's eyes. The two boxes that had been displayed earlier in his mind, the one from the doctor's eyes and the one from Kennedy's eyes had disappeared, the last one blanking out just after the bed had spun in front of the doctor's face as he had fallen toward it.

Quinlan had seen all that Spence and Flo had done. The one thing he hadn't seen was Christen. But neither had any view come from her eyes. He hadn't seen any image transmitted through her eyes since she had turned it off back at the laboratory.

He had thought she was coming for him—for him and Genowski.

But now he knew there was another possibility—a much more logical possibility.

36

QUINLAN STARED ACROSS the desk at Genowski.

"She's not going to come, is she?" Genowski said.

He spoke the words in the form of a question, but he was making a statement. Their conclusions, keyed by the identical amount of information stored in the chips implanted in their brains, had been the same. Christen *wasn't* coming. She was sending someone after them, even as they had sent people after her.

Quinlan nodded. "It's what *we* did. It would be her move, too."

Genowski's eyes closed. He was already concentrating. They would look through each of the newly implanted eyes, see who was coming in the direction of the complex. Then they would order them back, turn them back after her. If the ones ordered back didn't obey immediately, they would be eliminated.

Christen would be doing the same. It would be a game of moves and countermoves of human chess pieces. They would be clutching their heads and falling all around town. But Quinlan knew he had one ace she didn't have. There were two of them, he *and* Genowski.

Two minds working against one.

Two equals against one equal.

They would overpower her with numbers.

But first, he thought, *there is Spence Stevens and his lab assistant.* They had to be stopped before they could leave with the secrets of the complex.

He came to his feet, his automatic in his hand.

Genowski hurried to unlock and unbolt the door and swing it open.

"The dumb bitch," Quinlan said, and smiled as he strode through the doorway.

Genowski followed him.

Christen stepped from the hall bathroom twenty feet away—and fired two quick shots.

Outside the building, just as the two guards ran up the concrete steps to the main door, they suddenly grabbed their heads. The one in the lead screamed the loudest, but they both screamed, high-pitched screams of terrible pain, and then they fell backward down the steps. Gripping their heads, their heels kicked in agony against the sidewalk leading up to the steps.

And then they were silent, unmoving.

At that second, police chief Carlos Solomon's car, its blue lights flashing, sped through a red light on Clinton Boulevard, less than a quarter mile from the Biogenetics Research Center.

A moment later, a loud scream caused a driver of a pickup in an opposite lane to look toward the car. It began to weave, then rapidly went totally out of control and, at its same high speed, angled abruptly off the pavement, crashing into a large oak and bursting into flames.

Christen appeared in the double doorway.

She held her small automatic down by her side. Spence struggled under Kennedy's weight, lifting the stocky agent back onto the bed. Flo lifted the mask from the anesthesia and oxygen tanks.

"What are you going to do?" Christen asked.

Flo was the one who answered. "We're going to sedate him so we can handle him until we get him to the hospital."

"To remove the brain chip?" Christen asked.

Flo nodded as she began to lift the mask at the ends of the hoses running from the tanks toward Kennedy's head. "If it can be done," she said.

"There are actually three of them," Christen said.

At the words *actually three of them*, Spence looked toward Christen.

She had the automatic raised and pointed at him.

Kennedy's words passed through his mind: *You can't imagine what they're able to set up and make you believe.*

He glanced down at the automatic stuffed inside his jeans waistband. Christen shook her head no. "Among my other abilities, I would need only one shot to put a bullet anywhere I wanted."

As he raised his gaze fully to hers, she said, "A person with more intellectual ability than any human in the world . . . Should the Pulitzer be my main goal? No, Doctor, not a Pulitzer winner." She smiled then, her smile that was more of a grin. A cute grin. "Not even a rocket scientist," she said. "No. How about a world leader? How about, eventually, *the* world leader? Would you aspire to anything less if you had my mind? If you had my power to make things happen?"

She shook her head. She wasn't grinning now. "No, Doctor, I was only temporarily inconvenienced by Walter Quinlan's masculine sense of priorities. When we sought a woman close enough in appearance that I could take her place, we ended up with one whose ambition was to go into journalism. Other than that, she fit all the circumstances I required. She had no close relatives other than a father who hadn't seen her more than two or three times since she was a little child and a brother who was blind and had never seen her at all. And she *was* remarkably similar to me in appearance. I didn't even have to resort to any plastic surgery to make the final switch. Afterward, I could, of course, have changed my mind about her direction of study. That happens all the time among young people. But Walter Quinlan didn't wish that—and he thought he controlled."

Her grin was back. "Again, a typical male. He thought the luxuries he allowed me to have . . ." She held up her arm showing the diamond-studded bracelet at her wrist. "He thought this purchased my satisfaction. Purchased me. A woman. I think he realized how much of a woman I really was in that split second before he died. I hope he did."

She raised the automatic. "And now, Doctor, I must send you on your way. You and the *real* bitch," she added, looking at Flo.

Flo dropped her eyes in fear. One forearm was up across her stomach, her hand trembling, her other arm twisted partially behind her hips, like she wanted to turn on around and not look.

"And by the way," Christen said, still looking at her, "he's not that much of a lover by any definition of the word."

Christen's eyes turned back to his. "Just thinks he is, of course," she said, and pointed the barrel of the small automatic directly at his forehead.

Flo whipped the doctor's automatic up to her waist and fired, the loud roar of the heavy-caliber weapon deafening in the close space.

Christen, hit in the chest, flew backward to slam into the floor. She tried to raise up, then collapsed back to the tile and didn't move.

Flo started crying.

37

THEY BLINDFOLDED SPENCE after they met him at the airport in Washington, D.C. Flo also knew everything, so she had been required to make the flight, too. He felt her hand tremble slightly in his in the backseat of a limousine with windows you could see neither out of nor into.

The ride through the dark night had lasted for more than two hours, and the long vehicle had made several turns. During that time, Spence twice heard the sound of a boom-box tuned to the same station, and he wondered if the turns had meant only that the limousine was circling around in the same general area rather than making a trip of any distance.

You can't imagine what they're able to set up and make you believe. The only thing you can be absolutely certain of is that what you think you know is never what you get—if they don't want you to get it.

He quit trying to guess where they were going and leaned further back in the seat. His movement pulled at Flo's hand, and he felt her grip tighten suddenly, as if she were afraid he might move his hand away.

He tightened the pressure of his fingers against hers, and she moved closer, laying her head against his shoulder. She remained lying that way, her hand holding his tightly.

He thought about how much she had progressed the eye research by concentrating the impulses. He had wanted that, and more—the way to make vision work when the entire eye had been damaged. He had wanted to be able to make the impulses work when wired into the occipital lobe.

And he would keep working on that. Keep trying. But he had wanted even more than that, really. He had dreamed that the research with the conductivity of the nerves might someday allow him the way to actually implant thoughts.

Implant intelligence.

He shook his head a little, the movement causing Flo to shift her head against his shoulder. He squeezed her hand again.

Start with eye research and end up implanting intelligence, he thought. He wondered if all this had started the same way, with some military scientists making a breakthrough whose ultimate results they could not have possibly envisioned.

But *he* could. He knew now. He had seen it. He had seen the results. Maybe under other conditions being able to implant knowledge would be a good thing. He was certain that the college students he had thought of, bored with lectures and wanting an easier way, would think it was a good thing. Or was it that anything that came too easy carried a danger with it? Were the long periods of working to attain something what made a person disciplined enough to use it correctly once he had it?

And then he smiled at his thoughts and shook his head. He would certainly like to see another million dollars poured into his research and worry about handling it later. The limousine was stopping.

He heard the side doors open, and he was gently separated from Flo as someone led her away. As he followed the arm tugging his, he came out onto the pavement. Now, a person on each side guided him where they wanted him to go. He knew Flo was behind him from the sound of her uncertain steps sliding against the concrete.

Then they went through a set of doors into a place much cooler than it had been outside, and he heard her steps sliding behind him again.

They stopped after navigating several corners. He didn't

hear anything. Then the two were urging him forward onto an elevator. He knew it was an elevator because he felt the sudden rising motion in his stomach as it plunged toward somewhere down below. It had to be below ground level because they hadn't come up any steps after they had entered the building.

As the elevator continued to plummet farther and farther he knew they were going *way* below ground level. It had to be a nuclear-blast-safe area.

The elevator suddenly slowed its rapid motion, seemed to bounce gently on a cushion of air, and then stopped. He didn't hear the doors open, but the two were guiding him outside again.

A couple of minutes later, after a walk down a floor hard enough to be tile or concrete, but made of a material that muffled Flo's steps to the point he could no longer hear them, he was brought to a stop.

He stood there for a moment, and then fingers worked at the back of his blindfold.

It came off.

He stared into a wide, circular room that could have been the control center aboard a giant *Star Wars* spaceship. Screens the size of those in a movie theater glowed a light blue and white from every wall—and Special Agent Bob Kennedy stared back at him.

Spence wasn't certain of what to think for a moment. And then he was. "I knew it all along," he said.

Kennedy shook his head. "You didn't know."

The only thing you can be absolutely certain of is that what you think you know is never what you get—if they don't want you to get it.

He remembered once more the stocky agent walking straight to the entrance of the air shaft without angling a step one way or the other in any other direction. *They* would have known where it was. And now he remembered the night when he had heard about Joey's death from Patricia and had telephoned the agent. Kennedy had been so shocked by the news that he had let his guard down temporarily. He had said he would "be right over"—without asking for an address. He already knew. Spence knew now that *they* had been there from the beginning, watching, waiting.

He nodded. "If I had just gone with my thoughts, I would have known."

Kennedy smiled a little. Then he said, "When I was wrestling with you, I had to do it. I knew Quinlan and Genowski were watching. More important, I really wanted that gun. I knew they were in the building. With me being pretty certain John was dead when his transmissions started wildly hitting in my head and the doctor's at the same time and then vanished, I knew I had a chance to get the three of them that were left—if Christen would show up."

He shook his head. "I didn't know where she was, but the chips themselves were telling me there was a good possibility she was on the way there. I don't know how I knew that, but that was what kept going through my mind. But they had to be close together. I would have only two or three seconds before the chip started dissolving. Two or three seconds to get off three shots before they could react. I needed your gun, and in any case I had to go after you until the time presented itself that they were together—and hope that they didn't kill you before then."

Spence nodded. "But if they had, then I would have just had to pay the price."

Kennedy nodded. "It was all part of the big picture."

"Bob," Flo said, "did Colonel Weaver . . ."

"He's okay," Kennedy said. He touched one of three small areas of red and puckered skin on his forehead. The black stitches were evident. "The good thing about the chips is the knowledge contained in them allowed me to tell the doctors how to get them out. Weaver did, too."

Spence looked at the men to his sides and the control room surrounding him.

"You came back in because of Joey?"

Kennedy shook his head. "They wouldn't have let me back in for a personal reason. I never left."

Then he lifted a device similar in design to a TV remote control and pressed a button.

"This is why you're here," he said.

Each of the screens surrounding the room suddenly split into images of four screens, each glowing quadrant now displaying an aerial view of a different country. Spence could recognize most of them by their familiar shapes—the leg and boot of Italy, the long shape of Israel bordering the Mediterranean Sea, the vast wide mass of China, the spear-head-like shape of India, the obvious shape of the United States. . . . Dozens of countries, each displayed in a different quadrant of the large screens, each obviously an image coming from a satellite high above the earth.

The lenses began to zoom in for closer shots. The shapes of countries narrowed to those of states, provinces, and other regional boundaries. As the lenses continued to zoom in, individual cities and towns became apparent. Spence saw Jackson. Whole sections of city blocks, and then individual blocks and streets with people strolling them came into view as the lenses zoomed closer and closer. Finally, individuals themselves. The magnification was so great you could not only count their fingers and see their eyes clearly, you could see their hair rustling in the wind or lying flat on top of their heads.

Spence noticed that an inordinate amount of the people being shown were carrying umbrellas or walking sticks. Some just held a rolled newspaper, like the man crossing a lawn toward a small brick house in Jackson. The rear end of a police car projected from the garage near the rear of the house. The man went around toward the tree-covered backyard but stopped short of a fence there and angled toward a rear window. In a moment, the window was raised and he disappeared inside the house, his shiny shoes the last thing Spence saw.

A few seconds passed. No more than that amount of time, and Spence noticed that the people carrying the umbrellas, walking sticks, and rolled newspapers were each nearing a person walking ahead of them.

A man in one screen walked up behind another as they started over a short bridge across a creek, stuck the tip of his umbrella against the man's leg, then suddenly apologized as the man grabbed his calf, as if the tip of the umbrella had stung him. The camera lenses now moved from the man who had been carrying the umbrella and focused on the man who had grabbed his calf. He started walking again. The camera followed him. A moment later his hands flew up to clutch at his chest, he seemed to cough, spin wildly, and collapse to the sidewalk and lay still.

All over the screens people were dropping, mostly men, but occasionally a woman, falling to sidewalks, and sides of rural roads, and pavements, and at street crossings.

In seconds, there was no one moving.

The images on the screens suddenly shifted back to the view of each country as taken from high in the atmosphere and then faded away to be replaced once again by the blank, blue-and-white glow.

"We probably got all of them," Kennedy said.

Spence thought of all that had taken place, how the chips in Quinlan's, Genowski's, John's, and Christen's brains had each contained the identities of all who had ever been implanted. John's body had been found in the mobile x-ray van, where Christen had gone back inside for her purse and added an extra strip of tape up under his nostrils to cut off his breathing. She had hurriedly wrapped one last piece of tape tightly around his neck, cutting into his windpipe to make certain no one could awaken him again. Neither would Genowski or Quinlan ever wake after her accurate shots. Christen was currently still breathing, but, with her implants removed, was being held in a military stockade under tight security. She had pleaded that the chips had influenced her behavior, but no one had paid any attention. There hadn't been any acid chip in her brain that she had to fear. She had sold her soul to the devil based strictly on her own choice. She was breathing, alright, and would continue to breathe until she reached an old age and then breathe her last breath in the same small cell.

All starting from an experiment gone bad, and then Randle resembling his old boyhood friend, Alfred, and going after him. Each of the five had assumed somebody else's identity. The key to all they did, their building the genetics plant where they brought each victim for an implant and everything else, all came about because of the great fortune the real Walter Quinlan had made over his life. His great mistake among his many accomplishments had been his becoming reclusive as he grew older, like a modern-day Howard Hughes. With no family, seldom anyone who saw him, and being of the approximate needed height, it had been easy to assume his identity. A little plastic surgery around the eyes and the nose, and the old Quinlan had become the new.

"If we didn't get all of them, we will," Kennedy said. "And you don't have to worry about any new ones popping up. Not even new ones who might be working for us. The original scientists made certain of that. If their experiment worked, chips were to be inserted into the heads of intelligence operatives who could report directly what they saw and heard. Later, they would probably be inserted into members of certain combat teams, where each member of the team would be aware of what each other member faced. But such widespread implantation would also present a problem. If one of those implanted were captured or killed, the chips could be removed. The military didn't want the secrets to the chips falling into the wrong hands. So they were designed in such a way that if ever removed their information and circuitry were erased. I imagine that's where Quinlan got the idea for the acid—so that he could erase anyone who didn't follow his commands. Now that the technique has been proven, I'm sure we have scientists who are going to try to duplicate the chips. But they're going to have to start from scratch."

Then he looked directly at them. "You two know there can never be another word uttered about this. Anything you've heard here. Anything you already know."

He said what he had said in a soft voice, without any

emphasis on the words. He didn't have to. Spence understood and so did Flo. Their compliance would be taken for granted. And to be taken for granted by *them* meant there would be no violations of any kind.

It was all in *the big picture*.

"How do you know that's all of them if the chips didn't hold any information when they were removed?" Flo asked.

"From me," Kennedy said. "I had them remove the acid chip first." He smiled a little. "Just in case. Then I named them all."

Spence watched the stocky agent's gaze come back to his. "By the way, Spence. You couldn't have pulled loose from me to hit that doctor unless I had wanted you to."

Spence couldn't help but smile himself. "A little ego there, Bob?" He held his hands out to the sides, indicating the control room and screens surrounding them. "In the midst of all this perfect technology and . . . this perfect organization of yours?"

"Individually, we're still allowed our petty weaknesses," the agent said, and returned the smile.

As the men started to replace the blindfolds in preparation for the trip back out of the room, Kennedy held up his forefinger, stopping them for a moment.

"One more thing, Spence. I did all I could to scare you off right at first. I was worried you would be in my way. As it turns out, if you hadn't gone along, I wouldn't be here today." He touched one of the swollen places on his forehead to make his point. "At least not as me. You showed guts and a little craziness. That's a prerequisite for some things. If you ever get tired of what you're doing and would like to try a real job for a while . . ."

Spence's thoughts moved to the computer chip that nearly cost him his life. He had started to destroy it. But he hadn't. He had brought it with him in case he decided to finally give it up. But now he decided against that.

Not just yet, he thought. But maybe some day . . .

38

COLONEL WEAVER SAT on a side of his bed at the VA hospital. He had once been one of *them*, but, unlike Kennedy, had actually retired from service, as Joey had done. Because of that, he was no longer privy to special information and therefore didn't know Kennedy's status. The colonel had been told that the stocky agent had been kept in a room down the hall, recuperating in isolation as Weaver had been, both of them warned by the surgeons that the removal of the implants had left the brain tissue surrounding the areas in such a state that, for a few days, any movement at all, even speaking too loudly, could possibly cause a fatal hemorrhage.

Of course Weaver *did* know about the volunteers from the old experiment. He knew they had survived the explosion at the underground site and had been responsible for what he had faced. He had also been told that the volunteers had all been taken out. But that was the extent of his knowledge—the way it had to be.

"You don't know how sick you get of bedpans and being afraid to even turn over too fast," he said. "It's a relief to know that's all over now. Hopefully," he added, and touched his finger to one of the barely noticeable spots on his forehead where, with the stitches removed for several days, the red indentations had now all but disappeared. A bit of minor plastic surgery and the marks would be totally gone. He looked over at Kennedy, lying with his back against a pair of thick pillows at the head of his bed. Healed enough to be moved out of isolation, Kennedy had supposedly finally talked the doctors into letting him be moved into the room with his old friend.

Flo and Spence stood near the foot of the beds. "I wish we could have come earlier," Flo said. "But we just couldn't get an answer from . . ." She glanced at Kennedy, not certain how much she was allowed to say and didn't say any more at all.

Kennedy shook his head in irritation. "Bureaucrats," he said.

"Thank you again for the flowers," Weaver said, looking at the roses she had sent them, now arranged in a vase on the table between the beds. They looked a little bit wilted.

"Even the flower shops are run by bureaucrats in this town," Kennedy said. "But I guess it's better than if we were still working with *them*. The flowers would have been checked for biological agents, intentional chemical contaminants, and delayed explosives in the stems," he said. "Doubt if there would be much left of them by the time they got here."

Flo smiled. Spence asked the question he had been wondering about ever since Kennedy had said he had assisted in the operation to remove the chips. "Did any of the knowledge stay with you?" It was a medical question, asked by a researcher interested in what could be fed into the brain. More to the point, what could be recalled after it was fed into the brain. For everything a person saw and heard was absorbed through the senses into the brain. Intelligence was simply the ability to recall, and the more one could recall, the smarter they were.

"Do I look any smarter?" Kennedy asked, and shook his head no.

Colonel Weaver said, "In a way I wish it had. It was scary, but sort of intriguing during the operation when I realized I knew as much as the surgeon who was removing the implants."

"I don't miss the information," Kennedy said. "I prefer

not to know that from the height and intensity of an approaching storm that it probably contains a tornado."

A reflective expression crossed his face. "One thing though, it would have been nice if they had left in the transmitter chip and put one into my wife, too. When she was at the grocery store and I thought of something I forgot to tell her I needed, I could just click the message on over to her at the checkout counter."

Flo shook her head and smiled. "I'm sure Judy would have loved that, Bob. Where is she?"

The lighthearted look that had been on his face most of the time they were in the room, went away. "Waiting," he said. "Like she always does."

"Well," Spence said, glancing at his watch.

"Appreciate your coming by, Doctor," Kennedy said.

"Yeah," Colonel Weaver said, "the next time I'm down in the Jackson area to visit Bob, I'll stop by and see if you have time to go to lunch." He nodded his head toward Kennedy. "If you don't mind having to see him again."

"Not at all," Flo said, and looked at the agent. "I hope you don't end up being a stranger after you get back."

When they stepped out into the hall they walked a few steps. Then she glanced back across her shoulder and spoke in a low voice. "What about the administrative assistant—Alexander Raye?"

"They took his implants out, too."

"*They* trusted somebody then—besides us."

"If he makes it to the Senate he's going to be one well-informed man about Intelligence work."

"Maybe they offered him a job, too."

"Maybe."

"Any others?"

"You saw all the others on those screens."

"What about the doctor?"

"I didn't ask."

"It looks like they could have saved some of them," she said. "I understand why Kennedy and his people went after the original volunteers. They did what they did because they wanted to. But there were some like that man in Montana."

"Tommy Rhiner?"

She nodded. "You said he didn't want to be like he was."

Reaching the end of the hall, he opened the door. "I can understand they had no other choice," he said. "Just five of them had multiplied where they were spreading all over the world. Their game plan was obvious. They were going to take over. At least some countries. With their knowledge, it's scary what it could have led to. Kennedy and his bunch couldn't take time to pick and choose between the ones who might not have liked what they were and the ones who did. It had to be fast, taking them all out at about the same moment. If one of them had found out what was happening and got the word out, the others could have gone into hiding." He shook his head. "And then, who knows? With their minds, they might have eventually learned how to develop a chip that controlled the hearing and seeing of others, like the original volunteers could—they would have the *real power* once more. Then they would have started multiplying all over again."

Flo nodded. "That's why they hadn't already run when Quinlan and the other two were killed and Christen was shot. The new ones didn't know what had happened."

He nodded. "Until it was too late. With their minds they might have realized it when they were being taken out."

Flo nodded her understanding as she passed through the doorway. But as she moved down the steps to the sidewalk in front of the aging building, her expression told him she was still thinking about the fate of Tommy Rhiner and any others who might have felt like him.

He patted her shoulder gently, and let his hand lay there as they walked.

Then a pleasant expression spread across her face. "I saw in the newspaper that there's a play in town I've always wanted to see."

"Fine," he said. "What's its name?"

Instead of answering that, Flo's eyes narrowed in thought. "Christen disabled the generator in the x-ray unit," she said. "You had left her outside when you went into the lab. She knew John was coming. She knew she was going to stop him if you didn't. She was going to suggest x-raying his head to get you thinking about the implants. When the generator wouldn't work, and her telling you he was an executive at the genetics center, she knew she could talk you into going out there, use you as a distraction so she could get to the others. But why did she lock onto you in the first place—right after Dr. Lambert was murdered? She couldn't have known you were going to get so involved in everything."

"I imagine that first day she was just seeing what she could find out about what we knew about the murder. Me, the cops, anybody. Maybe Quinlan sent her, everything just kept evolving from that."

Flo suddenly stopped and shrugged his hand off her shoulder. Her eyes narrowed as she stared at him.

"What?" he asked.

"What did Christen mean by "He's not that much of a lover by any definition of the word?" she asked. "I was so scared at the time that it completely skipped my mind until right now. Did you two . . ."

He would never tell. Somebody would have a better chance of getting him to tell something about *them* than they could the answer to that question.

He shook his head no and added a little irritated expression to the gesture to make the lie stick. "Be serious," he said, "all I was thinking about doing that night was running for my life. When would we have had the time?" he asked.

Flo accepted that with her smile, and they started along the sidewalk again, walking slowly in the warm summer air.

But Flo really had accepted it only because it was past. She knew the correct answer, and even the date when the tryst had taken place.

Spence had said, "All I was doing *that* night . . ."

Christen hadn't mentioned any particular night.

Flo smiled at the thought. She didn't need an implant to be smart, and she didn't need one to help her with the next move in *her* game plan. She moved closer to Spence as they walked, slipping her arm around his waist, and he slid his around her shoulders.

She looked up at the beautiful sunlit sky above the city, and smiled again.

TURN THE PAGE FOR AN EXCERPT
FROM CHARLES WILSON'S
ELECTRIFYING NEW THRILLER

DEEP SLEEP

NOW AVAILABLE IN HARDCOVER
FROM ST. MARTIN'S PRESS!

NORMALLY, THE TALL iron gates leading into the grounds were kept closed, but they stood open now, stark in the dim moonlight.

Mark French drove onto the gravel entry road. The shirt of his deputy's uniform showed wrinkles. It was the one he had pitched onto the chair in his bedroom after ending his shift, then grabbed and put back on before hurrying from his apartment a few minutes before. He rested his elbow out his window. The night air, loaded with the moisture rising from the lowlands in this part of the parish, felt almost chilly when compared to the earlier heat of the day that had left him perspiring nearly as much as if he had been playing a game of handball at the gym. He looked off to the road's right, at the wide sign displaying the facility's name:

SOUTH LOUISIANA SLEEP DISORDERS INSTITUTE

Dennis Guitrau sat in the car's passenger seat. The stocky, forty-three-year-old deputy, his uniform sleeves stretched tightly around his heavy arms folded across his chest, stared ahead of them across the fog-cloaked uniformly flat land at a large antebellum house. Sitting a hundred yards back from the entrance, it was surrounded by massive, aging oaks draped with long strands of Spanish moss. "When this opened ten years ago, I didn't know what to think," Guitrau said. "Why would something depending mostly on out-of-state clients locate here? Why not around New Orleans, closer to the airport? Then I got to thinking, you open up something like this . . . maybe you want it in a place where it doesn't attract all that much attention."

Several cars sat in the circular drive in front of the home's tall white columns. The second floor was darkened, but the first-floor windows and big glass globes hanging down between the columns were ablaze with bright illumination. Mark could see someone standing on the deep porch. He knew that whatever Shasha Dominique's reason for locating the institute where she had, and despite the low profile those who worked there kept, it had become a point of contention among some in the mostly conservative, rural area. Not a sleep disorders clinic in the normal sense, but a place where clients could come to live out fantasies in their dreams. He remembered an older lady only a few weeks before asking him if he could imagine the kinds of fantasies some men would pay money to enjoy. She didn't like that idea and she didn't like those kinds of people coming into the parish. "From as far away as Chicago," he remembered the woman saying as she remarked about some of the license plates she had seen on cars driving out the blacktop toward the institute. But there had never been a problem associated with the place.

Until tonight.

He looked toward the glow of flashing blue lights illuminating the darkness in the distance behind the home, then turned off the gravel, and with the damp wind whipping at his face, drove across the grass toward the thick trees that marked the beginning of the vast swamp that spread out beyond the institute.

He parked beside the department's forensic van. Two deputies his age, in their early thirties, wore rubber boots fitting high around the legs of their uniform trousers as they slowly waded a few feet out in the shallow water. The flashing lights reflecting off their faces and the fog curling up around them, they played their flashlight beams carefully

over each patch of exposed mud and tall grass, looking for
any evidence that might lie in easy sight. He lifted his flashlight from the dash, opened his door, and stepped outside
as Guitrau climbed out the passenger side.

Dr. Poirier stood near the edge of the water. Short and
gray-haired, he had his dark sports coat unbuttoned and
spread open to the sides of his rounded stomach and held
a cellular phone to his ear. A black body bag lay on the
bank ten feet behind him.

Dottie waited next to the bag. Also in her early thirties,
her sandy-blond hair was cut above her collar, and she was
neither thin nor heavy but filled her uniform solidly; the
tautness of her neck and her smooth, tight arms gave evidence of how often she worked out with weights. Her full
lips and blue eyes pleasantly softened her look of strength.
As Mark drew near, she knelt on one knee and pulled the
bag's zipper down to expose the face of an attractive, young
black female. Streaks of mud smeared her skin. A small
laceration showed at a side of her forehead. Her shoulder-
length black hair was wet and twisted into thick strands
matted with decaying leaves.

"Hit one time with a blunt object," Dottie said. "Dr.
Poirier found fragments of bark embedded in the wound,
indicating a limb was used. He said the blow came when
she was facing her assailant. It might or might not have
knocked her unconscious. But the cause of death was stran-
gulation."

She switched on her flashlight and shone it close against
the young woman's neck, revealing two bruises, each
maybe a half inch wide, a little more than an inch long,
and horizontal across the throat. "Might be able to lift a
print from those," Dottie said.

He nodded. With the use of the technology called blue
light, forensic specialists now routinely picked up faint
traces of blood left on walls that had been repeatedly
scrubbed, and fingerprints off the skin of victims who had
only been barely touched. The nearest law enforcement
agency with that kind of expertise was in New Orleans.

Some of their people would have to come over.

Dottie closed the bag and came to her feet. "If we're not able to lift those, we don't have anything at this point," she added. "There's no sign she put up a struggle—no skin under her nails, none of them broken off, no other marks on her body." She looked back toward the swamp. "She was lying face down in the water, naked. The ground's soft there, but there's no shoe prints or footprints around where she was found—not even hers. It's almost as if she were thrown toward the water."

As Dottie paused, she turned her gaze in the direction of two men standing beside a department car off to the right. "Except for their prints," she said. "They pulled her out of the water."

One of the men was a tall black man in his mid- to late forties, wearing dark slacks and a red vest hanging open over a blue dress shirt. The other was a short white man of similar age with unusually pale skin. He was cloaked in an ankle-length black robe with its hood back against his shoulders.

"Samuel Johnson and Bennie Rogers," Dottie said. "Johnson—the one in the vest—is the one who actually discovered the body. He's an employee here. Rogers is one of the guests. They said she would have had on a robe like he's wearing."

Dr. Poirier walked up beside her. He nodded his greeting at Guitrau, then said, "No obvious sign she's been sexually assaulted, Mark. But I can't be certain until I get her back to the morgue."

Mark nodded. "Appreciate knowing as soon as you can."

"Only take me a little while," Poirier said.

"How did you get here so fast?"

"Mark, you don't know the work I got piled up at the morgue. Was determined to stay until I got caught up. I heard Dottie's call over the radio when I was on my way home. Sheriff still out of the country?"

"For a couple more weeks."

Dottie looked toward the two men again. "Johnson said

she had gone into her dream sleep a few minutes before
two. Dream sleep's the term they use when a guest is put
to sleep to experience his or her fantasies. He said she must
have awakened and wandered off down here right after that.
He said they found her within thirty minutes. Based on that,
she would have been attacked between an hour and a half
to two hours ago."

Dr. Poirier nodded. "That fits. No more than two hours
ago at the most."

Mark started toward the two men.

"Her name is Deloris Rivet," Dottie said as she walked
beside him. "She went by Missey. She lived in San Francisco, but her family is originally from this area. Johnson's
the one in the red vest," she reminded him as they neared
the two men.

He was around six-feet-two, with an almost gaunt build
and a dark face deeply creased with wrinkles that made
him look older than his trim body had caused him to appear
from farther away.

When Mark stopped in front of him, Dottie said, "Mr.
Johnson, this is Chief Deputy Mark French."

"You found the body?" Mark asked.

"Yes, sir," Johnson answered in a low voice.

"We both found her," the other man said. "My name's
Bennie Rogers, from Dallas. Did you see where someone
knocked her on the head?"

Up close, he was even shorter than he had first appeared,
maybe five-three or five-four, with a slight build. He had a
deeply receding hairline, with what hair he did have lying
in a thin blond layer on top of his head. His pale skin was
made to look all the whiter by his black robe and the reflection of the lights flashing against his face. He held his
glasses down at his side in his small hand.

"Yes, I saw it," Mark said and looked back at Johnson.
"Why did you come down here to look for her?"

"I was looking everywhere," Johnson answered in his
soft tone. "Guests sometimes get confused when they wake
right after being put into their dream sleep."

"Get disoriented," Rogers said. He had slipped his
glasses on, and his small eyes were blurred through the
lenses. "Tell him about Boudron," he said to Johnson.

Johnson glanced in the direction of the deputies wading
the swamp. "Have you heard of him?" he asked.

Mark nodded. He hadn't thought about it until now, but
the institute wasn't all that far from the landing. There
would be few people in the parish who hadn't heard of the
wild man of the landing, as he was called in both exag-
gerated and normal conversation—a child who had been
extensively deformed at birth and whose family had bought
property in the swamp and moved there years before to save
him from the stares of others.

"When we were on our way down here, I heard something in the trees," Johnson continued. "Over in there." He
nodded off to his right, in the direction where the swamp
veered in a gentle curve off to the north, away from where
the victim's body lay.

"When I called out, I saw him when he ran between
some trees. But Boudron couldn't have strangled Miss
Rivet."

"Couldn't have?"

"No, sir, he has only one arm. He couldn't strangle nobody and leave thumbprints."

"One arm?" That was something Mark didn't remember
hearing mentioned in the past.

"Yes, sir. That's what his parents said."

Mark looked at Guitrau. The stocky deputy shook his
head that he hadn't heard that mentioned either.

"He was up here one time," Johnson said. "Frightened
some guests who saw him moving around in the trees. He
ran when I came up."

"And you're certain it was him tonight?"

"Well . . . I just got a glimpse. But . . . yes, I got a good
enough look. It was him again."

"It had to be only minutes after the attack," Guitrau said.
"He could have seen it."

Mark looked in the direction of the deputies wading the

water. Past them, trees and stretches of dark water, separated by strips of muddy ground, spread out for miles to the sides. He judged the landing, a small section of higher, dry ground covered in tall pines, to be about a mile straight behind them, through the heart of the swamp.

"Do we need to take a boat to get back there?"

"No, sir," Johnson said. "You can walk in."

"Can you show us the way?"

Johnson nodded. "To where his parents live. He doesn't live with them. He cut everybody else off and then them, they said. He lives by himself in a place he's built somewhere on the landing. I didn't see him when I went in to speak with them. But like I said, I had seen him when he was up here by the guests."

Mark glanced at his watch. "We'll wait until it's light." He looked toward the big house a hundred yards in the distance. "Are there other guests here?"

"Two," Johnson said. "They've been in their dream sleep for hours. Missey was the next to last to be put into her sleep. Miss Shasha was preparing Mr. Rogers for his sleep when I found out Missey had left her room."

"I would like to speak with them," Mark said.

The home appeared even larger driving up from behind it than it had when they had passed it on the way down to the swamp. Guitrau stared at the oversized pool directly behind the wide structure. Thin plumes of mist curled above the water. Tall bushes ran along the sides of the pool and the rear of the house. A sidewalk lit with the glow of gas lamps wound past iron chairs and benches placed in areas surrounded by similar bushes planted to form privacy circles. Mark drove around the side of the home to its front, parking beside a Cadillac in the drive that curved by the wide steps leading up onto the porch.

As they walked toward the steps, Guitrau said, "Some families just live under dark clouds."

"Excuse me?"

"You've heard about Shasha's mother?"

"Being convicted of murder?"

"Yeah," Guitrau said. "Her and her boy—they killed Shasha's uncle."

Mark nodded as they moved up onto the porch. He had heard the story before.

Guitrau explained anyway. "It was Shasha who turned them in. She wasn't much more than six or seven at the time."

When they stopped in front of the expensive inlaid glass front door, Guitrau said, "From a foster home to this," and shook his head.

Mark glanced at his watch. Johnson and Rogers were walking the hundred yards from the swamp. He looked out across the sprawling, neatly kept grounds. The only thing marring the overall beauty of the surroundings was a massive pine on the far side of the drive that had died, its covering of needles brown now, contrasting vividly with the dark green leaves and needles of the other pines and oaks in the curving line.

"Wouldn't want to be inside if that fell over," Guitrau said, looking at the tree. It was at least three feet in diameter. "Go right through to the first floor. You know," he added, "I've been thinking. Sort of like the talk in the parish about the types this place might attract. Have some character with a twisted fantasy in mind, come here, get it pumped up a little more . . . and bang, pushed over the edge into trying it out in real life. That seems a lot more likely than a stranger wandering around out here in the middle of nowhere."

The door opened behind them.

"Gentlemen," Johnson said, and stepped back from the doorway for them to come inside.

Shasha Dominique, in her late thirties, waited in the spacious living room. Tall earthen vases filled with plants with their limbs drooping toward the floor sat about the walls. A large couch covered with a bright yellow fabric, a coffee table nearly the width of a queen-size bed, and two heavily cushioned chairs covered in the same yellow fabric served as the centerpiece of the room. She sat in one of the chairs. Her elbows resting on its arms and her hands clasped in front of her chest, she wore a white sleeveless blouse and short black skirt that displayed her slim brown arms and legs.

"Mr. French," she said, smiling politely up at him.

"Dr. Dominique."

Johnson said, "I'll bring the others down," and walked toward the carpeted staircase at the far side of the room.

"I find this deeply disturbing," Shasha said, bringing Mark's attention back to her. Her smile had gone away. "You've heard about my mother and brother?"

He nodded.

"Tonight makes me revisit my past in a most disturbing manner," she said in a voice so low it was almost as if she was thinking aloud rather than addressing him.

It took a moment and an obvious effort for her to bring a pleasant expression back to her face. She glanced over her shoulder in the direction of a man walking across the carpet toward her from a hallway at the rear of the room. Close to her age, maybe a couple of years older, forty to forty-one at the most, his head was shaved bare, he wore jeans and a T-shirt, and he had a muscular build, a sharply chiseled face, and skin much darker than hers. He carried a serving tray holding a half dozen cups brimming with coffee.

"This is our cook, John Paul," she said as he stopped in front of her. She lifted a cup from the tray and said, "If you would like one? It's strong."

"No, thank you," Mark said. "Are there any other employees who live on the premises at night?"

Shasha shook her head. She looked toward Guitrau, and he stepped forward and lifted a cup into his big hand.

Johnson took several minutes before he appeared at the top of the stairs with two men. Both wore the long black robes with the hoods back. As they started down the stairs, he held one's arm; the man seemed unsteady.

Shasha came up from the chair, met them at the bottom of the stairs, and looked back across the living room. "This is Mr. Dale Dutt."

The one she indicated was about five-ten and had a narrow face, thinning blond hair, and blue eyes. He appeared to be in his early fifties. The man next to him, the one Johnson had helped along, was about the same height and age but more bulky, with a pudgy face and black hair swept toward one side of his head.

"And this is Mr. Daniel Berry," Shasha said, indicating him with a nod of her head.

Johnson leaned forward and said something to her. She nodded, and he walked past her across the living room in the direction of the front door.

The others came across the floor. Shasha and Mr. Dutt remained standing as they stopped near the coffee table. Berry slowly lowered himself onto the couch. He still gave the appearance of someone dazed. Guitrau was staring at him.

"You will have to forgive Mr. Berry," Shasha said. "He was deep into his dream sleep. Sometimes it takes several minutes to come back fully awake. According to the individual, as long as fifteen to twenty minutes." Berry, his face devoid of expression, stared up from the couch.

"Missey's dead?" Mr. Dutt said in a subdued tone.

Mark nodded. Berry looked up from the couch for a moment longer, then lowered his gaze, pulled the hood of his robe up over his head, and snuggled back into the cushions, folding his arms across his chest and closing his eyes as if he were going to sleep again.

Guitrau moved his gaze from Berry to Shasha. "Why the robes?" he asked.

"Their softness against the bare skin is comforting. Along with an optimum temperature and the subdued lighting we maintain in the rooms when we start a guest into the process of dream sleep, they help create an environment of relaxation."

Johnson was coming back across the living room floor.

"His car is gone," he said to Shasha.

Mark saw her eyes tighten slightly; a quizzical expression crossed her face.

"I'm afraid we've had a guest leave," she said in a low voice.

At that moment, back past the rear of the house, past the deputies wading the water and farther into the trees, a dark shape crouched unseen behind a clump of willows. Part of the figure was thrust forward, maybe a head with eyes peering toward the deputies. Yet at the same time the part seemed too out of proportion to be a head. While rounded, it was unusually long from top to bottom, like the shape of a giant egg stretched even more oblong than normal. What could be thick hair hung down from the egg-shaped appendage and lay across what could be wide shoulders. A faint sound emanated from the figure, too low for any of the deputies to hear. A cross between a child's low crying and an animal's soft wailing.

The shape turned away from the willows.

Moving farther back into the swamp, it neared an open spot of ground bathed in the dim moonlight. Entering the patch of faint light, the figure now appeared more human, but with its shoulders stooped, its legs bowed, and one foot moving more awkwardly than the other. Continuing a slow almost painful-looking pace, it continued back into the trees.

Its wailing followed it into the darkness.

Six-year-old Paul Haines watches as two older boys dive into a coastal river...and don't come up. His mother, Carolyn, a charter boat captain on the Mississippi Gulf Coast, finds herself embroiled in the tragedy to an extent she could never have imagined.

Carolyn joins with marine biologist Alan Freeman in the hunt for a creature that is terrorizing the waters along the Gulf Coast. But neither of them could have envisioned exactly what kind of danger they are facing.

Only one man knows what this creature is, and how it has come into the shallows. And his secret obsession with it will force him, as well as Paul, Carolyn and Alan, into a race against time...and a race toward death.

EXTINCT
by Charles Wilson

"Eminently plausible, chilling in its detail, and highly entertaining straight through to its finale."
—Dr. Dean A. Dunn, Professor of Oceanography and Paleontology, University of Southern Mississippi

"With his taut tales and fast words, Charles Wilson will be around for a long time. I hope so."
—John Grisham

AVAILABLE WHEREVER BOOKS ARE SOLD
FROM ST. MARTIN'S PAPERBACKS